HOW
TO MURDER
A GHOST

Also by Charles Hampton —

BROTHERS OF TOMORROW
WIND HUNTER
WRITING GREAT STORIES

HOW
TO
MURDER
A GHOST

CHARLES
HAMPTON

BUSH PUBLICATIONS
BREA, CALIFORNIA

Published by
Charles Hampton Bush
Brea, CA

To my father,
the most honest man
I have ever known.

In the real of ghosts,
love and hate are the only forces
that transcend the barriers
of time and mortality.
— Unknown

ONE

PAUL DAVENPORT'S life was in a shamble, and now he had just done something foolish. He would win the idiot of the year award with no contest. The worst part? He could have avoided most of his problems by being smart and not so damned honest. But what was done couldn't be undone.

He pushed open the front door of the Pasadena Police Department and stepped aside to allow detective Sergeant Bill Johnson to exit first. The detective nodded his thanks and strode out onto the building's front portico. Paul followed but almost collided with the detective, who stopped without warning. He looked past the man and saw the reason. An odd group of people occupied the sidewalk in front of the station. Overhead, the Sunday afternoon sky swept the world below like a bright blue sea.

Three photographers, two video cameramen, several male reporters, one pretty young woman with short brown hair, and a few others had arrayed themselves on the cobblestone sidewalk in front of the building. They ignored the detective and gawked up at Paul.

Panic ripped through him like a sharp-pointed icicle, freezing his spine. The last thing he needed was to talk to reporters. He turned back, intending to escape, but Bill Johnson grabbed his arm. "Won't do any good to run," he said. "This is a big story, and they won't let you rest until you give them an interview."

"But who told them I was here?" He regretted even more his dumb decision to get the police involved.

"Good question. They got spies everywhere, and you can bet they know most of it already. When a young jogger finds an enormous amount of money and turns it over to the cops, that's big news. They'll buzz about it for days."

Dressed in navy-blue jogging sweats that were still wet in spots on his back and under his arms, Paul stood tall, ignoring the curious stares aimed his way. He brushed back a wave of black hair that fell over his brow and aimed deep blue eyes at the tough, gray-suited detective. His lean face showed doubt, but he said, "Okay, if you say so, but I'm pretty sweaty."

"Don't worry about it. They've seen runners before. I'll try to get them off your back, but you're a hero. They won't let go until they have something to take home."

Paul shrugged. "Okay, Sergeant, I'm game. Go ahead." He surveyed the reporters again. They were a pack of hungry dogs, starving for food, but the sergeant was right. Finding that much money was a big story. He spotted a couple of friendly faces and nodded his recognition of them. He resigned himself to answering a few questions and then hurrying home to his apartment for a shower and a nap.

The detective nudged Paul into the sunlight. Several reporters, waving hand-held mikes, came toward them. TV cameras targeted them. The photographers were busy eying him through their view finders and taking pictures.

Bill Johnson waved them back. They halted their progress.

"Okay folks, I'm not sure who leaked this, but I have nothing for you. You understand the procedure. If you want details, see the information officer."M

"Aw, come on, Sarge. Give us a break," one reporter called. "We know he found two suitcases full of money and turned it in.

How about a few tidbits, anyway?"

The detective pinched his brow, deciding, and then shrugged. He looked at Paul. "Sorry, they're onto us. Will you answer a few questions?"

Paul nodded.

Sergeant Johnson turned back to the reporters. "Okay, here's the story." He motioned to Paul. "This young man's name is Paul Davenport. He's thirty years old, and single. Paul jogs regularly at the Hahamonga Watershed Park. On this Sunday afternoon, he spotted something odd under a big rock. He investigated and found two large leather suitcases containing more than a quarter million dollars. He realized it was an important find. As a good citizen, he brought them to us. My guess is he stumbled on a pickup point for drug dealers, but we're uncertain about that. The department will draft a press release as soon as we learn more." Johnson paused. "Mr. Davenport has agreed to take a few questions, but don't overwhelm him. He did his duty by bringing in that money, so let's not punish him for it." The sergeant nodded to Paul. "All yours."

Paul squelched a nervous knot in his stomach and then mimicked what he had seen others do on TV. He chose an older journalist who was closest to him. The man's face was friendly, so he said, "Sir, I'll take your questions first."

The reporter climbed three of the seven steps leading to the portico. "Mr. Davenport, why did you turn in that money? Weren't you tempted to keep it?"

"Hell, yes, but it's not mine, so I brought it to the police." Paul tried not to look as stupid as he felt.

"I doubt many people would give it up so easily," the reporter said. "Are you a rich man?"

"I wish. I'm a freelance CNC programmer at an aerospace company. There's not enough money in my account to buy two tickets to Disneyland."

Someone yelled. "So what are you, some kind of overgrown Boy Scout?"

"No." Paul tried to pick out the questioner. "It's more accurate to call me a former jarhead who believes in doing the right thing."

There was a scattering of laughter. Paul relaxed.

"Hey, what's a CNC programmer?" someone shouted.

Paul looked around and spotted the shouter, an older man in a rumpled brown suit and battered hat. "Sir, CNC stands for computer numerical control. I write G-code programs that run advanced metal-working equipment. It's not very exciting, but it buys the bacon."

"Where did you go to school?" someone else called.

"Three years at UCLA."

"You saying they teach CNC programming at UCLA?" the first reporter asked, surprised.

"No, they may, but I studied mechanical engineering there. I learned to program in the Marine Corps and studied G-code at a local trade school."

"Hey, I was in the Corps," an older reporter said. "How'd you land working with computers?

Paul tossed the man a quick salute. "Sir, if you were in the marines, you know they test you to see where you belong. They sent me to electronics training school and then one day the opportunity to switch came up, so I took it."

The man chuckled. "You must be a smart dude then."

"Not according to my sergeant." Another smattering of laughter.

The dark-haired young reporter elbowed her way to the front. "Mr. Davenport, weren't you frightened by what you found? I would have been. Drug gangs are notoriously vicious."

Paul returned her smile. "No, though maybe a little nervous."

"What about the money? Did that surprise you?"

"Sure, but I figured it was counterfeit. Who finds suitcases full of actual cash? Detective Johnson thinks it's drug money, which makes sense now."

"Suppose you had kept it," the girl insisted. "What would

you do with it?"

Paul saw her question was serious. "Are you asking what I would do if I won the lottery?"

The girl giggled. "I guess I am? What's the answer?"

"Well, I'm like everyone else. You name it, and I've dreamed it."

"Does your family live in Pasadena?"

"No. I'm alone."

"Oh, sorry," she said.

"No problem." He looked around at his audience. "If there's nothing else, I think I need a shower."

Paul looked at the detective for agreement.

"Hey, Davenport. Why don't you tell us the whole truth?" The voice was caustic, accusing and loud.

His face turned ashen. What truth? He tried to locate the questioner. A young guy his own age stepped forward. Paul frowned. "What are you talking about?"

TWO

THE REPORTER, dark hair, lean, aggressive, wearing a blue sports shirt, held up a cell phone.. "Just got a call from my office. Research department looked you up. They say your father died three months ago at a local mental health clinic left you owing the clinic two hundred thousand dollars. So, my question is, can you prove you turned in all e money? Who's to say you didn't find half a million bucks?"

Paul's body stiffened. They had discovered his father had died. Had they also learned how? The hospital kept that information from the public. Several loud boos aimed at the questioner brought Paul's attention back to the man.

"Come on, Davenport! Tell us the truth." The reporter's face twisted with a cynical accusation.

Paul scanned the group. Every eye was on him, waiting for his reaction. He looked back at the station door. It was closed. He met the sergeant's eyes. He wanted an answer, too. A lone hawk soared high overhead, winging its way west. Paul yearned to join the bird, but knew he couldn't. His jaw muscles bunched. He had to answer. He took a breath to calm himself.

"Are you accusing me of lying?" His jaws pinched shut with the effort to remain calm.

The reporter's face went slack when he saw Paul's anger. "Uh, no. I'm a reporter trying to get the truth. Uh..."

"Okay. I'll tell you one more time. I took nothing for myself. And, yes, my father's illness left me in debt. He was ill, so the marines gave me a hardship leave to care for him. The hospital extended the credit I needed, which is why I owe them so much."

Paul looked at the young girl. Her eyes showed disappointment, as if he had somehow become tarnished. He felt ashamed and wanted to escape. Instead, he smiled at her, and said, "Miss, if I won the lottery, I would pay what I owe the hospital."

"That all sounds good, Davenport, but why should we believe your debt solution wasn't part of that money you brought in?" The guy with the phone took two steps toward him as he spoke.

Paul's temper rose like a hot geyser, ready to blow. "I don't give a damn what you believe, mister. You can believe up is down for all I care." The geyser in him exploded. "What I know is that somebody needs to teach you a lesson in manners." He balled his fists and started toward the man. The reporter's expression twisted in fear. He twisted around to find an escape route.

"Paul, stop!" Bill Johnson caught his arm. "He's not worth the trouble." He scowled at the reporter. "You're a jerk, pal, and you're now on my list. Get the hell back before I lose my temper."

The guy backed off, and Paul relaxed.

The detective swept the group with squinted eyes. "For your information, the Pasadena police department is satisfied that Paul brought in all the money. We applied the criminal forfeiture act to take possession of the funds. We've also begun an expanded investigation of the site where it he found it."

A reporter asked, "Sergeant, how do you know it's drug money and subject to forfeiture?"

"Because we found residual traces of heroin in the suitcases. You'll learn more when we release a statement."

The girl reporter raised her hand and said, "Mr. Davenport,

with all your problems, you strike me as still optimistic. What's your secret?"

"I sit quietly listening to music and read books." The moment was over. He sucked in a huge breath of relief.

"What kind of music do you like?" The girl stepped closer. She was even prettier up close.

Paul gave her a crooked smile and answered, "Vivaldi, mostly. And easy listening rock. I prefer quiet music that doesn't intrude on my thoughts."

"That's interesting. What type of books do you read, Paul?"

"I like the Greek classics, but I enjoy Mark Twain most."

The girl's eyes widened. "Why Mark Twain?"

"Because he's the wisest man I've ever read. He understood the real world, and he makes me laugh."

"Can you give us an example?"

Paul nodded. "Yeah. I guess my favorite Twain quote is, 'If you tell the truth, you don't have to remember anything.'"

Another ripple of laughter from the reporters.

"I'll check him out." The girl appeared impressed.

Sergeant Johnson raised his voice and said, "Listen. There's something else you need to know about Paul. He is a decorated hero with a Purple Heart and the Silver Star. If you want more, do your damned homework. Check him up."

He glared at the guy who attacked Paul. "People like you make me sick. You put your mouth in gear before you have the facts, and that makes you feel so smart. How many times have you laid your life on the line for our country?" The man withered under the sergeant's anger. "Yeah, that's what I figured." He ran out of steam. "Okay, that's it. You've got your story. That's all there is. Paul is an honest young patriot who did his duty as a citizen despite needing money. I doubt many of you would have done what he did. Now, back off and let us through." He whispered to Paul. "I'll walk you to your car. Where are you parked?"

"Half a block away." Paul swallowed his embarrassment.

"Sergeant, I should have warned you."

"Hey, forget it. You did good."

"But how did you learn about my service record? I've told no one about that."

Johnson patted him on the shoulder. "We're the cops, son. We checked you out. You have nothing to be sorry about. That creep is trying to make a name for himself. He's an idiot. Let's go."

At Paul's old Ford F-150 pickup, the detective shook hands and said, "Thanks again, Paul. For your bravery and your honesty. We appreciate that." He became serious. "One more thing. That girl reporter was right. Drug gangs are senseless killers. Somebody's gonna be pissed off because of what you did, so stay on the lookout for trouble. If you see anything odd coming your way, call me pronto, day or night. We'll get a car to you quick. Oh, and we may need to reach you if our investigation leads anywhere, though I doubt it will. These people are worse than ghosts."

"Thanks. I understand." He climbed in the truck and peered at the sergeant. "You've got my number."

"Kid, wait. If you don't mind my asking, what are you gonna do about that debt? It must keep you awake at night."

"Yeah. Sometimes, but the marines teach you never to give up, so I guess I'll try to find a way to pay it off. Others shouldn't have to suffer for my decisions. But—."

"What?"

Paul grinned. "Now and then I walk around with my fingers crossed, praying for a miracle."

The sergeant chuckled. "Don't we all."

"I have to pay the bill somehow."

"Not necessarily. Have you considered bankruptcy?"

"Yes, but I can't do that."

"Why not? Those laws are written for cases like yours."

"I know that, but I begged the hospital to accept my father. I gave the administrator my oath and signed a contract, saying

I would pay them no matter what. The administrator was a nice guy and trusted me. They accepted him based on my word and gave him excellent care. So—"

"You feel honor-bound to pay them."

"Yes."

"So, what will you do?"

"I haven't decided. I'll think of something."

"I bet you will. You're quite a man, Paul. In my business, I don't meet many like you." The detective stuck out his hand to shake. "It's been a pleasure."

"Thanks," Paul said, reddening. "I appreciate that."

"For what it's worth, son, I hope you make it. Take care."

"You, too."

The sergeant slapped the truck's roof and headed back to work.

THREE

IN A DARK MOOD, he burned rubber as he pulled away from the police station. That bastard reporter had invaded his privacy and paraded his dirty laundry on TV for the entire world to see. And for what purpose? To show important news? No. He did it to make a name for himself. Look at me. I'm a hard-hitting, two-fisted journalist.

And he was smart, too. No accusations. Just questions. A dirty way to attack without opening himself to a slander charge. Paul clamped his jaws in anger. He had read stories describing how reporters destroyed others to further their own careers, though they usually chose politicians as their targets. This time, he was the whipping boy, and it angered him.

A car horn and a noisy clatter ahead of him blasted into his thoughts. Paul screeched to a halt a foot from the rear of a shiny black Chevy Cruze. Multiple tire screeches came from behind him. Behind him, a bearded old man in the car behind him sat staring in shock.

The Cruze driver jumped out of the vehicle and rushed around the hood screaming four-letter words. An old woman with stringy gray hair struggled to her feet. The man charged toward her. "You crazy bitch! You hit my car!" Then he pushed her shoulders, sending her sprawling backward to the pavement.

"Damn!" Paul hopped out of his truck and yelled, "Hey! Stop!" What the hell?

The guy whirled as Paul reached him. Well dressed, he was twice Paul's age, four inches shorter, and wore a sizable gut. "Mind your own damned business. She scratched my car."

Paul brushed past him and helped the woman to her feet. Her arms were skinny, and his fingers sank through the soft flesh to her bones. Behind her, the contents of her shopping cart had scattered on the street. She was homeless.

She turned water blue eyes on h'm in surprise and whispered, "Bless you."

"No problem. You hurt?"

"No."

"You sure?"

"Yeah. He didn't hit me. I got scared and fell is all. Knocked my wheels over."

He lifted the heavy cart and helped her reload it. She fretted over her stuff, rearranging it as he picked it up. The driver stood glaring at them, his face showing wounded anger.

"Hey," he wailed. "Who's gonna pay for this?"

He pointed to a minor scratch on the front bumper.

"I suggest you try your insurance company. Or maybe you'd rather visit a judge about hitting a little old lady."

The guy's face wrinkled into a snarl, and he started toward Paul.

"I doubt you want to do that." Paul bared his teeth. The man stopped.

"Fuck you." He whirled and climbed into his car. "Get that bitch out of the way." He glared at Paul through the windshield and revved his engine to show he meant business.

Paul shook his head in disgust. Two jerks in one day were his limit.

The woman pushed her cart back to the sidewalk. Paul followed her and looked at her. Her face held more wrinkles than a prune. The Cruze peeled away.

"You sure you're okay?"

"Yeah, I shoulda used the crosswalk. I ain't too smart sometimes." She waggled a hand at Paul's truck. "You better git goin' before somebody else gets pissed." She grinned at him through wrinkled lips. She was toothless. A horn blared. "See?" she said. "Anyhow, I gotta go now" She giggle and hurried across the street.."

Paul patted her shoulder and hurried to his truck

The woman watched as he drove away. Oddly enough, the encounter lifted his spirits. Compared to her predicament, his problems were trivial, except for one thing. Everyone in Southern California now knew about his dirty financial underwear. And, beyond standing tall and facing the music, he could do nothing about it. The only solution was money and lots of it. He could skip out, of course, but he had done that to his mother when he joined the marines and left her to die alone. When he got the news of her death, he wanted to shoot himself, but instead, swore bitterly to never again abandon anyone. How had his life become so complicated?

His cell phone buzzed, breaking the downward spiral of his thoughts. "Yoshi, what's up?" Yoshiru Kawasaki was his best friend.

"Horee sheeto, Paul. Just saw you on TV. You found a quarter million bucks?" Yoshi's usually calm voice was up two notches in pitch and several decibels in volume.

"That's what the cops say, Yosh. I didn't count it though. They did."

"Did you get a reward?"

"No."

"Stingy bastards. You should have kicked that stupid reporter's ass."

"Didn't have to. The sergeant did it for me"Hai. So desu. Where are you now?"

"On my way home. Almost there."

"Good. Mr. Moto needs to speak with you about several matters. If it's okay, I'll drop by later."

"Can't wait, Yosh. I got a new bottle of Southern Comfort."

"No, no, Paul-san. You deserve a feast."

"What are you suggesting?"

"Sake and sushi. What else?"

"In that case, hyaku. I ran seven miles today. I'm starving."

"Ah, so. Then I will hurry. Almost four now. Can you hang on until six?"

"Sure, I'll nibble something."

"Great. See you."

Paul hung up and imagined his friend wearing the round gold-rimmed glasses he bought to help him mimic Peter Lorre in the Mr. Moto films. Yoshi was five-feet-four inches tall, but he compensated for his short size by having amazing determination and a sense of humor that made Paul laugh. They met while jogging and had become friends. Paul often tried to outrun him, but no matter how hard he ran, Yoshi always kept up. His short legs moved like high-speed pistons.

At four o'clock, Paul turned into the carport behind his apartment building. He looked forward to seeing his friend and telling him about his visit with the police. Yoshi's father owned luxury hotels in major cities in ten different countries. As a result, Yoshi came to America to study American hotel business practices, but elected to hang out and play in Southern California instead. His father gave him an allowance that was twice Paul's annual income, yet he remained polite and unassuming. He was generous, and he was goofy sometimes, too, but Paul knew he was brilliant. Yoshi held black belts in judo and karate and, off and on, taught Paul some of his self-defense techniques. Yoshi was a huge fan of John Marquand's Mr. Moto novels. He even claimed he resembled Peter Lorre, who played the international agent in eight black and white films. But he always added, "Except I'm taller and better looking."

Thought of Yoshi's upcoming visit lifted his spirits. He

relaxed. Detective Johnson was right. That reporter was a jerk and not worth worrying about. The world was full of self-centered, ambitious people who cared only about themselves.

"And I just met a doozy," he muttered to himself, laughing.

Paul put his financial problems out of his mind. They were pressing and had to be solved, but nothing could be done about them today, anyway.

He was smiling by the time he entered his apartment. He wondered what Yoshi had on his mind. His visits were always fun.

FOUR

PAUL RAN UP the front steps of the old duplex where he lived with his mother before joining the Marines. At the door, he adjusted his marine uniform. His visit would surprise her and make her happy. He would shower her with hugs and kisses to show her much he loved her. He banged with his knuckles and waited. No answer. He hit it harder. Still no response. Worried, he tried the knob. It turned. The door swung open. He caught himself and stopped just in time. Shiny, wet quicksand filled the living room wall to wall. One more step and he would have fallen in.

"Paul, help." He searched for the source of the cry. In a back corner, only his mother's grief-stricken face and thrashing right arm were visible above the quagmire. Her stringy gray hair floated on the surface of the thick goo. Her arm flopped around in desperation, trying to keep her afloat, but it wasn't working. She was sinking.

"Mom, hang on," he screamed. He scanned the room for a way to reach her, but found none. The quicksand was wall to wall.

"It's okay, son. Don't worry about me. I love you." Her voice was tired, and she tried to smile as her haggard face and arm sank under the muck. He screamed.

The mechanical bell on Paul's apartment door rang. Ring, ring. It sounded like a bicycle handlebar ringer, but it worked well enough to penetrate his nightmare and wake him. Groaning, he sat up, trying to sweep the fuzz from his brain. The nightmare was a recurring one that had plagued him ever since his mother died. He hated it. His encounter with the homeless woman must have brought it on.

Two more impatient jangles.

"Hang on. I'm coming."

His apartment was a sardine can, but the sofa was long and comfortable, perfect to lie on and watch TV. He had fallen asleep watching his own story being broadcast over a local TV station. The bell rang.

He scrubbed his face in his hands and yelled, "Okay, okay. I'm coming." His wristwatch said five-thirty. Too early for Yoshi.

The visitor was a tall man in his mid-fifties, dressed in a light-gray suit.

"May I help you?"

"Are you Mr. Davenport?"

"Yes. Who are you?" He was not a bill collector. He appeared too honest and friendly.

"Name's Frank Carlin, sir." He stuck out a business card. "I'm a private investigator working for a lawyer named Huckabee. May we go inside?"

Paul's heart took a swan dive off a tall cliff. "Is somebody suing me?"

The detective looked amused. "Not that I know of. Mr. Huckabee saw you on TV and asked me to contact you. He's an estate attorney. May we talk?"

The guy appeared friendly, and now his demeanor piqued Paul's curiosity. "Sure, why not? Come on in."

He sat in the rocking chair inherited from his mother and waved the detective to sit on the sofa. "What's this about? If I'm not being sued, why is an estate attorney interested in me? Is it about the money I found this afternoon?"

"Oh, yes. I heard about that. The news people called you a hero."

"Yeah, but I don't feel like one. I found two suitcases full of cash and took them to the cops. Why are you here?"

"A lawyer named Huckabee with offices in downtown Pasadena asked me to find you. May I ask where you were born?"

Should he answer? He decided. "In Arkansas."

"What was your father's name?"

"James Davenport."

"Is he still alive?"

"No. He died three months ago. Why the inquisition?"

"What about your mother?"

"She's gone, too. I'm an orphan. What's this about?"

"Lawyer Huckabee wants to see you. I had to be sure you're the right Paul Davenport."

"Am I?"

"Yep. Saw a copy of your driver's license."

"Where?"

"Mr. Huckabee's office."

"So?"

"Mr. Huckabee would like you to visit him tomorrow morning at 8:00 AM."

"I have a job."

"What time do you start?"

"Eight o'clock."

"Can you call in and be late?"

"That depends. What's this about?"

"Sorry, but that's above my pay grade. However, I know you don't have anything to worry about. Mr. Huckabee specializes in large estates. Who knows, maybe you struck it rich."

Paul chuckled. "I doubt it. I'm the last of the Mohicans. No home, no family, no rich relatives. Miracles don't happen to me."

"Sorry, but that's all I can tell you. Mr. Huckabee wants to give you the news himself."

"What news?"

"Like I said. That's above my pay grade."

Frank Carlin's blue-gray eyes matched the color of his hair and suit. He studied Paul and said, "If you don't mind my saying so, Mr. Davenport, you look exhausted. Are you okay?"

"Fine. Just tired. I ran seven miles this afternoon. And there was that stupid interview."

Carlin shook his head. "Seven miles? Makes me tired even to think about it." The detective pulled another card from his suit pocket, rose, and handed it to Paul. "That's Lawyer Huckabee's address. Will you be there?"

Paul hesitated. It had to be a case of mistaken identity, but his curiosity was splitting its seams. "Yes." He took the card. "You sure you can't say why he wants to see me?"

Frank Carlin's eyes showed distress. "It wouldn't be unethical, but I can guess.

"Guess then."

"Wish I could, but I enjoy working for Mr. Huckabee. He doesn't hire people who can't control their mouths. I'll tell you one thing, though. Most folks like what he has to say, so don't be late. Mr. Huckabee runs a tight schedule."

The detective shook hands and left.

Paul stared after him, allowing himself a moment's daydream. Could the man be right? He had a rich relative he didn't know about? Then he sighed. A stupid idea. He had no family. Still…

He walked into the kitchen, considered pouring a drink, but the doorbell rang again. Five forty-five. Still too early for Yoshi, who was obsessed with punctuality. Who else then? He went to the door.

FIVE

A STRONG WHIFF of perfume greeted him, along with a pair of flashing, long-lashed brown eyes when he opened the door. The eyes weren't smiling. They met his own gaze for two seconds and shifted past him.

"Aurora, this is a pleasant surprise. What—?"

"I have to talk to you. May I come in?" Her voice was frosty with and razor sharp.

"Sure, sorry." He stepped back, surprised by her brusque response.

Aurora Tagliano, long, glistening brown hair, built sleek and dressed to perfection in an expensive black dress, brushed past him like a bitter wind. No usual peck on the lips. he had dated her once or twice a month for almost a year, but on their last two dates, she kept trying to discuss marriage. In his mind, the idea was impossible, given his circumstances.

He motioned to the sofa. "Can I get you a drink?"

"No." She met his eyes. "Why didn't you tell me?"

"Tell you what?"

"That you're bankrupt and that your father hung himself. I trusted you, and it turns out I don't even know you."

"How did you hear about my father? That's private

information."

"Dad saw you on TV and called some people. He said you left your mother alone to die in poverty when you joined the marines. How could you do that?" Her lips protruded in a pout. "Anyway, that doesn't matter. My dad says insanity runs in families. He ordered me to stop seeing you."

"Then why are you here?" Her accusation was a battering ram. He retreated into the kitchen to put space between them.

"Because you told me you wanted to have a family someday. But that was a lie. You care about nothing. Dad says you dated me because he's rich." Her voice broke. "Was that it? You wanted my father's money?"

"Sure. What else would I be interested in? You?" He regretted his words as soon as he spoke them. "Aurora, I'm sorry. I didn't mean that."

Tears welled in her eyes. "You think I'm an idiot for wasting a year of my life on you. I hate you!"

"In that case, perhaps you should leave. My insanity might be contagious."

She glared at him. Paul walked to the door and held it open for her. She swung to slap him. He caught her wrist before the blow landed and urged her into the hallway.

"Goodbye, Aurora. Have a happy life." She hurried toward the stairway exit.

"Shit!" He went back into the kitchen. There, with his heart drumming in his ears, he stood for a moment and before retrieving the bottle of Southern Comfort. He poured a drink and took it to the living area and flopped into his rocking chair. He loved sitting and rocking in it, which he often did when he wanted to mull over a problem. Today was no different. The whiskey in the glass rolled back and forth like a tiny amber wave.

Her father figures I'm a candidate for the nuthouse. The idea drifted into his mind like an ominous cloud. Then an even darker cloud swallowed the first one, like a killer whale consuming a shark. She says I believe in nothing. He stopped rocking to examine the idea. Was she right?

Most of his deepest beliefs came from his mother and the Corps. He loved and trusted America, the Marine Corps, and its motto, Semper Fi, which meant always faithful. He believed in honor and duty and close families, though he was ashamed of his failure in that area. And he believed in loyal friends, too. Yet, he had inherited no rules or traditions from his family. They never owned a home. Like gypsies, they never settled in one place for long. As a result, he had no close friends. His father was a drunk who now and then beat his mother until he left them to fend for themselves. His mother's life had spiraled into a physical and economic struggle to survive. During those bad years, he had fended for himself, living like a tumbleweed rolling in the wind.

After high school, he began working his way through UCLA, but when his father left home, he gave up and ran away to join the Marines. His mother's last words to him had been, "Paul, write to me, please. You are an intelligent man, and I'm proud of you, but promise me you won't follow in your father's footsteps. Find a good woman and marry her. Be true to her. Men are not meant to be alone. A man alone is only half what God intended."

He had blown her off with a cursory, "Sure, Mom," and a quick hug, leaving her to die in solitude and poverty while he was in Afghanistan. Over the years, she wrote him many upbeat letters, never mentioning her own problems. In return, he had responded only two or three times. His notes were always short, with little about his personal life, more to fulfill a duty than to send love. When he got home, he found them tucked in a dresser drawer with a blue ribbon around them. The memory caused his throat to constrict with remorse.

The nightmare vision of his mother sinking in quicksand rose in his mind. He shuddered and stared at the whiskey in the glass. A cold emptiness stirred in his gut. Aurora's father said insanity runs in families, and that had made him angry. Why? He had worried about the same thing, enough so that on his last visit with the doctor who treated his father, he had broached the subject.

"Doctor Lanza, do I have anything to worry about?" he had asked.

"Like what, Paul."

"Well, you know. Doesn't mental illness run in families?"

"Most doctors would say yes, but in your father's case, years of excessive alcohol abuse caused his problem. Why? Are you feeling depressed?"

"Only about the size of your bills."

The doctor chuckled. "Do you drink?"

"Now and then, but—."

"How often?"

"Several times a week after work."

"How much?"

"One or two shots to relax."

"I see. To be honest, I do that myself, but I don't have your family history. Would you like my advice?"

Paul chuckled. "Sure, as long as it's free."

"Well, you look fit. Do you exercise?"

"Several miles a week."

"Good. Keep that up. Eat right and lay off the booze. You may be prone to alcoholism."

"Right. Thanks."

Paul lifted the whiskey glass. Untouched. He rose, walked to the kitchen, and stopped at the sink. "Promise me you won't follow in your father's footsteps." He dumped the drink into the sink and washed the glass.

The thought of his father's suicide was something he wanted to forget, but it lingered in his thoughts like dust in the corner of a big room. He ground his teeth. "I'll make you proud, Mom. I promise." Maybe.

What the hell is wrong with me? he wondered, returning to the rocker. Nothing. I'm the perfect piece of driftwood, with no money, no goals, no family, no home, heavy debt, and no future. He grew angry at his own sense of helplessness. Without a goal, a person was a rudderless boat adrift in a choppy sea. I won't be like my dad, he told himself. I won't. He clamped his jaws. I'll find a proper goal as soon as I pay off the hospital.

His thoughts returned to Aurora. Nothing about her had attracted him enough to want marriage or share a family. Even on their first date, she had been conniving and manipulative, plus she had pushed herself on him. But she had been an amiable enough companion and someone to help break the drudgery of endless work. He pictured the anger in her face when she tried to slap him, and an odd relief washed over him. She was out of his life now. His shoulders lifted as if a heavy burden had been removed.

He hoped Yoshi's visit would help cheer him up.

SIX

YOSHI POUNDED on the apartment door at six o'clock sharp. Paul let him in, and his friend handed him a giant bottle of sake and a wicker picnic basket. Then he bowed and said in his imitation of Peter Lorre's whiny voice, "Mr. Moto thanks you very much for gracious invitation."

Paul laughed, as always, at his friend's silliness. "No, I thank you for the food. Let's get this feast underway. I'm starving." The kitchen clock said six o'clock.

Yoshi peered at him through his gold-rimmed spectacles. His dark hair was trimmed and combed to perfection. "If you don't mind, I must speak with you about several things before pleasure."

Paul sat the bottle and basket on the counter and turned back. "Sure, what's up?"

Yoshi sat on the sofa. "I'm worried," he said.

"About what?"

"About you. You may be in danger. Drug gangs don't like people who appropriate their property."

"I didn't appropriate it. I took it to the cops. That may piss them off, but why would they be mad at me?"

"Because evil people live by a different code. You must be

careful."

"Well, why would they come after ne, The cops have their money. If they want it back, they can get it from them. You worry too much."

"No, no, Paul-san. I am in your debt. I must worry. You saved my life."

"That's an exaggeration. I helped a fellow jogger."

"Yes, by carrying me for three miles to your car when I broke my leg. If you hadn't done so, I'd be in a coffin, not here."

"Damn it, that was two years ago. We're friends."

"Yes, so I worryv Drug dealers are evil people. They could come after you for honor's sake. They lost a quarter of a million dollars."

Paul sighed and gave up. "You sound like Bill Johnson. He warned me, too. So, I promise. I'll watch myself and call the cops if I hear anything squeak or go bump in the night. Okay?"

"Yes, okay. But—"

Paul sat. Yoshi had more to say. "What is it?"

"Well, I was unaware of your service record and you never mentioned you had financial difficulties. I am saddened to hear that your otosan died. The shock must have been terrible."

"Yes, it was a nasty surprise, but it was also a blessing. I spent two years caring for him, and in the end, he didn't recognize me. He was miserable. At least it's over for both of us."

"I understand, except for your financial difficulties. I knew nothing about that. Please, let me help you. I waste more money than you know, and—"

Paul held up his hand. "Yoshi, you're the best friend I've ever had, and I thank you, but I don't believe friends should burden each other. Let's drop it, okay? It's my problem, and I'll handle it somehow. If you don't mind, I'd rather not talk about it." Paul reddened.

Yoshi looked stricken. "Paul-san, I'm so sorry. I will never mention it again. Forgive me."

"Damn it, Yosh. There's nothing to forgive. If you needed

help, I would say the same thing. Is it time to eat yet?"

"Ah, one more subject."

"Shoot."

"My father called last night from Tokyo. He will arrive in Los Angeles tomorrow afternoon about six o'clock. I must meet him at the hotel at seven. He says it's time for me to go to work and take responsibility. He plans to tour major hotels in the U. S. And I must travel with him to learn the business."

"You mean I'll lose my jogging buddy?"

Yoshi nodded.. "Yes. I am sorry to leave, but my father's patience has ended. He ordered me to go to work."

"Will you keep in touch?"

"Paul-san, we are best friends." Paul shoved up from the rocker. He waved to the basket on the kitchen counter. "In that case, what say we prepare this stuff? What do we need?"

Yoshi jumped up and hurried into the kitchen. "You need a pot to heat the sake, cups and a tray, plates and chopsticks to serve the sushi."

When they were done, they took their feast into the living room and sat. Yoshi did the honors of pouring the sake.

They lifted the small white sake cups Paul kept for Yoshi's visits. "Here's to good friends." He held up his drink.

Yoshi bowed and hoisted his cup. "To best friends. Kanpai."

As the evening wore on, Paul told Yoshi about Aurora.

Yoshi nodded and muttered something that sounded like, "Yoi yakkai harai desu."

"Huh?"

Yoshi chuckled. "I said 'Good riddance.' I never liked her anyway."

They both laughed long and hard.

At eight o'clock, Yoshi rose and said, "I have to go. I must pack and be ready for my father's arrival."

"Yoshi, wait. You need coffee before you drive, and there's something I want to discuss with you. Can you spare a few more minutes?"

His friend fell back on the sofa. "Make it black and bitter, dozo."

While he brewed two cups, Paul told him of Frank Carlin's strange visit. He finished at the same time the coffee was ready. He handed Yoshi a cup on a saucer. "So, what do you think Yoshi took a sip of the steaming liquid and then set it aside on a small circular table next to the sofa. After a minute, he said, "Sounds as though you have a relative who died."

"I have no relatives."

"You mean none you know of? The detective said you'd like the lawyer's revelations, right?"

"Yes."

"Then we must be there at eight o'clock sharp."

"We?"

"Hai, Paul-san. You need reinforcements when you visit a lawyer. Two heads are always better than one."

"But how can you spare the time? Don't you have to pack?"

"I'll do that tonight. I don't have to meet Otosan until seven P.M. Mr. Moto thinks you must have someone with you. If you don't mind, I wish to spend one last day with my best friend. If this Lawyer Huckabee bears important news for you, I want to be there to share it."

"Are you sure?"

"Yes. I have a good feeling about this."

Yoshi took a swig from his coffee, set the cup aside, and rose. "I'll be here at seven o'clock tomorrow morning. We will go in my Mercedes."

Paul stood. "Thanks, Yoshi."

Yoshi did a quick bow. "My pleasure. Paul-san."

Paul followed him to his car, where they exchanged hugs. He fought back tears as his friend drove away. Yoshi wasn't just his best friend. Mr. Moto was his only close friend. When Yoshi turned the corner at the end of the block, he climbed halfway up the apartment steps and sat.

A gentle breeze caressed his face and gave him a lift. Huge

old sycamore trees lined the street and soughed mournfully in the wind. On the distant corners, orange street lights cast warm circles onto the sidewalk. A young couple stood embracing under a tree. Peaceful and deserted.

Paul took a deep breath and leaned back on the steps. Today had been one for the books. On top of everything else, now his closest friend was leaving town.

His gaze returned to the couple. They were kissing. She had one foot up behind her. He felt empty and alone. He looked away, lifted his phone, and called his boss. To the answering machine, he said, "Bill, it's Paul. I'll be in late. I'll call you."

What could an estate lawyer possibly want with him? He was frowning when he went up to bed.

SEVEN

SAMANTHA DUET stood eyeing herself in her dresser mirror. Her expression resembled that of a hanging judge. Her blue eyes accused her of being a traitor. She turned away, not wanting to see the guilt in them. Instead, she examined the black shirt and pants purchased for tonight's undertaking. They hid any skin on her arms and body. She studied her face. Should she darken it? No.

She lifted the long navy-blue beanie lying on top of the dresser and pulled it over her golden, shoulder-length hair, now balled into a low bun. That should do it, she thought.

A dull thump came from her father's adjoining bedroom. She caught her breath and listened. His door opened and closed. The clock on her dresse said it was ten 'til midnight. She frowned. He was leaving the house again. Why? Where was he going? Ever since her return from college two weeks ago, he had left his room every night. Once, she asked him where he went, and he snapped at her, "You're mistaken, Sam. I never go out after dark. Mind your own business."

Why would he lie? Shaken by the anger in his voice, she vowed to discover the reason for his behavior. Several times she followed him but lost sight of him because she didn't plan for it. She took too long to get dressed. This time, though, she was ready.

Samantha hurried to her bedroom door and placed her ear against it. She heard her dad's feet clumping down the stairs. She waited thirty seconds and then tiptoed to the top of the stairway. From there, she watched him leave the cottage and disappear into the night.

Heart pounding, she hurried downstairs to the front door, opened it a crack, and peered out. A bright three-quarter moon hung low above Chateau Montmartre, which stood a hundred yards from the cottage. The mansion was a watchful guardian, brooding over the vast estate grounds cared for by her father. Its sharp-pointed spires resembled giant spears stabbing into the sky. At night, the chateau was an evil silhouette of the cheerful Victorian home that smiled a welcome in the daytime. She shuddered. The sight always caused foreboding to rise within her. She had begged hundreds of times to go inside, but Uncle Justin, the owner, ordered her dad to keep her away. In twenty years, she had never seen inside the house.

Samantha tore her thoughts from the mansion and sought her father's figure. She sooh she found him. In the moonlight, he was a tall, long-legged silhouette moving toward the mansion house. She slipped outside and pressed against the front door. The lunar brightness made her glad she had bought the beanie. The great yellow satellite seemed to point straight at her. She tried to make herself invisible.

Samantha stood, slowing her breath, waiting until he was far enough ahead of her, and then stepped onto the grass alongside the walkway that led to the big house. Heart thumping, she followed her father, prepared to dive to the ground if he turned to look back. She need not have worried. His movement resembled a zombie from one of the old black and white movies. Tears welled in her eyes. Where are you going?

When she first arrived at school, he had written cheerful letters to her. Now he was a frightening stranger.

Her father reached the left-hand corner of the wide porch that wrapped around three sides of the mansion. He rounded the corner and disappeared from view. Samantha quickened her step. She didn't want to lose him. She aimed for the same corner. Once there,she tepped into the open to find him. He was now fifty yards ahead of her, moving past a four-foot-tall stone water well long ago filled with dirt and used as a planter. She loved that old well. It had always seemed magical to her because of its explosion of colorful flowers.

She gulped air and hurried to duck behind the well. There, bending low, she peeked around the stone structure. To her surprise, he had vanished. She rose, intending to keep going, but stopped when his voice, mumbling, reached her from a distance. She clamped her mouth shut to avoid calling out to him. Instead, she crept toward the sound. A few steps later, she froze when she saw him standing with his back to her inside a tall, arched garden trellis loaded with grape-like clusters of Wisteria flowers. He was staring upward at the moon.

She moved closer until she could understand his words.

"Yes," he said. "Tomorrow." He became silent, as though listening. After a moment, he said in a loud voice. "No! I can't do that. I have my daughter to think about." Another silence, then, "No, you have to find another way." Pause as if he was listening, then, "You can kill me, if you wish, but I won't do it, and that's final."

Won't do what? Samantha stood with her mouth open. Who was he talking to? Who could kill him? There was no one there. She swallowed a powerful desire to cry out.

Suddenly, her father flew backward as if a powerful force had hit him in the chest. He stumbled several steps before tripping and falling. He landed on his buttocks. Before she could move, he scrambled to his feet and stared at the trellis. "Go to hell!" he yelled and turned in her direction. "Do with me what you will, but I won't do it."

Do what?

Samantha raced back to the well and ducked behind it. Looking straight ahead, her father walked past her, still walking as if in a trance. When he was gone, she hurried to the trellis. She looked everywhere but found nothing. He had been talking to himself.

"Oh, Dad," she sobbed. "What has happened to you?"

Her heart heavy, she walked toward the grounds keeper's cottage that had been her home since early childhood. It had always been a happy place, but no longer.

What was it her father thought his imaginary opponent wanted him to do?

"Damn, damn," she said in a soft tone. Then she gave vent to her frustration. "Dad, what's wrong with you?"

EIGHT

T HE LAWYER'S OFFICE occupied the entire top floor of a small four-story building in downtown Pasadena. Gold lettering on the glass entry doors declared: Thomas J. Huckabee, Attorney at Law. Its classic styling showed the lawyer was doing well.

What the hell am I doing here? Paul wondered. The detective said Huckabee wasn't a bill collector, so what did he want?

Yoshi rushed ahead and pulled open the door. Inside, they approached a plastic-looking, professional blond at the reception desk.

She glanced up from a stack of papers and smiled. "May I help you?"

"Paul Davenport for Lawyer Huckabee."

"One moment, please." The woman pushed an intercom button.

"Yes?"

"Sir, your eight o'clock is here."

"Excellent. Send him in."

The blond rose. "This way, sir." She walked to a heavy oaken door, opened it, and stepped aside.

Paul entered, followed by Yoshi.

A plump, pleasant-looking, pink-faced man with a shiny bald head jumped up and hurried around his sprawling polished desk with his hand stuck out.

"Mr. Davenport, I'd recognize you anywhere from seeing you on TV." His voice was a deep bass, which didn't go with his looks. "Thomas Huckabee at your service."

Paul shook hands and turned to Yoshi. "This is my adviser, Yoshiru Kawasaki. I asked him to accompany me. I hope you don't mind."

The lawyer's eyes brightened as he shook Yoshi's hand. "Kawasaki? Not—.

"Nope. I wish, though."

"Please, have a seat." Lawyer Huckabee gestured at two cushy leather seats facing his desk. He walked around to his chair. "We were planning to approach you today, but when I watched your interview on TV last night, I phoned Frank Carlin. That was quite a story."

"More than you know." Paul sat and leaned back.

The lawyer opened a thick file folder, studied it, and then smiled at Paul. "Has anyone told you why you're here?"

"Not yet. Your detective requested me to come, so I'm here to satisfy my curiosity. What's this about?"

"I see," the lawyer said, frowning. "Are you aware you had an uncle, Mr. Davenport? A man named Justin Davenport?"

"No. Never heard of him. As far as I know, I have no relatives. My mother and father are dead. I'm an only child."

"Yes, Iright Ah, just a formality, but may I see you drivers license? We obtained your birth records, and we need to see your driver's license. Do you have it with you?"

Paul dug his wallet from his back pocket, opened it to his license, and shoved it across the desk. The lawyer compared it to a document in the folder and returned it. "Thank you, that's fine." He studied his documents and then smiled by showing his teeth. "Sir, I have good news for you. Your uncle, your father's older brother, Justin Davenport, died three weeks ago.

Mr. Davenport accumulated a rather large fortune in his day, seventy-five million dollars. You are his only living heir. As a result, if you meet certain conditions, you stand to inherit his entire estate. What do you think of that?" The lawyer beamed at Paul, expecting an excited reaction.

Paul frowned instead. "I'm astonished, I guess. Seventy-five million? You mean I'm rich now? Or is this some kind of scam?" He squelched the hope bubbling in his breast.

The lawyer held up a hand. "I apologize, Mr. Davenport. This is no scam, as you called it, but I don't want to mislead you, either. You may become rich, sir, but there's a catch."

"How so?" Yoshi asked.

Lawyer Huckabee turned to Yoshi. "Well, Mr. Davenport's uncle was a rather eccentric gentleman. There are stipulations in his will."

"What does that mean?" Paul asked.

"Ah, well, you see, he owns an old house."

"What's strange about that? Millions of other people do, too."

"Yes, but your uncle believed ghosts occupy his."

"You're kidding!"

"I wish I were."

"How big is it?" Yoshi asked.

"Chateau Montmartre is a great Victorian-style home with sixteen-thousand square feet of space. The place has twenty-six rooms, including nine bedrooms, seven bathrooms, a large parlor, an even larger two-story library, a dining room, plus all the other essentials. There's a basement, too, with the same dimensions as the house. Mr. Davenport added a separate garage for five vehicles, a tennis court and a swimming pool. There are several other utility buildings, too. A twelve-foot high stone fence with a heavy iron gate blocks the entrance to Montmartre Valley. The estate occupies nine very expensive acres."

"That's a monster," Yoshi said.

Paul frowned. "What about servants? That sounds too big

for one man. How did he live?"

"Well, a grounds keeper named Gerard Duet has worked there for twenty years. Mr. Duet has a twenty-eight-year-old daughter, Samantha, who recently graduated with a degree in English literature and returned from attending Harvard University, I believe." The lawyer wrinkled his nose. "For your information, your uncle paid her entire tuition."

"That's it?"

"Not quite. Until a year ago, Mr. Davenport had a man living with him. Your uncle referred to him as a gentleman's gentleman. His name was Franz Heimlich. There were no other servants. Mr. Heimlich cooked for them and did other chores. They were close friends." He paused. "Oh, I should tell you. Your uncle left the place well stocked with food."

"What happened to Mr. Heimlich?"

"He died a year ago of a heart attack. Your uncle removed him from his will."

"Where is the property?" Yoshi asked.

"It's in the Santa Monica Mountains, a few miles inland from Malibu, California. It sits in a valley just off Latigo Canyon Road, which winds its way east through the hills from Coast Highway. A man called Fortune Montmartre, the original owner named the house and the valley. Montmartre was a Frenchman who struck it rich during the California gold rush. Your uncle believed the man's name was fictitious, though he may have been from the Montmartre district in Paris."

"How old is the place?" Paul asked.

"The chateau was built in 1890, but don't let its age concern you. It's in perfect shape and has all the modern conveniences. Your uncle spent a fortune rejuvenating the mansion and the valley. Montmartre is now an incredible oasis nestled in the Santa Monica Mountains."

"A haunted oasis," Paul said, not hiding his cynicism.

"Yes."

"Depending on traffic, Malibu is about forty-eight miles or

an hour and a half west of here," Yoshi said, studying his smart phone.

"You mentioned stipulations," Paul said. "You mean conditions I have to meet to get the money?"

The lawyer looked away, embarrassed. His face turned red. "Yes."

"What are they?"

"Your uncle requires you to live in Montmartre for two weeks and save a beautiful young female ghost named Helena Montmartre. He believed she is being tortured by the evil ghost of her husband, who also lives there. Those are his terms. If you don't agree, you get nothing. His entire fortune goes to charity." The lawyer paused. "One more thing. The time limit is not negotiable. You must meet your uncle's requirements in that time or lose everything."

Paul stared at the desktop to hide his thoughts. First his father, and now his uncle. "My dad says insanity runs in families," Aurora had said. Am I next? he wondered. He gritted his teeth and looked at the lawyer.

"Mr. Huckabee, how did my uncle die?" He prayed it wasn't alcohol related.

"Yes, I expected you'd want to know that. For the past year, your uncle has been dying of incurable cancer. His physician, a Dr. Reese, said he grew quite ill a week before he died. Apparently, his heart just stopped beating one night, which surprised the doctor, who said his demise was unexpected. He found odd bruises on your uncle's chest, as though he had fallen before going to bed or something heavy had pressed on his chest. The doctor found no evidence of foul play, however, and said your uncle's heart just stopped beating. As a result, he pronounced it death due to natural causes. Off the record, however, Dr. Reese said the case was strange. Despite the cancer, Justin Davenport's heart was strong."

"Who found him?"

"The caretaker. He phoned the house twice to get permission

to buy something, I forget what, but your uncle didn't answer. Duet went to the house, found him in his bedroom and called the doctor."

"I see." His pulse rate inched up a notch, and he frowned. "Sir, you said my uncle was eccentric. Was he insane?"

NINE

LAWYER HUCKABEE hesitated, avoiding meeting Paul's gaze.

"Well, was he or not?" Paul demanded. He needed an answer for the sake of his own sanity.

The attorney met Paul's eyes with a pained expression. "That's a matter of opinion, Mr. Davenport. I've known your uncle for years. He was astute and a pleasant gentleman. I guess I'd prefer to remember him as being a rich eccentric. This firm has handled his account for the past twenty-five years. Your uncle believed in his heart that the ghost of Montmartre and his wife haunted his home."

Paul squirmed in his chair. Yoshi, who seemed amused.

"Young man, I'm not allowed to advise you about what to do," the attorney continued, "but I can explain your options. There are only two. You can decline your uncle's conditions, and the entire estate goes to charity except for a small amount to another person. Or you can at least try to do as he asks and perhaps win the lottery."

Paul shook his head. This whole situation was so bizarre that only a crazy person could have created it, and yet this lawyer was real. These offices were real. Lawyer Huckabee wasn't laughing, which itself was crazy.

"Mr. Huckabee, why was it so important to Paul's uncle to save the ghost?"

Paul nodded his appreciation at his friend. Mr. Moto had gone straight for the problem's jugular.

Lawyer Huckabee cleared his throat and his pink face got even redder. "I hate to tell you, Mr. Kawasaki, but Justin Davenport fell in love with Helena, Fortune Montmartre's eighteen-year-old wife. He—."

"So my uncle was insane." Paul blurted. "How can a man love a ghost?"

"I can't answer that, but according to your uncle, the lady is a true beauty."

"Has anyone besides Mr. Davenport seen her?" Yoshi asked.

"I can't answer that either, sir. Mr. Davenport had few visitors."

Paul stood and said, "Mr. Huckabee, I—"

"Paul, wait!" Yoshi said. "Sir, who decides whether Paul has saved the ghost? If success depends on saving her, who's the referee? You?"

Paul sat.

The lawyer shook his head and clucked. "Good question. The ultimate judge is a woman who calls herself Madam Song, a psychic hired by Mr. Davenport's uncle."

Paul nodded thanks to Yoshi. At least his brain was functioning.

"Mr. Huckabee, this sounds like an expensive undertaking. Two weeks is a long time. If you watched the TV interview, you know I'm not only flat broke, I'm deep in debt and close to Chapter Seven bankruptcy. I couldn't finance three days living in that place with no income, let alone two weeks without income. So, I guess I'll say no... unless there's a way out."

The lawyer pinched his brows and nodded. "I saw the interview, and I understand your predicament. However, your uncle foresaw just this situation. His will accommodates your dilemma. I'm allowed to advance you all the money you need to purchase equipment or services you require in order to save the Helena from eternal torture. I'm also allowed to pay you one hundred thousand dollars as income for the time you are at the estate. The bottom line is, I'm allowed to pay for anything you can convince me is necessary to meet the conditions of the will."

"A hundred thousand? Dollars?"

"Yes. Whether you succeed or fail, that money will be yours."

"So, I have nothing to lose."

"Only a fortune, but considering your present circumstances, yes."

"Mr. Huckabee, I'm a computer programmer. I have no idea how to begin a project like this. Truth is, I don't believe in ghosts. How can I save something that doesn't exist?"

The lawyer looked at Paul with an apologetic expression. "You have my sympathy, Mr. Davenport. I agree with you, about ghosts, I mean. To be honest with you, presenting your uncle's terms is embarrassing, but as his attorney, I'm compelled to follow the letter of his will"How long has my uncle known about me?" Paul's curiosity was overwhelming.

"Sorry. I don't know that. Justin Davenport gave me a letter to open ten days after his interment, which was sixteen days ago. We learned of your existence in that letter."

"Where is he buried?"

"At the estate. Years ago, he received permission to create a family cemetery. He told me once he hoped to meet up with his lady love in the afterlife."

"Amazing." The idea made Paul sick. Suicidal father. Insane uncle. "So you learned about me yesterday when you saw me on TV?" he asked in a calm tone.

"Yes. No. We learned of your existence a few days ago. Your appearance on TV prompted me to contact you yesterday rather than today. We want to execute your uncle's will as soon as possible, to close our books on the case, you might say."

"Did Paul's uncle leave any kind of information that could

help him?" Yoshi asked.

"He did, Mr. Kawasaki. He left quite a few diaries detailing his efforts to save Helena, but they are not in our possession. Perhaps Madam Song can help with that." The lawyer lifted a sealed envelope. "It may be in this envelope addressed to Mr. Davenport."

Paul rose and reached for the envelope, but the lawyer pulled it back and dropped it into the folder.

"Sorry. I'm not allowed to give this to you until you agree to your uncle's terms."

"You mean about saving the ghost?"

"Yes."

"I see," Paul sat back. "So, what do I have to do?"

Lawyer Huckabee reached for another sheet of paper and held it up. "Sign this. Once it's witnessed, we can proceed."

"What is it?" Yoshi asked.

"It's a contract between Paul and my firm requiring him to comply with the terms of his uncle's will and make all efforts to save the young ghost. Once he does that, I can release his uncle's letter to him and half of the funds he will need."

"Give it to me. I'll sign."

The lawyer shoved the paper across to Paul along with a shiny-black, gold-rimmed pen.

"So what does Mr. Moto have to say.?"

"Mr. Moto says hell, yes. A hundred thousand bucks is a reasonable incentive, don't you think?"

"Yeah, I think."

"Mr. Moto?" Puzzled, the lawyer raised his brows.

"Inside joke. Sorry."

He read the documant and signed it. It was a simple agreement that didn't require study. He shoved it back to the lawyer and asked, "What's next?"

TEN

WHAT HAPPENED next was simple, too.

The secretary came in, witnessed and notarized the document, and then tucked it away in a corner filing cabinet. After that, smiling like a man who had scored a super-bowl touchdown, the lawyer shoved the letter from his uncle across the desk to Paul. "Would you like to read it in private?"

"No." Paul examined the envelope. On the outside in dark-blue ink, his uncle had written, "To my only heir." Paul grabbed a corner to tear it open, but the lawyer offered him a sharp-edged letter opener. He used it to slit the envelope and retrieved four folded sheets of watermarked stationery. With a trembling hand, he opened the pages. The penmanship was small and neat.

April 1, 20___

My dear nephew,

If you are reading this letter, I assume you are in Lawyer Huckabee's office, and that, by now, you are aware my net worth exceeds seventy-five-million dollars. It will all be yours, including Montmartre, my home in the mountains near Malibu, California... if you can fulfill my request to save the woman I love from eternal torture. You will learn more about that later, but first let me clear up one important point.

I am not insane!

I am certain Lawyer Huckabee would disagree, but, fearing losing my lucrative account, he has overlooked what he calls my "eccentricities." So, I ask you now to discount his belief and heed what I am about to tell you. It is all true.

Fifty years ago, at age eighteen, I left home and traveled to South Africa. There, I worked hard, made some important connections and over a few years accumulated a fortune in the gold-mining industry. When the South African mines played out, I made other connections with some not-so-savory people in the diamond industry. In that endeavor, I further increased my fortune, but encountered the displeasure of a group of nasty men who wanted me dead.

Twenty-five years ago, using a phony name, I escaped from South Africa and returned home. I sought a place to live that would allow me to live a private life and remain difficult to find. That is when I bought the Montmartre property in the mountains. Neglected for many years, it was in a sad state when I bought it. So, to make it habitable, I spent a small fortune on both the house and the property. It is now a shining example of decadent living and is an ideal hideaway for one seeking anonymity.

Now comes the crux of your situation.

After I settled in at Montmartre, I soon heard a young woman's agonized scream in the night. I investigated and learned that if I remained still and silent, I could see her moving about the house. She is eighteen years old, has long blond hair, blue eyes and skin that is creamy white and smooth as silk. The girl wears a sheer see-through nightgown that embarrassed me at first, but I soon succumbed to the pleasure of seeing her young body.

It surprised her to learn that I could see her, since no one else in the past ever did. Perhaps it is a capability uniquely mine, but it also may be something you can do. Once she understood I could see her, she often gestured with a pained expression on her face. I almost went mad trying to understand what she wanted.

Only after months of frustration, I learned she can manipulate small objects. I got the idea to buy a chalkboard. My first words to her were, "Can you read?" She nodded yes. I next wrote the words, "I want to help you. Can you use the chalk to write messages?" She understood and tried hard to manipulate the chalk. It took more than a month before she learned to do it. Her first message was worse than not understanding her gesturing. It was, "Help me! Please." After that, she explained the details of her plight. During this period, I found her to be intelligent and playful, unless she was in fear of being seen and tortured by her husband.

Her family name was Longmore. The Longmores were a wealthy San Francisco family. The man who built this house, a man named Fortune Montmartre, saw her traveling in a carriage. Thrice her age, his uncontrollable lust drove him to possess her. He hired thugs to kidnap and abscond with her to Montmartre as a toy for his depraved pleasure. There, he used her and sometimes abused her. After a time, he married her. Later, his son joined him there. Helena and the son often found themselves left alone in the house when the father was away. This led them to become lovers. The father returned home and caught them in bed together. In a rage, he murdered the girl and tried to kill his son, but failed. His son killed him instead and disposed of the bodies somewhere on the estate. Authorities, at one point, heard rumors of the murder and showed up to investigate. Their efforts led nowhere, as they never found the victims' remains.

Helena's punishment has been long and miserable. Montmartre murdered her in 1893. She has remained trapped in this house ever since. Montmartre gains his revenge by torturing her. Helena tells me that his strength has grown over the years until he now has the power to manipulate physical objects. As a result, she pleads with me to save her.

Trying to understand how Montmartre hurt her, I asked her many times to explain.. I told her I understood ghosts to be incorporeal, and, therefore, unable to feel pain. She does not know what he does or how he does it, but says he has the ability with his mind to crush her, like a giant foot a balloon flat. The pain is excruciating and she says that, if he did not stop, she would explode like a balloon, and her soul would forever vanish. She believes the only way to save her is to free her from the clutches of Montmartre, but she doesn't know any way to do it.

To my great regret, my years of effort failed to do so, though I tried everything imaginable. Over the years, I searched for and found a reliable psychic named Madam Song. She agreed to help, but other than advice, she had little to offer. After a single visit to Montmartre, she refuses ever to enter the house again. She fears what she calls the "evil spirit" of Fortune Montmartre and something else. I don't blame her for that. He is an evil and angry abomination, and he is much more powerful than Helena. He has tried many times to drive me from the house and once broke my leg. However, I couldn't bear to leave Helena alone with him, so I refused to go. We eventually reached accommodation. Since Madam Song was the only psychic I found with the ability to detect the ghost's presence, I have designated her to be the judge of your success or failure.

I am dying of cancer as I write this. The doctors say my time on this earth is short, so let me beg your forgiveness for the demands I have placed on you before you can inherit my fortune. I make those demands, not because I have anything against you, but because I have fallen in love with Helena and would sacrifice my soul to save her. The futility of my efforts to help her is maddening, but now I must die a broken failure. My investigations of you tell me that, unlike your father, you are a strong-minded man and capable. I admire you for seeking service in the U. S. Marine Corps where you received an award for heroism. I also understand that you requested a hardship leave to care for your dying father. Since you are as close to a son as I will ever have, I regret we have never met. I imagine we would have become friends.

In closing, I must do two things. First, I must warn you that if you undertake to save Helena, you will be in mortal danger. Fortune Montmartre is evil and filled with rage, and though I achieved a sort of accommodation with him, he tried many times to hurt me. He once caused me to break a leg, so he will do everything in his power to kill you or drive you away.

Second, why did I place a two weeks time limit for you to earn your inheritance? The answer is, I believe in incentive. My hope is the size of my fortune will spark your creativity, and you will save Helena. All my efforts over the years failed. As my only living heir, I pass that goal to you. I pray you succeed where I have failed. However, whether you succeed or fail, I have left a last letter to you with the lawyer. Huckabee will open it at the end of your efforts. That letter will contain my last wishes to you, my only heir.

I have requested interment on the grounds at Montmartre in the desperate hope I may meet my Helena in the afterlife. If I succeed, I will battle and destroy the evil Montmartre, though Madam Song says it is unlikely.

May God have mercy on all our souls.

With respects I am,

Your uncle, Justin Davenport.

Paul continued staring at the letter long after he finished reading it.

"Paul? You okay?" Yoshi asked after a few moments.

Paul looked at Yoshi, blinked, and then, oddly relieved, turned to Huckabee.

"My uncle said you have another letter to open at the end of the two weeks. Is that true?"

The lawyer blushed bright red. "Yes. However, I thought it was to be confidential."

"It wasn't. And, for what it's worth, my uncle doesn't sound crazy. He was just..."

"What?" Yoshi asked.

"I don't know. Delusional maybe, but not insane."

"You mean you believe him?" Yoshi asked. His tone was incredulous.

Paul shrugged. "I know he believed. Now you tell me." He passed the letter to his friend.

Paul and the lawyer remained silent on while Yoshi read the letter. When he finished, Yoshi said, "Horee sheeto!"

"Damn it, Yoshi. That doesn't tell me a thing. What do you think?"

Yoshi returned the letter. "I agree."

"With what?"

"He wasn't crazy, but…" Yoshi shrugged.

"May I read the letter, Paul?" Lawyer Huckabee asked.

Paul hesitated and then shrugged. "Sure, why not?"

They waited in silence while the lawyer read it. When he finished, he cleared his throat three times. He passed the letter back to Paul. "Remarkable," he said. "Remarkable."

"What are you going to do?" Yoshi asked.

"I'll investigate and try to fulfill his last wishes. Also, I'll use the money he left me to pay some of my dad's hospital bill. My uncle wasn't insane, and I intend to prove that, too." The letter had given him a rising hope. He looked at the lawyer. "Now what?"

"That's up to you, Paul. How do you want to handle this?"

"Can we push the start date off until after we meet with Madam Song?"

"Good thought," Yoshi said.

"Sorry, the contract started the minute you signed the agreement." The lawyer furrowed his brow. "When will you visit the Madam?"

"As soon as we're finished here,, if possible. I have only two weeks to solve this problem. Can you arrange for me to meet her?"

"Yes. She lives behind her little storefront parlor. She's always there."

"Good." Paul stood and shook hands with the lawyer. "How do we handle the money thing?"

"I'll have a Fifty-thousand dollar check ready for you when you return from seeing Madam Song. My secretary will give you her address."

"Fine." He turned to Yoshi. "An interesting problem, wouldn't you say, Mr. Moto?"

"Hai, so desu. Very interesting. I only wish I could be around to help you solve it."

"So do I, Yosh, but I'll manage somehow."

Yoshi's face became serious. "I want to go with you to visit Madam Song, and if there's time, I'd like to see that house. It sounds fascinating."

"You're welcome to hang out as long as your time permits."

The receptionist gave them Madam Song's address and a card bearing the phone number of Gerard Duet, the estate caretaker.

"You'll need that number to have Mr. Duet let you enter the estate," Huckabee explained.

They shook hands again, and, as they left, Yoshi said, "I wonder what help Madam Song will offer?"

Paul frowned. "Good question, Yosh. We'll find out soon enough."

ELEVEN

A SIGN ON the door's glass window said, "Madam Song. Questions of Love and Destiny." The words wrapped around a purple-blue painting of the zodiac. The parlor was small, occupying only half of a small stucco building on Fair Oaks Boulevard across from Pasadena Central Park.

Paul opened the door. A soft tinkle from a bell above their heads and a strong smell of incense greeted them. The waiting room was narrow and had several old, but clean, stuffed chairs placed against the walls for waiting guests. Across from the door, two glittering purple-blue curtains wavered from the breeze caused by their entrance. Yellow crescent moons, stars, and several small versions of the zodiac gave the room an exotic atmosphere. Paul's stomach took a sudden dive. What was he doing here? He didn't believe in psychics any more than he did in ghosts.

Yoshi closed the door. A rich female voice spoke from behind the curtain. "Please come in, Mr. Davenport, and you, too, Mr. Kawasaki." The accent was unfamiliar, unrecognizable, not Korean, and not American.

They pushed through the curtain into a dark room lit by the bright glow of a large-diameter crystal ball sitting on a circular table. A purple-blue velvet cloth that matched the entry curtains covered the table.

Behind the table sat Madam Song, wearing a purple scarf over shoulder-length black hair. Her visage was overpowering and memorable. The woman's face was long and thin; her nose was tall and sharp, causing her eyes to peer from deep within sunken sockets. Her eyebrows were thick and unruly. Only an occasional glitter on each eyeball signaled she was watching them.

She waved her right arm toward the two chairs across from her. Sequins on the loose sleeves of her purple robe gleamed in the light. "Please, young gentlemen. Be seated."

Paul took the chair on the right; Yoshi sat on the left. The room had the somber feeling of a darkened cathedral. The exotic odor of incense hung even stronger in this room. Yoshi seemed spellbound by Madam Song, who exuded an air of mystery. Paul tried without success to fathom Madam Song's expression.

"And now, Mr. Davenport, how may I help you?" Her voice had an undertaker's gravity.

"Well, I'm not sure. I hoped you could tell me. You understand the terms of my uncle's will, right?"

"Yes. You have two weeks to comply. I am under contract to serve you until you either fail or succeed. Your uncle and I spoke often."

"Then help me now. Tell me how to get rid of Fortune Montmartre. I'm at a loss here."

Two pale hands rose from the woman's sides and hovered over the crystal ball as if seeking warmth. Then they lowered palms-down to the tabletop. "I can understand that, Mr. Davenport. I presume you want me to provide a road map that will tell you how to save the young spirit trapped in your uncle's home."

"For starters, yes. Is that possible?"

"Possible? Perhaps. Probable? No."

"Why? Because the ghost doesn't exist?"

"Ah, so you doubt your uncle's sanity? You are here not to

find out how to save a tortured young spirit, but to learn how to collect your uncle's fortune. Is that not so?"

"No!" Paul checked his temper. He took a breath. "Questioning my motives is presumptuous of you, Madam Song. Until Lawyer Huckabee told me, I thought I had no relatives, much less a rich one. Justin left me a letter expressing his sincere belief that the ghost of Helena Longmore is being tortured. I came here to learn from you the basis of his belief. If you're not willing to help, we'll go."

"Also, Madam," Yoshi said. "Lawyer Huckabee said you are to judge whether Paul has met his uncle's terms. It would help if you told us what he has to do to satisfy you." He looked at Paul. "Sorry. Didn't mean to butt in."

"No problem," Paul said. "Thanks." He looked back at the shadowy face. "Well? What do I have to do? Ghosts don't exist, so I don't see how it's even possible for you to decide. Unless…"

"Unless what? You want to pay me to lie to the lawyer?"

Paul rose. "I think we'd better leave." He motioned to Yoshi.

Madam Song leaned closer to the crystal ball. When she did, Paul almost laughed in relief. Her eyes were friendly, and they were smiling at him. "The first thing, Mr. Davenport, is to accept my apology. I wanted to learn what kind of man you are, and now I am satisfied."

"You mean you were trying to learn whether I'm a gold digger?"

"Yes."

"Does that mean you will help me?"

"It means I will do my best to advise you." Her smile returned. "Will you lift your right arm, please?"

"Why?"

"I wish to see the flesh under your armpit."

"Is this some kind of test?"

"No. I wish to see if you have a birthmark there."

Paul shrugged, lifted his arm, and pulled back the sleeve on his short-sleeve shirt.

"Ah!" the woman said.

"What does that mean?"

"It means you are remarkably like your uncle. He also had three small red circles just below his armpit."

"Is that supposed to be significant?"

"Perhaps. It may mean you have some of his characteristics, too. He was an amazing man."

"Madam, until this morning, my only impossible problem was to find a way to pay off a two-hundred-thousand-dollar hospital bill. Until this morning, I didn't know I had an uncle. And now, I find myself facing an even more hopeless task, to clear my uncle's home of ghosts that don't exist. I know nothing of ghosts, nor, frankly, do I care to. My uncle, however, had great faith in you, so help me. How should I proceed?"

"The terms of your uncle's last will are quite clear. You must save the young ghost. As for gaining approval, you must save the young ghost."

"But where do I start?"

The woman leaned back, once more sending her face in deep shadows. "My advice, young man, is to start where your uncle left off," she said. "Do not waste time retracing old ground."

"Who knows where he left off? Do you?"

"I suggest you examine his diaries. Your uncle kept a detailed log of everything he did and attempted to do over the years. He told me so himself."

"So, you don't have his diaries?"

"No. They're somewhere at the house, but I don't know where he kept them."I see. Madam Song, do you believe my uncle was delusional?"

"You mean, was he insane?"

"Yes."

The woman tilted her head while her dark eyes studied Paul. "I can see the answer to this question is important to you. Why, Mr. Davenport?"

"Because my father hung himself at a mental institution."

"Ah, so you're worried about yourself, too."

"No...yes. Maybe a little."

"Well, stop worrying, Paul. Your uncle was not only sane, he was brilliant and the most dedicated person I've ever known."

"Dedicated?"

"He spent twenty-five years against frightening odds trying to save Helena Longmore."

A relieved laugh escaped Paul.

"You don't believe in ghosts, Mr. Davenport, but I can tell you for a fact that the ghosts of Helena Longmore and her husband Fortune Montmartre haunt your uncle's home." Her tone changed to one almost of admiration. "The creature is evil, dangerous, and incredibly powerful. He may be the most powerful ghost that ever existed, and I'm certain he will try to kill you, so I advise you to be cautious."

"You sound as though you admire him."

"Not admire, Mr. Davenport. I fear him. He is the most powerful presence I've ever encountered."

"How powerful?" Paul stifled another laugh.

"I don't know. He has been there a long time. Perhaps time strengthens a ghost."

Paul sat back, speechless. First his uncle. Now this woman.

"Let me warn you, young man. Fortune Montmartre will do everything in his power to prevent you from freeing Helena. He is a sadist who enjoys punishing his unfaithful wife. He almost killed your uncle on several occasions."

"How can you call her unfaithful?" Yoshi blurted. "He kidnapped her."

"In his mind she was unfaithful, Mr. Kawasaki. I said he is evil."

"So you have no specific advice to help me get started?"

"Specific? No. But I can suggest you read your uncle's diaries and this article from a small-town paper that once existed in Denver, Colorado. This may be of help." She reached inside her robe and retrieved an envelope. "I received this from your uncle a week before he died. He asked me to give it to you. His note to me said it's a newspaper clipping, though it did not say what it's about." She passed a sealed, white, number-ten envelope across the table to him. "After you read your uncle's diaries, you will have more specific questions for me. When you do, you may phone and I will give you another appointment. After that, with one exception, I will help you in any way I can."

Paul lifted the envelope and examined it. In blue ink, it said FOR PAUL DAVENPORT.

"What's the exception?"

"I will never set foot in that house again."

"Why not, Madam Song?" Yoshi asked.

"Because, young man, I value my life." She turned back to Paul. "Call me when you've read your uncle's diaries. Do that, and we can speak from a common ground."

The psychic rose and pushed back her chair. She was as tall as Paul, which shocked him. "Thank you for coming," she said. "Now I must prepare for my next client. Be very careful, Mr. Davenport. Don't let skepticism be the instrument of your death. Montmartre Chateau is deceiving. On the outside, it appears to be a happy place, but, trust me, it is also dangerous. Have a nice day."

Paul shook his head as they left. Madam Song appeared to be intelligent. How could she be so superstitious? Ghosts couldn't kill. They didn't exist.

He looked at the envelope? What else did his uncle have to tell him?

TWELVE

Paul spotted a coffee shop on the corner of Fair Oaks and another street. "I need to make a couple of phone calls, and I'm hungry," he said. "How about you?"

"Starving," Yoshi said. He turned off Fair Oaks and parked behind the restaurant. He opened the door to get out, but Paul stopped him.

"Hang on. Let's read this first."

Yoshi sat back and Paul tore open the envelope. Inside was a short handwritten note and a photocopy of a brief newspaper clipping from the Cripple Creek Beaver dated 1905.

The note was in his uncle's neat handwriting:

Paul,
Two things more:

First, you will need my diaries, which delineate my efforts over the years to save Helena. You will find them in a gray metal lock box in the bottom drawer of my library desk. Read them with care, and you will save much time and frustration by not repeating my own failed efforts.

Second. I received the enclosed clipping from a contact in Colorado. The Cripple Creek Beaver, which no longer exists, published the story. Though this clipping arrived too late for me, it may help you do what I could not do. Have a good life, Paul.

   Justin Davenport

PS. I ordered a new GPR you may find useful. It has not arrived yet.

Paul turned to Yoshi. "My uncle says he ordered a new GPR. Do you know what that is?"

"No, but I'll check." He took out his smart phone and began typing with his thumbs.

Paul lifted the clipping and read.

New Lead In Montmartre Murders
By Carter Franklin

Cripple Creek, Co.—This reporter happened upon information that may lead to solving the infamous disappearance of California's Fortune Montmartre and his beautiful young wife Helena. I learned that a dying man named Talon Montmartre was in a local hospice run by Benedictine Nuns near Cripple Creek. On his deathbed, he asked to speak to a reporter. I recalled the stories and notoriety of the Montmartre Murders, so your intrepid reporter rushed to the hospice posthaste. There, I found the man, shrunken from debauchery, pale and toothless. He opened his eyes upon my arrival. For your enlightenment, you will find my summary of the interview in the following paragraphs.

"I am the son of Fortune Montmartre," he said. "I want to tell you the truth. My father was an evil man. In San Francisco, he belonged to a cult of devil worshipers who kidnapped, abused, and murdered young women from the lower classes. The police learned of the cult and broke it up. My father left San Francisco and moved to Malibu, California. Later, he kidnapped and forced Helena Longmore, a beautiful sixteen-year-old girl, to marry him. Helena and I fell in love. My father found us together and murdered my Helena. He tried to murder me, but I fought him off and strangled him instead."

Your reporter then asked three more questions.

Question: "What have you been doing all these years, sir?"

Answer: "I'm a brick mason. I drifted around. Worked when I needed money. Mostly I did nothing."

Question: "Do you have any regrets about things you've done or left undone in your life?"

Answer: "Yes, I regret I failed to kill my father. I pray that when I'm gone, I can finish the job."

Then I asked a question that burned in the hearts of everyone familiar with the case. "Mr. Montmartre, where are the bodies?"

The man opened his eyes one last time and smiled at me. "I left an upside down clue on the estate," he said. "It's there for anyone of sufficient intelligence to think through the problem and apply what they learn." He closed his eyes and died.

This reporter attended his less-than-auspicious funeral and burial. And that ended this story.

Paul finished reading and looked up from the clipping. Yoshi said, "A GPR is a ground penetrating radar system. They're used on road projects, archeology digs, all kinds of things to detect underground objects. Some of them can detect objects as deep as twenty feet, depending on the soil conditions. Your uncle obviously planned to survey the estate looking for something. Wow!"

His friend's enthusiasm caused him to smile. "Probably bones, Yosh." He handed the note and clipping to Yoshi. "Take a look at this."

Yoshi skimmed it and handed it back.

"Well?"

"Mmmm…An upside down clue. I'd say you now have a

tantalizing goal to get you started, though you can bet people have searched that place a hundred times over the years?"

"I agree, which is likely the reason my uncle bought the GPR. A delicious puzzle, though."

"Yes, damn it, and I have to leave town."

Paul tucked the papers back into the envelope. "Speaking of tantalizing, the smell coming from this coffee shop is driving me nuts. My stomach's screaming for food."

Inside, the coffee shop was empty of customers. A pretty, young Mexican waitress came to their booth and placed coffee cups before them. Her name tag said, "Alana."

"I know what I want," Paul told the girl. "Two eggs over medium, bacon, French fries, white toast and a side order of pancakes."

The girl's eyes grew wide as she jotted the order on her pad. "Wow," she said, smiling at Paul. She turned to Yoshi. "And you, sir?" Her lack of accent said she was born and raised in the U. S.

"Fish-head soup and rice, please."

"What?" Eyes even wider.

Yoshi's eyes twinkled. "Just kidding," he said. "Do you have country-fried steak and eggs, biscuits with white gravy on top?"

"Yes, sir." The girl smiled in relief.

"I'll have that then. And coffee."

"Two coffees, Alana," Paul said.

"I saw you on TV yesterday," she said. "You want ketchup for your fries?"

Paul gave her an appreciative smile. "How'd you guess?"

"You look like a ketchup man," she said teasing. "Wow, a quarter million dollars, and you gave it away. I'll get your coffee."

"You're famous," Yoshi said. "I think she likes you."

"My crystal ball says she goes to a college close by."

"Why do you say that?"

"Just a hunch. Hang on a second." Paul dialed Huckabee's

office. The receptionist answered. "Attorney Huckabee's office."

"Paul Davenport," Paul said. "May I speak to Mr. Huckabee?"

"Sir, he's not here. He went to the bank to get a cashier's check for your first payment. You will receive the second payment next week. He said to tell you he'll be back by ten-thirty."

"All right, thanks. We'll be there."

"Thank you. I'll tell Mr. Huckabee."

"Ten thirty for the money," he told Yoshi.

Alana brought their coffee. She gave Paul another big smile.

"Uh, miss, are you in college around here somewhere?" Yoshi asked.

"Yes. Why do you ask?"

"Just testing a theory." Yoshi blushed.

"What's your major?" Paul asked.

"English," she said. "I'm going for a teaching credential."

An elderly man and his wife entered the shop.

"Excuse me," the girl said. She raced off to serve them.

"You were right," Yoshi said.

"Of course. Mr. Moto's not the only brain around here."

They sipped their coffee, and Yoshi said, "So, what's your plan?"

"I don't have one. How can you plan to achieve the impossible? I had hoped Madam Song would help, but that bombed out. I guess my only option is to find my uncle's diaries. After that, who knows? I see no way to win here."

"According to the lawyer, you have to live at the estate."

"I know. Damn. I have to call my work."

"Is that going to be a problem?"

"No. I'm just wrapping up a project. Their shop programmer can finish it."

Paul phoned his project supervisor.

"Paul. What's up?"

"Tom, something's come up. There's been a death in the family with unexpected complications. Can you get Tang to finish up for me?"

"Sure. How long's this going to take?"

"At least two weeks. Sorry."

"Shit." A sigh. "Okay, well, you gotta do what you gotta do. Call me when you're available again."

"Right, thanks."

"No problem. Take care."

Alana brought their food and put their check on the table. She eyed Paul's breakfast. "You really going to eat all that?"

"I'm a growing boy," he said.

She surveyed him with an approving eye. "I'd say you're just about done with that." Another customer entered. She hurried to seat him.

They ate in silence until their plates were near empty. Paul laid his fork on the plate. "You should drop me off at my place. I'll get my things, pick up the check, and head to Malibu. You need to get ready to meet your dad."

"I'm ready. My bags are in the car. I told you, I want to see Montmartre before I go. I'll drive straight to dad's hotel from there." Yoshi pushed his plate away. It was empty.

THIRTEEN

HIS FOOT SLAMMED the brakes hard. The tires squealed as his truck skidded to a stop. Paul checked the rear-view mirror. No cars in sight. He backed until he found it. Half hidden in weeds, it was a green, arrow-shaped sign with the word "Montmartre" painted on it in white letters. It sat atop a low metal post and pointed to a narrow asphalt road that branched to the right. He turned off the main highway and drove toward a bend in the road fifty yards ahead. The hills on each side of him were matted with dwarf oaks and gray-green sagebrush that filled the air with an unfamiliar, bitter, spicy smell.

He reached the curve and slowed. In front of him, the twelve-foot high stone fence and the tall iron gate mentioned by Lawyer Huckabee rose to make a forbidding barrier. Paul pulled ahead and stopped ten feet from the barrier. The fence showed its age. The gate, though rusty, was newer. On the other side, tall Live Oak trees with gnarled limbs lined both sides of the asphalt road. The trees blocked any view of Chateau Montmartre. He pushed a speed-dial button on his phone and waited. Thirty seconds later, a gruff voice answered. "Who is it?"

"Is this Mr. Duet?" Paul asked.

"Yes. Who is this?" The voice sounded annoyed.

"It's Paul Davenport, sir. I'm at the gate. Lawyer Huckabee said you're expecting me."

"Yeah, right. I'll open the gate for you. Drive in. I'll meet you at the cottage."

"What—?" The man was gone.

There was a clang, and the tall gates opened toward the estate. Paul waited for the gate to open enough to enter. So much for hospitality.

He drove in and found a tall, lean, somber-faced, dark-haired man wearing brown slacks and a khaki shirt stepped to the side of the road and waved. Just behind him was the "cottage" he had mentioned. It was a pleasant two-story stucco house with a red-tiled roof, green shuttered windows, and a second-floor balcony running full width in front. In the distance, Paul could see bits of the chateau's white trim, but nothing more. He stopped. The man came around to his window. Gerard Duet peered through the window and poked a latchkey and a small remote control through to him.

Paul smiled, but got nothing back but a dead pan. He stuck his hand up to shake. The grounds keeper ignored it.

"That's the house key," Duet said, "and that's the control for the gate. You're gonna need that if you want to leave." The man stepped back from the window. "One more thing. I'm the grounds keeper, not a servant. If you need help with the grounds, let me know. But I don't run errands, and I don't go in that house."

"Right, thanks for the explanation. Good to know." Paul hit the gas, leaving the man frowning and looking after him. Paul squelched anger bubbling at the man's unfriendliness. Stay calm, he told himself. He had fifty-thousand dollars in the bank, another fifty thousand coming in a week and a chance to gain seventy-five million. Not the time to blow his top.

He followed a bend in the road and the house rose into full view. He stomped his brakes and stopped, shocked by the sight that greeted him. Despite what the lawyer told him, he somehow expected something dark and evil, a haunted house. Instead, Chateau Montmartre was a bright, cheerful old mansion with dark blue-gray paint. It stood two and a half stories tall and had a captain's walk on top.

Built with double wraparound porches, the enormous home overlooked an expansive green lawn like the powerful ruler of all lesser things below. Live Oak trees dotting a vast expanse of lawn transformed the place into a beautiful private park. Broad entry steps lead from a curving driveway to a wide porch that wrapped all the way around the house. The house seemed to offer a welcoming smile.

Paul's mouth was agape. He snapped it shut. His family had never owned a home, and now he had a chance to own the most fantastic home he'd ever seen. "Yeah, right," he muttered. To own it, all he had to do was save a nonexistent ghost from a nonexistent evil ghost. Impossible.

Heart pounding with eager anticipation, he touched the accelerator and pulled ahead to park in front of the entrance. He stopped and looked left and right. The driveway branched on both sides into work roads that disappeared to the back of the estate. Tall juniper trees spaced close together stood guard on the outside of the work roads like walls designed to protect the place from any incursion from the ugly low mountains surrounding the estate.

He loved it.

Paul climbed out of the car and peered toward the ornate double front doors. He hefted the key Gerard Duet gave him, but hesitated as a wave of nervousness hit him. I don't belong here, he thought. He turned his head to check the gatekeeper's house. He was being stupid. Ghosts didn't exist. Nothing to be jittery about.

He hopped out of the truck, opened the back door, and retrieved his luggage. No sense procrastinating.

Moments later, loaded with the two suitcases that held everything he owned of value, he walked up the steps to the edge of the porch. The porch color was the same dark blue-gray paint as the house, but the paint was as shiny as glass. He hesitated to step on it and then did it, anyway. Porches were made for walking. He set down the suitcases and dug out the key. He aimed the key at the door, but his cell phone interrupted him. Startled, he looked back toward the front gate.

"Yoshi, where are you?"

"Fifteen minutes away. Have you gone in the house yet?"

"No, I just got here. Why?"

"Because I want you to wait for me. You need someone to watch your back."

"Damn it, Yoshi. I'm standing on the porch."

"I don't care if you're standing on your head. Don't go in until I arrive."

"So, you believe my uncle."

"No. Yes. Maybe. Mr. Davenport said Montmartre will try to kill you. You need a backup. Dozo, Paul-san. Wait for me."

"Don't be silly, Yosh. I'm here."

"Paul, wait—" He muttered something in Japanese, and then said, "Paul, dozo. Wait for me. Mr. Moto thinks waiting would be wise."

"Yosh, I'm standing on the porch." He turned and stuck the key in the lock. "I have to go. Honk when you get here."

Paul hung up.

"Mr. Davenport?"

"What?"

FOURTEEN

H E WHIRLED TO HIS LEFT and found an exquisitely beautiful young blond woman dressed in navy-blue slacks and a white blouse coming around the side of the porch. She reached the porch steps and stopped. Dark blue eyes, so tender and beautiful they stabbed holes in his gut, smiled up at him through black horn-rimmed glasses.

"I hope I didn't startle you," she said, smiling. Her voice, low and mellow, finished the job in his gut her eyes had started. "I'm Samantha Duet." She gestured toward the ground keeper's cottage. "I live over there."

Paul sucked in a deep breath and hurried down the steps. "No problem," he said. "Lawyer Huckabee told me about you, but he left out one important detail."

"What was that?" Puzzled.

"He implied you're some kind of studious, English-lit nerd. He missed that by a mile." Paul stuck out his hand. "Nice to meet you, Samantha. I'm Paul." He noted her left hand as they shook. Good. No ring. He felt his heart in his ears. Her effect on him was unbelievable, a first in his life.

She reddened a little, but seemed to appreciate the off-hand compliment. "My dad mentioned you were coming. Welcome to

Montmartre." Her hand was as warm as her smile. "Just moving in?"

"Sort of," he said, not releasing her hand. "For two weeks anyway." His eyes did a quick survey of her. Perfect figure. About five-foot ten, which was perfect for him. Silken gold hair pulled back in a ponytail. Full lips. High cheek bones. The black horn-rimmed glasses exaggerated the dark blue of her incredible eyes. A slight springtime smell. Perfect. "The lawyer said Harvard. Was he right?"

She retrieved her hand. "Yes. Thanks to Uncle Justin. He paid for it. I owe… owed him a lot." "Why only two weeks? Are you selling the house?"

"Not mine to sell. I don't own it yet."

"But, I — I'm sorry. It's none of my business." Her blush returned.

"No, it's okay. So you don't know about my uncle's will?"

"Only that you're the sole heir."

"There's a hitch. I have a chore to do in two weeks or I won't inherit."

"Chore?"

"How long have you lived here?"

"We moved here when I was eightPaul tilted his head to one side and eyed her with an amused grin. "How long ago was that?"

"Twenty years."

"So, you don't know my uncle believed Montmartre is haunted?"

"I..." Her eyes darted to the front door and then back to Paul. "Not really, though I've heard rumors. They never let me go inside. Uncle Justin and my father scolded me if they caught me trying to peek inside." She paused and studied the front door again. "Are you saying it's true?"

"No. I'm saying my uncle thought so. He wrote me a letter and claimed a beautiful young ghost who's tortured by the evil ghost of her husband jaunts this incredible place. If I want to inherit, I have to become a ghost buster and save her. Otherwise, nothing. So, in twenty years, you've never been inside?"

"No." She looked at her feet.

"Too bad. I was hoping you could give me a guided tour."

Her brows lifted in question. "We could explore the house together. I…"

Her manner said she hoped he'd invite her in. He didn't blame her. A twenty-year build up of curiosity must be ready to explode.

He copied one of Yoshi's little bows and said, "Ma'am, your wish is my command. Let's do it." As they turned to climb the steps, his hip bumped against hers. It hit him like an electric shock. She continued on, giving no sign she had noticed.

His phone buzzed. He answered, "Yoshi, what?"

"I'm at the gate. Let me in."

"Hang on a sec." He held up the remote. "You know how to use this?"

"Aim and push the button on the right," she said. "The gate closes automatically."

He did it. "Just follow the yellow brick road, Yosh. We'll wait for you on the porch."

They waited in silence, looking toward the gate. Two minutes later, Yoshi's silver Mercedes pulled up and stopped behind Paul's pickup. He peered up at Samantha through the car window, grinned and said, "Horee sheeto! Wow!"

He scrambled out of the car, raced up the steps, and stopped before Samantha. He did a grand bow, lifted her hand, kissed it, and then grinned. "Yoshi Kawasaki at your service, fair damsel," he said. Then he frowned. "You're not the beautiful ghost, are you?"

Samantha's face broke into a gleeful smile. "Nice to meet you, too, Yoshi. I'm Sam. And, no, I'm not the ghost. Welcome to Montmartre."

"Sam?"

"Short for Samantha. This silly man is my best friend." Paul said, laughing. "He's here to protect me from any big, bad ghosts we meet."

"Protect you?"

"Yes. He's the reincarnation of Mr. Moto, the famous international spy. He has black belts in judo and karate."

Samantha's eyes widened and then twinkled. "I read about you in a lit class. John P. Marquand. Mr. Moto. I'm impressed."

Yoshi's face split into a broad grin.

"My uncle left diaries detailing everything he has done so far to free his fictitious girl ghost," Paul said. "If I want to inherit his estate, I have to read those diaries as soon as possible so I won't make the same mistakes he did."

"I see. You don't really believe in ghosts, do you?" Sam's eyes were questioning.

"No, but he did. It seems silly as hell, but we have to play the cards we're dealt."

"We should start with a quick walk-through the house first," Yoshi said. "If we're planning to battle a ghost, we need to get the lay of the battlefield."

Paul nodded. "Right. I'll take point. Samantha will follow me. You bring up the rear."

Yoshi did a quick bow and said, "I concur. Let's go see the ghosts of the Montmartre mansion. Lead on."

Samantha smiled and looked at the door in anticipation.

FIFTEEN

PAUL WALKED through a long vestibule and stopped short at the entrance to a huge foyer. His mouth dropped open in surprise. Samantha bumped into him and giggled.

"Sorry," he said. "Brake lights aren't working."

Samantha blushed. "No problem. This place is amazing."

Paul studied a mass of wood paneling and dark-wood carvings. On his left, a large parlor held an ornate, natural wood grand piano against the far wall. On the right, he saw two heavy wooden doors with brass handles.

"I bet that's the library," he said. "Hang on."

He hurried to it and opened the right-hand door. It was the library. And what a library it was. He turned to his friends. "You have to see this," he said. He stepped aside to allow them to enter.

"Wow!" Yoshi exclaimed.

Even more impressive than the exterior of the big house, the library was two stories high and at least forty feet long. A spiral wooden staircase led up to the second floor, which was a four-foot wide walkway that circled the room. There were ladders up there to allow a browser to climb to the upper shelves. At the far end of the room, an enormous stone fireplace played host to a brown leather wingback sofa and two wingback chairs. Scattered around the room, various comfortable-looking chairs with tables and reading lamps beside them invited browsers to sit for a while. Across the room from the entrance sat an antique desk and chair. Beside it stood a large chalkboard on a stand. Paul's heart leaped when Samantha stopped close enough for him to feel the warmth of her body. He faced her and found her looking at him.

"It's wonderful," she said. "No. It's beautiful. I never dreamed this was here. Uncle Justin always talked about the library, but I never imagined it the grandeur of it."

Paul resisted an urge to take her in his arms. He took a deep breath. This was unusual for him and worrisome. Why did Samantha evoke such a powerful reaction from him? It never happened with Aurora or any other woman he had dated. To change his thoughts, he gave his right-side ear lobe a hard pinch and a tug.

"That makes two of us," he said. "I never dreamed such a library could even exist."

"Paul-san, I've changed my mind. I think we should start our search for your uncle's diaries right here and now," Yoshi said.

"No, Yoshi. We should save this room for last. You were right. We need to explore the entire house first, so we can understand what we're up against. We'd better get started."

They spent the next hour and a half examining the incredible details of the home. To Paul's amazement, the interior of the house belied any notion that ghost could haunt the place. On the first floor, the dining room with a huge breakfast nook off to one side was fit for a medieval king. The decorations we rich with flowered wallpaper set off with dark-wood trim and a monster chandelier that resembled a topsy-turvy mountain of crystal. Paul had seen such rooms in movies, but never in real life. Fortune Montmartre must have thought of himself as royalty, because his dining chamber was better suited for a king's feast than for simple dining.

They soon discovered that every room in the mansion was subdued, with exquisite dark-wood paneling or cheerful wallpaper set off by amazing wood carvings that in themselves were works of art. So far, nothing was frightening. Only the house's overwhelming size and grandeur was daunting.

At first, the three explorers toured in silence, not because of fear, but because of the awesome richness of the home. Along the way, they discovered nine enormous stone fireplaces, four on the first floor and four in the main bedrooms on the second floor. "The hallway stretching across the entire width of the house in front of the bedrooms was adorned with various statues and two suits of armor holding battle axes." Along the hallway, several uncomfortable-looking polished dark-wood benches were more for decoration than sitting. The hallway, like the dining room, seemed like it belonged in a medieval castle. Yoshi, being part comic, stopped and bowed to the two knights, causing Samantha to laugh.

Every time Paul opened a door and stepped into a room, his jaw dropped in awe. Behind him he heard an occasional "Wow!" from Yoshi and a whispered "Beautiful!" from Samantha.

On the smaller third floor, they found three servants' bedrooms nicer and more comfortable than Paul's own. A huge play room with a billiard table, a bar, a giant-screen TV and a ninth fireplace occupied most of the third level.

How could I ever own this place? Paul wondered.

At the foot of a narrow, paneled stairway leading upward from the play room, Paul stopped and turned to the two following him. His face and shoulders sagged.

Samantha saw his expression and said, "What's wrong?"

He forced a smile and shrugged. "Nothing. Somehow, I feel discouraged and a little sad."

"About what? This place is gorgeous, a dream." Sam said, puzzled.

"He knows it, Sam," Yoshi said. "He's sad because he just realized that it is a dream he can never own. Right, Paul?"

"So you're a mind reader, too. But you're right. I guess I'm down because this house is too beautiful. My uncle invested a lot of money into it and turned it into a happy home. No way is this a haunted house."

"Which means there's no girl ghost to save," Samantha said. "Is that it?"

Paul nodded. "Yes."

"Well, at least you have the hundred K," Yoshi said. "That's a decent consolation prize, isn't it?"

"Hundred K? You mean dollars?" Sam asked. Her brows were up a notch.

"My compensation for spending two weeks in a haunted house, succeed or not."

"So you have nothing to lose." Sam's blue eyes were wide, but tender and sympathetic.

Paul again resisted a powerful urge to wrap her in his arms.

"Only seventy-five million," Yoshi said.

"Hey, it's only money." Paul's spirits lifted as a new thought struck him. He now had a more important goal in life. Her name was Samantha Duet. Laughing, he said, "Come on. Let's see how this kingdom looks from the roof."

The stairway led to a door that opened into a ten-feet diameter turret with eight windows that gave a view of the estate in four directions.

Another door on its side led outside to a captain's walk that circled the turret. Paul hurried outside and rushed to a waist-high railing. The mountains to the west were only half as tall as the others surrounding the valley. A narrow gray belt of asphalt road circled the entire circumference of the estate. In the distance, Gerard Duet was a tiny figure riding a power mower, cutting the grass on the broadest lawn he had ever seen. The large California Live Oak trees scattered around the grounds made it all resemble a vast private part. The sight made him want to go jogging around the work road and the trees.. One large Live Oak stood near the back of the house twenty-five yards from a trellis covered with a blaze of purple flowers.

"How often does he do that?" he asked, pointing to the distant figure.

"Do what?"

"Mow this place."

"He mows a section every day," she answered, looking toward her father. "Montmartre Valley is about one and a half football fields wide where we are now and about four and a half football fields deep to where Dad is now."

"Football fields?" Yoshi asked. "What does that mean in real numbers?"

"The valley occupies three hundred and ninety-two thousand square feet of flat land, Yoshi. When I was a kid, I converted nine acres into square feet. It's about thirty-six-thousand, five-hundred square meters, if you prefer metrics."

Yoshi grinned and bowed. "Impressive, milady. Brains and everything else, too."

"What's that building over there?" Paul asked, pointing to a wide building shoved against the mountains on the left of the estate.

"The garage." Samantha moved closer to him, causing her right hip to press against him. Paul became acutely aware of her presence, but she gave no indication that she did. "It has room for five vehicles," she said. "Uncle Justin owns three cars, which are still there, I believe. There's an apartment above it with a kitchen, bath, living room and two bedrooms. When we first arrived, we lived there for two years."

"Why there and not the cottage?" Paul asked.

"Because it didn't exist. Uncle Justin had the cottage built especially for us. We loved it."

"So the apartment is still there?"

"Yes."

"What building is that beyond the garage?"

"It's dad's workshop and storage shed where he keeps all his tools. That fenced-in building further back is the pool house.

You can't see the pool from here because it's surrounded by shrubbery. Behind that building is a tennis court. Uncle Justin built the pool and the tennis court as a gift for my twelfth birthday."

"He built them for you?"

She turned to face him, again close enough for him to smell her perfume. "Yes. We're pretty isolated out here. Uncle Justin said I needed a place to invite friends from school and have fun. He was the kindest man I've ever known, Paul." Their eyes locked for a moment. "You're very much like him, you know," she added.

"I don't know that, Sam. I didn't know he existed until this morning. He must have cared a lot for you."

Samantha blushed. "I know he did, and I loved him. He said he wanted me to have the best of everything. He gave me a Honda Accord on my sixteenth birthday, and it was his idea to send me to Harvard. I—"

Yoshi coughed, breaking the moment. They turned to find him looking at them and grinning. "So solly for interruption, Paul-san," he said, "but I think I heard some diaries calling from the library."

"Right," Paul said. "Time's flying. We'd better get to them."

He turned back to Samantha. "I'd appreciate a full tour of the grounds tomorrow, if you can spare the time. I'd like to visit my uncle's grave site."

"My time is yours, Paul. Just say the word."

"Thanks."

He smiled and wondered how much of her time would be his? Forever would be nice, he thought.

SIXTEEN

WHEN THEY RETURNED to the library, Paul hurried to the antique desk and pulled open the bottom right-hand drawer where his uncle's note said he would find a gray metal box. It was empty. None of the others were large enough to hold a box. He opened them to verify the fact.

"Damn," he said. He turned to fSamantha and Yoshi waiting to hear. "Not here."

"You're looking for the diaries, right?" Samantha asked.

"Yes. His note said they would be in the bottom drawer of his desk."

"Maybe he forgot where he put them," Yoshi offered.

"I suppose… I was hoping this would be easy, but I guess not." Paul circled the desk to join his friends.

"What kind of diaries are they?" Samantha asked.

"We're not sure," Paul said. "Wait."

He pulled his uncle's letter and the note and newspaper clipping he had received from Madam Song and handed both to Samantha. "This is all we know."

Sam read them and returned them to Paul. "If Uncle Justin says they're here, they're here. I think Yoshi's right. Dad said he was sick. Perhaps he became confused at the end."

"We must search the library."

They stood scanning the vast library, and Paul groaned.

"It won't be so bad if we follow a system," Yoshi suggested. "I suspect the diaries are too big to be inside a book, but they may be on a bookshelf somewhere. Also, they're supposed to be in a gray metal box. It wouldn't make sense to scatter them around. Still, someone might have rearranged things. We should scan all the shelves for bindings that don't fit in."

"Good idea, Yosh." Paul said. "You guys take the downstairs. I'll take the upstairs, although I doubt they'll be up there."

Paul climbed the circular wooden stairway to the second floor, then walked along the wall, running his eyes and fingers over the books as he moved. The floor stopped at the fireplace. He peered below at the sofa and chairs, then walked around to the opposite wall. That side ended at the fireplace, too. He found nothing that resembled a diary. Every book he examined had an exquisite old leather binding. He guessed they were collector's items by now. The titles were in French. Could this be Fortune Montmartre's original library?

Paul leaned over the library rail. Yoshi and Samantha waved at him from the center of the room.

Yoshi turned up his palms to show they found nothing. Paul nodded and scanned the upper layers of books. His gut told him the diaries were not on the upper shelves. No sense wasting time. He hurried to rejoin his friends.

They walked to the fireplace and plopped on the sofa and chairs. Yoshi took one of the wingback chairs. Paul and Sam sat on the sofa. Paul sat first, but noticed Samantha sat close beside him. She seemed preoccupied.

"So, what now?" Yoshi asked.

"You tell me. We're looking for a needle in a gigantic haystack."

Samantha stood and said, "I have an idea. May I have another look at that note and the clipping?"

"Sure." Paul handed it to her. She opened and reread it. When she returned it to Paul, she said, "I want to check something. It won't take long. Will you wait for me here?"

"Sure. Where are you going?"

"To the cottage. Anybody want something cold to drink?"

"That would be great," Paul said. "What's on the menu?"

"Diet Pepsi and Seven Up."

Yoshi raised his hand. "Seven Up for me, dozo."

"Pepsi for me, thanks. Do you need help?"

"Nope. Be right back."

They watched with admiration as Sam hurried from the room.

"Wow!" Yoshi said. "I think you'd better marry that girl. Not many like her in the world. She's incredible."

Paul looked at his friend. "You are a mind reader, aren't you?"

SEVENTEEN

SAMANTHA STOPPED on the mansion porch and took a deep breath to prevent a flood of tears from pouring forth. She now knew where the diaries were. The day after returning home, she had seen her father carrying a gray metal box from the mansion to the cottage. She had asked what was in it. "Just some papers," he had said. She had forgotten the incident until now. Why would her father take them? Was this part of his recent pattern of odd behavior?

She checked to be sure Gerard Duet was not in the house. The sound of the big mower came to her from the distance behind the big house. She gritted her teeth and hurried to the cottage. Inside, she rushed up the stairs into her father's bedroom. Heart pounding, she looked around the room.

The bedroom was spotless. The bed cover was tight, the dresser was neat, everything in its place. She stepped to the dresser. Where would he put such a box? She opened the largest drawer. Nothing. She opened the other drawers. Still nothing.

She slid open the closet doors and found the gray box sitting on the top shelf in plain sight. Samantha lifted it from the shelf and placed it on the bed. She flipped open the lid, and there they were. Three worn spiral-bound notebooks. She opened the top book. Uncle Justin's neat script covered the first page. She noticed a white number ten envelope hidden under the other diaries. Addressed to her, it had no postage, and someone had opened it. She sat on the side of the bed to read. The brief note inside was from Uncle Justin. Dated a week before he died. It said:

To my angel, Sam,

I asked Gerard to give this to you after I've gone. Please do not mourn my passing. My life has been exciting, adventurous and happy. So, no regrets. Sam, I hesitate to ask, but I need a favor from you.

My nephew, Paul Davenport, will spend at least two weeks at Montmartre trying to fulfill the stipulations in my will. I will let him explain them to you. What I ask of you is that you befriend and assist him in any way possible during his time at Montmartre. Though I have never met him, his record in the marines, his effort to care for his father, and other information I have gathered tell me he is a person worthy of respect. I hope you, too, will find him so.

I have always cared for you and wanted the best for you. Watching you grow into a beautiful young woman has blessed my last years on earth. One more thing you should know about. There is a sealed codicil to my will held by the attorney, Huckabee. The codicil instructs him to provide a bequest of $100,000 to you to help you along in your life. The lawyer will open the codicil only at the end of Paul's effort to fulfill my wishes.

Sam, I have loved you as my own daughter. I pray you will have a wonderful life. Perhaps with Paul. I have never met him, but I understand he is a fine, honest young man and not at all bad looking.

Now I am tired and must rest.

Love,

Uncle Justin

Tears poured from her eyes as she folded the letter and put it and the diary back in the metal box. Her heart pounded as though ready to burst with pride and love for Justin Davenport. It made her sick to learn her father had taken the diaries and had hidden the note from her. Why would he do such a thing? She heard a sudden thump outside the house. Fearing discovery, she shut the closet doors and hurried from the room Downstairs, at the front door, she remembered her promise to get drinks. She turned back into the kitchen, grabbed three drinks from the fridge and stuffed them into a plastic bag. Then, as an afterthought, she moistened a paper towel and wiped at her tears. What can I tell Paul? My dad stole your uncle's diaries? No, no. Uncle Justin wanted her to help Paul, not burden him. That wouldn't help. She would tell him her father took them to keep them safe. She glanced around and stepped out of the cottage to the sidewalk.

"Sam, what are you doing?"

Sam froze. Her heart skipped a beat, taking away her breath. She turned to see her father charging toward her from the side of the cottage. Anger contorted his face.

"Dad, I…" She was a burglar caught in the act.

"Where did you get that box? What were you doing in my room?" His tone was almost a growl.

"Dad, Uncle Justin left the diaries for Paul. Paul received a note saying they were in the desk drawer, but they weren't there. I remembered seeing you with them and came to get them." She took a breath. "I don't understand."

"You were in that house?" Gerard Duet's eyes opened wide in shock.

"Yes, Paul gave us a tour. It's beautiful. Why didn't you ever let me go inside?"

"You damned fool! I told you never to go in that house." Gerard Duet's face showed fear. He glanced around as if to see whether anyone was listening. He met her eyes. His shoulders slumped. "Sam, why did you go in there? I… never mind! It may be too late now. Oh, God, why didn't you listen?" He reached out. "Give me that box! You had no business meddling in things you don't understand."

"Dad, no!" She jumped back and jerked the box away "This belongs to Paul, and there's a letter addressed to me from Uncle Justin. Why did you hide it from me? What were you thinking?"

Her father's posture collapsed. His expression changed to resignation. "That's none of your business. Sam, please, give me the box. Don't do this?"

"Do what? Return Paul's property? Read Uncle Justin's letter?" Anger rose in her. "Why are you acting this way?"

"Please, Sam. If you won't listen, it's on your head. I warned you. You should have stayed in the East." He shook his head and pushed past her, muttering, "I warned you."

"Dad, wait! I want to invite Paul to the house for dinner tonight. It's his first night here."

Gerard Duet turned and glared at her. "If you bring that man anywhere near this house, you'll have to move out. If you don't obey me, I don't want you around. Do you understand?"

"Dad, no! I don't understand! Please, what's wrong with you? Why are you acting like this?"

Gerard left her standing bewildered, her question unanswered, and entered the cottage.

Sam walked the rest of the way to the mansion. She wanted to run and hide. What had happened to her father? He threatened to throw her out of her home. This was impossible. Surreal. Something terrible was wrong with him. But what? She remembered his muttered conversation with the moon on Saturday night and his threat if she followed him again. Was he losing his mind? Despite his threats, she had to know.

Sam climbed the steps and stood at the Montmartre front door for several minutes before recognizing where she was. She removed her glasses and patted her eyes with the palms of her hands. She took a deep breath and squared her shoulders.

No matter what her father said, she had to help Paul.

EIGHTEEN

WHEN THE LIBRARY door latch clacked, Paul and Yoshi both looked up. Paul spotted the gray box she carried and hurried to meet her.

"You found it," he said, taking it from her. "Where was it?"

"My dad took it home for safekeeping," she said. "I remembered seeing him do it, but I wasn't sure." She held up the plastic bag. "I brought the drinks."

Yoshi took them from her. Eager to read the diaries, Paul hurried to the desk. There, he lifted the lid and examined the box's contents. He saw Sam's name on a white number ten envelope that rested on top of the diaries. He handed it to her. As he did, he noticed the redness around her eyes. "Are you all right? Were you crying?"

She held up the envelope. "It's Uncle Justin's note. It made me cry." She tucked it in her purse. "I'm okay now."

"He made you cry?" Yoshi looked puzzled.

"Not him, Yoshi. His words. Something he wrote to me before he died. He was a kind, sweet man." She stifled an embarrassed laugh. "And I'm a sentimental idiot. Let's look at the diaries."

Yoshi's cell phone chimed. He lifted it to his ear and said, "Hello?" His eyes widened in shocked surprise. "Otosan!"

Silence, followed by, "Ah, so desuka? Ah, so. Hai. Hai." He looked at his wristwatch and cut loose with a rapid-fire string of Japanese. He listened for another half minute and said, "Hai, sugu ikimasu." He hung up and turned.

"Yosh, who was that?"

"My father. He caught an earlier flight. I must go now. Sorry."

"No problem. Stay in touch and let me know your itinerary."

"You can count on it, but I hate to leave you. You need someone to guard your back."

"I'll do that," Samantha said.

A happy warmth spread through Paul. "Anyhow," he said, "there's nothing to worry about. This place is as tame as a kid's zoo.

"I hope so. Dad booked a suite at the Hilton. I'm have to meet him for dinner. We're flying to New York on the red-eye."

"Then you'd better go."

Yoshi bowed. "I'll call you every day."

They walked with him to his car. Yoshi shook hands with Sam and said, "It's been a great pleasure. Take care of my friend, please."

"Don't worry. I will."

Yoshi opened the car door, but before he climbed in, he gave Paul a bear hug. "Watch out for the boogie man, Paul-san."

"What boogie man? Be careful on the road. It's a lousy drive to the airport."

"The gate will open automatically for you," Sam said. "Take care."

"Right."

They watched as he pulled away.

"He's a great guy," Sam said.

"My best friend."

They stood without speaking for several minutes before they returned to the library. Soon, drinks in their hands, they sat in front of the fireplace. Paul slouched back on the sofa and Sam perched on one of the wingback chairs.

"So what are your plans?" Sam asked. "It's almost six o'clock."

Paul would have been content to sit and stare at her forever, but she expected more. "To be honest, I have no idea what to do. I'll read my uncle's diaries, I guess, and play it by ear. What do you have in mind?"

"Well, I thought I'd help you get moved in, and then, if you're hungry, I'd like to take you to dinner. There's a nice seaside restaurant in Malibu? What do you think?"

"That's sounds great, Sam, but I understand the kitchen here is well stocked."

"I'm sure it is, but—wait."

She sat her drink on a chair-side table and joined him on the sofa. She opened her purse and handed him the note. "Read that before you say anything else."

He read it slowly. It was in his uncle's handwriting. He looked up. "Damn, he really loved you. Congratulations."

"For what?"

"Your bequest. That's a lot of money."

Her face became serious. "Uncle Justin gave me a better life than I ever could have dreamed, including sending me to a high-priced university."

"I understand, but how can you spare the time? Don't you work?"

"No. Yes. I do now. Helping you win your inheritance."

"So, you're sponging off your father?"

"No. I live at the cottage, but Uncle Justin owns that, or rather, you do. Uncle Justin gave me a large allowance for school, and I saved most of it. I can live a year or more on my savings if I wish. Besides that, there's the bequest. You only need help for two weeks."

"Yes, but—"

"Paul, don't be stupid. I want to help. I owed him and now you."

"You don't owe me anything."

"You're wrong. Uncle Justin's last request was for me to assist you. If I didn't fulfill that wish, I couldn't live with myself. Understand?"

"Yeah, okay, got it." Paul's face turned impish. "You can help me get rich on one condition."

She brightened. "Name it."

"Well, I want to know whether you agree with him."

Her beautiful lips opened. "About what?"

"That I'm not a bad-looking young man."

She giggled and tilted her head sideways. "The truth?"

"Yes, I think."

"I'd say I've seen worse."

"Where?"

"Harvard."

"Is that good?"

"Maybe."

"Maybe?"

"Yes. Now answer me."

"I forgot the question."

"About getting you settled and having dinner with me."

He leaned close to her, but stopped himself within kissing distance.

"I'm good for half of your suggestion."

She turned bright red, but didn't back away. Instead, she asked, "Which half?"

"Getting settled. I have to look at my uncle's diaries. He tried for twenty-five years to save his imaginary girl ghost. I have thirteen days to do what he tried all those years trying to accomplish. May I take a rain check on the dinner?"

"I have a better idea. Do you like pizza?"

"Pizza?"

"Yes. I went to school with a boy named Tony Licata. He owns a pizzeria four miles from here, just off the Pacific Coast Highway. He makes delicious pizza. If I ask him, his guy will deliver. He's done it before."

"You're serious, aren't you?"

"About what?"

"Helping me."

She hesitated, studying his expression. Then, "You've been alone most of your life, I can tell. You have trouble accepting help, don't you?"

"I… maybe a little."

"Well, I suggest you get used to it. You have a helper now. What kind of pizza do you like?"

"Cheese, topped with pepperoni, black olives, fresh tomatoes and bell pepper. How about you?"

"That's perfect. Wait. What drink?"

"Coke's fine."

"Right. I'll order, and then let's get to work."

Paul wished he had a tail to wag.

NINETEEN

AND GET TO WORK, she did. As soon as she finished the call, she headed straight to the old desk and, one after the other, searched the drawers. Paul hurried to follow her.

"What are you looking for?"

"Found them." She came up with two brand-new spiral-bound steno pads from the desk's middle drawer and tossed them on the desk. She smiled at Paul. "We need pads to take our notes on, don't you think?"

"I do." He searched and spotted an old cane-bottomed chair against the wall near the door. He took it to the desk and sat.

"No, sorry, that won't do." She came around the desk and tugged him up from the chair. "You're the master of the manor now. You sit behind the desk."

As he stood, he brushed against her, causing an electric shock to zap him. She felt it, too, because her mouth opened in surprise.

"What now, miss efficiency?" he asked.

"We read the diaries and take notes."

"Right. No, wait." He dug out the letter he got from his uncle at Huckabee's office, handed it to her, and dropped into his chair.

"If you intend to be my partner, you need to read this first. You might change your mind." He leaned back to enjoy the sight of her working.

When she finished, her lower lip quivered. "Poor Uncle Justin. He never let on to anyone." She scanned the library as if looking for Helena Longmore. Frowning, she examined the chalkboard before returning to Paul. "He makes Helena sound so real."

"Yeah, it's spooky. No pun intended."

She giggle. "But she can't be, can she?"

"No. Ghosts don't exist. My uncle was delusional. Something might have happened to him in Africa. Or living here alone for all those years caused him to fantasize. Maybe he became senile."

"No. He was as normal as anyone I know."

"Except that he fell in love with and became obsessed with a half-nude, nonexistent ghost.

Samantha's face showed doubt. "So, this is just an exercise? A waste of time?"

"I'm afraid so."

"Then what are we going to do?"

He squelched a grin. He liked she said we, not you. Having her around was like standing next to a warm fire.

"Well, I agreed to do as he asked, but you didn't. In return, I'm being well paid for my work, so I'm honor bound to follow through, but you're not."

She giggled. "So you are a Boy Scout."

"That was a stupid interview?"

"I don't agree. You were great. Very poised." She pulled the metal box to her, lifted out the top diary, and shoved it at him. "You do that one and I'll do another one. When we're finished, we'll swap. Okay?"

"Aye-aye, sir. Did Harvard make you like this?"

"Like what?" She looked puzzled.

"Like being incredibly beautiful and highly efficient."

"Harvard taught me to be efficient, anyway. You really find

me beautiful?"

His face became serious. "If I were better educated, I'm sure I could come up with more appropriate words to describe you. Beautiful doesn't come close. You take my breath away." He took a breath to prove it.

"Wow!" she whispered. "You're as romantic as Uncle Justin. Now I'm embarrassed."

"Sam, I'm sorry," he said, "but if we hang around together, you may as well know how you affect me."

She reached across the desk and patted his hand. "It's okay, Paul. One of these days, I'll tell you how you affect me."

Her phone rang. She answered and listened. "Hi, Tony." Pause. "Already? Did you tell him to beep at the gate?" Another pause. "Yes. I finally graduated. I'm home for good now. Right. Me, too." She hung up. "Pizza will be here soon. We have to let him in."

Paul stood. "Let's do it."

The pizza came along with the cold drinks and paper plates. Sam Paul moved the pizza box to the coffee table in front of the sofa. Paul wolfed down four big slices, then sat back and said, "You were right. Tony, make great pizza."

"Told you." Sam said. She put the paper plates on top of the pizza at one end of the coffee table. "Right now, we'd better get back to work."

On the way back to Justin's desk, Sam spotted a small library table with two chairs. "Let's move there," she said. "Turn on that lamp next to it and I'll get the diaries.

When they were all set up, Sam sat across the table from Paul and shoved half the dairies over to Paul and said, "Uncle Justin said we should learn what he's tried so far. Is that what you want to do?"

"Sure," he said. "My uncle hired a psychic named Madam Song. I met her this afternoon and asked how to proceed."

"Madam Song?"

"She appears to be Korean and is well educated. She said the same thing. Read the diaries to learn what my uncle has tried, so I won't repeat his mistakes."

"I see. So that's what we want to note and list. Things he did trying to save Helena Longmore."

"Yes."

"Got it." She glanced at her wristwatch. "Six-thirty. I suggest we skim-read the diaries for forty-five minutes, take a fifteen-minute break, and repeat the process until we finish." She hesitated. "Sorry. I guess I'm being presumptuous."

"No, no. You're doing fine. You learn that at Harvard, too?"

"No. From Miss Thomas, my eighth-grade science teacher."

"Smart lady."

Sam brightened as she remembered. "She was smart and the best teacher I ever had, including all the stuffed shirts at Harvard."

At ten P.M., Samantha slapped her pencil on the desk and sat back in her chair. Her expression was one of distress mixed with sadness. "This makes me want to cry," she said. "Uncle Justin loved her so, and he was so sad, and yet he let no one see it, especially not me. He considered himself a failure."

"I agree," Paul said. "You must be tired. Would you like to quit now? Tomorrow is another day."

"No. We have to combine our notes and get a comprehensive list. I can do it, if you like."

"You sure you're up to it?"

She sat up straight. "Sure. This was standard procedure at school. I'm good at it. Give me your list."

He shoved his pad to her and sat back to watch. She tore out the pages from her note book and started a new list. Then she read, checked, marked, and combined the lists. Although he cared about what she was finding, he was more interested in watching her work. Once again, the thought struck him that even if he didn't win his uncle's fortune, he couldn't allow himself to lose her. The problem was how to make her a want a flat broke former marine programmer.

"Do you want me to read the list?" she asked. She had finished and was watching him. "You seemed far away. Are you all right?"

"Yeah. Just thinking. What's the verdict?"

"He was pretty creative, more than I would have imagined." She aimed her pencil point at the pad and said, "Okay, here goes. Over the years, he consulted with thirty different parapsychologists, several numerologists, fortune tellers, ghost hunters and others. He held fifty-seven seances. Seven different clergy from a variety of religions, including Catholic, Protestant, and Buddhist Monks from the Himalayas, visited him. He had several charlatan holy men whom he tossed out on their ears. None of the clergy or psychics detected Fortune's existence because he always remained quiet during their visits. Madam Song was the only one who sensed Montmartre's presence, which is why he kept her as a consultant. He learned from Helena that Fortune loved Mozart's music and frequented concerts in Los Angeles. So, he rigged the house with speakers and blasted horrible, raucous rock and roll music twenty-four hours a day, hoping to drive Montmartre away. No luck.

Samantha took a breath and frowned. "He hired men to search the grounds using metal-detection and X-ray equipment." She stopped. "I remember that. I kept asking what they were doing. Uncle Justin patted me on the head and said they were looking for gold, and I believed him."

Paul chuckled.

She returned to her pad. "He hired several electronics engineers to design a wave detection machine, hoping to detect ghosts. The machine was supposed to detect the strong emanations of a ghost's presence. None of the machines worked. Also, along that line, he bought a dog named Max and a big green parrot called Francine, whose sellers claimed they could sense a ghost's presence. The dog was lovable, but detected nothing. Francine, however, squawked at anything that moved. Drove him crazy, so he gave them back. He also wrote letters to several people asking for information about Talon Montmartre, but never received an answer." She hesitated. "Oh, this is interesting. He came to believe that Fortune Montmartre had a

limited territory close to the house within which he could move
about."

"How close?"

"He didn't say."

"That would be useful info if Montmartre existed. But…"

"This may be his most important entry," she said, turning
back to her notes. "On the last page of the third notebook, he
wrote that someone told him that to remove a ghost, he needed to
find their bones and give them a proper burial. If he had lived, he
intended to search deeper all over the grounds." She dropped the
pad and pencil. "That's about it. Poor thing. He was so unhappy.
If I had known, I could have helped him."

"I doubt it. I understand him now. This was his personal
battle. It gave him a reason to live. It's weird, I know, but I
understand it."

He backed his chair away from the desk and walked to the
big dusty chalkboard. He stared at it and then turned to find
Samantha peering over his shoulder.

"What are you thinking?" she asked.

"I just wondered what kinds of delusional conversations he
created on this board. They would be a brilliant case study for
psychiatrists."

"No, don't say that. Uncle Justin was the nicest, sanest man
I've ever known."

"Right, a nice eccentric who now and then wrote notes to a
ghost on a big blackboard."

She looked distressed.

"Sorry," he said. "Guess all this has blown my mind."

She touched his arm. "I understand. What's next on the
agenda?"

"Madam Song, I guess. She said to call her after I read the
diaries. So…"

"What time do we leave?"

"We?"

"Sure. I promised Yoshi I'd watch your back."

"I feel safer already."

She snickered.

"It's late," he said. "I'd better walk you home."

TWENTY

A S THEY NEARED the cottage's front stoop, Samantha stopped and turned to Paul. "Are you all right?" she asked.

"Sure, why?"

"You haven't said a word since we left the library."

"Sorry."

"If you're worried about Uncle Justin's will, don't. We'll meet his requirements somehow. We must. You belong here."

"That not it," he said. He looked into her eyes and he felt the same stirring in his gut again.

"What then?"

"You. You seem as far out of reach as my uncle's fortune."

"Don't be silly. I told you. We're a team. I'm here for the duration, no matter how it turns out."You mean that?"

"Of course. In for a penny, in for a pound."

She lifted his left hand and examined it. "Good?"

"What's good?"

"None of your business." She let go his hand. "You'd better get some rest. I expect we'll have a full day tomorrow."

She turned away, then surprised him by giving him a quick kiss on his right cheek. "Sleep well," she whispered.

She hurried to the front door and disappeared inside. He

examined his hand. What was good about it? Could it be she was happy he had no ring?

The light went off.

TWENTY-ONE

O NCE INSIDE, Samantha hurried up the stairway. At the top, she hesitated. A soft orange light oozed from under her father's door. She considered knocking and trying to make peace, but discarded the idea.

In the past, she would have tapped and called a cheerful "Night, Dad," and even stopped in to chat. But not tonight. She no longer knew him, and he frightened her. Samantha tiptoed into her room to avoid alerting him. She closed the door and sat on her bed. Last night her father had spoken to the moon as if to a real person. Then today, she learned he hid Uncle Justin's diaries and, for some bizarre reason, hated Paul. He ad threatened to throw her out of the house if she invited Paul to dinner. Why? The puzzle held her mind fixated until she realized the truth. There could be no answer until she confronted him.

She turned on the bedside light, opened Justin Davenport's letter, and reread it. She read one line several times. "I pray you will have a wonderful life. Perhaps with Paul."

She stopped reading. Her impulsive kiss on Paul's cheek surprised her as much as him. Why did she do it? Because he seemed so lost, and she wanted to cheer him? Or because she was attracted to him from the moment she met him? She called him silly, but that wasn't true. He was a calm man with sensitive blue eyes and a gentle nature. He resembled a young, handsome version of Uncle Justin, whom she loved dearly, which was a disturbing complication.

She reread the part of the letter about Paul. Uncle Justin said he'd heard Paul was not bad looking at all, which she considered an understatement. Paul was deliciously handsome, and she found his own yearning for her almost irresistible.

I wanted to kiss him, she told herself in a burst of honesty. I kissed him because his desire to kiss me was magnetic, and I wanted to kiss him. But what if she had encouraged him to go further? Where would that have led? Excitement raced through her as she considered the idea, but a flash memory of her father's angry face drove it away. She tucked the problem of Paul in a mental compartment for later consideration.

As much as she loved Uncle Justin and appreciated all his efforts to help her and her father, Samantha still yearned to have a home of her own. She thought back to the girls at school. Most left school to go home on vacations and returned happy. She hung around school during holidays because she wanted to save her money, and travel to California cost too much. For her, there was nowhere else to go.

Tears welled in her eyes. She fought against sobs. Why did her father act this way? If it weren't for her father's strange behavior, she would be happier than she had ever been. She loved the challenge of helping Paul win his fortune. But her dad's attitude toward him created an irrational pall that hung over her like a threatening thundercloud. Paul might someday be his employer. Why would he hate him? And why would he treat her like an interloping stranger? She stared unseeing at the letter in her hands as she tried to imagine an answer, but there was no answer.

"I have my daughter to think about," he had said into space last night. He also had said, "You can kill me, but I won't do it?"

Do what? What?

A bump against the wall in her father's room broke her reverie. Impelled by anxiety, Samantha stood. Was he going out again? The bedside alarm clock said eleven-thirty. She looked with yearning at her bed. No. She had to learn the cause of her father's strange behavior. She vowed to follow him if he left the house. She had to know what was happening.

She removed from her closet the dark clothes she had worn last night. No sense taking chances. The moon was bright and ready to spotlight her on the world. She would need camouflage.

TWENTY-TWO

PAUL SAT DOWN on the side of the most enormous bed he had ever seen. Unable to resist the impulse, he bounced up and down the edge, testing it. It was the most comfortable he had ever tried. He studied its expanse, wondering why any unmarried person would need that much bed space?

The master bedroom was almost the size of his entire apartment, and it was so richly decorated it was overwhelming. He continued to toggle the room's luxury, then lay back to stare at the ceiling. He felt drained and numb emotionally. The ceiling twelve feet above him seemed to say, "You don't belong here, little man," but the expensive mattress welcomed his body with a soothing warmth. His uncle had lived well.

Paul awoke at five A. M. and now, in half an hour, it would be midnight. Nineteen surrealistic and unforgettable hours. He inhaled a deep breath. Sleep threatened to engulf him. No. Get up, change clothes, brush his teeth and take care of business first. He rose and tossed his suitcase on the bed, intending to get his travel kit. As he reached to open it, a loud thud and a crash came from next door.

Puzzled, he listened and a moment later heard it again. He frowned. What could it be? Except for him, the house was empty.

Another louder thump left no doubt. Someone was in the next room. But who? And what were they doing?

Ghosts? Having a party?

He suppressed a laugh at his own foolishness. What the hell? He rose, hurried into the hallway, and turned left. At the next room, he stopped to listen with his ear to the door. A loud crash caused him to jerk back. He yanked the door open and stared into the darkness. He fumbled to find the light switch. But, before he switched it on, he imagined he saw a reddish glow passing through a wall into the next bedroom. When the light came on. He was alone.

The room was a mess. Several large chairs and two bedside tables stood in the center of the floor near the foot of the bed. A heavy antique dresser with a tall wood-rimmed mirror had tipped over and lay face down on the floor. The mirror had broken loose and hit the floor, leaving scattered shards of glass.

He examined the room, searching for clues, but found nothing to account for the mess before him.. He stopped at the wall in the corner where he saw the glow. It was the same. Nothing there. He shrugged. A puzzle and a half. He walked to the bed and sat down to think.

Earthquake? No. The entire house would have rocked. It didn't. So what had done this? Ghosts?

He laughed and kicked himself. Ghosts don't exist. He tugged his right earlobe and looked around the room. No answer popped into his head. He scrubbed his face and walked back into the hallway. To hell with it. Tomorrow. He started toward his bedroom, but an impulse caused him to check out the third bedchamber where the glow had gone. He stood at its door, flicked on the lights, and peered inside. Empty.

He shook his head at his stupidity, closed the door, and returned to his bedroom. Right now, he needed sleep.

TWENTY-THREE

ICY WIND ATTACKED Paul's face and body. Wet with stinging slivers of sleet, it penetrated deep into his body. He shivered and staggered in the wind. Frozen snow crunched on the sidewalk beneath his feet. He lifted his hand to touch his face with his bare fingers. They were numb sticks thumping his cheek. I'll freeze to death if I don't get warm! He scanned the street for a house where he might find shelter. The homes on the street were rich and inviting, with yellow light spilling from their windows onto the snow-covered lawns. They don't want me.

He spotted a small cottage with orange tiles on the roof. Oddly, there was no snow on its roof or in its yard. The light from its windows beckoned him like a friendly siren. They'll let me in. They'll help me.

He raced across several frozen lawns to reach the front door of the cottage. He stopped and banged on the door with the heel of his fist. "Help, please! I'm freezing!"

The door opened, and Samantha was there, smiling at him. She was naked except for a thin nightgown.

"Paul, come in," she said. "I've been waiting for you."

His cell phone buzzed on the bedside table. Samantha

vanished. The phone buzzed. He pushed up on one elbow and reached for it.

"Hello?" He blinked, trying to see the phone number of the caller. The display showed no incoming calls. He lifted it anyway. "Hello, who is this?" No answer. He punched off and lay back. As usual, he had slept without using the bed covers because of the warmth of the evening. Now he was freezing. He shivered. Something was wrong. He sat up and swung his feet over the side.

A bright light appeared near the foot of the bed. He frown and stared at it. The light wavered for a moment before coming into focus. It resembled a hologram of a young blond woman wearing a thin, see-through neglige. He stared in a dumb trance for a few seconds at a sexy, near-perfect woman's body before his brain got into gear. "Helena! Are you Helena?"

The ghostly young girl nodded and looked surprised that he saw her. Suddenly, her eyes opened wide in fear and something jerked her away from the bed and pinned her against the distant wall next to the bedroom door. She screamed in terror and pain, unable to move. Her screaming became a terrifying, throat-shredding sound tore holes into his soul.

Paul grabbed his pants from the bedpost as another holographic figure, a man this time, appeared in front of the girl. His aura was red and even brighter than the girl's. The man wore dark trousers and a long coat with one sleeve torn off at the shoulder, revealing a frilly long-sleeved white shirt beneath it. Fortune Montmartre. Uncle Justin was right! This is how the ghost tortured the girl.

"Hey! Leave her alone!" Paul yelled, struggling into his pants. He stuffed his feet into his shoes.

The ghost of Fortune Montmartre turned and glared at him. Then it looked toward the wall. A huge oil painting lifted off and flew straight at his Paul's head. Paul ducked and finished buttoning his pants as the painting crashed against the bed's headboard. Before he recovered, a second missile, a large white vase, flew at him. He raised his right arm as a shield. The vase hit his arm, flipped past, and struck the side of his head. It shattered and dropped to the floor. Paul cried out and fell back onto the bed.

A raucous laugh echoed through the room. He pushed up in time to see Fortune Montmartre's face change shape into that of a horrible monster with glowing red eyes and long white fangs. Ignoring Helena, the apparition floated toward him.

"You're a dead man," the creature mouthed. Paul jumped up and raced toward the figure. As he reached it, he swung as hard as he could, but his fist passed through emptiness. The ugly monster laughed, and a smaller vase came from nowhere and hit Paul on the left side of his head. He heard the vase hit the floor and roll. He staggered back, caught his balance and swung at the leering face, hitting nothing but air. "You're dead, you son of a bitch," he yelled, "and soon you'll be buried, too."

A heavy bedside chair slammed into Paul's back. He yelped in pain, but grabbed the chair and swung it at the ghost. The chair sailed through the apparition as easily as his fist, throwing him off balance. The face of Montmartre returned to normal and Paul could see he had a thin mustache below his nose. Montmartre grinned at him and lifted his hands. Something hit Paul's chest like a battering ram and sent him flying back onto the bed. He bounced up and raced through the apparition of Fortune Montmartre to the bedroom door. The ghost had no physical body, but Paul had the sense of passing through a cold, dry fog.

At the door, he turned right and, driven by panic, raced to the stairway and pounded down them to the foyer. Unable to stop soon enough, he slammed against the heavy front door and jerked it open. Then he stopped short. He was running like a coward. One of his favorite Mark Twain quotes rose unbidden and blocked his fear. "Courage is resistance to fear—not the absence of fear."

"What am I doing?" he growled. Anger exploded within

him. He slammed the door shut and raced up the stairs two at a time. He entered the master bedroom and halted.

"Montmartre, you son of a bitch!" he yelled. "I'm not afraid of you. You're nothing. A ghost! No body and no soul. Where are you? Show yourself!" He gave no thought about what to do if the ghost showed up, but in his anger, he didn't care.

He searched for the apparitions. They had vanished. "Show yourself," he shouted again. "You coward! You can't hide from me forever." No response.

He turned on the light. The room was as he left it. The large portrait was lying on the bed. There was a white gash on the dark-wood headboard where the heavy picture frame hit it. Fragments of the white vase lay scattered on the floor. A splotch of blood stained the bed where he fell. The smaller vase lay on the floor five feet away. The heavy chair strangely sat upright before him. He lifted it and returned it to its position beside the beside table. Without warning, his energy deserted him. He plopped into the chair and leaned back. Pain in his back caused him to jerk upright.

He considered spending the night in the house, but vetoed the idea. Montmartre could murder him in his sleep. Only a fool would leave himself vulnerable in an enemy's camp. Is that what happened to my uncle?

A warm trickle ran down the side of his face. He touched it and winced. His finger came away bloody. He walked into the adjoining bathroom. Blood oozed from a slight cut in front of his right ear. The wound sat on top of a sizable lump. Not too bad. He washed his face with lukewarm water and then used antiseptic cream and a wide Band Aid from the medicine cabinet to dress the cut.

Back in the bedroom, he gathered his belongings. He would spend the rest of the night in his truck and make a longer-term plan tomorrow.

Minutes later, he tossed his bag on the floor of his truck, climbed in, and drove halfway to the cottage. He did a three-point turn and parked off the road. His uncle's diary said Montmartre's ghost had a limited range. Paul hoped he was right.

He gazed at the mansion through bleary eyes. What had happened? A nightmare? Stupid question. Nightmares didn't throw heavy oil paintings or vases.

He touched the side of his face and considered the facts, as he now understood them. Fact one. His uncle was as sane as anyone. Fact two. Everything he claimed was real. Paul had seen and felt the proof first hand. Fact three. At least two ghosts existed. He had met both of them, and that meant winning his uncle's fortune was now possible. If he could figure out how. Fact four. He now had three clear goals. Save Helena by getting rid of Montmartre, gain his uncle's fortune and win the love of Samantha. He wondered which one would be the most difficult.

Satisfied that his life was now much simpler, he locked the car doors and cracked the windows for ventilation. He adjusted his seat to give his legs room to stretch out room and reclined it as far as it would go. The Band Aid tugged at the skin on his face. He thought of Samantha and Yoshi. What would they say when he told them what happened? Yoshi would accept his report as a fact, but what about Sam? Would his revelation drive her away? He would have to think about that.

He settled back in his seat and closed his eyes. It didn't matter what others thought. He knew the truth now. He smiled as he remembered Fortune Montmartre's apparition. Those red eyes and white fangs were a funny touch. The ghost didn't know it yet, but he had made a major mistake. He had turned Paul into his worst enemy. If it was at all possible, Paul vowed to destroy the evil creature.

Paul went to sleep counting pain pulses in his head and thinking of Samantha and what measures he could take to find Montmartre's and Helena's bones.

TWENTY-FOUR

WITH ONE EXCEPTION, Gerard Duet followed the same pattern he had set the previous night. Soon after his bedroom door opened and closed, Sam ducked behind the old stone-well planter to wait.

She listened. Her father made no sound. She rose and approached the garden trellis, expecting to find him under it as before, but he wasn't there. Dad, where are you? As if to answer her, his voice drifted to her from somewhere to her left. She turned and spotted his silhouette under a huge Live Oak twenty-five yards from the trellis. She hesitated. Should she take a chance crossing the open space between the trellis and the big tree? If he saw her, would his face contort in anger as it had earlier? A loud shout interrupted her thoughts. "Leave my daughter alone!" And then she heard a scream of pure agony from her father.

Shocked by the sound, Samantha froze for a second before bolting into a run toward her father's shadow. He emitted another throat-stripping scream of agony and flew backwards further than he had the night before. As she approached him, he lay writhing and rolling like a madman. She dropped to her knees beside him and caught his shoulders in her hands.

"Dad! What's wrong?"

He opened his eyes and glared at her. "Run!" he screamed. "Run!" He shoved her away, scrambled to his feet, and raced toward the cottage. Stunned, she rose and stumbled after him. A sudden freezing gust of wind blew against her face, and then something brushed against her breast. She yelped and searched in panic for the cause. Nothing. Tears welled in her eyes, blinding her.

"Oh, Dad," she moaned.

Stricken with worry and fear, she realized now that somehow her father's mind had become addled. What other explanation could there be?

She stopped walking. Could she help her father? Or was it too late? Should she tell Paul about it? No. He had problems of his own. Sobbing from the anguish of having lost everything that mattered in her life, she stumbled home, seeing only the dark worry clouding her vision.

What was she to do?

Her father's bedroom light was on when she returned. Not wanting to face him tonight, she tiptoed into her bedroom. The clock on her dresser showed Tuesday - 12:05 A. M.

She sat on her bed, staring at the floor. All day today he worked at his normal chores, riding the powered mower to trim another section of the estate's giant lawn. All normal. But at night, he acted crazy. Why? She had read about full moons causing people to become crazy, which was the source of the word lunatic, but the moon wasn't full. Bright, but not full. Was midnight madness an illness?

Deep in worry, she unbuttoned the top two buttons on her black shirt. A loud knock on her door caused her heart to leap. Hope rose in her breast. Perhaps her father wanted to apologize?

"Just a minute." She re-buttoned her blouse and hurried to the door. "Dad?"

"Who else at this time of night?" His voice was not friendly.

She opened the door and his expression startled her. He looked even grimmer than she felt. "Dad, are you all right?"

"Yes. I want to talk to you." His voice was dead.

"Sure," she said, trying to sound cheerful. "Come on in. What's wrong?" She stepped back to allow him in, but he remained standing like a statue. His face said something terrible was wrong.

"Nothing. I just wanted to tell you. If you follow me again, you won't be welcome here. You'll have to move out." The words droned out like computer speech.

"Dad, why would I have to leave?" Her throat constricted and her heartbeat ramped up. She couldn't breathe.

"That's not your business. Either obey me or leave. Make up your mind."

"But... Dad, please. I don't understand."

"You don't have to." His face contorted with sudden anger. "That's clear enough, isn't it"No! Damn it! I want to know why you're acting this way. What happened to you? You're acting crazy."

"Bullshit. You don't know what you're talking about." He glared at her with hate-filled eyes. "No more discussion. You have a choice. Obey me or leave. That's it." He turned and clumped down the stairs.

"Dad, wait! Please!"

He ignored her.

Samantha wasn't sure how long she stood looking at nothing, but when she turned back into her room, her legs were too weak to remain standing. She fell onto the bed and buried her face in her hands. She had been wrong about her father. He wasn't having a nervous breakdown. It was something else. Something terrible.

She fell back, ignoring the tears running down her cheeks.

What was wrong with her father?

She cried herself to sleep.

TWENTY-FIVE

HE WAS STANDING in front of the caretaker's cottage door. Frosty wind buffeted his face. His body shivered violently from the cold. In desperation, he lifted his fist and pounded on the door.

"Samantha, please! Let me in. I'm freezing."

The door opened. Sam was standing in the same see-through nightgown as before. Her eyes widened, and she slammed the door in his face. He knocked louder. "Sam, let me in. Please."

"Paul, are you all right?" The door pounded back at him.

He stared at the door.

"Paul, wake up." Pound, pound, pound.

He opened his eyes. Bright morning light blinded him. He closed them.

Loud pounding came from his left. He opened his eyes again and blinked away the sleep fuzz.

"What?"

"Are you all right? You were dreaming. Wake up!"

He realized where he was and tried to sit up, but the reclined truck seat made doing so difficult. He grabbed the side lever and raised the seat back. The window was fogged. He pushed a button and lowered it to be met by the face of an angel..

Samantha's face, with a worried ssmile peered in at him.

"Paul, what happened? There's blood on your face."

He opened the door. She stepped back. He climbed out with a small groan. His back and legs complained.

"You really want to know?"

"Yes."

"I'll tell you on two conditions."

"What conditions?"

"Number one, you go to breakfast with me."

She turned his head to examine at the cut.

"No deal. At least not until I dress that wound. Come with me."

"Where?"

"The cottage."

"Where's your dad?"

"Right now, I don't care. I need to dress that cut." She grabbed his hand and tugged.

"Okay, you lead. I'll follow."

She turned and headed for the cottage. He lagged back just enough to admire the view. Dressed in dark-blue jeans and a blue and beige blouse with rolled-up sleeves, she had the most perfect figure he had ever seen. She walked with the elegant grace of a swan. He wondered how she would react if she realized he planned to marry her.

Once inside the cottage, she pointed to a door. "Guest bedroom and bathroom. I suspect you'll want to wash up about now. When you're done, the kitchen is straight back. I'll wait for you there."

He nodded headed for the bathroom. A short timelater, joined her at a small breakfast table in the kitchen. On it he found a cup of steaming black coffee, a bottle of peroxide, cotton swabs, a tube of antibiotic ointment and a box of Band Aids. He sat in front of the coffee. "For me, I hope."

"For you. I figured you'd need that about now, too."

"You figured right." He took a long swig of coffee.

She stood close beside him. "Now be still. I want to redress that wound." She gently pulled the old Band Aid off and leaned closer to examine the cut. "Wow, that's a whopper. Don't move."

The fresh odor of her bath soap was pleasant. "You smell good," he said.

"Glad you think so. Wait here."

She hurried out of the kitchen and returned with a washcloth. She ran water in the kitchen sink until it steamed and soaked the cloth. "The blood on your face has dried," she explained when she returned to him. "I want to wash it off."

She lightly dabbed his face. Twice her body pressed against his shoulder, and he wondered how it would feel to hold her close. "There," she said finally. She lifted the peroxide and a swab and applied the peroxide. It burned, but was an enjoyable experience. When she finished, she applied the antibiotic cream and another Band Aid strip.

"How's that feel?" she asked, stepping back.

"Good as new."

She walked around the table and sat across from him. Leaning on her elbows, she said, "I'll make breakfast for you in a minute. First, tell me what happened. Why were you sleeping in the truck?"

He studied her face, sincere and concerned. "You promise not to laugh?"

"Yes."

"I caught Fortune Montmartre attacking Helena and yelled at him to stop. He threw a vase and hit me in the head. I tried to hit him, but there was nothing to hit." He expected the news to surprise her, but it didn't.

"So, you're saying he's real? Uncle Justin was right?"

"Yes. He's powerful and dangerous. He also threw a heavy painting at me."

"Were you frightened?"

"You mean because a real live ghost tried to bash out my brains?"

She giggled. "Were you?"

"Hell, yes. He's no Casper. I ran like a scared rabbit down the stairs to the front door. When I got there, I realized what I was doing and got mad and rushed back upstairs to challenge him, but, by then, he was gone. I decided not to stay there because I'm sure he would try to kill me. He's not a friendly ghost."

"Paul, we have to discover a way to destroy that monster."

"I agree. My uncle tried a lot of things and they all failed. But there was one thing he never tried, at least not seriously."

"What was that?"

"You mentioned it last night, remember? Someone told him if he wanted to remove a ghost, he should locate the bones and give them a proper burial. I have one week and six days to do that one thing he never did. Find their bones."

"Paul, you're right. But how? He hired men to search the grounds using metal-detection and X-ray equipment. They failed, too." Her face showed worry. "What can we do they didn't do?"

"Justin said he ordered a ground penetrating radar device before he died. It should have been delivered by now. We'll need it to locate the buried bones, so we have to find it."

"What is it?"

"Yoshi says it's a device used to search for objects as deep as twenty feet underground. I read about them once. Police use them to search for buried corpses and other things." He sucked in a breath. "I doubt Talon had the energy to dig graves more than twenty feet deep."

"So, we might still have a chance to win your fortune?"

"A chance, yes. May I ask you a question."

"Of course. What is it?"

"You don't seem too surprised by my story about battling Montmartre. Why?

She giggled. "Because I grew up around Uncle Justin. He wasn't crazy. He wouldn't say it if it wasn't true. And…"

"What?"

"I don't think you're crazy, either." She hesitated. "This means you need a safe place to stay."

"You have any ideas?"

"Yes. Remember I mentioned there's an apartment over the garage?"

"Yes." He swigged his coffee.

"Well, it's still in good shape. Everything works, but…"

"What?"

"Well, If I were choosing, I'd pick the pool house."

"The pool house?"

"Yes. It has everything. An upstairs bedroom and bath, a second bedroom and bath downstairs. There's also a fully equipped kitchen and a pleasant living room with a view of the pool. It's setup for a computer, too. Uncle Justin and Mr. Heimlich often stayed there. It's brighter and more cheerful than the garage. When I was in high school, we used to have slumber parties there."

"Sounds perfect," he said. "How big is the pool?"

"Eighty feet long, sixty feet wide. Great for parties."

"Wow," he said.

She smiled and rose. "We'll look at both places after breakfast. How do you like your eggs?"

"Over easy, but wouldn't you rather go out?"

"No. Go get your truck and bring it closer. We can use it to tour the property after breakfast."

"Aye, aye, ma'am." He rose and left.

Half an hour later, Paul dropped his fork and leaned back. "I didn't know Harvard girls learned to cook like that. That was great."

"You're being silly, but I like it. Nobody calls eggs over easy, bacon, toast and a few French fries great."

"Well, maybe not. Guess I had the cook in mind."

Her face flushed. "Paul, may I be serious for a minute?"

"Of course, I've never yet turned down a gorgeous damsel in distress. What is it?"

"I'm worried about my father."

He became serious, too. "Worried how?"

She played with her napkin and then gushed out the story of her last two nights following Gerard Duet, including the truth about the diaries. She concluded with, "He twice threatened to throw me out of my home. At first, I thought he was having a mental breakdown. But considering what you told me, I fear that creature has done something to him."

"You mean like a possession?"

"Well… yes, but is that even possible?"

He chuckled. "When I went to bed last night, I didn't believe in ghosts. This morning, I do, so yes, I believe it's possible."

"I — " Her distress was palpable.

"You said it sounded like someone wants him to do something, but he refused?"

"Yes. He said, 'You can kill me, but I won't do it.'"

"If he's talking to Montmartre, it sounds like he's fighting him. That's a good sign."

She met his gaze. "Paul, I think Montmartre asked Dad to kill you, and Dad refused."

Paul rose and took the dishes to the sink. "That makes sense, especially after last night. But, before we confront your father, we need more information. I suggest we move me into the pool house, take a quick tour of the property, and then pay another visit to Madam Song. I want her to read our notes."

She lit the room with a bright smile and hurried to join him at the sink. "Sounds perfect. Thanks for understanding."

"You're welcome, but—"

She bumped him away with her hip and took over the rest of the KP duty. He returned to the table, sipped his coffee and enjoyed the pleasure of watching her work.

Mostly one question dominated his thoughts? What would it take to win her love?

TWENTY-SIX

PAUL STEPPED OUT of the shower, dried and wrapped himself in a large beach towel. It always amazed him how refreshing a clean shave and shower made him feel. He studied himself in the mirror. Passable, but good enough for Samantha? A wave of doubt plagued him.

Refreshed, he walked into the bedroom, dug in his bag for clean slacks and a dark-blue sports shirt. He sat on the bed to put on his shoes. Sam called this place a pool house, but compared top his little apartment, it was a luxury hotel. It even had a sliding door leading to a balcony overlooking the pool.

His phone jangled on the bedside table. "Yosh! I was just going to call you."

"Hey, Paul-san. You couldn't reach me, anyway. I've been in a conference all morning with my phone off. We're breaking for lunch now."

"So how's New York?"

"Terrible. I'm bored to death. I'd much rather be in Malibu with you and Sam."

Paul heard the misery in his friend's voice. "Hang in there, Yosh. You'll live."

"Yeah, I guess. Listen, I have to go soon. I called for an update. Mr. Moto is dying for a report on what's happening."

"Are you sitting down?"

"Hai. In the conference room."

"Okay, here it is. Fortune and Helena are real. Fortune threw a vase at me last night. Almost knocked out my brains. My uncle's description of the ghosts was right."

"You could see them?"

"Yes."

"Horee Sheeto. Are you okay?"

"I'm fine, Yosh. We're trying to figure a way to get rid of him, but it won't be easy. My uncle tried everything at least once."

"Ah, so. I—"

The sound of loud voices cut drowned Yoshi's own. One voice called, "Yoshiru, ikou."

"Paul-san, sorry. My dad's calling me. I'll try to phone you tonight."

"Right. Take care. We miss you."

"Thanks. How's Sam?"

"Use your imagination."

Yoshi chuckled and cut the connection.

He scribbled a check to the hospital for twenty-thousand dollars. That left thirty thousand in his account.

The enticing smell or coffee reached him. Sam was in the kitchen. He stuffed the check in his wallet and hurried downstairs. Anxiety followed him.

"Hey, you clean up good," Sam said when she saw him.

"Thanks." He relaxed.

"Sit. We'll drink coffee while we make our plans."

He sat and let his eyes feast on her. "I figured out a rough itinerary while I was in the shower."

She placed a steaming cup in front of him and joined him at the table. Her left leg brushed against his when she sat. "Should I take notes?"

"It's not that complicated. It's what we discussed earlier.

Tour the estate, but with an addition."

"What?"

"Remember the newspaper clipping you read?"

"Yes."

"Talon Montmartre said he left an upside-down clue to help determine where he buried the bodies. Maybe we can spot it from the car, though that's a long shot. A thorough search will have to wait.

"What kind of sign would it be?"

"I doubt it would be a cross. Talon said his father was into devil worship. Does that ring a bell?"

"Are you suggesting a pentagram or an upside down cross?"

"Why not?"

"Remember, I've lived her most of my life. I've walked or played on every square inch of these grounds. Everything always seemed normal."

"Except the house."

"Right."

"Anyway, Yoshi suggested Talon's words could be a last dirty trick on the world, so—"

"You mean to send people out chasing wild geese?"

"That's what Yoshi believes."

"Well, the work road encircles Montmartre. It won't hurt to check it out. Perhaps your fresh perspective will see something I've overlooked." Her blue eyes bored through him to his toes. "What else is on the itinerary?"

"Madam Song, for starters. She owes me some answers."

"In Pasadena, right?"

"Yes."

"We'd better hurry then. It's almost nine now."

"Sam, I don't want to impose. You must have other things to do."

"We settled that nonsense last night. Until we get rid of Fortune Montmartre, I go where you go. What else?"

"I want to stop in at the hospital and pay some on my father's bill. After that, I'll just play it by ear. To make a proper plan, I need more information."

"I agree, but you meant we have to play it by ear, didn't you?"

"Yeah, I must have."

"I have a question." She stood and took their cups to the sink.

"What?"

"What was the second condition?"

"Second condition?"

"This morning you said you would tell me what happened, but only if I met your two conditions. One was breakfast. What was the other one?"

"Are you always this persistent?"

"Yes. Tell me."

If you don't lie, you don't have to remember anything, thought. He had to tell her the truth. "Okay, you asked for it. Explain to me why you kissed me last night."

"Is that all?"

"Isn't that enough?" So far, so good. She didn't slap him.

"Why do you want to know?"

"Because I liked it."

"Well, I wondered about that myself, but I figured it out last night."

"And?"

A twinkle appeared in her gorgeous eyes. "I did it because I thought it would be pleasant."

"Was it?"

"Yes, very."

"In that case, I should tell you. I'm available anytime you want to have another try."

"Well, thanks, kind sir. I'll keep that in mind. Now we'd better get to your truck and go."

Moments later, they were at the far end of the estate when Samantha grabbed his arm and pointed through the truck's passenger window. "I've never seen that before."

Paul slowed from ten miles an hour to a complete stop. He followed her pointing finger. They were as far from the front gate as possible. Thirty yards away at the base of a tall Live Oak sat a box that resembled an old-fashioned pine-box coffin. Next to it was a mound of fresh dirt. "Looks like a coffin," he said.

"Yes, and a grave."

Paul got out, intending to open the door for Sam. She beat him to it. "Duh. I can work a door handle."

She hurried to the box, with Paul right behind her. He bent closer. Its lid was closed. He caught the edges and tugged it open. "Empty."

"That's odd." Sam dropped to her knees on the grass and scraped at the pile of dirt. When she hit bottom, she said, "Weird."

"What?"

She stood and looked at him. "The hole is about four inches deep. Dad just started work on it, I guess. He never wastes time or energy."

"We can ask him later," Paul said, grinning at her expression. "Let's go."

"Wait! Why dig a hole here?"

"I'd say he plans to bury something? Let's move on." He didn't tell her his real opinion , that Gerard Duet planned to bury a body. But whose?

Several minutes later, Paul hit the brakes hard. The car stopped parallel to the rear of the mansion. He strained to see past the perimeter row of Juniper trees. He backed the truck until he found what caught his eye. It resembled an old gold mine cave entrance.

"What is it?" Sam asked.

"It looks like a rotted wooden door."

"A door? Oh, that's nothing. It goes nowhere."

"You've seen it before?"

"Many times. I never thought it was important."

"Mind if I check it myself?"

"Not at all."

They climbed out and walked to the edge of the road. Paul ducked past the wall of Junipers that hid the door from view. Needles and spider webs clawed at his face.

The door was mounted in a frame of rotting four-by-four timbers. It was a full-size old door, grayed by time and decay. No door knob. Only a hole where a knob might once have been.

Samantha ducked under the tree on the opposite side. "Why would anyone put a door here?"

"To hide something, I'd say. I wonder if anyone's at home." He knocked hard. A dull thud answered.

"It doesn't sound hollow," Sam said.

"It isn't." He pounded again in a different location. Same thudding sound.

"What do you think is in there?"

"A mountain of dirt, and, of course, ghosts. What else?"

"You really are silly. Can we open it?"

"Let's see." He stuck two fingers in the knob hole and jerked. A six-inch piece of rotted wood came off in his hand. He grabbed another section and ripped. The termite-eaten wood crumbled in his hand. He dug his fingers into the soil behind the door and brought forth a handful.

"Nothing there," he said, brushing the dirt from his hand. "Just mountain."

"Weirder and weirder," Sam said. "Why build a door to nowhere?

"Perhaps he planned to dig later, but abandoned the project."

"That makes no sense."

"I agree. One of the world's great mysteries."

"So, Madam Song now?"

"Yeah, I'll call her, pick up our notes from the library, and follow the plan."

Samantha maneuvered backward out onto the road. Then, using both hands, brushed dried Juniper needles from her hair. Paul followed and then stepped forward to pull a strand of spider web from her ear.

"Thanks," she said.

"My pleasure."

TWENTY-SEVEN

MADAM SONG'S inner sanctum hadn't changed. The powerful odor of incense permeated the place. They found her at the table with her crystal ball casting an eerie glow over everything in the room.

"Welcome," she said when they entered.

The woman waved them to the chairs in front of her desk. When Samantha sat, she said, "You must be Samantha Duet. Justin was right. You're beautiful."

"Thank you," Sam said.

"Madam Song, thanks for seeing us."

"Did Fortune do that?" The psychic gestured to the side of Paul's face.

"Yes. He threw a large portrait and a vase at me. I didn't dodge in time."

"Ah! Just as I suspected. He has telekinetic powers. Do you still doubt ghosts exist, Mr. Davenport?" She didn't bother to hide the sarcastic edge in her voice.

"No. But I... we have questions and time is short." Sam opened her purse and handed Paul the notes they had made the night beforeHe turned back to the psychic. "We read and summarized everything my uncle tried over the years to defeat Montmartre. Perhaps you should read them before we talk." He pushed the pages across the desk.

She touched a hidden button. The lights came on. Sam did a quick intake of breath when she saw Madam Song in full light. The impact of the fortune-teller's visage was astonishing. A smile washed over her long face as she retrieved spectacles from the folds of her colorful tunic. She lifted the pages and read with interest. When she finished, she pushed the notes back to Paul and removed her glasses.

"Fascinating. Your uncle was a determined man. Many items on your list are my ideas, but not all. You said you have questions. How may I help you?"

"Well, number one, my uncle believed Fortune Montmartre has a limited operating range. I wondered whether that's true, and, if so, what is it?"

"Why does that matter?"

"Because I want to set up a safe working zone outside the house."

"I see. So, you want me to tell you how far his powers extend from the house?"

"Yes."

"I wish I could. No one can."

"Why?"

"Because ghosts are like people. They come in many varieties and different capabilities. Some are more powerful than others. Some so-called experts say ghosts attach themselves to objects or places and can't leave the vicinity of their attachment. Others hold different views. But the truth is, I don't know whether any of that's true."

"But—"

"Paul, your uncle was the most experienced ghost fighter in the world. He spent twenty-five years battling Montmartre. I suggest you trust his judgement."

He glanced at Sam. She gave him an encouraging smile.

Madam Song raised her brows. "Anything else?

"Yes. Someone told my uncle that if he finds the bones and gives them a proper burial, Montmartre will go away. Can you verify that?"

"No, sorry. Many ghost hunters believe that, though. I know only one way to find out."

"What's that, Madam," Sam asked.

The woman twisted her face into a wry smile. "Find the bones and bury them. If the ghost of Montmartre disappears, it's true."

"You're not being much help," Paul said, not trying to hide his ire.

"What would you like me to do?"

"Help me. You said if I read the diaries, you would answer my questions."

"I'm trying to do that, young man. The problem is, you don't like my answers."

"You read our notes and you can't suggest anything else we can try?"

"No." She sighed. "Mr. Davenport, I've never purported to be an expert on ghosts. Your uncle understood that."

"Then what was he paying you for?" Paul demanded.

"He seemed to gain comfort from the knowledge I sensed Fortune Montmartre's existence, and that I sympathized with his efforts to save the girl, though not his desire to remove Fortune Montmartre. Most people thought he was eccentric, perhaps insane."

Samantha touched Paul's arm to ease his frustration. "Madam Song, does such a thing as a ghost expert exist?" she asked.

"There are people who claim to be. But—"

"Can you give us a name?"

Relieved to change the subject, Madam Song said, "There is one man, a PhD, a retired professor of parapsychology named Mathias Sage. He wrote a controversial book called *Immortality of Ghosts*, which outraged even his most extreme colleagues. He may have the answers you need."

"What was controversial about his book?" Sam asked.

"The book's premise is that one can become immortal by becoming a ghost. He claims he knows more about ghosts than any other living human." Her gaze bounced from Samantha and back to Paul. "I have his phone number and address if you want it."

"Have you met him?"

"No. He called me once, asking for an introduction to your uncle. He said he learned about the hauntings at Chateau Montmartre from a colleague."

"Did you give it to him?"

"Yes. Justin met him one time only and refused his services."

"Why?"

"I'm not sure. Perhaps Dr. Sage can tell you."

"What services does he offer?" Sam asked.

"You'll have to ask him that, too, if you're interested."

"It sounds like you have little else to offer," Paul said, his voice disappointed.

"I fear you're right, Mr. Davenport. I've tried for years to solve your uncle's problem with no success. As much as I'd like to help, I'm all out of ideas. I'm sorry."

"But you still took his money, didn't you?"

"You can believe me or not. That's your choice. I offered to cancel my agreement with Justin two years ago, but he refused to allow it. He was a kind man. The contract ends in thirty days, anyway. I will return the money if you wish."

Paul was sorry for pushing so hard. "No, my apologies, Madam Song. I guess I'm frustrated because I don't know how to proceed."

"Understood, but I'm confident you'll find a way forward."

Paul gave her a weak smile. "I wish I was."

"Paul, let's talk to the professor," Samantha said. "What do we have to lose?" Sam's eyes sparkled with excitement for a moment. He could tell she was eager to meet the man. How could he say no?

"I guess we'll take that number and address, Madam," he said. "Thanks."

"You're welcome and don't forget to call me tonight."

"Right."

Back in the truck, Sam said, "To the hospital, right."

"Yes. It's five minutes from here tops."

He started the truck.

TWENTY-EIGHT

PAUL DROVE to the hospital and Sam accompanied him into the front office. The girl there saws him and smiled. "May I—oh, hi, Mr. Davenport. Haven't seen you in a while."

Paul returned her smile. "Hi, Annie. I've been busy."

"Saw you on TV Sunday. You were awesome."

"Thanks. I didn't feel awesome. This is Samantha Duet. Sam, Annie Coburn. Annie runs this place."

The girl snickered. "Not really. Dr. Lanza helps a little." To Paul, she said, "Dr. Lanza is not here. He's…" Her eyes filled with worry. She studied her desktop, blushing. "He's talking to the collection agency."

"About me?" Paul's heart sank.

"Yes. Paul, I'm sorry, but I overheard them talking. They intend to get every penny they can."

"Damn. I was afraid this would happen. I came here to give him this." Paul retrieved the check from his wallet and handed it to her.

"Twenty-thousand dollars," she whispered as she read the numbers. She stared at it a moment and then shoved it back to him. "I… you better save this for lawyers." She hesitated. "I shouldn't tell you this, but you're a nice guy. You'd be amazed at what I see and overhear sitting at this desk. I'm aware of the sacrifices you've made for your father. You don't deserve to be hounded." She looked at the door and back. "Collection agencies sometimes settle for pennies on the dollar, so you can use this as part of negotiation. If you pay this now, you lose your ability to fight."

"Annie, I..."

Samantha touched his arm to stop him. "I think she's right. I suggest you do as she says."

Annie smiled at Samantha. "Between us chickens, they already wrote your account off on their taxes anyhow. Saved them a bundle."

"Annie, will this get you in trouble?" Sam asked.

"Only if you tell on me. Paul, the collectors can be nasty. I'm not sure what deal they're making with Dr. Lanza, but they'll hound you into bankruptcy. They get fifty to seventy-five percent of every dollar they collect."

Paul put the check back in his wallet. "Annie, thanks. I owe you."

She glanced at Sam and smiled at Paul. "Consider it my good deed for the day. You'd better leave before they come back. Take care."

"I will. Tell the doctor I'll call him in a few days, okay?"

"I wouldn't call," Annie said. "You didn't come here today, and we didn't talk."

Paul bent to give her a friendly peck on her forehead. "You're a sweetheart."

The phone rang. Annie grabbed it and waved them away. "Go! Shoo!"

Back at the car, Sam said, "That girl has a big crush on you. She's nice, and she's smart, too."

Paul frowned as they got in the car. "Yeah, she's unusual. What she did just now could get her in deep hot water."

"If they found out, but you won't mention it, right?"

"Not even if they torture me. She gave me a blueprint for

handling them, too. I think I just got a reprieve. Are you hungry yet?"

"Not really."

"I'm not either. What say we give Mathias Sage a try?"

She moistened her lips. "Let's do it."

Paul called the professor. He enjoyed having Samantha hanging out with him. The question was, how could he make it permanent?

The phone rang twice and a powerful tenor voice answered. "Hello?"

"Professor Sage?"

"Yes, who is this?"

"Sir, my name is Paul Davenport. I—"

"Davenport! Are you related to Justin Davenport?"

"Yes. He was my uncle."

"I met him once. I heard he died."

"Yes. Professor, I want to talk to you about the ghosts living at Chateau Montmartre. I need help."

"Ah, ha! I knew it. Are you saying you have ghosts?"

Paul suppressed a laugh at the man's exuberance. "Yes. Like you wouldn't believe. If you're free, I'd like to see you right away."

"Sure, but I'm surprised by your interest in me. Why is that?"

"Madam Song said you are one of the greatest experts on ghosts and hauntings in the country. I've inherited my uncle's estate. I need your help."

A happy cackle sounded on the other end of the phone. "Madam Song was wrong on one count, Mr. Davenport."

"What's that?"

"I'm not one of the greatest experts on ghosts. I am the greatest."

"Sorry."

"No problem. Where are you now?"

"Pasadena. May I visit you?"

"Hell, yes. Do you know my address?"

Paul read the address Madam Song had given him, which was in a pleasant neighborhood of Old Pasadena.

"How soon can you be here?"

TWENTY-NINE

THE WIZARD'S EXCITEMENT on the phone was real. Dr. Mathias Sage was standing outside, pacing alongside his old Chevy, when they slowed and turned into his driveway. The house was a typical Southern California yellow-beige stucco home with green shutters and a gray wooden-tile roof. Before they braked to a stop, the old professor scooted around to Paul's window. In his eagerness, he tried to open the door, but could not.

"Welcome, welcome!" he said through the glass. "Come in. Come in."

Paul lifted a hand to say thanks. He cut the engine and set the brake. He turned to Sam. "He looks happy we made it." They opened their doors and got out.

Dr. Mathias Sage, dressed in black trousers, a white shirt open at the collar and a dark vest, was as tall as Paul. He wore a ragged full-face white beard with a matching mustache and bushy eyebrows. His face was gaunt and wrinkled, but brown eyes sparkled as he beamed at Paul. Curly white hair poked out of his nostrils and around his collar.

Paul climbed out of the car, and the man grabbed his hand and shook it with exaggerated enthusiasm. His grip was bony but strong.

"Glad to meet you, Mr. Davenport. Glad. Thanks for coming. You've made my day."

Paul retrieved his hand. "Thanks for having us, Professor." He pointed to Samantha, who was watching them. "This is Samantha Duet, Professor. She's—"

"The caretaker's daughter!" The professor charged around the car and shook Sam's hand. "Wonderful. Twenty years living near a famous haunted mansion. I envy you. Welcome to my home."

"Nice to meet you. Thanks for inviting us."

"Let's go in. I made fresh coffee. He spun on his heel and hurried to open the front door for them.

Ten minutes later, Paul finished his coffee and sat the cup and saucer on a pecan-wood coffee table in front of the sofa where he and Sam were sitting.

"More coffee?" The professor, perched on the edge of an overstuffed easy chair across from them, fidgeted nonstop. As Paul sipped the coffee, the man made him nervous, watching every sip he took like a cat stalking a canary.

"No, thanks," Paul said. "That hit the spot. Professor, I have questions I'd like to ask you, if I may."

"Of course you may. But first, you said Fortune Montmartre tried to kill you. Did he give you that bump on your face?"

"Yes."

"Was he visible to you? I mean, did he have form? My understanding is that both Fortune and his wife made themselves visible to your uncle. That's very rare."

"Yes. my uncle was aware of that. What do you mean, they made themselves visible??"

"From what I've learned, depending on their power, ghosts can control whether they are visible to the living."

"I'm not sure that's true. Helena seemed surprised to learn I could see her."

"She may not be as powerful as her husband."

"Are they visible to each other?"

"I've studied texts from all over the world. Ghosts are not weird, mindless manifestations floating around like empty-headed zombies. They are sentient creatures who live in another plane of existence. I believe they are not only visible to each other, but can communicate via telepathy. You encountered Fortune Montmartre. Did he strike you as being mindless?"

Paul relived his ghostly encounter for a moment, and then said, "No, I'm certain he was aware of what he was doing to me, and that he enjoyed doing it."

The professor cackled. "I knew it. I was certain of it!"

"Professor, Madam Song thinks seeing them is a special talent possessed only by me."

The professor shrugged. "I doubt that. The entire field is fraught with expert disagreement about everything. Maybe we're both right. We're not dealing with any known science here."

"So, you think Montmartre deliberately made himself visible to me?"

"Yes, and he wanted your uncle to communicate with him, too. Otherwise…"

"One correction, Professor. My uncle didn't converse with Montmartre. Only with Helena. He wrote messages on a chalk board, and she responded the same way."

"Incredible! But you saw Fortune. What did he look like? Please, tell me."

The notion struck Paul that the professor's interest was more than simple curiosity, but he decided that fairness required him to exchange information with the man. "All right. I'll tell you what happened, and then it will be my turn. Okay?"

"Yes, yes."

Paul sat back and described the events of the night before in vivid detail. He concluded with, "That's it. When I went back upstairs to confront him, he was gone."

"Amazing." The old professor gulped. The Adam's apple on his skinny neck bobbed like a fishing cork getting nibbles. "He must have lost his coat sleeve in the fight with his son. That's a detail I've never heard before. Did Helena speak?"

"Helena screamed and Fortune burst out with a wild laugh like a mad man. He mouthed words to me. He said, 'You're a dead man.' Helena didn't speak."

"And you say Fortune's face changed?"

"Yes, at first it was normal, and then it changed?"

"How?"

"It looked like a phony Halloween mask, with long white fangs and glowing red eyes."

"Good Lord!"

"What?"

"That means he is extremely powerful and can shape shift. He may even have become a demon. If so, your uncle had no chance to win his fight against Montmartre."

Paul's hopes plummeted. "A demon? I don't understand."

Mathias Sage pinched his brows as he considered his next words. "The bible is full of references to demons. And, as you might expect, evil people and spirits serve as magnets for such hellish entities. Sometimes, if they are evil and angry enough, they become demons themselves. Scholars have documented this since the time of Christ."

"But—"

"Trust me, sir. I know whereof I speak."

Paul sat back, trying to assimilate this new problem. Samantha gave him a sympathetic gaze.

"Dr. Sage, where did you learn so much about Chateau Montmartre?" Samantha asked. "I grew up there, and no one ever mentioned ghosts to me."

"Ah, yes. Justin Davenport hired quite a few psychics and mediums over the years. Some of them are my friends. I've questioned several of the others and even paid one man two hundred dollars to reveal what he learned during his visit. And, as a scholar myself, I have scoured everything in print about the chateau's history."

"Sir, I've answered your questions. I'd like to ask mine now, if I may."

Mathias Sage sat back in his chair for the first time since their arrival. "Please accept my apologies. As you can see, I have a great interest in Fortune Montmartre. What do you wish to know?"

"I have three questions. Number one, are ghosts free to roam anywhere they wish, or are they limited to a certain territory they can haunt? My uncle believed Fortune has a limited operating range."

"Excellent question. Your uncle is correct. Earthbound spirits or ghosts often attach themselves to places or objects, like houses, dolls or familiar things they left behind. How far they can range depends on their power. Trial and error may be the only way to determine their ability to roam. Ghosts often gain power over time, and from what you tell me, Fortune Montmartre has become quite powerful and dangerous."

"Doctor, do ghosts ever eave the places they haunt?" Sam asked. "I mean because they want to leave."

"Good question, young lady. I suppose it's possible, especially with a vengeful spirit."

"Vengeful spirit?" Paul said, frowning. "What the devil is that?"

THIRTY

THE PROFESSOR GRINNED broadly. He hopped up and hurried to a wall of old books jammed into a built-in bookcase. His fingers scanned the volumes like a kid dragging a stick across a picket fence. He found what he was looking for and pulled out an old leather-bound book. He flipped pages as he started towards them, but then changed his mind and replaced it in the bookcase. As if angry at himself, he rushed to his seat. He hopped in, leaned back all the way, then jerked forward. His body was as spastic as his brain.

"Ah, sorry," he said. "You want quick answers? And I was about to launch into a long lecture. Vengeful spirits are special types of ghosts created under special circumstances. And they're the most fearsome of all ghosts possible. They are the spirits of people who died during such powerful emotion that they refuse to pass on when they die. Fortune Montmartre died in an angry battle with his son. He tried to murder Talon, but he died instead. That alone qualifies him as a vengeful spirit. He was, without doubt, filled with rage, jealousy, and hatred when he died. From what I've learned over the years, he remained behind because he desires to exact revenge on his son."

"Professor Sage, you didn't answer my question," Sam said.

"Do ghosts ever leave the places they haunt?"

"Sorry, my dear. You know how garrulous old men are. No one knows for sure. But I suspect they can once they quench their thirst for vengeance. They also might leave if they can do so by leaving. However, I see no way for Fortune to satisfy his desire for revenge. I doubt he knows where his son is, so…" He turned palms up and said to Paul. "You asked about Fortune's range of operation. Why is that important to you?"

"Do you know the kid's game, King of the Hill?"

"Of course. One kid goes to the top of a hill or to the center of a circle. Other kids try to knock him off the hill or out of the circle. Whoever succeeds becomes the new King of the Hill. It's also called King of the Mountain or King of the Castle. Pretty rough and tumble old game. Why do you ask?"

"Because Fortune can't come out to fight. So, to boot him out of the mansion, it seems necessary for me to go in after him. It also means I need a safe zone for retreat. He's mean and tough."

"Ah! Exactly like the game." The professor chuckled. "Except in this case, I'd call the game King of the Mansion. And your second question?"

"What happens if you find a ghost's bones and give them a proper burial? Will the ghost go away then?"

The professor cackled, which appeared to be his laugh response, when he became excited. "Is that your goal here? Get rid of Fortune by finding and burying his bones?"

"Yes. It's the only thing possible in the time I have."

"That could be very dangerous."

"I know. What's the answer?"

The professor considered the question it for a moment, then asked, "Do you believe Fortune Montmartre is a sentient entity?"

"You mean, did he seem to be aware of what he was doing?"

"Yes. Would you say he has goals and desires?"

"I suppose he must. He tried for years to get rid of my uncle, and now he wants me gone too."

"Have you considered the possibility you are planning to

murder Mr. Montmartre?"

"Murder!" Sam exclaimed. "How can you murder a ghost? The idea is absurd, professor."

The professor chuckled. "It seems so on the surface, doesn't it? But it may not be. My long-held view is that ghosts are actual people living on a different plane of existence. If Fortune has goals, if he has anger and a desire for revenge, he exhibits all the traits of living human beings. Therefore, it's obvious he's alive in a form other than corporeal. If you destroy him, that would meet all the requirements of murder, wouldn't it?"

"Damn it, professor, I don't want to murder him," Paul said, "but if that's what it takes to get him out of my house, that's what I'll do. I just want to send him to wherever all the other ghosts go." He frowned. "You haven't answered my question"Right. Sorry. The answer is it might work, but it depends on many factors. A ghost may do everything in its power to prevent you from finding its bones. That is especially true of earthbound ghosts that don't want to move on. Why is this important to you?"

"Because my uncle's will stipulates I must clear chateau Montmartre of ghosts in two weeks. Otherwise, I get nothing."

"So you're in desperate need of help."

"Desperate? No. I have another life. But I get nothing if I don't succeed."

"Do you have any volunteers to help you?"

"Only two. Samantha and a close friend of mine who can't be here."

"I see." The professor scooted to the edge of his seat and wiggled with excitement.. "How would you like a volunteer for your little ghost-buster army?"

Paul couldn't help himself. He laughed at the professor's enthusiasm. "Are you volunteering?"

Mathias Sage jumped to his feet and saluted with a Cheshire-cat smile. "Dr. Mathias Sage at your service, sir." He clicked his heels together and dropped into his chair, grinning.

Samantha giggled. Paul chuckled. "So what's the going rate for retired professors these days?"

"Pshaw! I have all the money I need. Hell... excuse me, Miss Duet... I'll pay you to let me help. That place has intrigued me for years. This is a fantastic opportunity."

"Did you once offer your services to my uncle?"

"Yes, but he turned me down."

"Why?"

"I'm sure it was because Madam Song disapproved of the book I wrote."

"Immortality of Ghosts?" Sam asked.

"Yes. Have you read it?"

"No."

"Ah, too bad. If you had, that would have given me three readers." He grinned at Paul. "Sorry. Your uncle didn't say so, but I'm certain the good madam poisoned his mind against me because of the book's premise. She was wrong." He gazed at Paul with pleading eyes. "What do you say, young sir? I need only a place to sleep."

Samantha touched his arm. "Paul?"

He looked at her. Sage was weird as hell, but they needed help. "What do you think?"

Gorgeous blue eyes blasted him to his soul. "It's the best offer we've had all day, and the garage apartment is ready and waiting, so I say yes."

Paul turned back to Mathias Sage. "When can you start?"

The man looked at his wristwatch. "How about six o'clock?"

"Tomorrow morning?"

"Tonight, if that's okay."

"Great, thanks. Do you need the address?"

"Are you kidding? I've driven by there a hundred times."

"Right. Turn in at the sign. Drive to the gate and honk your horn. We'll open it for you."

"Mr. Davenport, you won't be sorry. I promise."

"I believe you." Paul stood to leave, but the professor stopped him.

"Wait, you said three questions. What's number three?"

"We wondered whether a ghost can take possession of a human being?"

"Is someone at the Chateau acting as though possessed?"

"Yes. Sam's father."

"I see. How long has he worked there?"

"Twenty years." Sam's voice broke with emotion.

"I'm sorry, miss Duet. It can happen and often does when there's a demon involved." The professor frowned. "Why do you think he's possessed?"

"He's turned against me," Sam said, "and he seems to hate Paul. He's never acted that way before. How can you tell whether Fortune has possessed him?"

"Well, there are several clues. The most obvious ones are higher than normal strength, the sudden ability to speak strange languages, and an aversion to holy symbols. Others include inexplicable behavior, speaking to invisible companions and irrational anger. Have you seen any of those things?"

"Yes. My father was talking to something in the air behind the chateau. I thought he was losing his mind. Whatever it was, it pushed him to the ground." Her lip trembled. "Can you help him?"

"Sorry, but that's difficult to answer. It's possible, but I would have to meet him first."

"Should we confront him?" Paul asked.

"I don't recommend it. He could be dangerous."

Paul stood up. "We appreciate your help, Dr. Sage. Thank you."

"No, no. Thank you. You're helping me fulfill a twenty-year-old dream. I can't wait to visit the chateau."

Samantha stood and shook the doctor's hand.

The professor beamed almost with joy. "See you at six."

"Where to now?" Sam touched Paul's arm as he started the car.

"I have an idea."

"What?"

"That, miss nosy, is a secret. First, we need food."

THIRTY-ONE

A FTER A QUICK lunch at a nearby coffee shop, Paul slammed on his brakes and pulled to the side of the street.

Surprised, Samantha asked, "What's wrong?"

"Nothing. I just realized I need some information."

"What?" She tilted her head to study him.

"When were the first typing schools opened in the U. S.?"

"Typing?"

"Yes."

"I have the answer, but I won't tell until you tell me why it's important."

Paul gave her an impish look. "You drive a hard bargain, but I'll tell you my idea soon. I promise. When did they start?"

Sam stared at the roof of the car, remembering. "Let's see, Remington introduced the first commercial typewriters with QWERTY keyboard around eighteen seventy-three." She pursed her lip as she tried to recall the answer.

Paul's eyes were drawn to her lips, moist, pink, slightly puckered. A brilliant idea popped into his head. He had been wanting to find an excuse to feel those lips without making her mad. Now he had it. He leaned toward her and planted a light kiss on her puckered lips. She jerked back, eyes wide.

"Why did you do that?"

"I realized it might be pleasant."

Her brows went up, followed by a smile and a high-pitched laugh. "Was it?"

"Almost."

"Almost?"

"Yeah. I think I needed a little longer sample to be sure."

"How long?"

"I'm not sure. Longer."

She sighed. "Okay, try if you must. I won't stop you."

She met him halfway. Their lips touched. Her hand slipped around the back of his neck and pulled him tighter. He had a hard time keeping his hands on the steering wheel, but he did it. A minute later, she backed away and took a deep breath. "Well?"

"Oh, yeah," he said. "In fact, I'm already addicted."

"Good." Her eyes twinkled. "Now, back to your question. As I recall, early typewriter manufacturers like Remington offered typing courses to promote sales. You know, if nobody knows how to type, who'll buy a typewriter? Anyway, it worked, and typewriters became common in offices by the mid eighteen eighties.

"What are you, an encyclopedia or something?"

"I read a lot. Behave. Tell me your idea."

"Not yet, but I'll show you. We're off to see a marine buddy of mine about a computer."

The sign on the storefront said, "Computer-IT Services, Inc." Beneath the big letters, in smaller type, it said, "Jack Davis, prop."

Three parking slots were open. Paul picked the one closest to the front door.

"Jack and I were in the marines together," Paul explained. "His parents had money. Mine didn't. He mustered out of the marines a year before I did and started this business. I've written software for a few of his customers."

"I'm still waiting for an explanation," Sam said. "What are

we doing at a computer store?"

"Sorry, it's still a secret. Let's go in, but watch yourself. Jack's a wolf in wolf's clothing."

"Don't worry. I've handled his type before."

The storefront was narrow. A cowbell sounded as they entered. A counter ran the width of the shop dividing front from back. Several long, shelf-filled aisles divided the space behind the counter. It resembled an auto parts store. Shelves displaying a variety of laptop and desktop computers and accessories lined the walls, left and right. The store was empty of people.

Suddenly, a loud voice blasted from the shadows behind the counter. "Damn, Davenport! Where did you find that angel? My God, she would make Helen of Troy cringe in a corner." Jack Davis, almost as tall as Paul, lean, with muscles bulging through a thin polo shirt, crew cut, deep-set brown eyes, came toward them into the light. He spoke to Paul, but his eyes were locked on Samantha.

"Hey, Jack. Keep your eyes and hands to yourself. This lady is my future fiancé, Samantha Duet." Samantha's brows shot up in surprise, but she said nothing.

Jack ignored the normal exit from behind the counter. Instead, in one smooth leap, he vaulted over the counter and landed light as a cat. "Future fiancé? Great. That means there's still a chance for me." He did a corny bow. "Jack Davis at your service, beautiful lady."

Samantha smiled and shook his hand. "Nice to meet you, Jack. Paul told me you're a wolf, so I'll be fair and put you straight up front. I'm not interested. Okay? Nice shop you have here."

Jack Davis guffawed and waved his hand around the shop. "Thanks, Samantha. As you can tell, we're busting with customers, but I think I can fit you in." He turned to Paul. "Social visit or business?"

"Business."

"So, how can I help you?"

Samantha studied Paul with interest. He could tell her curiosity was popping its seams about what he had said about her and about why they were there.

"I need the smallest Windows Pro computer you have, the largest flat-screen monitor you have, and a soft-touch keyboard with large letters." Paul turned to Samantha. "You said the house has internet, right?"

"Yes, Uncle Justin spent a lot of money setting it up. There's a wireless modem in the pool house, and there's one on a shelf in the library."

"So what do you say, Jack? Can do?"

"When do you need it?"

"Now."

"Now? That's a damned weird order for you, Paul. What's this about?"

"If I told you, I'd have to kill you, so I won't. I like you too much."

Jack Davis guffawed again. "See what you're getting into," he said to Samantha. "Now if you were engaged to me…."

"Come on, Jack, can you help me or not?"

"Yeah, I've got a hot mini with everything you need. It's pricey, though."

"Did I ask about the price? What about the keyboard?"

"Yeah, I got one of those somewhere. Customer ordered it, then changed his mind. The keys are bright yellow with large black letters."

"That works. What about the monitor?"

"Is twenty-seven inches okay?"

"Perfect."

"You'll need at least two HDMI cables."

"I'll take four."

"Right. What else?"

"Will you take a check?"

Jack Davis grinned, showing a mouthful of big white teeth. "I'd rather have a handful of that drug money. Easier to skip problems with the IRS, you know."

Paul grinned at his friend. "Sorry, I gave all that to the cops."

"Yeah, I know. I saw the interview." Davis glanced at Samantha. "Some hero, huh?"

"No argument here."

"Give me a minute to get it together." Jack Davis vaulted over the counter.

As soon as he disappeared into the back of the store, Samantha turned a fierce gaze on Paul and said, "Future, fiancé?" Her eyes held a tentative twinkle.

Paul flushed. "Sorry about that. I wanted to get his mind on business instead of you. I hope it didn't upset you."

"It didn't. I figured it was something like that."

Jack came back with a large cardboard box, which he placed on the counter. He disappeared once more and came back with a larger box holding the monitor. He showed and explained each item to Paul. Paul paid him.

When he finished, Jack leapt over the counter and held the door for Paul. Paul arranged his purchases in the back seat of his truck. Then, as Samantha got in, Jack Davis called out, "Hey, Samantha. Don't forget. If you change your mind about that knucklehead, I'm right here."

Sam waved, and Paul started the car.

As they pulled away, Sam said, "I'm still waiting."

"For what?"

"Your plan. Why the computer?"

Paul grinned. "Simple. I plan to teach a beautiful young ghost how to type on a computer. If she can lift pieces of chalk, she should be able to punch keys on a keyboard. It'll be much faster than writing one letter at a time on a chalk board, don't you think?"

Sam giggled. "What a clever idea. Brilliant, even… if it works."

"Yeah. If…"

THIRTY-TWO

TWO AND A HALF hours later, Paul, seated at his uncle's library desk, leaned back and said, "Pretty good time. Less than an hour for the entire setup."

"I followed most of what you did," Sam said from her chair to his right, "but you lost me in the end." She had said nothing the entire time he worked.

"Not much to it. I installed a word processor and wrote a macro that saves anything typed in my cloud storage account. Then I programmed the F12 function key to call my cell phone and link to this computer. With this setup, she'll be able to call me when she wants to talk. This lets us message back and forth." He stood and backed away from the desk. "That's it, I guess. The biggest hurdle now will be to teach her how to type."

Sam stood, too. "There's still an hour before Professor Sage will arrive. If you're finished, we should try to find Dad."

A small, hard object hit him in the neck and fell to the floor. It was a stick of chalk. He turned toward the blackboard. Helena, young, beautiful and beaming with a cheerful grin, was standing beside the board staring at him.

"Hello, Helena." He should have given her a welcoming smile, but the close-up sight of her nude body was like a magnet for his eyes. Realizing he was staring, he concentrated on her face her face and smiled. "I was hoping you would show up. We need to talk."

Helena's return smile showed she understood her impact on him.

"Helena is here?" Sam said. Her eyes swept the area where Paul was looking.

"She's standing next to the blackboard.

Helena drifted close to Paul, still smiling. She floated to the desk and lowered into the chair. She lifted her hands to the keyboard and bent to locate the home keys, then typed. The letters A S D F J K L; appeared on the monitor. She typed more. "You're related to Justin, aren't you?" she said. "You look just like him."

Paul nodded. "I'm Paul Davenport, his nephew. And this is Samantha Duet. We're trying to learn how to save you from Fortune."

"Hello, Samantha," Helena typed. "I've seen you on the grounds many times. You are beautiful."

"Thanks. I can't see you, but Paul says you are beautiful, too. You don't seem surprised to see us. Were you expecting Paul?"

"Not really. I never expect anything. Justin says all disappointment comes from over expectation. But I'm excited to meet both of you. If I could shout about how happy I am, I would, but I can't. It's boring here without Justin." She studied the keyboard for a moment, then typed, "This makes typing easy. What is this machine called?"

"It's called a computer, and it's powered by electricity. It will send anything you type to another location. I can read your messages no matter where I am. And, if you press the key marked F12, the computer will telephone me. I can send messages from my telephone to that screen before you. That way we can talk."

"So, this is for me?"

"Yes, we made it especially for you. It's easier than using chalk on a blackboard, don't you think?"

"Yes, and I love it, thank you. It's wonderful."

"We think you are wonderful," Sam said. "You type well."

"I was the fastest typist in Miss Taylor's secretarial school. Eighty-six words a minute. My father wanted me to learn a skill. These keys are easier to push than a typewriter, so I bet I could go even faster than that."

Helena pushed the F12 function key. Paul's phone rang. He answered and said, "We can now exchange messages on the phone. See? What I say is showing up on your big screen there. What you type will show up on this little screen wherever I am. Do you understand?"

She typed, "Yes. I learned about cellular telephones from Justin." The typing stopped for a second. "This is incredible."

"No more incredible than talking to you."

"You mean because I'm a ghost?"

"Yes, you're an amazing young lady." He cut the phone connection and said, "Helena, we want to help you, but we need information."

She looked sad and lost, then typed, "It won't do any good. Justin tried everything. Nothing worked. Did he ask you to keep trying?"

"Yes. I have two weeks."

"What kind of information do you need?"

"I have read that if I can find and give Fortune's bones a proper funeral, he will cease to exist as a ghost. Is that true?"

"Justin asked me that, too. Even though I am one, I'm pretty ignorant about ghosts. I've lived here ever since Fortune killed me."

"I understand, Helena. You're doing great. Did he ask where Talon buried your bodies?"

"Yes, but I knew nothing about it until Justin told me."

"That makes sense." Paul hesitated. "I have another question, if you don't mind.

"I don't mind, Paul. It's so lonely here. I love having someone to talk to." She looked back at him and smiled.

Paul nodded. "Thanks. Does Fortune travel outside the chateau?"

"Yes. Sometimes."

"How far can he go?"

"Why is that important to you?"

"He tried to kill me last night, so I can't stay here. I need a safe place to sleep."

"Oh. Justin worried about that, too. He used to sleep in the house by the swimming pool."

"Thanks. That's important information."

"I'm stuck inside these walls, but Fortune isn't. His power has grown since Talon killed him. He can lift things and move them around. He loves to catch and torture me."

"I know that first hand," Paul said.

"Do you know in advance when he's after you?" Sam asked.

"Sometimes, but not always."

"Are you able to escape from him when he comes after you?"

"Most of the time. It's kind of like playing hide and seek, but there aren't many places to hide. He attacks me whenever he finds me."

"Damn," Paul said.

"Helena, is there any way we can help you?" Sam asked.

"Ha, ha!" she typed. "I would love a cup of vanilla ice cream with hot chocolate syrup on top. We had a wonderful ice-cream parlor back home. As a ghost, I can't eat or drink or feel, but I can remember things."

"But you must feel something. You scream in pain," Paul said.

"Only when Fortune tortures me."

"Where is he right now? Do you know?"

"No. He may be near the big oak."

Paul's phone rang.

"Excuse me." It was Mathias Sage. "Hello, Professor."

"Paul, I finished my business early. I'm at the gate?"

"Great. I'll open it for you. Follow the drive to the main

house. We'll wait for you on the porch."

"Right, thanks.

Paul dug the gate remote from his pant's pocket and turned to Sam. "Will this work from inside the house?"

"I'm not sure. Let me have it. I'll go outside and let him in. You stay with Helena." She took it and hurried out of the library.

The keyboard clicked. "I wish you had kidnapped me instead of Fortune. In that case, I wouldn't mind being trapped in this place. You're a beautiful man."

Paul tried not to grin. She was still young with adolescent dreams. He said, "Helena, to be with you, I would first have to die, wouldn't I?"

"Yes, but it's not so bad unless he tortures me. The worst part is there's no one to talk to." Her face grew somber. "I loved Talon, and I get very lonely. I miss Justin."

"Helena, my uncle told me you were trying to end your existence. I hope that's no longer the case. We're here to free you from all this."

She smiled at him and then typed, "I was until you arrived." She smiled at him again. "I'll tell you the truth. Just before you showed up, I figured out how to do it."

"You did?" Paul's heart sank. "How?"

She gave him a mischievous smile. "I call it death by husband. He always stops torturing me just before I would die. I think if I make him angry enough, he won't stop, and that would do it."

"Helena, please say you won't do that."

She beamed at him. "I promise, Paul. As long as you're here and we can talk on this machine, I'll try to be happy."

"Thanks, Helena. We care about you and—. "

She stuck up a hand to stop him and typed, "Paul, go. He's coming. Run!"

Paul rushed out of the house to the porch. Samantha was there watching the professor's old Chevy approach. "What happened?"

"Had to leave," he told her. "Helena saw Fortune coming

and vanished. I ran. I don't think she will be much more help."

Samantha smiled. "She likes you."

"Yeah, I'm afraid you're right. She said if I could join her, she wouldn't mind staying at Montmartre. I told her that to do that, I'd first have to die."

Mathias Sage parked his car behind Paul's, hopped out, and waved.

THIRTY-THREE

THE PROFESSOR bounded up the steps, pumped Paul's hand with enthusiasm. "I can't wait to tour Montmartre," he said. "I've wanted to visit this estate for years." His eyes danced with excitement. "Can we do that firstPaul hated to stick a pin in the man's enthusiasm, but did so anyway. "I'm sorry, professor. Helena warned us to get out. It's too dangerous right now."

"You can communicate with her?"

"Yes. We will give you a tour when it's safe. In the meantime, I have a lot to tell you."

"I see." Disappointment. "W   ell, you know best. What's next?"

"We'll take you to your quarters, and then we'll go to mine. I'll show you a transcript of our conversation with Helena. Okay?"

"Yes. Thank you."

The professor followed them to the garage and into the upstairs apartment. He eyed the place in surprise and said, "My goodness, this is perfect. Kitchen, bath, bedroom, sitting room, TV. Wonderful!" He had one suitcase for his clothes and three boxes of food. When Paul raised his eyebrows at the food, he explained, "I'm on a special diet, so I brought enough food for several days. Hope you don't mind."

"That's a good idea, professor," Samantha said. "We're pretty isolated up here."

"Time's a-wasting, Paul. Shall we get on with it?"

Paul nodded. "I like your attitude, Professor. Let's do it."

They took Paul's car to the pool house and parked in back. When they reached the living room, the professor joined Samantha on the sofa. "You mentioned a transcript of your conversation with Helena?"

"Yes, hang on." Paul hurried to his bedroom to get his laptop, the notes from his uncle, and the summary of his diaries. Back in the living room, he powered up and tried to link to the pool-house Wi-Fi, but it asked for a password. "Password?" he said to Samantha.

"It's a tough one," she said. "Poolhouse999. No spaces, initial caps."

"Got it." While he was connecting to his cloud account, he explained to the professor what he had set up to communicate with Helena.

"Amazing. You knew she could type?" The professor's eyes were wide.

"No, considering her age, gambled she might have learned to type, but if not, we planned to teach her."

"Very creative."

As soon as he connected to the document on his cloud account, Paul placed the lightweight computer in the professor's lap. "Are you familiar with laptops?"

The professor ignored the question, donned his spectacles and scanned the document. He read it three times before he said, "Incredible. What makes you think this isn't phony?"

"It's real," Samantha said. "I witnessed it." His skepticism amused her. "And Paul watched her typing it."

Mathias Sage glanced at Paul. "Why is it that only you can see her?"

"You tell me, doc. My uncle could, and now I can. Perhaps

it's genetic."

"Well, at least we can communicate. How do you contact her?"

"I don't, but she can call my smart phone when she wants to talk. We can text back and forth."

The professor chuckled. "This is a fascinating concept. Who set it up for you?"

"Paul did," Samantha said. "He's a computer genius." She smiled at Paul.

"Well, judging by this transcript, I predict you'll hear from her a lot more than you'd like."

"Why is that?" Samantha asked.

"Didn't you read the last few bits of dialog between Helena and Paul?"

"No, I was outside waiting for you."

"Read this and you'll understand." The professor handed over the laptop.

Samantha skim-read the document and then stopped and read aloud, "I wish you had kidnapped me instead of Fortune. In that case, I wouldn't mind being trapped here. I know you like my body, so I'm sure we would fall in love. You're a handsome man." She looked up, smiling. "And what did you say to her? 'I'm sure we would.' Is she that alluring?" Her voice held a tinge of jealousy.

Paul coughed. "Well, she said it herself, didn't she? To men, all naked women are attractive."

"Aw, she has a crush on you. Too bad."

"Okay, that's enough of that." Paul walked to the easy chair facing the sofa. "Professor, there are two other documents you should read before we get down to the problem at hand." Paul sat and handed over his uncle's letter and the note containing the newspaper clipping. "These are notes from my uncle. I'd like your opinion once you've read them. And then I have questions."

"Right."

The professor first read Justin Davenport's letter and then the note and news story covering Talon Montmartre's death. When he finished, he removed his glasses and looked at Paul. "Did you find your uncle's diaries?"

"Yes. We spent several hours reading and summarizing them. We listed all the things he tried over the years."

"May I see those?"

Paul handed them over and waited in silence while the professor read. When he finished, the man returned to them. "Your uncle was very thorough."

"So that's it? You have no ideas beyond what my uncle tried?"

Mathias Sage squirmed in his chair. "I didn't say that. I need time to think about it. And, I would like to question Helena. I may learn something from her you haven't."

"What about Talon's upside-down clue?" Sam asked.

"That's possible. Have you searched?"

"Not yet. However, that's on the agenda."

"Good. I think you have an excellent chance of succeeding where your uncle failed."

"Why do you say that?"

"Because you already have been more innovative than your uncle."

"What do you mean?"

"You're a modern man. Your uncle wasn't. Your communication system proves it."

Paul stood and crossed the room to peer at the pool through the sliding glass door. Then he hurried back to his chair, sat and leaned forward. "Professor, maybe what you say is true, but step one in solving a problem is to have accurate information. I need information."

"Of course you do. That's why I'm here."

"Then help me. My goal is to get rid of Fortune Montmartre and save Helena. You say you're the world's greatest expert on the subject. Prove it. Give me the information I need. I can't create a solution without understanding what I'm up against. I need facts."

The professor chuckled. "Facts are nonexistent in this field, Paul, but I can give you my ten-minute lecture about the huge amount of extant conjecture, if you like."

"Please, do."

"Right." Mathias pinched his brows. "I've already answered three of your questions, so I'll start with the basics. Do either of you know where ghosts come from?

"Where they come from?" Sam's brows shot up. "I thought they were the spirits of dead people."

"Sorry, I meant what causes a dead person to become a ghost. Many students of ghosts call them earthbound spirits, which is fine by me. A rose by any other name still smells as sweet." Mathias Sage brought the fingertips of both hands together in a thoughtful gesture. "Ask any so-called ghost expert and you'll get a range of causes for a ghost's existence. For example, a ghost may remain among us because he or she had unfinished business. Pure anger or a desire for revenge may do it. Or love for someone left behind. People who die without warning may not realize they're dead, so they hang around in a confused state. The number of causes proposed by experts is limited only by their imagination."

Paul stood and sat again. "What about Fortune Montmartre? He died in a fit of jealous rage, trying to kill his son and his wife. He succeeded with Helena, but not his son. Where would you place him?

"I can see two causes for his remaining behind. First, as you say, is his jealous rage, his desire for revenge against Helena. There are cases reported about angry criminals vowing to come back for revenge. And his anger may have been strong enough to keep Helena with him. Second is what Talon said in the newspaper clipping. Fortune belonged to a cult of devil worshipers. An evil spirit may have attached itself to him before he died. Most likely, his rage has kept him behind."

"Helena says he is much more powerful than she is."

"Which makes sense. He died in anger, trying to kill his son. Helena died in fear. I have to admire his strength. It's unusual for a ghost to hang around for more than a hundred years. It shows a powerful will to survive. I find him to be amazing. I—"

"You admire him!" Paul stood and stared at the man. "Professor, if that's the best you can do, perhaps you need not waste anymore of your time by remaining here. I need help, not a Fortune Montmartre cheer leader."

"Paul, wait, please!" The professor's face had turned white. "I didn't say I can't help. I need time to study and analyze the problem. This is a complex situation. Please, don't send me away. I—"

A loud blast from a car horn interrupted the professor. It came from the parking area behind the pool house.

"That's Dad's truck," Sam said, standing. "I'd better go."

"No." Paul stood, too. "We'll all go. I want the professor to meet him."

"You mean I can stay?" Mathias Sage clasped his hands, almost in a pleading gesture. "Please."

Paul frowned. Why was the professor near panic? "Yes, for now," he said. "Let's go."

THIRTY-FOUR

GERARD DUET had parked his pickup truck alongside Paul's F-150. They found him leaning against it with one hand hidden behind his back. He resembled a man recovering from a debilitating illness. His eyes had sunk deeper and his cheeks were thinner than Paul remembered.

When he saw them approaching, Duet came to a slow attention and said, "Stop. That's close enough."

"Dad, what's wrong? Are you sick?" Sam took a step forward, but Mathias Sage caught her arm and said, "I wouldn't, Miss Duet."

Duet glared at his daughter and bared his teeth. "You went back into that house," he accused. "I told you not to, and now he knows about you."

"Who knows about her, Mr. Duet?" the professor asked. "Fortune Montmartre?"

Duet turned his head to glare at the professor. "Who are you?"

"Mathias Sage at your service, sir. I asked you who knows about your daughter. Fortune Montmartre or the other one?"

Gerard Duet blinked. "Fortune. There is no other one."

"I know the ghost of Fortune Montmartre haunts the chateau,

and that he is evil and malevolent. Do you confirm that?"

Duet's eyes grew hard and wild. "I ain't saying anything. This is none of your business. Butt out." He turned back to Sam. "He wants you, Sam, and I can't stop him. If you stay here, he'll kill you. If you want to live, leave now."

"I will, if you will," Sam said. "Please, Dad, let's leave this place."

"I can't."

"Why, sir?" Mathias demanded. "Does he own your soul?"

"I told you to shut up!" Duet brought his hidden arm forward and aimed a thirty-eight police special at them.

Sam's eyes locked on the pistol for a second, and then she met her father's eyes and pleaded, "Dad, let us help you. Please. I won't leave unless you do. Please, what can we do?" Tears were pouring down her cheeks.

"Nothing. I... nothing. It's too late for me. I tried to break free, but I can't. He's too powerful."

"Mr. Duet, I know something of these matters," Mathias said. "Perhaps I can help."

Gerard Duet swung the gun toward the professor. "I told you to shut up. Say one more word, and I'll put a bullet through your head."

Paul used the lapse in Duet's attention to grab the barrel of the pistol and twist it skyward. The weapon came free with surprising ease. He flipped it in his hand and aimed at Gerard Duet's gut.

"That's better," he said. "Don't move. I want answers."

Surprised, the man stared at the pistol and then at Paul. "You want to kill me, Mr. Davenport? Go ahead. I'm dead already."

Samantha stood staring at nothing, her mouth hanging open in shock.

"I don't want to kill you, Mr. Duet. I need help and so do you. Why can't we help each other?"

Duet bared his teeth at Paul like a snarling animal. "You think you're gonna inherit your uncle's fortune? Well, you're not.

You're a dead man, and dead men can't inherit anything. He's going to kill you. If you were smart, you'd take my daughter and get away from here."

Paul felt trapped. He wanted to smash Duet's face in, but for Sam's sake, he couldn't. He said, "I'm not leaving, Mr. Duet. You should leave and take Sam with you. I'll cover any expenses you have."

"Fuck you. Give me my gun."

"Dad, no!"

Duet lunged at Paul, reaching for the gun. Paul stepped aside and pushed him toward the concrete. The man sprawled onto his stomach and let out a loud yelp of pain as his face hit the cement. He scrambled to his feet and raced past Paul to the driver's side of his pickup. "You'll pay for this," he screamed as he got in. "Both of you."

He glared one last time at Sam. "If you come home again, I won't have a choice. I'll have to kill you." He squealed tires as he backed up and roared away.

THIRTY-FIVE

T HEY WATCHED the truck speeding around the work road. At the far end, it screeched to a stop and Duet climbed out. He lifted a shovel from the back of the truck and took it to the tree where they earlier found the pine box. He glanced once toward them before stabbing the shovel into the ground. After that, he began digging like a madman.

Paul touched Samantha's arm. "We'd better go now."

She didn't respond. She stared at her father's truck with her mouth open. Her eyes were glassy, and tears made tiny rivers on both cheeks. He had seen that reaction once in Afghanistan. One of his Marine buddies had watched a close friend's head explode from a sudden bullet through his skull. Sam was in shock. He stepped around in front of her.

He caught both shoulders in his hands and pulled her close. "Sam, we have to move your things to the pool house. Okay?"

"He said he would kill me." Her voice was low with subdued fear.

"No. He came because he loves you and wants to save you from Montmartre. He came to warn us."

She pushed away and met his eyes. "What am I going to do?"

"You're moving to the pool house. Let's get your things and move you before your dad returns. Otherwise, there might be serious trouble."

"The pool house?"

"Yes. The upstairs bedroom. I'll live downstairs and protect you until this is over. We'll help your dad."

"He's right, Samantha," Mathias Sage said. "You can't stay at the cottage. Your father admitted Fortune controls him. It's too dangerous."

Paul urged Samantha into the passenger seat of his truck. She climbed in without protest. "You'll go with us," he said to the professor. "You'll stand guard and warn us if you see Duet returning."

"Right!" Mathias Sage got into the backseat of Paul's truck. "I'm ready. Let's go."

Paul backed out and drove toward to the cottage. They hurried inside and up to Sam's room.

"Get your suitcases," he said. "I'll help you pack."

She sat on the bed. "This isn't right. I'm deserting my father."

Paul sat beside her. "We're not deserting anybody. Right now, I want you safe while we search for a way to help him." He touched her cheek. "Please, Sam. Pack whatever you need. We'll talk about this when we're back at the pool house. We'll save him. I promise."

Tears welled in her eyes, yet there was sudden hope, too. "You mean that?"

"Yes."

A weak smile formed at the corners of her mouth, and she whispered, "You're like Uncle Justin. I feel safe when I'm with you. Thank you."

"My pleasure, ma'am." Paul stood and offered his hand. She took it and rose, too. Their bodies came together, causing him to suck in a quick breath. He backed away and touched her cheek. "We have to hurry," he said. "Tell me what to do."

When they left the cottage, he learned they need not have

rushed. Gerard Duet was still digging. What was he digging? Paul wondered. Was he finishing the grave he had started? He pushed his curiosity aside. His primary concern was Samantha.

Twenty minutes later, they were back in the pool-house living room. Sam's stuff was in the upstairs bedroom, Paul's downstairs. Sam, refreshed, sat beside Paul on the sofa, and the professor had perched on the edge of the big chair.

"That was amazing," the professor said. "I've read about such things, but never experienced it firsthand. Amazing!"

"I'm glad you're enjoying yourself, Professor," Paul said in a dour tone. "What's your opinion of Mr. Duet? Are you certain he's possessed?"

"No question about it. He has all the signs. His eyes are glassy and wild. They never once blinked. His voice sounded strained, too. He seemed to fight against saying the words he spoke. And, as you said, I'm pretty sure he came to warn us against the wishes of Montmartre. But the real giveaway is that he threatened you, Samantha."

"Okay, we agree he's possessed," Paul said. "So, what do we do about it?"

"What do you mean?"

"How do we free him?"

The professor chuckled. "I doubt that's possible, Paul. The Bible tells many stories about demons and how Jesus confronted them. Unfortunately, in this case, we don't have Jesus available. We could call in a priest, if you like. Many Catholic rituals exorcise demons. But that can be a long process. Also, we would need Mr. Duet's acquiescence, which I doubt would be forthcoming."

"Then what can we do, Professor?" Sam's voice held a hopeless note.

"I suggest we follow your original plan. Find Fortune's bones and give him a proper burial. If he moves on, your father should become free of him."

"So, that's the best you can suggest?"

The professor shrugged. "Yes. Find the bones. Get rid of Fortune Montmartre."

"You said that before. Tell us how?"

"Paul, we're not dealing with science here. I have research material at home that might provide useful information. I should go get it tonight, so we'll have the benefit of it tomorrow." Paul glanced at his watch. Six fifteen. "I was thinking of taking us all to dinner. It's been a long day."

"No, no thank you. You two go ahead. As I mentioned, I'm on a special diet, and I'd prefer to go after that research before it gets too late, if you don't mind."

"I don't mind. I hope you find something that will help."

"So do I." The professor stood and said, "I'm sorry about your father, Sam." The professor stood and took Sam's hand. "We'll do our best to help him. I promise."

"Thanks, professor."

Paul rose, followed by Sam. "The gate will open when you leave," he said. "Call me when you return, and I'll let you in."

"Right." Mathias Sage spun on his heel and left them with a wave of his hand.

THIRTY-SIX

PAUL HURRIED to Sam and took her face between his hands. She tilted her head up to him and he gave her a gentle kiss. She melted against him as he wrapped his arms around her. Offering no resistance, she laid her head on his shoulder. She remained in his arms for a moment, then pushed back and whispered, "Thanks. I needed that. With Uncle Justin gone and now my father, I'm feeling alone and vulnerable."

"Anytime you need a friendly shoulder, say the word I'll come running."

"Paul... I... thanks. I appreciate it. I..."

His arms yearned to hold her again, but the deep worry in her eyes stopped him. "Sam, there must be a way to help your father. Fortune doesn't have full control over him or he wouldn't have tried to warn us. That means there's still hope. Okay?"

"Yes. Sorry, but I need to sit down." She dropped onto the sofa.

"You sure you're okay? You've had quite a shock."

"Yes, I'm fine... just a bit disoriented, but..."

"What? Can I get you something?"

"No. I... would you mind if we stay home?"

"Stay home?"

"I mean not go out to eat. I'm too upset to handle a lot of other people right now."

"Fine with me. Were you and your dad close?"

"I thought so. But when I went to school, something happened. He changed."

"Like now."

"Not at first. I... I used to write him two or three times a week from school and Uncle Justin at least once a week. At first, he answered within a few days, but after the second year, I was lucky to get a letter once a month. By the third year, he stopped writing altogether. After that, when I heard from him, it was via short, blunt text messages." She hesitated and wiped at a trickle of tears. "I called him pretty often, but he always seemed distracted and too busy to talk. I've been worried sick."

"Sam, I'm sorry. I'm sure we can figure out a way to help him. There has to be a way out for him." Frustrated. he stopped and said, "I wish there was more I could do to help you."

"Paul, you are helping me. If you weren't here, I'd probably climb a tall tree and jump out."

He sat beside her. "We'll save him from that bastard, I promise."

She leaned back away from him and met his gaze. "May I ask you something personal"Sure. I'm an open book."

She took a deep breath. "I know you find me attractive, but is it more than that?"

"You mean more than wanting to take you to bed and make wild love to you?"

She smiled. "Yes."

"May I ask what brought on that question?"

"Because back at Harvard, the guys were too serious to notice anything, or they wanted to sleep with as many girls as possible. I hated the entire scene.

"So you're not one of those modern, super-liberated girls?"

"It seems not."

"How did that happen?"

"It's the way Uncle Justin raised me. He was kind, stern, loving, and he always taught me how to be a respectable young lady. Even at school, I always imagined he was watching me, looking over my shoulder."

"That's a father's role, isn't it?"

"Yes, but Dad is a quiet man. He never lectured me or tried to guide me. Uncle Justin was different. He was old-fashioned and pretty outspoken about his beliefs. He always wanted the best for me. And now here you are. You're so much like him. It's kind of spooky."

Paul tilted his head to look at her. Something was happening between them. He didn't understand it, but he liked it. "You still haven't answered my question."

"Which question?"

"Why did you ask about something happening between us?"

"Forget it. I shouldn't have asked."

"Sorry. Not acceptable. Tell me."

She reddened and then capitulated. "Because I was hoping you'd say yes."

"Oh, I see."

"So?"

He stifled a laugh. "So, yes. There's a lot more to it. Otherwise, I—"

Paul's phone rang. "Yoshi!"

"Good, Paul-san. You're still alive. I was worried."

"I'm fine, Yosh, and so is Sam."

"How about Mr. Montmartre?"

"Some interesting developments. We found a professor who claims to be a ghost expert, and we believe Montmartre has possessed Sam's father. We're trying to figure out how to help him."

"So, no progress on the primary problem?"

"Well, yes and no." Paul explained his set up and connection with Helena.

"Horee sheeto, Paul-san. That's fantastic. I can't wait to talk to her."

"Talk to her?"

"So sorry." Yoshi switched into his Mr. Motto voice. "Forgot to tell number-one friend. Otosan relented. I told him you would soon become very rich and would be a great business contact. I'm flying back to California, so do nothing foolish until I get there."

Paul laughed. "Sorry, Moto-san. You know I can't promise that. When are you coming?"

"Thursday morning, early."

"How long can you stay?"

"Until it's over."

"That's great, Yosh. We can't wait."

They hung up, and Paul turned to Samantha. "He'll be here the day after tomorrow. Early."

"I'm glad, Paul. You need another ally."

"Wrong pronoun. We need another ally." She stood and said, "I'm cooking. What's your favorite frozen dinner?"

"What are you offering?"

"I haven't checked lately, but Uncle Justin used to keep fried-rice dinners, chicken, beef, and a variety of desserts."

Paul rose, too. "I'm a bachelor, remember? And a halfway decent cook. Let's check the fridge and make dinner together. Shall we?"

"I'm game."

THIRTY-SEVEN

THEY SOON SAT DOWN to enjoy a meal of chicken-fried rice, baked sweet potato, sweet iced tea and rice pudding. They dined at a small breakfast table in the kitchen. When they finished, they tossed away their paper plates, rinsed their glasses and utensils, and went into the living room to sit on the sofa.

"That was good," Paul said. "Best fried rice I ever ate."

"Uncle Justin ordered it made especially for us. He liked good food."

"Don't we all?"

"I know I do. Especially when eaten in good company." She smiled at him.

"You feeling better."

"Yes, thanks to you."

To change the direction of his thoughts, Paul waved toward a TV hanging on the wall across from the sofa. "Does that work?" he asked.

"I'm sure it does. I used it a few days ago."

"Want to watch a movie? Or are you too tired?"

"No, I'm fine, but I'd rather sit out by the pool, if you don't mind."

Paul rose and took her hand. "That's a great idea. I love

looking at the moon and dreaming about the future."

Outside, he moved two lounge chairs into position so they could see the moon and the stars, which tonight were brilliant diamonds against a purple-black sky. He eyed his work and moved the chairs closer to make it easy to hold hands, which he hoped would happen. When they were both seated, Sam gazed into the night sky. "What do you dream about when you see the moon?"

"Is that a conversation starter or a serious question?"

"Serious."

"Do you like Mark Twain?"

"Yes. He's one of my favorite writers. Why?"

"A quote of his just popped into my mind."

"Which one?"

"Wherever she was, there was Eden."

"That's from Adam's Diary. What brought that on?"

"You sure you want the truth?"

"Yes, always."

"You did. Ever since I met you, you've been part of my dreams about the future."

"Oh." Samantha grew silent. Then her hand spanned the short distance between their chairs and caught his. "I'm flattered," she said. "But it's odd. We met only yesterday. Yet, you and the future have been on my mind, too, ever since I read uncle Justin's note. Remember what he wrote, 'I pray you have a wonderful life, perhaps with Paul.'"

"Smart man."

Sam giggled. "Yes, but is such a thing possible?"

"I hope it is," he said. "I dreamed about you last night."

"What kind of dream?"

"Well, sorry to say it wasn't romantic. I was outside in the freezing cold. I pounded on your door to let me in. You opened it, but when you saw me, you slammed it in my face."

"Why on earth would I do that?"

"You tell me. I was miserable. You woke me by banging on

my car window."

"Sounds like I rescued you from a bad dream."

"More like a nightmare, I'd say."

She grew serious. "Paul, I'm confused. What are we talking about here?"

"You mean the real conversation?"

"Yes."

Paul hesitated. He didn't want to say anything out of line. Finally, he said, "My guess is it's about chemistry."

"Chemistry?"

"Yeah. Pheromones. Boy meets girl. Boy smells girl. Boy loves girl. That kind of thing."

"Are you talking about love at first sight?"

He grinned. "I suppose I am. It's the only explanation I have for how I feel about you. Hope you don't mind."

"I don't mind, but it seems too crazy to be real."

"Yeah, that's a good word for it. I—."

Paul's cell phone vibrated in his shirt pocket. A message from Helena. "Paul, please come. I have a problem, and I have important information for you. I have to hide now. Hurry."

He typed, "Coming. Hang on."

"Helena wants to see me in the library," he told Samantha, rising. "Says she has important information. I have to go."

Samantha scrambled to her feet. "Wrong pronoun. We have to go. My job is to watch your back, remember?"

"We'd better take the truck," he said.

"Why? It's a short walk."

"We might need a fast getaway."

"Good thinking."

Ten minutes later, they entered the library and turned on the light.

Samantha looked around. "Is she here?"

"I don't see her. She said she had to hide."

They walked to the computer. Her message was still on the screen.

"Helena?"

Helena appeared behind them, stopped near Paul. She gave Paul a coquettish smile and stretched out her arms as she did a slow, graceful pirouette.

Paul grinned. "Helena, we came because your message sounded urgent. What's the problem?"

She floated to the computer. She typed, "The problem? I'm lonely. It's been over a hundred years since I've had any young people to talk to." She stopped typing to eye Sam. Then she turned back and typed, "Samantha, you're so lucky to have Paul. I wish I could borrow him for a while."

Paul reddened, but before he could answer, Samantha said, "He's not mine to loan. It would be up to him."

Helena's grew wide in surprise. She typed, "You're not a couple?"

"No."

She typed furiously. "Sam, what's wrong with you? If I was alive, he wouldn't get away from me."

"Helena, you're embarrassing me," Paul said. "You said you have important information. What is it?"

Helena frowned and typed. "Killjoy. I'm teasing."

"Helena, please."

Sam touched his arm and said, "Helena, I'm sure you're frightened and lonely, and I understand your feelings, but we're trying to help you escape. We need your help. Won't you cooperate?"

Helena stared at Sam for a few seconds, and then typed, "You seem nice, Sam. I'm sorry. I'm starved for someone to talk to. This machine Paul made is a miracle."

"I understand," Sam said. "I think you and I would become friends, given the chance. But—"

"OK, I'll tell you," she typed. "I don't trust Mathias Sage." She kept her eyes on Paul, typing without looking at the keyboard. "He's your enemy."

Startled, Paul said, "Why do you say that? We didn't

introduce him to you."

"I overheard him talking to Fortune and Mr. Duet."

"Are you saying that Fortune can hold a conversation?"

"He can say things sometimes, but it's difficult. He uses Mr. Duet to speak for him. I'm not sure how he does it."

"What did they talk about?"

"He offered to help kill you if Fortune showed him how to become a ghost."

"The premise of his book, Immortality of Ghosts," Sam breathed.

"Yes, the bastard. I knew something was fishy." To Helena he said, "Did Fortune agree?"

"Yes."

"When was this?"

"Just before I sent you the message."

"Where is Sage now?"

"They left. I was too frightened to follow them. I thought you should know."

"You mean my dad and the professor? They left together?"

Helena nodded. Paul told Sam, "She said yes." Tears were welling in Sam's eyes again.

"Helena, you're a brave girl to spy on Fortune for us. We appreciate it," Paul said. "Thank you. This is important information."

"You're welcome." She continued typing without looking at the keys. "You two are perfect together. It makes me want to cry. It's so lonely here."

"I'm sorry for that," Paul told her, "and I agree that Sam and I belong together. But, in modern America, a woman controls everything related to love."

"Do you love her?"

Paul hesitated and then said, "Yes."

Looking at Sam, she typed, "What about you? Do you love him?"

"I... don't know. We just met. I—"

Helena's fingers flew. "Don't be stupid, Sam. You love him. I can tell by the way you look at him."

Paul grinned and asked Sam, "Do you think she's right?"

Sam blushed. "Paul, I—."

Helena rose and approached Paul with her arms wide. She blended with his body for a moment. His eyes widened in surprise. A sudden warmth spread through him, and then it vanished, gone along with Helena. He grinned at Sam and shook his head. "That young ghost has a real problem."

"Poor thing. I can't imagine being trapped for so long. She must be miserable."

A loud footstep in the foyer interrupted them. They both turned toward the door.

"Stay here." Paul hurried into the foyer. He halted and Sam bumped into him.

"Oops, sorry," she said.

"Senor, senorita, don't move or I will kill you both." The voice came from behind the stairs.

THIRTY-EIGHT

H E SPUN AROUND to face the speaker. His heart shot toward his throat. Three Hispanic men stood glaring at him without mirth. One of them, the leader, held a forty-five automatic aimed at his heart. Dressed in a black shirt and pants, the leader was clean-shaved and wore a sharp goatee and a black mustache. Dark, humorless eyes glared at Paul, daring him to make a move. Paul remained frozen in place. The man bared straight, bright-white teeth in a phony smile. Except for the goatee, he reminded Paul of a young Geraldo Rivera. "Ah, good senor. You are not a stupid man."

His compatriots were bigger and looked mean. One of them was huge. Their expressions said they were waiting for word from the leader to pounce on him.

"What do you want?" Paul demanded, stepping between the men and Samantha.

"You know, Mr. Davenport."

"No, I don't. Tell me."

"Of course you do. And you want to stay alive, right?"

The man's English was perfect but spoken with a thick Hispanic accent. Paul had several Mexican acquaintances. This man was not Mexican. Colombian? It didn't matter. He was the leader. The other two men resembled angry attack dogs. They also wore black, but their clothes weren't as neat as those of their boss. Their expressions said they were eager for a pound of flesh.

"Paul, who are these men?" Samantha whispered in his ear.

"They're drug dealers. They want their money back." Yoshi and sergeant Johnson had been right.

"Bingo, Mr. Davenport. You figured it out, so let's make a deal. Give us our money, and we'll let you live. Otherwise…" The man wiggled the forty-five and shrugged. "You're a smart man. No smart person wants to die, and I'm certain you don't want my men to harm that beautiful lady of yours."

"You bastard. Touch her and—."

"What? You'll kill me?" The man showed a mouth full of gleaming white teeth. "You forget who has the gun, senor."

"Look, the police have your money," Paul said. "I found it and turned it over to the police."

"That is irrelevant." The man with the gun stepped in front of him. "You stole our money. Two-hundred-fifty thousand dollars. You gave it away. We want it back."

"That's impossible. Where would I get that much money?"

"Not our problem. It's yours. You stole it. You gave it away. You owe us. Nothing else matters."

Paul's thoughts were reeling. He had to stall. "How much time will you give me? I'm just an ordinary working guy. I'm always broke."

The man's face twisted. "How sad. Okay, maybe you're not so smart, after all, so I'll explain it to you." He pointed the gun at Paul's face. "You return our money in two weeks or we will kill you. Comprende?"

Paul clinched his fist. A two-inch-long white scar snaked down the cheek of the biggest man. He grinned and shook his head as if to say, "Don't try anything." Paul shrugged in resignation, looking from one ugly pair of unsympathetic eyes to another. Finally, he settled on the boss. "You might as well shoot me now," he said. "You're demanding the impossible."

"No, no, Mr. Davenport. We won't shoot you now. There is no profit in that. We will give you two weeks. Desperate people find desperate ways to stay alive. Rob a bank. We don't care. Of course, if you don't, you won't care either. You and your lady will be dead. One minute you're alive. The next you're dead. We can find you wherever you are. Wait." He nodded to the biggest of his henchmen. "Mario, let's give them a sample of what will happen. I wonder what she's got under that pretty shirt."

"Uh, you mean you want me…"

"Yes. Show me."

Samantha took a frightened breath.

The big man grinned, revealing a mouth filled with yellow teeth. His hand snaked out and squeezed Sam's breast. She screamed, and that was the trigger. Paul burst into action, doing two things at once. He shoved Samantha backward and smashed the man's face with his fist. It landed with a meaty crunch, sending the man reeling into his partner. Paul whirled and kicked the leader's gun hand toward the ceiling. It was one of those frozen moments he had experienced several times in Afghanistan. He could see and hear everything happening at once.

The big man tripped over his partner, sending both flailing backward. The forty-five flew across the foyer and landed with a deafening explosion. That didn't stop the Geraldo clone. He pulled a thirty-eight special from his inside coat pocket and aimed it at Paul.

Samantha cried, "Paul!"

Paul froze for two seconds, and then Helena was in front of the leader. She had shoved a sheet of stationery paper in his face, covering his eyes. Paul leapt forward and slammed his foot through Helena into the man's gut. He fell with a groan. The thirty-eight revolver skittered across the floor to join the forty-five. Paul turned. Samantha stood at the top of the stairs, mouth open in shock.

The Geraldo clone rose, intending to a make a dash for the

gun. Paul swung his foot and slammed his toe under the man's chin. He hit the floor with a groan. Paul moved toward him for another shot, but the leader scrambled up and dove headfirst to slam Paul with a shoulder block. Paul staggered backward, struggling to regain balance, but before he did so, the boss man was through the still-open front door, screaming, "Vamonos! Vamonos!" His two compatriots raced after him, each fighting to be first through the door.

Paul scooped up the forty-five automatic and rushed after them, but stopped at the porch. The three thugs were already halfway to the cottage, moving at high speed toward the gate. He considered chasing them, but decided the smarter course would be to call sergeant Johnson. The way they ran, he doubted they would make another try tonight.

He tucked the automatic in his belt and returned to the foyer. Sam was waiting for him at the foot of the stairs. He picked the thirty-eight off the floor, unloaded it, and put it in his pocket. Helena was standing in the library door, watching him. He grinned at her. She did a silly little curtsy and smiled.

Sam touched his arm. "Paul, are you alright?"

"Fine. I don't think they'll be back tonight."

She put both arms around his body and clung to him. He held her for a few seconds and then pushed her away. "The real question is, are you okay?"

"Yes. I... that was incredible. How did you do that?"

"I got mad. They shouldn't have threatened you.

"I... thanks."

He touched her cheek. "I have to call Sergeant Johnson.

"He was the detective with you at the interview, wasn't he?"

"Yeah. He's a good guy." Paul dialed the sergeant's private number.

Twenty seconds later, the sergeant's voice said, "Johnson."

"Sergeant. Paul Davenport."

"Hey, Paul. What's up?"

Paul told him.

"Son of a bitch!" the detective said when he finished. "Are you okay?"

"Yeah, I'm good."

"Great. Can you describe the men?"

"Yes. One of them, the leader, was a young, well-dressed version of Geraldo Rivera. A second one is a giant the leader called Mario. He has a long scar running down his face. No one mentioned the third man's name."

"I know them, Paul. They're local members of a Colombian drug syndicate. The big guy with the scar is a Guatemalan named Mario Ganza. He's the muscle of the outfit. The third guy could be anybody, but we'll know him soon enough. The sharp dresser is a Cuban named Dante Bueno. He and Ganza have been in our jail more than once. We'll pick them up easy." The detective chuckled.

"What's so funny?" Paul demanded.

"Well, those suitcases had more than money in them. They also had a dozen sets of fingerprints that may lead us to some of the higher up bosses. I laughed because Dante must be in deep shit right now. He lost a quarter million bucks. The cartel won't take that."

Paul grinned, too. He wondered what kind of thing a desperate Dante would do to stay alive. "So, what's the next step?" he asked.

"Nothing until we have them in lockup. After that, we'll need you to come in and press charges."

"Right. Let me know."

"Will do. Watch your ass, kid."

"You can count on it. Thanks."

The sergeant hung up. Paul held up his wristwatch. Almost ten. Helena was still in the doorway. "You'd better keep hiding," he told her. "We want our favorite girl ghost to be safe. Okay?" She beamed and nodded. He turned to Sam. "I'll drive you back and then have a little chat with the professor."

"Nope. Sorry. We'll have a little chat with the professor."

Sam closed the gap between them and gave him a long, sweet kiss. His arms pulled in, but she pulled back.

"What was that for?"

"Sorry. That was for me. I was scared to death."

He grinned. "Hey, I was scared, too. How about something for me?"

"I'm thinking about that. Where is Helena?"

"Standing in the library door watching us."

Sam turned toward her and said, "Good night, Helena. Stay safe."

Helena curtsied.

"If you need help, just call," he said to her. "We have to go now. Take care."

Helena vanished, and they went out to the car.

Another incredible day.

THIRTY-NINE

A S THEY ROUNDED the bend on the work road, Samantha pointed ahead to the garage. "He's awake," she said. "Time for our chat."

"You sure?"

"Yes. I want to hear his explanation. Besides, you might need backup. I didn't help you much with those thugs. Helena was more useful than I was."

"Forget it. They caught me by surprise, tooPaul pulled in alongside the professor's car, and they got out. With Samantha leading the way, they climbed the wooden stairs to the apartment entrance. Paul pounded on the door. Footsteps approached, followed by the rattle of a night latch. Paul was mulling different ways to send the professor packing when the door opened. Mathias Sage peered out at them.

"Well, well, come in," he said. "I just made tea."

They followed him into a small living room and sat on a beige-colored stuffed sofa. The professor beamed effusively at them and said, "How about some tea?"

"No thanks," Paul said. "We have questions that need answers."

The man took a chair across a low table from them. "Sure,

what can I do for you?"

"We understand you had a chat with Mr. Duet and Fortune Montmartre tonight. You told us you were going back to your apartment in Pasadena. Perhaps you'd like to explain."

"Ah, you spoke to Helena."

"Why did you lie to us?"

"I didn't lie. I decided that if I could convince Mr. Duet to let me speak to Fortune, I might learn something to help you. My intention was to tell you in the morning."

"Is that why you offered to help kill me in return for learning how to become a ghost?"

The professor squirmed in his chair. "Paul, please believe me. I did that to gain his confidence. Fortune is no fool. It was necessary to give him a credible reason for wanting the meeting. Otherwise, he would've killed me on the spot."

Paul relaxed. The professor's answer was plausible. "So, what did you learn?"

"I learned a lot. For example, Fortune has no clue where he's buried, but if you search the estate trying to find the location, he will fight you with all his power."

"We figured that. What else?"

"He's not worried about you because he's sure his bones have turned to dust by now. He says they would be impossible to find."

"What about my father?" Samantha demanded.

The professor frowned and shook his head. "I'm sorry, Sam, but Fortune has full control of your father. I'm not sure we can save him. He used Mr. Duet like a puppet to speak to me. He has ordered your father to kill both of you."

"So, what do you suggest?" Paul could not hide the suspicion in his voice.

"You should leave the estate. He is determined to kill you. His power is far stronger than I imagined. I doubt we can defeat him. If we try, we'll be risking our lives."

"You'll forgive me, Professor, but it's my opinion you told

Fortune the truth, not us. You're looking for some sick form of immortality. I don't agree we can't defeat him. It seems possible you're under his control, too."

"I understand your feeling that way, but I'm not. How can I convince you otherwise?"

"You can't. I want you to leave the estate tomorrow morning and not come back."

The professor jumped to his feet and stared at Paul with a panicky expression. "Paul, please! I'm trying to help you. I have Fortune's confidence now. They want me to meet with them tomorrow night under the big oak behind the house. Please, trust me. Give me a chance to learn more."

"What do you think?" he asked Sam.

She caught his hand. There were tears in her eyes. "I'm not sure, but if he agreed to help kill you, it seems too dangerous to let him stay."

"No! I told you. I agreed to that only to gain his confidence. I would never hurt another soul. It's not in my nature. Please believe me. I want to help, and I want to study this situation. This case can be a fantastic new book for me."

Paul rose and glared at the professor. "Okay, I'll trust you and give you one more day, but if you're conning us, you may become a ghost earlier than you'd like. We'll meet at the pool house at eight o'clock tomorrow morning to plan how to proceed."

He pulled Sam to her feet. "Let's go."

Mathias Sage followed them to the door and said, "You won't be sorry, Paul. I promise. Thank you."

The professor stood on the upstairs porch and watched them until they vanished behind the garage. Overhead, the moon was brilliant. All was well with the world.

"I'm with Helena," Sam said. "I don't trust that man."

FORTY

IN THE POOL-HOUSE living room, Paul stopped, snapped his fingers and said, "Damn!"

"What?"

"I forgot to ask him about the holes your dad was digging."

"What if he was digging our graves?"

"Yeah, that was my first thought, but didn't mention it. I didn't want to frighten you."

"Don't worry. I'm not frightened."

"You're not?"

She came to him and leaned her body into his. She lowered her cheek to his shoulder. "Not when I'm with you. I was amazed by the way you handled those drug-dealer thugs."

"Hey, I'm a marine, remember? And Yoshi has been teaching me some of his karate tricks."

Paul held her and let the warmth of her body seep into his own. Holding her was all the fulfillment he had ever dreamed of having. She belonged in his arms, and they belonged around her. He wanted the embrace to last forever, but she tilted back her head, lifted herself on tiptoes and kissed him. Unable to hold back, he crushed her body to his own and devoured her mouth. He felt his manhood growing, but she didn't pull away. Instead, she moved even harder against him.

"Samantha," he murmured.

"You're telling me something," she said. "Helena was right. I was too stupid to admit it, but I am attracted to you and…"

She leaned back and their eyes locked.

"And?"

"Remember, you asked me how about something for you, and I said I'm thinking about it?"

"Yeah."

"Well, I've decided. It's a present for both of us, if you want it."

"A present?"

She smiled at his puzzlement. "Yes."

"If it's from you, I'll want it. Where is it?"

"Upstairs."

He grinned and squinted at her with one eye as he understood. "Upstairs where?"

"In the bedroom. That bed is big enough for two, don't you agree?"

"Sam, are you sure?"

"I'm positive. You deserve it, and so do I."

He pinched his brows together and tried to look indecisive. "Well, I don't know…"

"What!"

He gave her a silly grin. "Just teasing. This is not one of those try-before-you buy deals, is it? I have something a little more permanent in mind."

"Paul, so do I, but I can't plan long term until I know dad is safe. I hope you understand."

"Whatever you say. I'm yours to command."

She moved against him and said, "In that case, answer me. What's it going to be? Upstairs with me or downstairs?"

He pulled her to him and kissed her with all the love and passion in his soul. After several minutes, she pounded his shoulders and backed away. "Well?"

"You promise not to hate me in the morning?"

She grinned at him. "I might start hating you right now. What took you so long to decide?"

He grinned. "My old sergeant said I'm not too bright. Anyhow, that settles half of my number-one goal. That leaves only goal number two."

"What's that?"

"To win my uncle's fortune and lay it at your feet. I—"

She cut him off with another kiss and then tugged him to follow her.

"Where to now?"

"Upstairs."

At the bedroom door, they stopped and kissed. When they broke apart, he said, "Sam, I'm a mess. I have to take a shower."

She giggled. "Wrong pronoun again."

FORTY-ONE

PAUL OPENED his eyes to the bright morning light streaming in through the bedroom window. He remembered where he was and rolled over to reach for Samantha. She wasn't there. He checked his watch on the bedside table. Eight-thirty.

Surprised he had slept so late, he swung his feet off the bed, wondering where Sam was. Then he smelled coffee and relaxed. She was in the kitchen. He stood, intending to get dressed, but stopped as the enormity of his evening with Sam struck with full force. He dropped back.

She had invited him to make love with her. A present for both of them, she called it. He had worried about spoiling their relationship, but now, as he recalled the incredible night that followed, he loved her more deeply than he thought possible. A fantastic series of dreamlike events had embedded themselves into his heart forever. The amazing shower together, the silken smoothness of her skin, the loving touches, the whispers of love, and the last moments of making love. He lowered his head, trembling in disbelief as a sudden wave of worry swept over him.

Her father had thrown her out of her home and threatened to kill her. She was frightened and vulnerable, and he had used her fear and depression to satisfy his selfish desire for her. He groaned. His love for her washed over him with the power of a tidal wave, causing him to hate himself. He stood and broke his own speed record for getting dressed. He had to see her, speak to her to see how the evening had affected her.

In the kitchen, he found Sam at the stove wearing jeans and a blouse. A white apron with red roses on the front protected her clothes as she worked at the counter next to the stove. He tiptoed to her and gave her a surprise hug and a quick peck on the lips.

"The prettiest cook in the universe."

She smiled. "How did you sleep?"

"Fantastic. Better than ever, but—."

She cut him off by wrapping him in her arms and pulling him close. "I wanted to thank you," she whispered in his ear.

Surprise. "For what?"

"The greatest night of my life yesterday, I found you very attractive. Today, I'm pretty sure I'm in love with you."

"Does that mean I have your permission to ask you to marry me?" His grin was so wide his ears wiggled.

She pushed him back. "Paul, no. I can't think about marriage until I save my dad from that evil creature. I want us to start our lives happy, not with me frantic with worry. Can you live with that?"

"If there's hope I can have you, I can live with anything."

She sniggered. "Trust me. There's enough hope for both of us to deluge this kitchen. Okay?"

Relief and powerful love left him speechless. He pulled her body to him and said, "Hell, yes." He met her lips and said, "I love you, Sam. I've loved you my entire life."

She giggled and pushed him away again. "That's pretty amazing. We only met two days ago. Go sit down. Your breakfast is ready. We'll settle this later."

Overwhelmed with the relief that comes when a joyful surprise replaces worry, he obeyed and sat across the table so he could watch her finish preparations. She placed a cup of black coffee, a plate with three eggs over easy, crisp bacon, and white buttered toast in front of him.

"Anyhow, why didn't you wake me when you got up?" he asked, grabbing the salt and pepper.

"You were sleeping so peacefully, I couldn't do it. You needed the rest." She looked happy, refreshed and delicious. She brought her breakfast and sat at the end of the table. Her knee touched his under the table. She smiled to let him know it was no accident.

Three loud knocks sounded at the back pool-house door.

"Professor?"

"Yes."

"Come on in."

The professor entered and sat across from Paul.

"Coffee?" Sam asked.

"No thanks. I've had my breakfast. So, what's our plan for today?"

"I figure we have only one viable possibility for saving Mr. Duet and getting rid of Fortune." Paul took a sip of coffee. "We have to find his bones, give him a burial, and pray that does the trick. So, my new goal is to do whatever it takes to accomplish that. Speed is essential."

"Why?"

"Nothing complex. If it doesn't work, I need time to try something else. The clock's ticking. I have only twelve days left."

"Ah!" The professor nodded. "I mulled the problem last night. I've read there's a basement under the big house that matches the dimensions of the mansion. It might be a good idea to start the search there."

"That sounds right." Sam smiled. "In the movies, a lot of skullduggery takes place in haunted-house basements. Why not Montmartre?"

"Most basements have two entrances." Paul said. "One inside the house and one outside."

"There's a slanting outside door, but it has a huge padlock on it. Dad keeps the keys in the tool shed."

"What's wrong with the inside door?" the professor asked. "I doubt it's locked."

"Probably not, but I don't want Fortune to know we're in. I'm hoping the outside entrance will buy us a little time."

"Ah!" The professor shrugged.

"Professor, did you learn anything about why my father was digging holes under the big tree? That has puzzled us since yesterday."

"Sorry. The subject didn't come up. Just being there scared me to death. The frightening thing was knowing Fortune was there, but I couldn't see him. I spoke to him through your father. Weirdest experience of my life."

"I'll bet," Paul said.

When they finished breakfast, Paul helped Samantha clean and wipe the dishes and store them in the dishwasher under the sink cabinet. While there, he leaned to her and gave her a kiss on the neck. "You look gorgeous this morning."

"Well, thank you. You weren't too bad last night in your birthday suit, either," she whispered back.

He almost choked on his stifled laugh and turned to the professor. "I think we can get started now."

FORTY-TWO

THEY ENTERED the basement through the exterior door. Far from being haunted, it was neat and well lit, and organized. The room was half the width of the main house. Across from the outside entrance, double doors, now closed, led to the other half. Paul entered first to examine the room. He saw nothing that didn't belong. On the right-hand side stood four long rows of shelves loaded with cardboard boxes, paint cans and equipment, coils of electrical wire, junction boxes, light switches and a variety of other household repair goods. To his left, the floor was open, though empty shelves lined walls on both sides. Against the far left-hand wall, several old sofas, two dining tables with chairs, three worn-out stuffed chairs, and several standing lamps created an impenetrable barrier to the wall. Everything seemed normal. He waved to Sam and the professor to come in.

When they joined him, he smiled. "So far, so good. No bones anyway."

"Darn. I'm disappointed," Sam said, looking around.

"Why?"

"I was hoping for a scary dungeon."

The professor chuckled. "Perhaps the other half will do better."

"Let's check it out."

Paul crossed to the other side of the basement. As he stepped past the doorway, motion-sensor-operated overhead fluorescents flooded the room with light. "Nothing here but nothing," he called. Except for more square concrete pillars supporting the floor above, this side of the basement was vacant. As a result, it seemed much larger than the other side.. Like the storage side, white acoustic tile covered the ceiling and light gray epoxy paint protected the floor. Aged brick lined the distant walls. A scattering of square concrete pillars supported the floor above. The professor came in, followed by Samantha.

Paul frowned and tugged his right ear. Something wasn't right. He walked back to the doorway, stopped and peered toward the ends of both rooms.

"What is it?" Sam asked.

"The lawyer said this basement has dimensions identical to the house."

"So?"

"It doesn't. These basement rooms are shorter than the house."

"How can you tell?"

"I noticed it when I came down."

Sam struggled with the idea. "Why does it matter?"

"Because hidden rooms down here," the professor said. "Right, Paul?"

"Yes. That's possible." He turned to Sam. "Have you noticed any other outside entrances?"

"No."

"During our first walk-through the house, did you see anything resembling a trapdoor in the floor?"

"No, but I wasn't looking. Why?"

"Because I'm certain there's a room beyond those end walls. Hang on."

He hurried to the far end of the room and walked along the brick wall in search of a telltale sign. He found nothing but brick. A surge of hopeful anticipation struck him. What was beyond this wall? Had Talon sealed the bodies in the basement? Could the answer be this easy?

"Uncle Justin paid a fortune to refurbish this place." Sam volunteered. "He must have known about a hidden room."

"Not necessarily. He didn't mention it in his notes."

"What are you thinking?" the professor asked.

Paul grinned. "I think this wall needs a door in it about here, don't you?"

"What do you think is there?" Sam's eyes were wide with wonder.

"Fortune's bones, I hope. Let's go. I need tools."

At Paul's insistence, Sam and the professor waited outside the basement while he dashed around the house to check for other entrances. He found none, so he changed course and jogged across the grounds to the tool shed for things he needed. When he returned loaded with tools, he led the way back to the wall in the basement.

Now, at his feet were a portable L-E-D work light, a short piece of two-by-four lumber, a whisk broom, a wire brush and several other tools. Most important was a heavy-duty flat chisel with a shield on top to protect bare knuckles and a three-pound sledge hammer. Behind him, Samantha and the professor stood holding flashlights, waiting for him to knock a hole in the wall.

Paul examined the brick at eye level for a soft spot in the mortar, then lowered the safety glasses over his eyes. He grabbed the hammer and chisel and aimed the chisel at one end of a brick. "Okay, stand back," he said, "and protect your eyes. These chips can fly like bullets."

Four heavy blows later, the chosen brick moved a quarter of an inch. He lifted his glasses and backed away. "The other side is empty. Maybe we hit the jackpot."

Sam gave him a worried smile, but said nothing.

"Can we help?" the professor asked.

"No, thanks."

Paul lifted the two-by-four and placed one end against the

loosened brick. He took careful aim and hit it hard twice. The brick flew out. They heard a loud thud as it hit the floor on the other side. Musty sweet air from the hole hit his face. He backed away. "Flashlight, please."

Samantha handed him her light. He aimed its beam through the hole and peered past it. In the distance, he saw another wall, but nothing else. He had to remove more blocks.

With Sam and the professor peeking over his shoulder, he pounded bricks with the hammer and chisel until the entry was large enough to step through. Then he dropped to his knees and cleared away the fallen bricks. The concrete floor inside the hidden room was moist and dark.

"Wait here until I make sure it's safe," he said, standing.

Sam came to him and, with a brief kiss, whispered, "Be careful."

"That's a promise."

Holding the heavy work light in front of him, he stepped through his homemade door into the middle of a cluttered room.

"What is it?" Sam called.

"Looks like a work room."

Mathias Sage joined him and looked around. "You're right, Paul. It's a workroom, but not the kind you're thinking of. This is a chamber of horrors, a torture chamber."

"Oh, God," Samantha said. "I can't believe it. That's an iron maiden in the corner. I read about those in school." She shivered.

"Want to leave?"

"No, I'm okay, but this place reeks of evil."

"It is evil, Samantha." Mathias Sage walked to the iron maiden, undid a latch and opened it. "This is not an iron maiden, Samantha," he said. "No spikes inside. It's just an iron box used to frighten victims by locking them inside." He closed the door on the iron coffin and walked to the wall beside the long table.

He rattled a set of shackles. "Talon wrote Fortune was into devil worship and torturing young women in San Francisco. Looks like he brought his predilection with him to Malibu." He lifted an odd-shaped iron tool from a hook on the wall. "As part of my paranormal studies, I've made a study of torture. This little invention was used to grip and tear tongues from the victims' mouths." He lifted another strange tool. "This one was used to pinch and tear the breasts of female victims."

"That's disgusting, horrible." Sam looked stricken.

"Yes, and it's one of the milder tools. Look on the wall there." He pointed to a wooden frame that held a variety of tools. He walked over and touched the items one by one. "Hacksaw for removing limbs. Thumb screw for delivering sheer agony. Oh, and this one is juicy. It's placed over the victim's neck and tightened to drive these pointed iron spikes into the neck. Talk or die." He returned to the table. "And this piece of furniture is the pièce de résistance. These iron straps allowed the executioner to lock down the victim's feet, waist and neck and perform whatever evil they wished. Fortune Montmartre must have been a demon even before he diedThe horror showing on Sam's face grew with each of the professor's descriptions. Paul intervened. "That's enough lecture for now, professor. We're looking for bones, remember?" He scanned the room. "No bones here." He crossed to a flat iron door that led to an adjoining room. The door was rusty and had a rotating iron latch with a tarnished bronze knob below it. He lifted the latch and gave the knob a twisting tug. It broke off in his hand. "Damn!"

He retrieved the hammer and returned to the door. "Hold the light up," he told the professor. Then, aiming with precision, he pounded the chisel into the wall where the throw deadbolt should be. One blow drove the blade through the wall. The door popped open with a squeal of rusty iron hinges.

The professor lifted the work light high over his head. "Well, young man, looks like you found your bones."

"Oh, dear God!" Samantha said.

FORTY-THREE

ALTOGETHER, three-dozen full-body skeletons lined the walls left and right. They all sat on the floor and leaned with their backs to the wall. Several skulls lay on the floor beside their bodies. Others, still attached, rested in an attitude of prayer. Stunned, Paul stepped aside to allow the professor to enter with the work light. He had seen atrocities in Afghanistan, but nothing to match this. These skeletons were small, almost child size. Samantha caught his hand and squeezed it.

"This is a nightmare," she whispered. "None of these skeletons can be Fortune or Helena. They're too small."

"Yeah, some of Fortune's handiwork."

"They're most likely young teenage girls," Mathias Sage said from the middle of the room. "Fortune Montmartre was a serial child abuser and rapist who enjoyed torturing his victims to death. I think we're seeing the results of his depravity. He was a sick man."

Samantha sobbed. "But who are they? Where did they come from?" She choked.

"He was a rich man," Paul said. "If he followed the pattern he set in San Francisco, I imagine he kidnapped lower-class girls from Los Angeles and other towns and brought them here." Paul pulled her to him. "Do you want to leave? You don't have to see this."

"No. If you stay, I stay."

"You sure?"

"Yes."

"Hey, look here." The professor called. He shined the work light into the far left-hand corner, highlighting a waist-high wooden lectern with a book on it.

Paul and Samantha hurried to join him. Their footsteps caused two teetering skulls to fall to the floor and roll. The professor placed the work light on a ledge above the lectern. The book was an old-fashioned account book with a green cover.

Mathias Sage stepped back and gestured. "Your house, your book. You do the honors."

Paul opened the cover to the first page, which was a ruled accounting sheet with standard columns. The page was blank. He opened the next page, which had a title.

Beautiful Girls Delivered to My Lord Satan
Fortune Montmartre

After the heading was a list of girl names, age, date and location of capture and brief comments like "Delicious, but died hard. Tight and sweet, but angry and loud. Cut out her tongue." He ran a finger down the age column. Four were nine years old. Two were eight. The rest ranged in ages from eleven to fifteen.

Paul growled in disgust. Even the terrorists in Afghanistan hadn't been so sick. He thought of the ugly face Fortune showed him his first night. Paul shuddered as a raging desire to tear the creature apart roared through him.

Sam craned to see past Paul's shoulder. "Paul, what is that? What's wrong?"

He slammed the book shut. "Fortune listed the name of every girl here and where he kidnapped them. He included sick comments about what he did to them. The youngest was only eight years old. The oldest was fifteen." His stomach did a flip-flop. "I have to report what we've found to the authorities."

"Sorry, but I can't allow that," Gerard Duet said from behind them. He had entered the room quiet as a cat and stopped three yards away. He had found another gun, an old Army forty-five, and now aimed it at them. "Sam, I told you to leave. Now you will die along with the others."

"Dad, what are you doing?"

"Hey wait!" the professor cried. "You can't kill me. I made a deal with Fortune."

Gerard Duet snorted his contempt. "You're a fool, Sage. He changed his mind."

In a coward's move, the professor grabbed Samantha and tried to use her as a shield, but Duet fired twice. The first bullet grazed Sam's left shoulder, passed through and blew a hole in the professor's chest. The second hit him in the throat. Blood spewed from his neck as he fell backward, carrying Sam with him. Blood sprayed Sam's face and neck and hair as she fell. Duet swung his weapon toward Paul, intending to murder him next.

Paul ducked low and lunged toward the man, grabbing for his gun hand, and driving his right shoulder into the man's solar plexus. His momentum carried them both to the floor. Duet gasped as Paul's elbow hit his chest and blasted the air from his lungs. The strength of Duet's grip on the gun surprised him. Paul squeezed his wrist, trying to dislodge the weapon, but Duet twisted his arm around until the weapon pointed at his own head. His eyes glared at Paul. "God forgive me," he wheezed. "I'm sorry." He pulled the trigger. The opposite side of his head exploded outward, scattering his brains and blood across the floor. Lifeless, the man went limp. Paul rolled away, fighting rising nausea. Dazed by Duet's insane action, he stumbled to his feet and tried to focus.

"Paul, help me!" An anguished cry from Samantha. The

professor's hand had landed on her waist, holding her down.

He rushed to her, tore the old man's arm away, and lifted her to her feet. Blood oozed from the top of her shoulder. "Don't move!" he ordered. "You're bleeding."

She stared past him at the body of her father. "Dad!" The word ripped from her throat by sheer anguish. She stared at Gerard's body in disbelief. and then stumbled past Paul. She fell to her knees beside her father and shook his dead face. She rocked back and forth several times, crying, "Dad, wake up! Please!"

Paul stood behind her and touched the side of her face. "Sam, please, you're bleeding. Let me help you."

She twisted around and glared at him through eyes blinded by shock and tears. Her face was a mask of terror. "You killed him," she said. The words hit him like a spike through the heart.

"Sam, please, I didn't. He—."

She didn't hear him. She turned away and fell across her dad's body, hugging her face to his chest like a little kid. "Dad, please don't leave me. Please!" Racking sobs destroyed her pleas.

Paul stood frozen for a moment. Shock and grief had taken full control of her, causing her to be immune to reason. The blood oozed in a slow trickle from her shoulder. He bent down to the professor's body and ripped both long sleeves from his white shirt. Then stepped over the body to stand in front of Sam. "Sam, get control of yourself. You can't help him. He's gone." She ignored him. He caught her good arm and pulled.

She jerked back and glared at him. "You killed him. Why didn't you save him? Why?"

"Sam, please listen to me. I didn't kill him. He tried to shoot me. We wrestled, and then he said, 'God forgive me. I'm sorry.' and shot himself in the head."

Her expression changed. Doubt and hope replaced the terror and the fear. "He said, 'God, forgive me?'"

"Yes, I think in the end, he had the courage to free himself from that devil. He was a good man, Sam. Fortune forced him to do what he did."

She looked down at Gerard's face, then turned back to him. Her expression had changed to understanding. "Sorry," she said. "I don't know why I said that. I... I'm sorry."

"Forget it. He shot you and you're in shock. Please, Sam. I have to stop the bleeding." He stepped over Duet's feet to help her. She reached for his extended arm.

"Steady now. Can you stand?"

She nodded.

He helped her up and led her to the corner lectern where the work light was still shining. Speaking in a gentle tone, he said, "Hold on to the lectern while I stop the bleeding."

She nodded again.

He peeled her blouse away from the wound. Her bra was soaked, so he peeled that away, too. "Good," he told her. "It's a minor flesh wound. The bullet grazed the upper trapezius. Didn't penetrate the muscle. Don't move now. This may hurt, but I have to stop the bleeding."

He folded one of the professor's sleeves and pressed it hard on the wound. As he did so, he lightly kissed her forehead. "Can't have my best girl bleed to death. Hold this tight for a minute."

"Paul..."

"Shush. Let me do this. Then we can talk."

He lifted her arm enough to slip the long shirt sleeve under her arm pit. Then he tied it up and over the other sleeve. He pulled tight until she winced. "That will hold for now, I think."

"Paul, I don't know why I said that. I know you didn't kill him. I'm sorry. "

"Sam, you just lost your dad. I understand. And I can tell you he didn't suffer. Death was instant. It took a lot of courage to do what he did to free himself from Montmartre. You should be proud of him."

"I... thank you for saying that."

"You're welcome. How do you feel?"

"Not much. My whole shoulder is numb."

"Yeah, that's typical. A forty-five slug hits you like a battering ram. We have to get out of here. If I help, can you walk?"

"I think so, but—." She looked at the professor's corpse. "He was lying all along, wasn't he?"

"Yes, but I doubt he got the immortality he wanted. Do you have bandages at the cottage?"

"In the bathroom."

"Good. I want to bandage that wound and call 911. Then we have to talk." In the back of his mind, he wondered what these events would do to his project. He was certain it would delay things.

Sam held onto him as he helped her through the torture room into the basement.

"If you can't make it, I'll carry you," he said.

"Don't be silly. I'm as strong as a..." She passed out.

Paul caught her, lifted her in his arms, and headed for the exit.

She weighed about the same as Yoshi. But she felt much better in his arms.

FORTY-FOUR

SAM AWOKE when they were halfway to the cottage. She wiggled one leg and said, "Paul?"

He stopped walking and said, "You're awake."

"What happened?"

"You passed out. We're almost at the cottage now."

"I'm sorry. Put me down, please."

"You sure?"

"Yes. Put me down."

He lowered her legs until they touched the ground, then steadied her as she stood. She frowned. "I'm so stupid."

"Don't. You had a hell of a shock. I've seen marines faint from less."

She gave him a weak smile. "What are we going to do?"

"First, I'll stop that bleeding and bandage your arm. Second, we'll have coffee and a talk. Once we've decided what to tell the police, I'll call 911. After that, we sit and speculate about the future until the cops arrive. Let's go. You can lean on me."

Paul worked fast until he was satisfied with his first aid. He put a giant Band-Aid over the wound and then sat beside her. Two cups of steaming coffee rested on the table before them. He took a sip and leaned back. "You ready to talk about what happened?"

"Yes, but to be honest, my brain seems lost somewhere in another dimension. I'll do whatever you say."

"Good. In that case, here's how I see it. If we tell the paramedics you got shot, they'll send you to a trauma center, which is a good idea. But they won't let me go with you. The police will want to question me. At least until they're satisfied, they have an accurate picture of what happened."

"My wound is not bad. You said so yourself. I won't go until we can leave together. Can they force me to get treated?"

"No, but I suggest we let the paramedics examine your arm, then decide. Okay?"

"Okay." She pinched her lips, still in shock, but trying hard to stay with it. "What do we tell the police?"

"We'd better not mention anything about ghosts. Otherwise…"

"They'll call the men in white coats. So, what should we say?"

"You said your dad had been acting funny the last two years and even worse since you returned home, right?"

"Yes, but…"

"Sam, I understand, but we have to give the police a plausible story or they'll question us forever. I think we should tell them your father resented my coming to Montmartre and disapproved of my interest in you. You might say he had been acting angry ever since you got home. You could tell them he came to the basement gunning for me, but I ducked and he hit you and Professor Sage. I struggled with him to get the gun, and he shot himself. Can you live with that story?"

"Yes, and it's close to what happened. It's simple and easy to remember." She broke into a sob. "Oh, Dad!"

Paul touched her hand and waited for her to gain control. Then he said, "They're certain to ask why the professor was here. I'll say he approached me because he wanted to help find Fortune's bones. His research led him to believe Talon buried them in the basement and wanted to help find them. I agreed. I won't mention Uncle Justin's will unless they ask. How does that sound to you?"

She stared at her coffee, then up to meet his eyes. "It sounds fine," she said. "Whatever you say, I'll follow your lead."

"Sam…"

"I'm okay, Paul. Just in shock. I think what happened to Dad was inevitable, but right now I feel like my brain is riding a wild tornado." She hesitated, and her eyes filled with tears.

"What is it?"

"I'm an orphan now. I feel lost."

"We're both orphans, Sam. And you're not lost. I'll always be here for you."

Tears welled, causing her eyes to sparkle like liquid sapphire. She gave him a grateful smile. "You mean that, don't you?

"Yes, with all my heart."

"I read about knights in shining armor in school, but you're the first one I've ever known." She straightened her shoulders. "You'd better call 911 while I clean off this blood and get a new blouse."

She rose and climbed the stairs upstairs to her room.

He watched her until he was certain she was okay, and then lifted his phone and dialed 911.

"911, what's your emergency?" A man's voice.

Paul hesitated for a breath. "I want to report a murder suicide."

"What's your name, sir?"

"Paul Davenport."

"Where did this happen?"

"At the old Montmartre estate on Latigo Canyon Road, four miles east of Malibu. The entrance is hard to find."

"Do you have the address?"

"I'm sure there is one, but I don't know it. Sorry?"

"Don't worry. We'll find you. Are you there now?"

"Yes."

"Are you armed?"

"No."

"What are the victim's names?" The man's voice was robotic.

"The suicide-shooter was a man named Gerard Duet. His victim was a man named Mathias Sage, a retired university professor."

"What weapon did he use?"

"An army forty-five automatic."

"Where is the weapon now?"

"On the floor near the bodies."

"Where are the bodies?"

He held back the information about the room full of skeletons. Time enough for that when the detectives arrived. It wasn't relevant to the case he was reporting. "In the basement of a sixteen-thousand square-foot mansion," he said.

Paul took a deep breath to remain patient at the man's slow pace. Complaining would do no good, anyway. The dispatcher had to get through his list of questions.

"When did this happen?"

"Forty-five minutes ago.

"What is your current location, sir?"

"In the caretaker's cottage a hundred yards from the mansion. One of the caretaker's shots went wild, and the bullet grazed his daughter's shoulder. I brought her to the cottage to dress the wound. I stopped the bleeding, but we need the paramedics."

"What's the daughter's name?"

"Samantha Duet."

"How old is she?"

"Twenty-eight."

"Is her wound serious?"

"No. I told you. I stopped the bleeding and dressed the wound. How long before the police arrive?"

"An L. A. County deputy sheriff will arrive at your location soon. What caused the shooting?"

"Ms. Duet told me her father seemed depressed. That's all

I can tell you. Look, how long before the paramedics arrive?"

"They're on their way, too, sir. Is the estate owner available for questioning?"

"Yes."

"What's his or her name, sir?"

"You're talking to him. I'll leave the front gate open. Do you need my phone number?"

"I have it."

"Fine. We'll be waiting. I have to go now."

Paul hung up.

The phone buzzed. This time it was Yoshi.

"Hey, Yosh."

"Paul, you sound terrible. What happened?"

Paul told him the entire story, including what they planned to tell the Sheriff.

"Sounds good. Is Sam okay?"

"Yeah, she's okay, but she's still in shock."

"Damn, what a turn of events!"

"It's crazy, Yosh."

"No kidding. Listen, I called to tell you I'll arrive around eight o'clock tomorrow morning if that works for you."

"Perfect. I can't wait."

"Wish I was there now."

"So do I, Yosh."

"See you, mañana."

"Right. Have a pleasant flight."

Paul hung up and sat for ten minutes sipping coffee and pondering. How long would the police investigation take? They had to secure the scene of the crime and ask a million questions. The coroner had to get involved. Then there was Fortune Montmartre's collection of skeletons. How long to clean up that mess? Two, three days?

He had twelve days left to meet the terms of his uncle's will. It seemed even more impossible now. He emitted a low growl as he thought of the pain Fortune Montmartre had dumped on

Samantha, her father and Helena, and at least thirty-six girls. His anger drove him to his feet, knocking over his chair. Even if he didn't win his uncle's fortune, he'd have to make that evil bastard pay for his crimes. No more digging for information. He wanted action.

"Paul?" Samantha had changed into a light-blue, long-sleeved blouse and navy blue slacks and returned. "What happened?"

"Sorry. Got up too fast. How's your arm?" He righted the chair and sat down.

"I can tell it's there, but it hurts only if I move it the wrong way. Did you call 911?" She sat beside him and made a face as she sipped her coffee, now cold.

"Yep. They'll be here soon. Is there a way to open the gate and keep it open?"

"Yes. Push the button on the controller's bottom corner."

"Right. Yoshi called. He'll be here tomorrow morning about eight o'clock."

"Great."

"Sam, what about arrangements for your father? I want to help you with that."

"We never discussed what to do. Uncle Justin said we could use the cemetery here. I never gave it much thought."

"Is that what you want? I ask because if the coroner agrees it's a murder-suicide, he'll release the bodies in a few days. And there's another consideration, too."

"What?"

"What if I fail? I lose everything, including the cemetery. What would happen to the grave sites? Maybe you'd rather bury your father somewhere else."

"I... what should I do?"

"Perhaps we should find a pretty place for him elsewhere. Someplace where they'll take care of the site."

"That sounds right. Paul... I can't think straight right now. Can we save that for later?"

"Of course. I shouldn't have brought it up. Sorry."

"No apologies needed. You're being practical. What do we do now?"

"Nothing. We wait."

FORTY-FIVE

THE SIRENS coming up Latigo Canyon Road were out of sync and sounded as if they were engaged in an angry argument. Paul checked the time. Forty-five minutes from call to response. Not bad.

He pushed back his chair and stood. "I'll go out to meet them. Maybe you should stay here and rest until they need you."

She stood. "No. I'm going, too. You do the talking, and I'll follow your lead."

He smiled at her determination. "All right. Come on, then."

They reached the side of the work road and stood looking toward the gate. Moments later, four black and white L. A. County sheriff's patrol cars came into sight and snaked their way toward them. Sam covered her ears to mute the noise. Paul waved. The front car slowed and stopped. The driver cut the siren and the other cars cut theirs, too, leaving welcome silence.

A tall man wearing a rumpled brown suit got out on the passenger side. He nodded to them. He was in his mid-fifties, Paul guessed, but well-conditioned. His face was sun-bronzed and crowned by close-cropped salt and pepper brown hair. His suit coat flopped open, showing a gold badge that dangled from a chain around his neck. He gave Paul a quick inspection, eyed

Samantha appreciatively, then smiled and stuck out his hand. "Josh McKenzie, homicide division," he said, flashing his ID, which was in a black leather holder laced around the edge"You got here fast," Paul said. "Are you from the local sheriff's station?"

"No. Monterey Park. I was at the Lost Hills station when the call came in. The report said the call came from a Paul Davenport. I wondered if it was you and here you are."

"Yep, it's me," Paul said. "Nice to meet you."

"Saw you on TV." The detective turned to Samantha. "You must be…"

"Samantha Duet." She stuck out her hand.

"The report said you got shot. You okay?"

"Yes. Paul patched me up, but I plan to have it checked by a doctor."

"The ambulance will be here soon. They can examine it. You can wait inside until they come, if you like."

Sam frowned. "No. I want to stay."

"Your choice."

"Her dad shot her," Paul said. "He took us all by surprise. We…"

The detective held up his hand. "We'll get your statement in due time.. First, are you armed?"

"No."

"Where's the murder weapon?"

"Still in her dad's hand."

"What is it?"

"Looks like an antique army forty-five. Three rounds fired."

"Right. You were a marine. Thanks. Where are the bodies?"

Paul gestured toward the chateau. "Over there in the basement. Entrance on the outside."

The other cars spilled deputies wearing light brown shirts and green-trouser uniforms. They stood beside their cars, awaiting orders. Paul watched with interest. Their eyes were on Paul, Sam and the detective, though mostly on Sam.

The man driving the detective's car joined them. He was Hispanic and about Samantha's height. His chest was thick and muscular, but without a bulge around the waist. Paul guessed he was in his mid-forties.

"This is Sergeant Ramirez of the Lost Hills Station," McKenzie said. "He'll accompany us to the scene and take charge of security."

Paul nodded and shook hands.

The sergeant swung his gaze around the estate. "This place is something else," he said. "I've driven past here several times, but imagined nothing like this."

"That makes two of us, Sergeant."

"Which brings up a question, Mr. Davenport. What are you doing here? I thought you lived in Pasadena."

"I do, sir, but it's complicated."

Paul explained his meeting with lawyer Huckabee and the conditions of his uncle's will. He left out any mention of ghosts, saying, "A man named Fortune Montmartre built this place. Later, he murdered his wife and tried to kill his son. The son killed him instead and hid the bodies of both victims. My uncle's will says to inherit his estate, I have to find and give the bones a proper burial in two weeks or I get nothing."

"Shit!" McKenzie said.

"That's a weird requirement," Sergeant Ramirez said. "Why would he do that?"

Paul shrugged. "I'd like to ask him that myself, Sergeant. I wasn't aware I had an uncle until two days ago. Lawyer Huckabee called him eccentric. We were looking for the bones when Samantha's dad came in shooting."

McKenzie glanced at his notebook. "The other victim was a man named Mathias Sage?"

"Yes. He's… was a retired professor. Apparently, he studied this place for years. His theory was that Talon Montmartre, Fortune's son, buried his father and his young stepmother in the basement. He offered to help me find them, and I agreed."

The detective nodded. To Samantha, he said, "Was your father acquainted with the professor, Miss Duet?" he asked Sam.

"No. Dad was very reclusive. He left the estate only to buy supplies and things. I've been away at school for the past four years. When I returned two weeks ago, he seemed angry and depressed. I was worried about him, and, frankly, he frightened me."

"Do you know why he shot you and the professor?"

"No. I think he intended to kill all three of us. I got the idea he hated to see Paul inherit the estate. His attitude was strange and frightening. I begged him to tell me what was wrong, but he wouldn't. He told me to mind my own business."

Sergeant Ramirez saw tears forming in Sam's eyes and touched the detective's arm. "We better get going. This case is crazy enough to draw as many reporters as flies on road kill."

"Damn. I hadn't thought of that," Paul blurted. "Mr. McKenzie, can you keep them out of here?"

"While we're working, yes. After that, it's your problem, I'm afraid." To Samantha, he said, "Are you sure your father is dead? We don't want another shootout."

Samantha nodded.

"What about the professor?"

"He's dead, too," Paul said. "He took two shots, one in the chest and one in the neck."

"Okay, let's have a look then."

Paul led them into the basement and to the empty side. There, he stopped and said, "One thing I haven't told you. We found the skeletons of thirty-six other bodies, too."

"Skeletons? Where?" Sergeant Ramirez's eyes widened.

Paul pointed toward the hole in the brick wall. "We found two sealed-off rooms. One is a torture chamber. The other is a prison. I broke open a section of the wall to reach them."

"They were all young girls," Samantha added. "Ages eight to fifteen. Fortune Montmartre abused, tortured and murdered them."

"How about the bones you were after? Were they there?"

"No. Just the girls and a book with their names. The creep kept careful records of where he kidnapped the girls and what he did to them. I expect you'll find solutions to a lot of old unsolved cases in there." Paul said.

"Jesus!" Ramirez frowned.

"Show us," McKenzie ordered.

They walked to the end of the basement and into the torture chamber. McKenzie shined his flashlight around the room. When he saw the skeletons, he stopped. "Son of a bitch!" The work light was now only a dim glow.

Detective McKenzie played his flashlight along the two walls of skeletons and then spotlighted Gerard Duet and the professor. The light stopped to dwell on Gerard Duet's gun hand and the forty-five. "Christ!" He sucked in a quick breath and turned to Ramirez. "Call the crime scene investigation team and seal off this basement. I'll call the medical examiner. This is one for the books. Christ!"

Ramirez nodded and left. The detective turned to Paul. "Is there another entrance to the basement?"

"There might be one upstairs in the house, but I can't tell you where. I'm sleeping at the pool house."

Surprise. "Why?"

Samantha was looking at everything but Gerard Duet's body. "Because I live in a small studio apartment in Pasadena, Mr. McKenzie. This place is too big. It gave me the jitters. The pool house is pleasant and convenient."

"Who else lives here?"

"No one."

The detective nodded. "Okay, you two wait in the outer room. Once I check the scene, we'll leave and let the medical examiner take over."

"How long will that take?"

"I'm not sure. Could be several hours. They have to come from L. A."

"Mr. McKenzie, are we under suspicion?" Sam asked.

"No, ma'am. I believe your story, but the medical examiner will have to agree before you're off the hook. Just a formality."

The detective's phone rang. "McKenzie." Listening. Then, "Okay, thanks." He turned to Samantha. "The ambulance is here. They know you're coming."

"Thanks. Where?"

"Somewhere up front. You'll find it."

"Mind if we wait at the pool house when we're done?" Paul asked.

"Where is it?"

"Fifty yards from where we entered the basement. You can't miss it."

"Okay. Go ahead. I've got your number. Just don't get lost."

FORTY-SIX

TIME PASSED IN PEACE after the paramedic gave Sam a shot and changed the dressing on her shoulder. Detective McKenzie had disappeared on busines, so they made ham and cheese sandwiches and moved out to sit beside the pool to eat them. They relaxed and watched a slow parade of people moving in and out of the basement entrance. Two bored-looking deputies stood chatting and guarding the door.

Most of the medical examiner's people wore civilian clothes. Several of them wore white face masks. Paul could only imagine what they were doing until they brought out the bodies on separate stretchers. He watched as they carried them around to an ambulance waiting at the front of the house. He wondered what Fortune Montmartre thought about the small army that had invaded his domain.

For the past half hour they had sat in silence observing the police at work, but when the med guys removed the bodies of Gerard Duet and the professor, Samantha stirred and asked, "Paul, do you believe in an afterlife?"

"Afterlife?"

"Yes. Heaven and hell, purgatory. That kind of thing."

Paul saw she was serious. "My mother did. She often prayed

at night after work. I never gave it much thought. I stayed too busy, and we didn't go to church, except once or twice at Easter when I was a kid. My mother's life was hard."

"What about now?"

"You mean after all that's happened?"

"Yes."

"That's a tough one. Until Monday night, I considered ghosts to be a fantasy. Now I realize they're real. If ghosts are real, I guess heaven and hell are possible, too. Why do you ask?"

"Because I'm worried about my dad. I hope he doesn't get trapped like Fortune and Helena. That would be horrible."

"A fate worse than death?"

She nodded. Paul saw she was ready to cry. "Sam, I'm sorry about your father. My coming here has been a disaster."

She reached across for his hand. "Don't say that. None of this is your fault. I realize now I lost Dad two years ago, possibly even before that. It's obvious he was a slave to that evil creature. I'm glad he's no longer suffering."

"I understand that," Paul said. "When my father died, I felt the same way. But, to answer your question about life after death. I hope there is a heaven. Because if there is one, I'm sure my mother is there. She worked hard to make a home for us despite my father. And she kept trying until she died."

"She sounds like quite a woman."

"Yeah… she was." He clamped his jaws to keep from gushing the truth about himself. "She wrote me a hundred letters while I was in the service. She always said she loved me and worried about me. Never once did she complain about her life or told me she was ill. I… was in Afghanistan when she died." He stopped. "Sam, I'm sorry. You don't need my problems."

"No, please, I want to hear." She reached for his hand again. "And I think you're being too hard on yourself. You were in Afghanistan fighting a war, but… Uncle Justin hoped to become a ghost to be with Helena. Is that possible?"

He forced the debilitating guilt from his thoughts. "I don't think so. He also said Madam Song doubted it. Remember?" The worry deepened on Sam's face. She had just lost her father, and he was sitting here wallowing in self pity.

"Yes." She sat silent, staring at something beyond her eyes. "We can't let that creature destroy more lives. I keep picturing those young girls locked up in chains and how terrifying it was for them. It makes me want to cry." She shuddered.

"Sam, we'll stop him. I promise I—."

"Mr. Davenport. Miss Duet!"

Startled, they turned. Detective McKenzie hurried toward them from the gate. He was beaming. "Nice place you got here. Sorry it took so long, but I bring good news! The M. E. cleared you both. He checked the bodies and declared it a murder-suicide. He'll make it official in a few days.

"That's a quick decision, isn't it?" Paul asked. "I figured he'd want to check me for powder residue."

"We talked about it, but the M.E. says it's unnecessary. It's an open and shut case."

"That's unusual, isn't it?"

"Yes, but Mr. Duet's hand still gripped the gun. and the M.E. couldn't pry it loose. He says there's no way you ut it in his hand after death."

"Right. Thanks for telling me."

"No problem. The medical examiner found powder burns on his hand, his sleeve, and the side of his head. You're in the clear, though they may want your testimony later on." He nodded to Sam. "Sorry, ma'am."

"So what's next for us?" Paul asked.

"The M. E. will finish removing the skeletons. They're bagging them now."

"Won't they need to search the house, too?"

"They have men doing that now. Do you have a problem with that?"

"No. Have at it. I live here."

"How long will all this take?"

"I overheard one of the med guys say they'll finish by noon tomorrow."

"What about the media? When this story breaks, they'll swarm this place trying to get in. I have only eleven days left to satisfy my uncle's will. I can't waste time dodging those people."

McKenzie nodded, understanding. "I can't help you with that. We'll keep them out until the medical examiner finishes his work tomorrow. After that, you're on your own. If I were you, I'd hire a couple of gate guards."

"Good idea. I'll think about it. Thanks."

"So, are we free to leave?" Sam asked.

"Yes, our guys will be here another couple of hours, but you're not needed. Oh, wait. These are yours." He handed Paul a gate remote and a loaded key chain. "These were in Mr. Duet's pocket."

"What about his cell phone?" Sam asked. "They won't destroy its contents, will they?"

"Depends on what's in it," McKenzie said. "Why?"

"I... it doesn't matter."

Sam's eyes were tearing up.

"It may have information she would like to keep," Paul explained. "It's one of the few things of her father's she owns."

"Ah, yes. Sorry, ma'am. I'll talk to the M.E. and see you get it back."

"Thank you."

"We also have his wallet and that madman's journal. I read it. He was a sick puppy. We'll return all three as soon as forensics is done with them."

"Right, thanks."

The detective stuck out his hand. "Well, I'm out of here. I have a report to write. I hope you heal soon, Ms. Duet, and I hope you find those bones, Mr. Davenport. This place is fantastic."

They watched him leave.

"I have to report," Paul said. He dialed Madam Song and turned on the speaker so Sam could listen. The psychic answered on the second ring.

"Mr. Davenport?"

"Yes." He told her what had happened.

When he finished, she said, "I told you he was dangerous. Please give Miss Duet my condolences. Anything else?"

"That's it?"

"What else would you have me say?"

"Nothing, I guess."

"Until tomorrow, then." She hung up.

"Damn." He did likewise.

"Cold-blooded lady," Sam said. "You said she wouldn't be much help."

"Yeah, I did, didn't I?"

After that, they sat for a time, enjoying a sense of peace. The afternoon was pleasant, and Paul was positive he could sit there forever with Samantha. But she had other ideas.

"Paul, we have to move back to the cottage," she said. "Will you help me?"

"Sure, but why?" he asked, surprised.

"Because there's three bedrooms at the cottage. My dad's room for you and the downstairs bedroom for Yoshi. That's more convenient for all of us, don't you think?"

"Yes, of course. When do you want to do it?"

"Now, if you don't mind. I want to search my dad's room and take a shower."

"I don't mind," he said. He rose and offered his hand. She took it and stood. "But I have a condition."

She smiled as if she knew what it was. "Okay, what?"

"That I get a kiss now, plus a chance to steal kisses while Yoshi's here."

She giggled and allowed his arms to encircle her body. He pulled her tight. The kiss lasted more than a minute before she broke away.

"I love you, you know," he said.

She hesitated, then said, "Yes."

When she didn't respond, a cloud of worry passed through him.

She noticed the change in his expression. "Paul, please be patient. I need a little more time to get my head straight. I don't want to hurt either of us." He knew his face showed his disappointment. Tear bubbles rose in the corners of her eyes. "Can you wait a while longer?"

"Sure. Whatever you want. Sorry." He looked toward the two deputies, hoping to hide his feelings from her. Once again, he had acted like an impatient school boy, unable to cope with his fear of losing her. He said, "I'd better check on those guys. They might need help. I'll be back in a while." He turned to walk away.

"Paul, wait!"

He turned back, feeing like a selfish fool who had moved in like a hungry piranha. He wanted to crawl under a rock where he belonged.

She pulled his arms around her, kissed him once, twice, and then a third time, deeply.

"Sam, I…"

"Please, Paul, I'm right here.

He turned back. Her eyes were pleading. He felt himself melt. "I'm such a fool," he said.

"No. I'm the fool. I love you, but…"

"You don't want to hurt me. I understand."

"No, you don't. My mother didn't die. She ran away after I was born. She told my dad marrying him was a mistake, including having me. I…"

"That can never happen to us." He shut her mouth with a kiss.

She pushed back. "Why? How can you say that?"

"Because I'll never let you go. If you marry me, it will be forever."

"How can you know that?"

"I'm psychic. I know such things."

She giggled. "Can you?"

"What?"

"Wait a while."

"Twain said, 'Love is a madness. If thwarted, it develops even faster.'" He smothered her with another kiss. "So, I'll do whatever you wish, and I'll try not to go mad while I wait. If you tell me to wait until you're a little old lady, I will. Can you live with that?"

She snickered. "You're the most romantic and lovable man I've ever known."

"Only with you, Sam. Throughout Afghanistan, I faced whatever danger came, but now I walk around terrified that I'll lose you." He raised his brows. "Hey, how many lovable, romantic guys have you known?"

"Oh, hush. There aren't anymore like you." She closed his mouth with a passionate kiss that lasted for a moment, that suspended time.

"Sam, you're starting something we might have to finish," he breathed when they broke apart. "Maybe we should go upstairs."

"No. Let's move my stuff first. I'll phone you when I'm ready and you can visit me at the cottage."

"Okay, but don't lock the door. I don't want to break it down."

"Yes, master."

She turned, laughing, and went into the pool house.

Paul gathered his stuff, and they drove to the cottage. He stowed his gear in Gerard Duet's bedroom. A quick glance told him the room and bathroom had everything he needed for the rest of his time at Montmartre. When Sam got settled in, she asked Paul to help her search her father's room.

"What are we looking for?"

"Anything that might help. Several times I heard him moving furniture around at night. He hid Uncle Justin's diaries in the closet. He might have hidden something else that will help us."

After more than an hour of detailed searching, they came

up empty. Samantha, discouraged, sat on the side of her father's bed and said, "I could have sworn he was moving furniture in here, but I guess not." She rose and gave him a quick peck on the lips. "Sorry about that," she said. "Now for my bath. I'll call you, okay?"

"I'll be next door. Just snap your fingers."

She watched him walk down the stairs and waited for him to reach the front door. Paul looked back and resisted telling her he loved her. She blew him a kiss. He grinned as he closed the door.

He whistled an off-key tune on his way back to his truck. He felt unbelievably hopeful for the first time in his life.

FORTY-SEVEN

TWILIGHT HIT Montmartre's little valley early because of the surrounding mountains. A bright yellow-orange glow had formed over the western peak, and a brisk night chill turned the air fresh and invigorating. The sky higher above the mountains was now a beautiful, deepening purple.

The evening air smelled fresh with a tinge of sagebrush and was a pleasure to breathe. He paused at the door of his truck and eyed the chateau. A rectangle of light from inside the basement highlighted two deputies chatting outside the basement doors. They spotted him. Paul waved. They waved back.

He drove his truck as far as the garage, parked, and walked across the lawn to chat with them.

"How's it going?" he asked as he approached them.

"About to wrap up," the taller of the deputies answered. He stuck out his hand. "You're Paul Davenport, right?"

Paul nodded and shook hands.

"I'm Deputy Jackson and this is Deputy Gomez."

He peered into the basement. "How are they doing?"

"They're getting there." Deputy Jackson motioned into the basement. "I'm glad it's them, not me."

"Bagging the bones?"

"Yeah. It's disgusting. What kind of person does a thing like that?"

"A monstrous, sick devil worshiper," Paul answered. "I'll be around if you need me. If not, when you leave, the gate will open automatically, but tomorrow you have to call me to get in. Also, if you don't mind, I'd appreciate it if you hit your siren once when you go. Okay?"No problem. We have your phone number."

"Great. You guys take care."

"You, too, Mr. Davenport."

Paul headed back across the grass to his car. Halfway there, something nagged at the corner of his brain. He stopped midfield and swept the entire estate to find the source of the nag. Suddenly, he understood what was troubling him. The sheer vastness of the land could thwart his efforts to find the bones in the meager number of days remaining to him. He shook his head. Size of the place didn't matter. He had to try. He brushed away the negative thought and continued on his way.

At the garage, when he approached his car, Gerard Duet's keys jangled in his pocket, giving him a sudden inspiration. Time to open the garage and see what goodies lay hidden there.

Paul spotted a door in the right-hand corner of the building. He hurried to it and stepped inside. Bright overhead fluorescents flooded the room with light. He blinked at the glare and then glanced around in amazement.

The garage housed a shiny black Cadillac Escalade, an older black Lincoln Continental Mark IV, and a near-new Honda Accord Sedan. The cars were were in immaculate condition. But what caught his eye was a flash of something bright green in the back corner of the big room. He wound his way around the passenger cars toward it. When he saw what it was, he smiled at his uncle's foresight. It was the answer to half his problem of digging up Fortune's bones... a brand-new, shiny, bright-green John Deere model 1025 R tractor with a front shovel and factory-installed backhoe for digging. He was certain his uncle bought it at the same time he ordered the ground penetrating radar. He turned his head to the sky and said, "Hey, Unk, thanks. This is perfect."

The tractor was brand new. A user's manual hung from the steering wheel on an S-shaped hook. He lifted it and flipped through it until he found a page with call-outs showing the locations of the operator controls. The ignition key was in the switch on the dash. He searched for the backhoe and and the front-end shovel controls and found They looked easy enough to handle, it would take some study and practice to learn to use them properlyHe walked around to the fuel tank behind the operator's seat, removed the cap, and sniffed. Diesel. He stuck a finger in the tank. Full. Good. He checked the backhoe, which was the handy tool grave diggers used in large cemeteries. Perfect for digging out old bones. The backhoe bucket hanging on the rear of the tractor resembled the arm on a one-armed praying mantis.

The unit had two stabilizer legs that were lowered to counterbalance the pull when the shovel dug into the ground. They prevented the opposite end of the tractor from lifting off the ground. The backhoe had its own folding operator seat. He checked to see if the operator could handle the tractor's movement from that seat, but learned it couldn't be done. That meant changing seats whenever he needed to move the machine. A minor nuisance, but doable.

Super happy with his find, Paul replaced the manual, and then checked inside the cars for their ignition keys. Not there, but it didn't matter. He didn't intend to use them. They weren't his yet.

As he left the garage, his spirits were high, and he felt optimistic. His uncle had bought that tractor for the same purpose he intended for it. He wondered whether the vendor had delivered the GPR and where Gerard Duet had stored it. The tool shed? If Yoshi was right, the GPR was essential to finding Fortune's and Helena's burial site.

He closed the garage door and got in his truck. The dash clock showed he had left Sam less than forty-five minutes before. He backed onto the work road and made another decision.

It was time to find out what Gerard Duet had been digging.

FORTY-EIGHT

HE PARKED with his headlamps aimed toward the big Live Oak. The beams lit the area with interesting patterns of light and shadow. The first thing he noticed were three piles of dirt, not just one. He retrieved a flashlight from the glove compartment and walked over to stand beside the closest trench. The loud cricket song from the Junipers and the oak stopped suddenly, as though they all followed the same conductor. Paul looked up in curiosity. He had always wondered how they did that.

He shined his beam on the ground. The three holes were long, rectangular, and three feet deep. Shallow graves. Fortune had ordered Gerard Duet to murder them as early as yesterday. Duet dug the graves in preparation, but the coffin they had seen yesterday had been taken away. Paul frowned. Duet planned to dump their bodies in these holes and shovel dirt on top. No coffin needed.

Paul swept his light around, looking for the pine box. No box anywhere. Puzzled, he stepped to the opposite side of the tree and scanned the grounds toward the chateau. Nothing. He walked further out from under the tree and squinted toward his car. Still no coffin.

The sound of breaking branches in the treetop above him startled him. What? He scanned the low branches and saw nothing. He backed further away from the tree and spotted it.

"What the hell?" He blinked his eyes at an inconceivable sight.

The coffin rested in the thinnest branches at the extreme top of the tree.

He aimed his flashlight at it, but at that distance, he could see no detail. Still, he knew it was the pine box. To his surprise, the coffin rocked side-to-side like a boat in a slow rolling sea. Even stranger, the box seemed to be floating in the air, not resting on a tree branch. "Impossible!" he muttered.

The short wow of a siren split the silence from the front gate. A signal from the deputies. He squint toward the gate. The only light visible anywhere came from an upstairs window of the cottage. It was a warm, orange invitation to rejoin Samantha, but he ignored it. First, he wanted to solve the mystery of the flying coffin.

He backed away from the tree another ten yards and searched for the floating coffin. It was no longer there.

He aimed his light toward the ground under the tree, thinking it might have drifted to a landing somewhere. No box. He turned to check the chateau. Nothing. Was he seeing things? No way.

The quiet sound of rushing air coming from behind him caused him to spin around and drop to the ground just as the box swept past his head like an attacking fighter jet.

"Damn!" he yelled. This was crazy.

He scrambled to his feet and watched the box stop midair and dive nose down toward him. He remained in place until the last second, and then jumped aside as it rushed past him. Its speed was slow enough that if he saw it coming, it would be easy to dodge. But it was also fast enough to knock his head off if his timing wasn't perfect. He kept his light and his gaze glued to the box. This time the coffin stopped and floated motionless, as though assessing him. But that idea was laughable. Pine boxes couldn't assess a gnat.

Without warning, the box sped up and plummeted straight for him, this time moving much faster. Paul jumped aside. The box scraped his shoulder and bumped him sideways. He watched in fascination as the coffin slowed and reversed direction. The thing seemed determined to kill him. Time to take cover.

He turned and sprinted toward the big oak, intending to put its thick trunk between him and the box. The coffin followed him, but halted at waist height when Paul maneuvered to a position behind the tree. The thing circled the tree, keeping its nose aimed at him like a wolf preparing to pounce.

This was nuts. The box had no eyes, no sensors. It was a damned pine box. Someone was controlling it. Fortune! The bastard had thrown a heavy painting and a vase trying to kill him, so why not a pine coffin? Where the hell are you, he wondered, giving the area around the chateau a quick scan.

He inched around the tree. The coffin followed him like a cat toying with a mouse. It was vying for another try at bashing out his brains. Paul chuckled at the bizarre situation. He was playing a game of hide and seek with a floating pine box. He was hiding, and it was seeking to kill him.

Paul moved with the coffin, keeping the thick trunk between them. He wondered how long Fortune could keep the game going? Keeping that box suspended and moving had to require a lot of energy. Or maybe since ghosts had no bodies, they never got tired.

The coffin inched closer and stopped to float, motionless, two feet from him. Its proximity gave Paul an idea for an experiment. Did Fortune have a weight limit to his lifting power, or did he have unlimited power? He eyed the floating coffin, counted to three, and then jumped out to land crossways on the box. As he hoped, his weight drove it to the ground.

"Gotcha, you bastard," he said, expelling air.

The box tried three times to lift him, but he was too heavy. After a while, it quit trying and lay still. Or rather, Fortune did, he thought.

He waited for Fortune to make a move, when the box didn't move, he got up and put the tree trunk between himself and the predatory anomaly. He played his light back and forth along its length. It lay motionless. He turned toward the chateau and found the source of the attack. A reddish glow floated under the old oak tree near the stone well. It was the same aura he had seen on Monday night. Fortune in all his shining glory.

Paul stepped out and waved his flashlight at the distant figure. "Go to hell!" he yelled. "You're a dead man!" His words reverberated in the crisp coolness of the evening and he felt stupid. Of course, he was a dead man. He was a ghost.

He heard a motion behind him. Surprised, he spun around. The box lifted from the ground and shot into the sky. Paul rushed from under the tree to keep it in sight. The box rose fifty yards into the sky and stopped. It sat motionless for more than a minute and then dived toward him at high-speed, like an old Douglas SBD Dauntless bomber aiming to destroy a ship. To avoid being crushed by the coffin's weight and speed, Paul timed his move and jumped aside.

This time, the box didn't slow or maneuver as he expected. Instead, it kept coming and crashed hard into the soft earth like a kamikaze pilot committing suicide for a holy cause. The impact plowed up a large gouge in the turf. The coffin broke open and splintered several of its planks. After that, it stopped moving and lay still, as though dead.

Paul turned back to the mansion in search of the ghost. The aura winked off as he did so.

"Fortune, the friendly ghost, has a tempe." he told himself, laughing. He kicked the side of the box to check whether Fortune was trying to trick him. It didn't move. Fortune had abandoned it, which meant the end of conflict for now. He turned away and walked back to his car. Thinking about what he had just experienced sent a chill through him.

He climbed into his truck and sat peering at the distant

chateau, trying to understand the consequences of what had happened. One thing was certain. Danger had now gone three dimensional. Carelessness would be fatal. Fortune's personal range had limits, that tree next to the big house, but his ability to levitate objects didn't. How far could his power reach? It extended to this tree, which meant the pool house was in his range, too. Paul pounded the steering wheel with the heel of his fist. How could he fight a monster with this kind of ability? His goal seemed even more impossible now.

His phone rang. Samantha. "Hi," he said in a cheerful tone. "What can I do for you? Something nice, I hope."

Samantha giggled. "I can think of several things. Right now, though, I want you to come to dinner before it gets cold. Where are you?" Her voice was soft and beckoning and sent a warm glow through him.

"At the big oak where your dad was digging."

"What are you doing there? It's dark out."

"You ordered me to go away, so I did. I used the time to look around. We wanted to know what your dad was digging. I found out."

"What was it?"

"Three graves." He didn't mention the flying coffin. He would tell her about that later.

"One for each of us, right?"

"That's how I figure it."

"That's what I thought, too. Paul, hurry please. The cottage feels lonely without you."

"That sounds promising," he said. "On my way."

She laughed and hung up. The sound of her voice gave his battery a powerful recharge. He squared his shoulders and yelled at the chateau, "Go to hell. You're dead, and I intend to see you're buried, too."

He hurried.

FORTY-NINE

THE COTTAGE DOOR was locked. He pushed the doorbell button twice. A poor copy of London's Big Ben sounded inside the house, followed by the latch clacking. The door opened.

Samantha stood before him in a low-neck, light-blue, button-down-the-front cotton dress with a matching belt pulled tight to accent her incredible body. His jaw dropped in awe. Her long, golden hair fell like a shining waterfall over her shoulders and framed her face and eyes. She was an angel come to earth. She smiled at his expression. "Hope you're hungry."

He stepped inside the door and pulled her close. "I get hungry just looking at you. You're incredible."

She backed away to allow him to enter. "Behave yourself. Dinner's waiting in the dining room."

She led him, not toward the kitchen, but turned left into a pleasant living room with an adjoining dining area. The table had an unlit chandelier above it and a lacy white tablecloth on it. Two place settings with utensils on folded maroon napkins adorned one corner of the table. Nearby sat a butter dish, a knife and a bottle of red wine and two bulbous glasses. A tall silver candlestick with three burning candles provided the light.

"Sit here." She patted the chair at the head of the table. "I'll bring dinner." She hurried to the kitchen and returned, carrying two large dinner plates holding sizzling brown sirloin steaks drowned in gravy, large baked potatoes split and buttered with a dash of sour cream and chives. For a vegetable, she had green beans fried in butter and a large French roll for bread. It was beautifully prepared and made him realize he was starving.

She sat a plate in front of Paul and another on his right. Then she eyed her handiwork and said, "Best I could do, I'm afraid. Hope you like it."

"I'm impressed. Did you graduate from a chef's school, too?"

"No.," she said, sitting beside him. "This I learned at the do-it-yourself school of hard knocks. For most of my life, I've been Dad's housekeeper and chief cook. As a kid without a mother, you learn all kinds of things. Care to pour?" She pointed to the wine bottle.

Paul rose and said, "My pleasure." He lifted the bottle, popped the cork and poured a splash of wine in his glass, which he then lifted and sipped. "Mmmm, excellent," he said. He rose and lifted the bottle. Grinning, he poured for both of them with the panache of an elegant French server. "Madam," he said. She laughed at his antics. He re-corked the bottle, sat and hoisted his glass, preparing to propose a toast.

"Wait," she said. "This is our first proper dinner. We have to do it right."

"I agree. May I?"

She nodded. "Please do."

He hoisted the glass again, met her gaze with a serious face and said, "To my morning sun and my evening hearth, I hereby offer my honor, my protection, and my love forever. And may our lives together have no room for bickering, apologies, heartbreaks, recrimination, only time for loving,"

"Wow," she said. "You are a romantic. I love it." They touched glasses and sipped. "That last sounds familiar.

"It should. It's a paraphrase from a Mark Twain letter to Clara Spaulding."

"You really enjoy his work, don't you?"

"Wisest, funniest and most practical man I've ever read."

"You're a man of interesting depths, Paul."

"So was he."

"We'd better eat before the steak gets cold," she said. "Wait, I forgot." She hopped up and hurried to the living room. Seconds later, she returned accompanied by soft dinner music coming from the living room.

The meal lasted an hour, but to Paul, it felt shorter than that. He spent half his time cutting steak and taking bites of food, and the other half watching her eyes sparkle in the candlelight. In his eyes, she was more elegant than a snow-white swan.

When they finished, he leaned back, satisfied beyond belief, and Sam said, "Paul, I'm sorry. I don't have a thing in the house for dessert."

He gazed at her. "Oh, yes, you do. I can't wait to try it."

"Behave," she said. "We have things to talk about. Go sit in the living room. I'll bring coffee."

He got up and held her chair while she stood. A push aimed him toward the living room, and she headed to the kitchen. She returned soon with two steaming cups on saucers. She placed them on the table in front of the sofa and sat beside him. He turned to embrace her, but she raised a hand to stop him.

"Paul, what happens if we fail? Have you thought about that?"

"Yes. You'll marry me. We'll rent a one-room shanty, raise a house full of noisy brats, and conquer the world together."

"Paul, I'm serious."

"Sorry." Her expression proved her words. "Look, I'm a good programmer, and once I solve the debt problem at the hospital, I'll have time to build my business. With the money I'm getting from Uncle Justin, I can set up a decent shop and hire some help. After that, I'll spend the rest of my life making you happy. How's that?"

"Sounds good, but don't forget the money Uncle Justin left me. When we get married, we can use that, too."

"Right, but I'd rather hold that in reserve," he said. He smiled. She had said when, not if. "Anyhow, I don't intend to fail. After what he did tonight, I'm more determined than ever to beat him. Sorry."

"Tonight?"

He hesitated, debating whether to tell her, but chose not to lie to her. He gave her the story, leaving nothing out.

When he finished, she asked, "But... but how can we fight that kind of power?"

"I'm working on that," he said. "We'll find a way. I won't walk away this time, though I think you should stay away and handle logistics."

"Forget that. I'm in. Just tell me what to do."

He tilted his head and smiled at her. "You're a stubborn girl, aren't you.?"

"About some things. This is one of them."

"Guess I'll have to get used to that, huh?"

"Yep."

"Okay, you can help, but if I yell, I want you to run like the devil is chasing you. Okay?"

"Agreed."

He paused. "Do you recall the note Uncle Justin attached to the news clipping about Talon?"

"Sure, why?"

"He said he ordered a GPR, remember?"

"Yes, but didn't understand it. What's a GPR?"

"It's short for a ground penetrating radar system. Yoshi found it with his phone. It's used for scanning the underground in search of whatever. People use them to find buried cables, sewers, fuel tanks, bodies, anything buried."

"Ghostly bones?"

"Right. Have you seen one anywhere on the estate?"

"No. Well, if I did, I didn't know it."

"It may resemble a lawn-mower frame with the radar attached. It wasn't in the garage."

"Did you check Dad's tool shed?"

"Not yet. I'll do that in the morning."

Paul's phone rang. Helena. He answered, punched in dictation mode and held it so Sam could see, too. "Helena, hi. Are you okay?"

A two-second delay, and then, "No. I'm afraid. I've been hiding all day."

"What happened?"

"Fortune has been lifting the heavy furniture and dropping it back. He's planning something.

"Can you guess what it is?"

"No."

"I'm sure he's practicing to harm you."

"You're right. I got a taste of his new power today."

"Did he hurt you?"

"No. He's powerful, but slow and clumsy. Do you need me at the library?"

" No. It's too dangerous, but I miss you. Is Samantha there?"

"This is Sam. Are you all right?"

"Yes. Just lonely."

"Maybe Paul can fix the computer so you can call me, too. That way we could girl talk."

"Oh, wow. That would be wonderful. I hope he can. Wait! He's coming. I have to go." She stopped typing. Paul hung up.

"Poor thing. I wish we could help her."

Paul pulled her to him and whispered, "I do, too, but right now, I feel sorry for me. Wasn't I supposed to get dessert?"

She gave him a long, loving kiss, and then tugged him to his feet. "Come on," she said. "I'll do the dishes in the morning."No, let's do them now. I want your mind only on me."

She did her silly curtsy and said, "In that case, follow me."

"Anywhere," he muttered.

FIFTY

ONCE AGAIN, the siren call of fresh-brewed coffee greeted
Paul as he finished dressing. Samantha was an early riser, he
thought. He hurried to the kitchen, eager to wrap her in his
arms once more before Yoshi arrived.

When he entered, she sat a cup on the breakfast table, turned
to him and whispered, "Thank you."

"For what?" He pulled her against him.

"For last night. I loved every second." She was back in jeans
and a subtle white blouse accented with swirls of navy blue.

"That makes two of us," he said, laughing. He tried to kiss
her, but she pushed him away.

"I love your one-track mind," she said, "but look at the clock.
Yoshi will be here soon. I'd better start breakfast."

"Sam, no. You're not here to be camp cook."

"Don't be silly. I enjoy cooking. Breakfast is my favorite
meal."

He nodded and took a sip of coffee just as his phone rang. He
answered, "Yoshi, where are you?"

"At the front gate behind a patrol car, one black car with two
guys in it, and a blue and white coroner's ambulance with two
men in front. Who are they?"

"The County Medical people. They're here to remove the skulls I told you about. I'll let you in. We're at the cottage."

"Can't wait."

Paul took a swig of coffee. The view of her working at the stove was irresistible. He rose and walked to stand behind her. He pulled her to him and said, "I love you, Sam."

She turned and gave him a quick peck. "I love you, too. Now go let Yoshi in. I'm busy."

Paul waited beside the work road. The patrol car stopped when they spotted him. Deputy Jackson and Gomez smiled through the window. Jackson was driving.

"Morning," Jackson said.

Paul shook hands. "You can park in front of the chateau. The basement door is still unlocked."

"Right. The M. E. Guys said we'll finish around ten o'clock. We'll give you another code 3 when we're leaving."

"Thanks. If you need anything, call me."

"Right. We better get to it."

Paul watched and nodded as they rolled past him and then waved Yoshi into a carport behind the cottage. When he climbed out of his car, Yoshi gave him a bear hug.

"Man, am I happy to see you," Paul told him, grabbing his suitcase. "Come on. Sam's making breakfast. I'll fill you in while we eat."

"Can't wait. I'm starving. How's Sam doing?"

"She's amazing, Yosh. Despite what her father did, she's determined to help us."

"Paul-san, I told you. You'd better marry that girl."

"Way ahead of you, Yosh. I asked her to marry me."

"What did she say?"

"She's thinking about it."

"Don't worry. She'll come around. You're a good man."

"Let's go eat."

Paul tugged his friend's arm and led him into the cottage, where they spent time bringing him up to date. But Yoshi was impatient. He wanted to put Mr. Moto's analytical powers to work on their problem. He dropped his gear in the living room and gulping a cup of coffee and listening to their story, he said, "Now Mr. Moto must see those coffins."

Soon Yoshi was on his hands and knees examining the busted pine coffin. After a moment, he stood and asked, "I wonder how much this thing weighs?"Yoshi was on his hands and knees examining the busted pine coffin. He stood and asked, "I wonder how much this thing weighs?"

"About sixty-five pounds," Samantha answered.

"How do you know?" Yoshi asked, surprised.

"I majored in trivia at school."+++"You did?"

She giggled. "No, I didn't go home for the holidays, so I read a lot of books. One of them was about burial practices in the old west. That's just a trivia that stuck with me. They ranged between fifty and eighty pounds, depending on the casket length and how wet the wood was."

"I told you she's amazing," Paul said, grinning. "Why do you ask?"

"Because I wonder about the Fortune's power. How long did you say it remained in the air?"

"Fifteen or twenty minutes. It flew up about thirty feet above this tree and it zoomed at me several times like a dive bomber. I hid behind that tree trunk. It followed me and stalked me. Weirdest thing I've ever witnessed. I saw Fortune standing under that oak over there. He didn't seem to get tired, if that's what you're getting at."

"How much do you weigh?"

"Two oh five last time I checked."

"Ah, so. Okay, we now have knowledge of his power's limit. Your weight plus this box's weight were beyond his capabilities. So..."

"What, Yoshi?" Sam asked.

"So, we now know his power has a limit. That might be handy to know. Will you show me the mysterious door now?"

"Sure, come on."

They walked back to the road and piled into the truck. Samantha offered to sit in the back, but Yoshi refused. "Beautiful woman must never ride in back. This is America."

They laughed and chatted during the drive around the work road to the mountainside door that went nowhere.

When they reached it, Sam waited on the road while Paul led Yoshi under the Junipers to examine the strange door. Paul showed him there was nothing behind it but mountain dirt.

They backed out and stood looking at the odd construction. "This is strange," Yoshi said, "Mr. Motto thinks this is not a joke or an accident. This man, Montmartre, was no fool. He would not build a door to nowhere that served no practical purpose. He built this for a reason. We must find out why."

"We can dig into the mountain with the backhoe," Paul suggested. "The ground here is pretty soft."

"Yes, but we need a plan first. May I examine the torture room you mentioned?"

"The medical examiner's people may still be at work. How about I introduce you to Helena?"

Yoshi beamed. "Even better, Paul-san. Do you think she will see us?"

"If I can reach her, she will. She's lonely and may propose to you."

"It's quite an experience," Sam added. "She's eighteen years old with a bagful of romantic notions, and according to Paul, she's beautiful."

"Horee sheeto. What are we waiting for? Let's go!"

FIFTY-ONE

THEY TIPTOED into the library, where Paul led them to the computer setup on his uncle's desk.

Yoshi and Sam examined the room. "Is she here?" Sam asked.

"Not yet. She hides when she senses danger. Maybe we should leave and try again later."

Helena jumped out of the bookcase that lined the wall behind the desk. She made an ugly face and mouthed, "Boo!"

"Helena, are you trying to give me a heart attack?"

She grinned.

"She's here?" Yoshi asked, wide-eyed.

"Yes."

"What did she say to you?"

Paul gave them an impish grin. "She said, 'Boo!'"

Samantha and Yoshi laughed.

Helena floated to the seat before the keyboard and typed. "Who is this handsome man with you?" She was smiling at Yoshi.

"Helena, this is my friend, Yoshi Kawasaki. He's here to help free you."

She typed, "Hello, Yohshee. Nice to meet you. Are you an

oriental? I met a Chinaman once."

Yoshi bowed. "Yes. I'm Japanese. Pleased to meet you."

She put her hand to her mouth to hide a giggle. "You're handsome. Are you married?"

"Not yet."

"Engaged?"

"Not yet."

"You should get married. You're a beautiful man."

Yoshi cackled and bowed low to her. "Thank you, ma'am. Paul says you're a beautiful girl."

"I'm not a girl. I'm a woman."

"So sorry. I meant to say woman."

"It's OK. I'm eighteen. Paul, will you turn the picture around so I can watch your faces while I type?"

"That won't work, Helena. If I do that, we can't read the screen."

"Oh, OK."

"Helena, we need information. What's Fortune up to?"

"He doesn't tell me anything. Right now, he's too busy to worry about me, but I'm scared. I know he's planning something. He scares me, which is why I was hiding."

"Do you know what he's doing?"

"No, but he acts tired. He worked hard yesterday, lifting heavy objects in the house."

"Yes, and trying to kill me."

"I'm sorry, Paul. He's evil."

"Helena, do you think lifting those heavy objects tired him?" Sam asked.

"Yes. I wish it would make him tired enough to die. He used to get tired after he punished me, but not anymore. He's much stronger now."

"Helena, I want to show Yoshi what Fortune did in the bedroom. Do you need anything before we go?"

"No, but… will you come back soon? I have no one else to talk to, and your machine makes talking fun."

"We'll try," Sam said. "Take care."

"OK. Bye." She disappeared.

Paul led them upstairs. At the top, a sudden notion struck him. He walked to the suits of armor. One was much taller than the other. He hit the tall one with his knuckle. It sounded hollow.

"What are you thinking?" Yoshi asked.

"That we might need these later on, if Fortune's attacks get too wild."

"You're kidding," Sam said.

"No, I'm not. You didn't see—oh, crap. Run!"

With Sam in the lead, they ran for the front door, and moments later, they were roaring around the work road.

Paul stopped alongside the tool shed.

"What was that all about?" Sam asked.

"Fortune was coming toward us."

"You scared me."

"Sorry. He scared me."

"Paul-san, are you sure we were talking to Helena?" Yoshi asked. "That was an incredible experience, if it was real."

"It's real, Yosh. She's an excellent typist."

"I'll say."

"We just lost another round, didn't we?" Sam said.

"Another round?" Yoshi looked puzzled.

"Paul says fighting Fortune is like a game of King of the Hill. We've learned that Fortune's telekinetic reach is pretty long, but his ghost body, if there is such a thing, has to stay close to the chateau."

"So, if we want to do battle, we have to go in after him."

"Hai, wakatte! That will be dangerous, though."

Paul chuckled. "No choice, Yosh."

Sam asked, "What now?"

"Let's see if we can find the GPR." He pointed to the tool shed. "I was in there yesterday, but I didn't see it."

"It's a big shed," Sam said. "It's so cluttered, it's easy to overlook things."

"We won't find it sitting here." Yoshi hopped out of the car and opened the door for Sam. He offered his hand to help her. She took it and smiled at Paul.

FIFTY-TWO

S AM FOUND the GPR after ten minutes of search. It sat hidden under a huge tarp in a back corner. "Hey, is this it?" she called, waving away a cloud of dust that swarmed like gnats in the light pouring in from windows on four sides of the shed.

They hurried to examine her find. "Sam, you did it," Yoshi said.

Paul knelt to examine the unit. The cart, labeled EasyRoll, had four large-diameter wheels. Sitting on the base of the cart, unattached, was the radar unit labeled SHERLOCK in large, bold letters. Paul stood up.

Attached to the lawnmower-type handle was a large, easy-to-read control panel. A user's manual and a brochure hung from a wire hook. He read the brochure cover. The title said SHERLOCK, Designed to Find Buried Evidence. Paul turned to Yoshi. "Let's take this to the pool house and study it in comfort."

"What about these?" Sam asked, pointing to two black poles standing in the corner behind the GPR. "They look like attachments for the GPR."

Paul rolled the cart out of the way to gain access to the corner. Then he examined the two handles. He lifted the SHERLOCK and estimated it weighed ten or twelve pounds. A plug-in battery

He flipped it over and examined the underside. He found two connections for quick release and to lock the unit into place. "You're right," he said. "This one with the wheel lets us pull the radar through narrow places, and this one seems to be a manual handle to lift it off the ground to scan vertical surfaces."

Paul handed the two pole units to Yoshi. "We'll walk," he said. "Sam, would you mind taking the truck? I'll pull the unit to see how it rolls."

Later, they returned to relax in the pool-house living room. Sam and Yoshi were leafing through the GPS color brochure while Paul studied the user's manual.

Paul tugged his earlobe and looked up at his friends. "This thing is easy enough to operate. It has digital buttons to set the depth you want to scan up to twenty feet and controls to set the dimensions of the grid you want to scan. You roll a crisscrossing grid to collect sufficient data. There's a button on the control panel to allow you to analyze the data in the field by showing a color rendering of the information. It has a way to email the scan results to other locations. Uncle Justin chose well."

"That won't be so hard then," Yoshi said.

"Yeah, but we still have to learn to recognize a buried skull when we find one. Otherwise, we could dig holes for nothing."

A brief wail came from the front gate.

"What was that?" Yoshi asked.

"Signal, the cops are leaving. They estimated a ten o'clock wrap up. Not bad. Only half an hour late."

"So, the basement is open now?"

"Yes."

"Good," Yoshi said.

"Paul, is it safe?"

"Probably, but there's a risk. If I see him first, we can run. If I don't, he could clobber us. Things changed last night. I was charger lay beside it.

He flipped it over and examined the underside. He found two connections for quick release and to lock the unit into place. "You're right," he said. "This one with the wheel lets us pull the radar through narrow places, and this one seems to be a manual handle to lift it off the ground to scan vertical surfaces."

Paul handed the two pole units to Yoshi. "We'll walk," he said. "Sam, would you mind taking the truck? I'll pull the unit to see how it rolls."

Later, they returned to relax in the pool-house living room. Sam and Yoshi were leafing through the GPS color brochure while Paul studied the user's manual.

Paul tugged his earlobe and looked up at his friends. "This thing is easy enough to operate. It has digital buttons to set the depth you want to scan up to twenty feet and controls to set the dimensions of the grid you want to scan. You roll a crisscrossing grid to collect sufficient data. There's a button on the control panel to allow you to analyze the data in the field by showing a color rendering of the information. It has a way to email the scan results to other locations. Uncle Justin chose well."

"That won't be so hard then," Yoshi said.

"Yeah, but we still have to learn to recognize a buried skull when we find one. Otherwise, we could dig holes for nothing."

A brief wail came from the front gate.

"What was that?" Yoshi asked.

"Signal, the cops are leaving. They estimated a ten o'clock wrap up. Not bad. Only half an hour late."

"So, the basement is open now?"

"Yes."

"Good," Yoshi said.

"Paul, is it safe?"

"Probably, but there's a risk. If I see him first, we can run. If I don't, he could clobber us. Things changed last night. I was lucky."

"Perhaps it would be better if you stay here," Yoshi said to Sam.

Sam frowned at Paul. "Don't even think about it," she warned.

"But…"

"No buts. You can be our ghost detector while I show the place to Yoshi."

"Good thinking," Yoshi said.

Paul gave Yoshi a helpless grin and shrugged. "Guess I'm outnumbered."

"Yep." Sam looked happy.

They spent half an hour in the torture room and dungeon, allowing Yoshi to walk around and ask questions. When he had seen enough, they returned to the pool house.

Now they were sitting with solemn faces in the living room.

"How can such evil exist?" Yoshi asked. "Thirty-six young girls tortured and imprisoned in chains. It's sickening."

"I agree, Yosh, but I always wonder why there aren't more like Fortune."

"I believe there are two reasons," Samantha said. "One is thousands of years of religion trying to tame humanity's worst instincts. The second is law enforcement that strikes fear into the hearts of evil men. Fear of death or imprisonment makes people behave better than they might otherwise."

"Those rules don't apply to everyone," Yoshi said. "Very wealthy men with power can always hide their evil. I've seen that in many places around the world, including Japan."

"Men like Fortune Montmartre," Paul added.

"Yes." Yoshi looked out past the pool. "We have to decide where to start the scan."

"I suggest we do what Sam's dad did when he cut the grass," Paul said. "Block it out and scan in sections."

"I think we should start at the trellis behind the house," Sam said. "And if that fails, move to the area under the big oak."

"Why, Samantha-san?"

"Because that's where my dad met Fortune at least twice. Those locations may have some significance."

"Sounds good," Paul said.

"Also, we could try the cemetery," Sam added. "I know that seems obvious, though."

"It's worth a try," Paul said.

"It's eleven-thirty now, and we have a plan," Yoshi said. "Let's go to lunch. After that, we can get underway. What say?"

"Wait. I want to recharge the battery while we're gone." He found an electrical outlet and plugged in the GPR battery for charging.

When he stood, Sam said, "I know a fast food place with great food."

Yoshi said, "I'll drive."

FIFTY-THREE

JAKE'S PLACE was a madhouse. They walked in the front door, and Paul groaned. The food smelled delicious, but they were out of luck. The place was packed with lunch-goers. They looked for a free booth. None were empty.

"Sorry," Samantha said. "Jake's business has boomed since I left."

"Jake?"

"A high school friend. We should go." She turned to leave, but a booming voice stopped her.

"Sam! Come on in."

Sam turned. A huge man with a giant belly covered by a greasy apron hurried toward them from behind the counter. When he reached them, he spread his arms wide and gave Sam a bear hug.

"Damn, girl. You're a sight for sore eyes. Where have you been all these years?"

"At school back east, Jake. Meet my friends Yoshi Kawasaki and my fiancé, Paul Davenport." She smiled.

Jake wiped his hands on the front of his apron and shook hands. To Paul, he said, "Fiancé, eh? Lucky guy."

"I agree," Paul said. Jake's eyes were working overtime,

checking out Sam.

"Jake, you seem to be full up," Sam said, "and we're in a hurry. Maybe we should come sometime when you're not so busy."

"Like hell!" He turned and yelled, "Hey, Rosie, set up number two for three." He grabbed Sam's arm and led them to a door at the end of the cafe. He ushered them in and, still staring at Sam, said, "This is for my special guests. God, you're even more gorgeous than when you were in highschool."

Paul grinned. "She's smart, too, Jake."

"Hey, don't I know it? She got straight A's all the way through school. Put all of us slobs to shame."

The room was for private dining. Rosie came in, smiling. She turned out to be a Chinese woman in her late twenties. "Don't listen to Jake. My name is Roseanne, but that's too hard for a big, dumb ox like him to remember. Please, have a seat."

Jake guffawed. "Sam, gentlemen, meet Rosie, my wife, and the love of my life."

"Congratulations, Jake. You needed someone to take you in hand," Sam said.

Rosie smiled and gave them place settings, utensils, and menus. "You said you're in a hurry, so I'll speed things up. What would you like to drink?" They all agreed on iced tea.

"Do you still offer delicious the fried-chicken plate with cornbread, mashed potatoes and gravy? I always loved that," Sam said.

"Sure, that's our specialty. People still like home cooking."

Paul and Yoshi agreed, and Rosie turned to Jake. "Stop ogling this lady and get going. They're in a hurry. Go get the drinks."

Minutes later, Jake came in with three tall glasses rattling with ice cubes. "Man, can you believe it? A murder-suicide right up here on Latigo Canyon Road. The reporter said they found thirty-six skeletons of little girls in a basement dungeon."

Paul cringed. "Which reporter?"

"Hell, some news guy. That's all they been talking about on TV. It's the craziest thing. I mean, really weird. Back with your chicken in a minute." He hurried away.

Paul envisioned a swarm of reporters waiting at the front gate on their return. "I have to call Huckabee," he said. He dialed the lawyer's number. Two rings later, the blond secretary answered.

"Lawyer Huckabee's office."

"Hi, this is Paul Davenport. I need to speak to Mr. Huckabee. This is important."

"I'll ring him, sir."

A click and the lawyer said, "Paul, good Lord! I just heard the news. It's incredible."

"That's why I called you, sir. I may need to hire guards to keep out the reporters. I want to know if what you called necessary expenses includes guards."

"Why the guards?"

"You saw how the reporters acted on Sunday. I wouldn't be able to work with them bugging the hell out of me."

The lawyer was silent for two breaths, then asked. "Do you think you can meet the terms of your uncle's will?"

"Yes, but not if I'm fighting off reporters."

"Guards, eh." He could almost hear the lawyer thinking. Then, "Okay, Paul. Send me the bills. I'll cover them."

"Thanks, sir. I'll do that."

Samantha handed over her phone. Paul put it to his ear. A woman answered, "Private security services."

Paul smiled. Sam had guessed what he wanted. "Yes, I want to hire six guards to work in three eight-hour shifts."

"May I ask your name, sir?"

"Paul Davenport."

"Where would you want the guards, sir?"

"It's a private estate four miles east of Malibu. I need one guard at the gate and another one to keep watch on the surrounding hills. Someone may try to go around the gate."

"When would you need them, sir?"

"As soon as possible. How soon can you have them there?"

"Why do you want them?"

"To keep out nosy reporters."

"I understand, sir. We do that often. How long will you need them?"

"Two weeks. They should bring stools, water, and brown bags for meals."

"So you don't have a guard shack?"

"No, sorry."

"No problem. We'll bring a portable one. What about restroom facilities?"

"Sorry. The caretaker's cottage is a long walk from the gate."

"We'll furnish that, too, the"Great. Looks like I called the right place."

"Hold, please." She came back. "All our men are bonded and experienced, Mr. Davenport. I can have two men there in an hour. They know what to do."

"Perfect. We'll see them there."

"Sir, what's the address?"

"That's a problem. I—hang on a second." Yoshi stuck his cell phone under Paul's nose and mouthed 'GPS coordinates.' Paul nodded and asked, "Can your guys use GPS coordinates to find it?"

"Yes, sir. We often do that to find mountain locations. Our rates are twenty-five dollars an hour per person. We require a week's payment in advance."

Paul's heart sank. His credit card was maxed out, and he only had two-thousand dollars in his wallet for emergencies. "Hang on a second," he said. Then he said, "Duh!" He had forgotten about the fifty-thousand dollars now sitting in his bank account. He lifted his phone. "Can you take a check?"

"Yes."

"Wait. Hang on."

Yoshi stuck his credit card under Paul's nose. "I'll pay them. You write me a check. Okay?"

Paul nodded and spoke to the woman. "My friend will pay you with his credit card. I'll repay him. Can we do it that way?"

"Fine, sir."

Paul handed the phone to Yoshi, and they watched while he gave his information to the woman. When he finished, he said, "Thank you, ma'am," and hung up.

"How much for the week?" Paul asked.

"Four thousand for the week, plus tax.

Paul smiled at his friends.

"Well, we're off to the races," he said. "Now let's go win."

FIFTY-FOUR

PAUL'S WORST FEARS became a reality when they returned to Montmartre. At the bend in the road leading to the front gate, Yoshi slammed on his brakes. Two TV mobile units and one bright-red Ford Escort blocked their way. Several men with video cameras and two thin female TV reporters turned to stare when Yoshi's brakes screeched.

"Damn!" Paul said.

"What do you want to do, Paul-san? We can get out of here."

"I'd like to, but it won't do any good. Like Sergeant Johnson said, this is a big story. I'll handle them this time." He turned to Sam. "What was that British writer's name who wrote about his six friends?"

"Six friends?" Yoshi's brows pinched in puzzlement.

"Rudyard Kipling," Sam explained. "He wrote, 'I keep six honest serving-men. They taught me all I knew; Their names are What and Why and When And How and Where and Who.'"

"That's it, Sam, perfect. Told you she's a genius, Yoshi."

"Yeah, and handy as a reference book, too. But I still don't understand."

"Simple, Yosh. I'm going to answer those six simple

questions and then order them to get the hell off my property."

"Not bad," Sam said.

Paul got out and walked toward the reporters. The cameramen aimed at him. The two reporters hurried toward him.

"Mr. Davenport, what—?"

"Please, stop," he ordered. "I'll answer six questions for you, and then I want you to leave."

"What questions?"

"One. Who did it? Answer. Mr. Gerard Duet, who was the groundskeeper for this estate for twenty years. Mr. Duet entered the basement of the Montmartre mansion and attempted to murder three people with an old army forty-five automatic. His intended victims were his daughter Samantha Duet, a professor of paranormal psychology, Dr. Mathias Sage, and myself. He shot his daughter in her shoulder and put two bullets into Mathias Sage. I struggled with him, knocking him to the ground. He turned the weapon on himself and shot himself. That answers the who, what, where and how of the matter."

One woman tried to butt in, but Paul stopped her. "Next question is, why did he do it? The answer is only he and God knows. His daughter, who has been away at school the last four years, says he became severely depressed after his long-time boss and my uncle Justin Davenport passed away. But that's speculation. When did it happen? Yesterday morning about ten-thirty A.M. Now I'd likeyou would get off this property."

"But what about the skeletons?" the youngest girl asked.

"They've been there since the eighteen nineties. Ask the police."

"Mr. Davenport, why are you here?" one of the two reporters blurted. "I thought you were broke."

"I was. An uncle unknown to me died recently and left the place to me. That's the story. No more questions."

The cameras kept targeting him.

Yoshi's horn sounded behind him. Two guards in khaki uniforms with patches on their shoulders and weapons on their hips came towards him. Both were Hispanic and looked as tough as his old marine buddies.

"I'm Juan and this is Roberto, sir. May we help you?" one of them asked, eyeing the reporters.

Paul shook with both of them. "I've just given these people all the information I have. Now I'm going to open the gates, so it would be nice if you can make sure they don't follow us inside." He turned back to face the cameras. "I'm sure you have better things besides wasting time here. This interview is over."

Paul called Yoshi's cell phone. "Yosh, come on forward. I'll open the gates. The vans are leaving now."

"You can't treat us this way," a woman said.

"What way? I've given you all the details."

"But—,"

"Sorry. There's nothing else to say."

The girl looked angry, but turned and said, "Okay, that's it."

Paul punched the remote and led the guards to the gate. He walked through and told them, "Nobody in unless I say so. I'm paying for privacy. Once they're gone, you can set up inside the gate and have a picnic. Weren't you going to bring a guard shack and a Porta Potty?"

"They'll be here soon," the one called Roberto said. "I think we'll set up outside the gate. Plenty of room here."

"Sounds good." He handed Roberto his gate remote. "You'll need this. You know how it works?"

"We'll figure it out, sir."

"Don't worry, sir. We've got you covered," Juan added.

"I believe you. You have my number?"

"No."

Paul gave it to them and said, "Call me if if I get visitors."

"You got it."

Paul nodded his satisfaction. The guards were competent. Yoshi stopped to pick up Paul, and they drove to the pool house.

All was going well, except for his primary problem. How to kill a ghost with telekinetic powers.

FIFTY-FIVE

AFTER PULLING THE GPR from the truck to the trellis, Paul dropped to his knees under the arch to connect the battery, the ground radar unit, and the external GPS. The GPS would tell him his exact location at any time during his scan.

Above him, early blooming wisteria hung like clusters of grapes from all sides of the trellis. The Wisteria's perfume, concentrated as it was under the trellis, was almost dizzying. Honeysuckle has always been his favorite flower to smell, but now he was having doubts. In his book, these gorgeous purple flowers were in the running for number one.

A gentle tap on his shoulder caused him to look up. Yoshi and Samantha stood over him. A pair of binoculars hung around Sam's neck. He stood.

"You told me to bring these," she said in a puzzled tone. "Now tell me what to do with them?"

"Well, you agreed to be our lookout and lookouts need binoculars, don't they?"

"But what am I looking for? No Indians around here. I checked. And I know I can't see ghosts. So…"

"So, you're our long-distance early warning system of unidentified flying objects."

"You mean like coffins?"

"Yes, or bricks or rocks or pieces of wood. I'm more worried about flying bricks, though. We left a pile of them in the basement. If he finds them, he might decide to use them as ammo. The binoculars will help if you need a closer view."

"You think he will attack?"

"Yes, I'm positive. I made him angry yesterday."

"How can you tell?"

"I don't know. Maybe it was the way he crashed the coffin into the ground. It seemed to be a temper fit."

"Where do you want me to set up your Norad system?" Sam asked.

Paul nodded in appreciation. She was a walking-talking encyclopedia of information. How many young women knew that acronym? "Under the big oak," he said. "Fortune had trouble moving the coffin around the tree trunk fast enough to do any damage with it. It was easy to dodge. But bricks and rocks are small and heavy enough to kill us if they hit us. He hit me in the head with that vase the other night."

"Good plan, Paul-san," Yoshi said. "We need as much warning as possible. What do you want me to do?"

"Thanks. Right now, stand lookout with Sam while I scan this area. If I find something, I'll yell, and we can move to the next step."

"You mean the tractor?"

"Yes. I'm pretty sure Fortune's attack will come from somewhere around the chateau, so I would concentrate your lookout on the house."

Sam touched his arm. "You don't have any protection. I don't like it."

"I don't either, which is why I need good lookouts. Just yell if you see anything coming at me, and I'll duck."

"Don't worry. I'll scream my head off."

He smiled over her shoulder at Yoshi. Yoshi beamed his approval. "Sounds perfect. Now I suggest we get this done."

Paul watched until Sam and Yoshi reached the big oak and took up their positions. Then he turned back to the GPR and studied the control panel. The manual had said the grid setting was best for forensic uses, such as scanning for buried corpses, weapons and other evidence.

He eyed the ground under the trellis. About four feet wide. Too narrow for a crisscross scan. He set the grid width to match.

Next, he set the resolution and depth of the scan. The manual said the higher the resolution, the less depth he could get, but it would yield more detail. Which was fine, he thought. He doubted Talon Montmartre would have buried Helena and Fortune over three or four feet.

He set the scan depth to four feet at maximum resolution and began rolling the unit back and forth under the trellis, overlapping the ground the way he did when he mowed his neighbor's lawn as a kid.

Next, he backed out and ran the scanner in a diagonal patter over the area. Satisfied he could do no better, he touched a button on the control panel to bring up a colored 3-D display of the area within the grid. It showed no objects resembling a skeleton. Only a few bright red spots surrounded by yellow-orange auras. He was certain they were small rocks buried in the soil.

Paul pushed the cart over to where Sam and Yoshi were under the tree.

"I need some pegs or flags to mark our areas for scanning," he said when he reached them. "Too much area to eyeball it."

"What did you see under the trellis?" Sam asked, peering at the GPR control panel.

Paul turned on the unit and showed them the 3-D display. "I set the scan for a depth of four feet," he said. "Those bright red dots are down about two feet."

"What are they?"

"My guess is small rocks and pebbles."

"So, what's next?" Yoshi asked.

"I think I saw some flags at Home Depot once," Sam

volunteered. "I visited their garden center with my dad."

"Good idea," Paul said. "How far is it?"

Yoshi checked his phone. "About five miles. They're called irrigation flags. They're multicolored and fifteen inches tall." He looked up from his phone. "They have them in stock. How many do you need?"

"Your guess is as good as mine, Yosh. How much are they?"

"They'll bankrupt you. Couple of bucks per bundle. Fifteen flags in a bundle. I suggest we buy them out."

Paul chuckled at his friend's exuberance. "I like it. Let's go."

"No, no, Paul-san. I'll go. You stay here and read the manual some more. I'll be back in forty-five minutes."

They walked back to the pool house with Paul pushing the GPR. Sam put her hand on the handle, too, just close enough to touch him.

Yoshi went to his car. Paul pushed the GPR into the living room.

They sat on the sofa. He tugged Sam's hand and said, "Yoshi's not here. We had a deal, didn't we?"

"Yes, I believe we did." She leaned in and kissed him.

FIFTY-SIX

PAUL COMPLETED the twentieth crisscrossing grid with the GPR near the big oak and stopped. He wiped his forehead on his arm. Colored flags rose from the green lawn, waving in a gentle breeze like a happy crowd, causing his recent search area to resemble a miniature medieval jousting field.

But the flags didn't represent celebration. Rather, they showed off his failures. Twenty four-foot by four-foot scans had yielded nothing but lots of small pebbles. He sighed and, without hope, hit the 3D button.

Yoshi stood beside him, holding even more flags. "What's wrong, Paul-san?"

"We won't find them this way, Yosh." He waved at the small field of flags. He swept his arm around the Montmartre estate. "Look at the size of this place. It's impossible in the time we have."

Yoshi grinned. "Ganbatte, Paul-san. It's the way of the world. One minute, things are calm. The next a tornado strikes. Remember what Thomas Edison said about failing?"

Paul smiled at his friend. "Yeah, I remember. He said after a thousand failed attempts, he was now a thousand materials closer to finding the right one. But Edison didn't have eleven days left to find it."

"Go on. Push the button. This may be the one. The display shows something down there."

Paul looked over at Samantha, who stood under the tree watching the chateau. A powerful urge demanded he quit this insane undertaking and take Sam some place safe. He touched the 3-D button and his pulse sped up a notch. The screen showed something big and long under his feet. One piece was about the size of a large skull. The longer piece was below it on the screen, as a body might be.

"What do you think?" Paul stepped aside.

Yoshi bent over the display and frowned. "It could be bones," he said, "but we must examine it. How deep is it?"

Paul tapped a button. "Three feet."

"That's shallow enough to dig with a shovel," Yoshi said. "And the ground here is soft."

"No. Let's get the tractor. We have to learn to use it. This will be a good way to do that."

Yoshi did a quick Japanese bow.

Paul marked the spot with six flags, and then, with Paul pushing the GPR, they all walked together back to the pool house.

"You think you found something?" Sam asked as they walked.

"Maybe, Sam-san. It could be a skull and bones or a couple of big rocks."

"We're going for the backhoe to dig it up," Paul said. "I suggest you get a folding chair to sit on. This could take a while."

Sam nodded and headed for the pool house.

Forty-five minutes later, with Paul driving the tractor, they cut across the lawn from the garage to the big oak. Samantha sat on the backhoe seat holding a canvas folding chair while Yoshi walked alongside. They stopped at the tree to allow Samantha to take up her lookout and then drove to the spot Paul had marked with flags.

Paul maneuvered the tractor until the backhoe shovel hovered over the dig site. Then he hopped off.

"You drive, Yosh. I'll dig," he said. "It'll be faster with the two of us."

"Drive where, Paul-san?" Yoshi asked, puzzled.

"Nowhere. The way it works is I dig and dump the dirt off to one side. When I've finished one place, you back the tractor a few inches, and I'll dig more."

"Ah, so," Yoshi said. "I've never done this before."

"That makes two of us. Get on and try maneuvering back and forth a bit. It's easy."

It took half an hour for them to develop a rhythm, and get the feel of working the backhoe bucket. His heart did a tympanic thump when he heard a clank under the bucket. Working with care, he cleared away most of the dirt.

"Back up a few feet, Yosh," he said.

Yoshi obeyed, and Paul jumped into the trench he had dug and dropped to his knees.

With his adrenaline pumping, he brushed dirt from the top of what he hoped was a skull. "Damn!" he said. Just a large stone. "Damn, damn!" More wasted time.

"Eeyai! Help!" Yoshi's terrified scream shattered the afternoon stillness.

Paul jerked upright. "Son of a—!" Yoshi was hanging on the tractor steering wheel with one hand while his feet pointed skyward at a forty-five degree angle. His legs were pumping like those of a drowning swimmer. His eyes, popping out, stared in fear at Paul. Wild panic showed on face.

Fortune!

"Hang on!" Paul scrambled out of the trench and onto the tractor. Yoshi's grip on the wheel let go at that instant. He rose upside down toward the heavens. His face pleaded with Paul. In desperation, Paul dove upward toward his friend. Yoshi reached toward him, and they locked hands like two trapeze performers. Their combined weight was too much for Fortune, and Paul sank feet-first to the ground.

Yoshi, his feet continuing to point into the air, grinned at Paul. "Velly intellesting, Paul-san," he said. Blood draining into his head caused his eyes to bulge. Paul didn't return the grin. His thoughts flew as he tried to figure a way to get Yoshi to the ground.

Samantha appeared in a flash beside him and jumped up to grab Yoshi's right leg. That did it. Fortune released all upward pressure on Yoshi, allowing to drop like a bag of wet cement. Paul caught him under the shoulders and held him until he regained his balance. Then he said, "Let's hold hands. He can't lift us all." As he suspected, he spotted Fortune's reddish aura floating next to the stone planter.

"Fortune, you go to hell!" he shouted. If his anger had been a mortar shell, Montmartre would have exploded into oblivion. Instead, the aura vanished. Samantha and Yoshi followed Paul's gaze. Seething, Paul turned back. He had almost got his best friend killed.

"It was Fortune," he said. "I saw him floating near that stone planter. I think he's done with us for now. Are you okay?"

"I'm fine, Paul-san."

Paul frowned and shook his head.

"What is it?" Sam asked.

"This changes everything. We're no longer safe from him in the open air."

"Paul-san, I'm sorry. He caught me by surprise."

"I can believe that! Make sure you're both holding tight onto something. He may not be gone. He may be trying to get us to lower our guard."

"How can we fight that kind of power?" Samantha asked in a worried tone.

"Good question, but no answer yet. I have to think." Scowling, Paul continued to stare at the old stone well.

"He is very powerful, Samantha-san. I could not hold on. I wish to thank you both for saving me."

Paul turned to Samantha. "Yeah. Thanks."

She patted Yoshi's cheek. "My pleasure. Can't afford to lose out, best friend."

Yoshi, having regained his composure, grinned.

Paul climbed onto the backhoe seat, lifted the bucket, and raised the stabilizers so they could move the tractor. "Let's go," he said. "Damnation!"

Yoshi hopped onto the tractor. Samantha climbed on, too, and held onto the back of the seat. Yoshi shifted into reverse and headed for the parking lot behind the pool house.

"Come on, Yosh. You're driving like a little old lady. Step on it." His heart pounded like war drums in his ears, and his body trembled from the seething anger threatening to consume him.

"Hai." Yoshi pushed the throttle all the way forward.

Paul's thoughts raced furiously as they bounced over the lawn. Fortune had tried to kill his best friend, and he would keep trying until either he succeeded with one or all of them, or they beat him. But beating the ghost seemed impossible.

A dark cloud of shame again engulfed Paul. He had failed to help his mother. Ditto his father, and now he had endangered his best friend and the woman he loved. So, what was the solution?

A sinking feeling in his stomach gave him the answer, one he didn't want to face. There was no solution. You can't kill something that's already dead. A low growl rumbled in his throat. He should forget the money and drop the entire business. She was as beautiful as an angel silhouetted against the afternoon sky. He clenched his fists. He would never allow that evil bastard to harm her. In that instant, he decided on the only safe course.

"Paul, are you all right?" Sam asked.

"I'm fine." His face was rigid, frozen into a frown. To Yoshi, he said: "Park in back. I'll wait for you in the living room."

FIFTY-SEVEN

HE REACHED the pool house before them and sat waiting in the over-stuffed easy chair. They came in, sat on the sofa and watched him with worried expressions.

He took a deep breath, held it, and then said in a blunt tone, "I've changed our plans. From now on, I will work alon"Paul-san, why? I don't understand." Yoshi exchanged glances with Sam.

"Paul, why?" Sam said. "You need us. You can't do it alone."

He refused to meet her gaze. "Because Fortune tried to kill Yoshi and you might be next. That's not acceptable. There's no telling where that bastard might try. I—." He stopped himself. They deserved the truth, not some made-up excuse. "Look, my uncle's money doesn't mean enough to me to risk your lives. I won't do it."

"Paul-san, wait, please," Yoshi blurted. "I have an idea. What if—?"

Paul's phone rang. He lifted a hand to shush Yoshi. "Davenport." It was Roberto, the gate guard.

"Mr. Davenport, you have a visitor."

"Reporter?"

"No, sir. A man named John Franklin. Says he received a

letter from Justin Davenport."

"Hang on a second." Paul turned to his friends. "Does the name John Franklin ring a bell?"

Yoshi shook his head no. Sam said, "The reporter who wrote that newspaper story about Talon. His name was Franklin, I believe."

"Damn, you're right." Paul's heart leapt.

Yoshi grinned at Sam in admiration while Paul dug the clipping and the letter from his wallet. At the top of the clipping it said 'by Carter Franklin.' He spoke to Roberto, "Roberto, ask him if he knows the name Carter Franklin."

"Yes, sir. Hold on." Paul heard a muffled discussion. Then Roberto said, "Sir, he says that was his great grandfather. He says he has information for Justin Davenport."

"Is he driving?"

"Yes, sir. A VW bus… I think."

"Great. Let him in. Tell him to take the work road. We're at the pool house. I'll wait for him outside."

"Uh, sir, are you sure?"

"Of course. Why wouldn't I be?"

The guard's voice became a whisper. "Well, he's kind of different, sir."

"Different how? Never mind. He may have information I need. Send him on."

"Consider it done, sir."

"Carter Franklin's great grandson," he told his friends. He has a letter from my uncle. "Let's go out to meet him. Maybe our luck has turned."

Some of the heaviness lifted from his heart.

John Franklin arrived at the pool house belching black smoke and banging out a variety of noisy backfires. Tying the noise together was a musical variety of squeaks and rattles emanating from a Volkswagen hippie bus covered with yellow flowers.

Yoshi's eyes widened when he saw the antique old wagon. "Wow!" he said.

Samantha giggled as the old bus pulled in beside Paul's truck. The bus's engine popped and clattered as it dieseled to a stop. When it did, a man three inches taller than Paul and skinny enough to disappear if he turned sideways, climbed out and grinned at them through a thick black beard. His long black hair was an unruly mess. Paul waved hello.

John Franklin ambled toward them like a tall giraffe, grinning broadly as he came. He raised thick eyebrows in surprise when he met Sam's smiling blue eyes. She offered her hand and said, "Samantha Duet, Mr. Franklin. Welcome."

Yoshi nodded and said, "Yoshi Kawasaki." Paul smiled. His friend's head was tilted far back to meet Franklin's eyes. Franklin nodded and turned to Paul.

"By a process of elimination, I'd say you're Mr. Justin Davenport," Franklin said. He stuck out a giant's hand to shake with Paul. It swallowed Paul's.

Paul smiled. "Well, you're close. Justin Davenport was my uncle, now deceased. I'm Paul Davenport. Come on in."

Paul led the way to the pool-house. "Take a seat. We're eager to see what you brought."

John Franklin searched the room for a place to sit, then chose the easy chair and lowered his lanky body into it. "Hope you don't mind, but them sofas are so damn low I almost can't get up." His teeth were straight and clean, and his smile was engaging.

Paul grinned. He liked this guy. "I have that problem myself sometimes, though not to the extent you have. How tall are you?"

"Reckon I used to be six-eight. Haven't measured in a while, though."

"I like your car," Sam said.

"You got weird tastes, ma'am. And it ain't my car. It's my house. I've been living in it more'n a year. I don't have enough bread to buy another one. Got that piece of junk from a guy in Denver. He paid me fifty bucks to take it away."

Paul noticed that the man's clothes were clean, but ragged at the edges. "Would you like something to drink?"

"I like white wine, if you got any."

"I'll get it," Sam volunteered. "Anybody else?"

Paul and Yoshi shook their heads. Sam hopped up and headed for the kitchen. A minute later, she returned with a tall water glass half full of white wine. She handed it to John Franklin and returned to her seat. Franklin's eyes watched her every movement.

"Thank you, ma'am. I was kind of thirsty." He took a sip and smiled.

"Do you have my uncle's letter?"

"Yep, right here" John Franklin pulled a letter out of the Manila envelope. "But…"

"What?"

"Mr. Davenport, uh, your uncle mentioned he might pay a reward for any information my dad had. My dad died six months ago, and I found this stuff in his desk drawer. Been hauling it around ever since."

Paul eyed the man. "Did you read the information you brought?"

"Hell, yeah."

"So what do you think it's worth?"

Franklin hesitated and blushed. "Uh, I don't rightly know. It's some pretty weird stuff."

"Weird how?"

"About ghosts and stuff. Weird."

Paul nodded. "I see. Tell you what, John. Let me read it. If it helps me, I'll give you fifteen hundred dollars. If it's not helpful, I'll give you five hundred for your trouble. How's that?"

Shocked, the man stood as if to leave, then dropped back, grinning. "Hell, that'll be great. Really great." He handed the letter and the manila envelope to Paul.

"Thanks, John. Enjoy your wine while I read. Okay?" "Hell, yeah." He took a big gulp of wine.

Sam took off and brought back a tray of crackers and cheese.

She sat the tray and the rest of the wine on a table next to John Franklin. He smiled his gratitude and grabbed up a handful of crackers and cheese.

Samantha sat close to Paul and peered over his shoulder as he read.

Paul ignored the others and read his uncle's letter, which also included a clip from The Cripple Creek Beaver. Written in the same neat penmanship as Justin's previous notes, the date on the letter was nine months earlier. It letter said:

> *Dear Mr. Franklin,*
>
> *I recently hired a private detective to locate any living relatives of Carter Franklin, the reporter who wrote the enclosed news story. He reported your great grandfather was the author. Therefore, I am writing to you with a request.*
>
> *If you have any additional information about the contents of the above news story, I would pay handsomely to get it.*
>
> *If I don't hear from you, I shall presume you have no further information.*
>
> *Thanks in advance for any help you might offer.*
>
> *Yours truly,*
>
> *Justin Davenport.*

Paul looked up. The letter was brief and to the point. His uncle had tried this approach as a last resort. Paul doubted he expected anything to come of it. He passed the letter to Sam.

"Already read it," she whispered. She passed it on to Yoshi.

John Franklin hungrily munched crackers and cheese and sipped wine while Paul pulled four typewritten pages from the manila envelope and began reading.

FIFTY-EIGHT

PAUL INHALED a deep breath. Hope rose in him when he read the first lines. A scribbled note at the top of the page said:

"Original story turned in to the editor of The Cripple Creek Beaver. He slashed the story, saying he didn't want such unholy claptrap in his newspaper."

Paul held the typewritten pages with trembling fingers and began reading.

New Lead In Montmartre Murders

By Carter Franklin

Cripple Creek, Colorado—This reporter happened upon information that may lead to solving the infamous murders of California's Fortune Montmartre and his beautiful young wife, Helena. I learned that a dying man named Talon Montmartre was in a local hospice run by Benedictine Nuns near Cripple Creek.

On his deathbed, he asked to speak to a reporter. Since I knew of the stories and notoriety of the Montmartre Murders, your intrepid reporter rushed to the hospice posthaste. There, I found the man, shrunken from debauchery, pale and toothless. He opened his eyes upon my arrival. Following is a summary of the things he reported.

"I am the son of Fortune Montmartre," he said. "I want to tell you the truth. My father was an evil man. In San Francisco, he belonged to a cult of devil worshipers who kidnapped, abused, raped and murdered young women from the lower classes. The police learned of the cult and broke it up. My father left San Francisco and moved to Malibu, California. Later, he kidnapped and forced Helena Longmore, a beautiful sixteen-year-old girl, to marry him. Helena and I fell in love. My father found us together and murdered my Helena. He tried to murder me, but I fought him off and strangled him instead."

This reporter then asked several more questions.

Question: Have you forgiven him?

Answer: You must be joking. I hate him so much that when I die, I will not move on to heaven or hell. I will stay here and wait forever to meet and destroy him.

Question: You mean you will become a ghost?

Answer: Yes. Why not? He did. I had to leave our home in Malibu. If I had not, he would have killed me.

Question: You mean his ghost would have killed you? You think ghosts are real?

Answer: (weak laugh) He's real alright. He's still alive at the mansion.

Question: Mr. Montmartre, where did you hide your father's and his wife's bones? People speculated about that for years.

Answer: Sorry, I won't say, but I'll tell you one thing. The man opened his eyes one last time and smiled at me. "I left an upside down clue on the estate," he said. "It's there to tell anyone who finds the bodies which grave is which. I also wrote a poem about it, and I'm proud of it.

He then whispered the poem to me:

My father worshiped the Devil as a god.

He raped and tortured young girls as well.
He murdered my beloved and tried to kill me,
But I buried his bones at the door to hell.

Startled, Paul looked up. The door to hell? Was he talking about their door? What else could it be? Heart pounding in anticipation, he returned to the manuscript.

Question, sir: At the door to hell? What does that mean?
Answer: You figure it out. I'm tired and have to sleep now.
Question: May I visit you again tomorrow?
Answer: Sure, if I'm still here.
Your reporter visited him the next day. He was weaker yet, near to death, the nurse reported. On my second visit, I asked. "What have you been doing all these years, sir?"
Answer: "I'm a brick mason. I drifted around. Worked when I needed money. Mostly doing nothing."
"Sir, do you regret anything you've done or left undone in your life?"
Answer: "Yes, I regret I left my father to haunt Chateau Montmartre and to torture my Helena. I pray that when I'm gone, I will meet him on the other side and destroy him."
He closed his eyes.
I said, "Sir, thank you for sharing your story with me.
He opened his eyes one last time and smiled at me. Then he closed his eyes and died.
This reporter attended his less-than-auspicious funeral and burial. And that ended this story.
Note: unlike the abbreviated report published by the editor, this is a full and true account of the death of Talon Montmartre. May he rest in peace.

Addendum: Years later, I revisited the cemetery where Mr. Montmartre was buried. The hospice had fallen into decay, but the cemetery remained. While there, I heard many stories claiming the cemetery was haunted. The locals were afraid to go near the place, claiming that an angry ghost lived there and occasionally frightened passersby. I surmised that Talon Montmartre got his wish and awaits there, hoping to exact revenge on his father. A very strange story indeed.

Paul passed the last page to Samantha and sat mulling what he'd read. Buried his bones at the door to hell. Was he referring to the door behind the Juniper trees? It had to be. No other interpretation made sense.

He sat back and tried to imagine how, working alone, he might tackle the problem of excavating that part of the mountain. He sighed. It wouldn't be easy.

John Franklin coughed. Paul blinked and looked toward the man. Franklin grinned. "Pretty interesting shit, huh?"

"That's an understatement, John." He turned to Sam and Yoshi. "What do you think?"

"I think our search is over," Yoshi said.

Sam nodded. "I agree."

"The poem, right?"

They both concurred. Paul turned to Franklin. "I offered fifteen hundred, didn't I?"

Franklin nodded. "Yeah, you sure did. So, it's good, huh?" He gulped the rest of his third glass of wine and wiped his matted chin beard.

"That remains to be seen, John, but it seems so. We have our fingers crossed. Hang on. I'll get your money." Paul stood and went upstairs to his get his wallet.

They watched and waved as Franklin's VW banged alive and pulled away. Then they returned to the pool-house where they sat sipping white wine from a fresh bottle. Paul was in the easy chair while Sam and Yoshi sat on the sofa watching him. His thoughts were back on the problem of excavation.

"Paul, what's going on?" asked

"Nothing. Just thinking."

"About what?" Yoshi asked.

"Different ways one man could excavate the door to hell."

"Forget it. There are none, and we won't let you try. I figured out a way to solve our problem. Will you listen?"

"I always listen to my best friend. Shoot."

Yoshi grinned. "Good. We know Fortune isn't strong enough to lift you, so you're no worry. We know he can lift me and probably Samantha as well, so why can't we tie ropes around our waists and anchor ourselves to something heavy? If he tries to lift us, he won't get far. We'll yell and you can come to our rescue. Also, we can wear hardhats in case he throws stuff at us."

Yoshi sat back, grinning. "Well?"

Paul laughed. "Sounds pretty high tech to me. That should work, though I'm not sure about the hard hats stopping bricks."

"I'd still be on lookout duty," Sam said. "Yoshi's idea will work. Five days are gone already. This is our last chance to succeed. Please."

Paul checked his watch. Four-thirty. Too late to do more today. "Okay, how can I argue? You guys are tough."

"Great," Yoshi said. "We'll go to Home Depot for the equipment. Then we'll grab a meal on the ocean and come home to rest."

"Love it." Sam hurried to Paul and whispered, "And you." She planted a soft kiss on his cheek.

"I'm driving." Yoshi grinned at Paul and headed outside.

FIFTY-NINE

BACK IN THE COTTAGE living room after a successful shopping sortie at Home Depot and a wonderful dinner of steak, lobster and red wine at one of Malibu's famous ocean side restaurants, the friends sat relaxing the peace only good food and good company can bring. At their feet lay a long coil of soft white rope, topped with three white hard hats.

Yoshi, occupying the stuffed chair, said, "I'm ready to burst. I'll never eat again. That lobster was as big as me."

Sam giggled, bent down and lifted one of the hard hats and placed it on her head at a rakish angle. "These should do nicely, don't you think?" She banged the top of her head with her knuckles to illustrate her point.

Yoshi grinned, but didn't answer her. Instead, he fired a slurred question at Paul. "Have you decided what you're going to do with all your uncle's money? Start a business, take a long vacation?"

Paul smiled. His friend had drunk a bit more than his liver could filter. "I don't have it yet, Yosh. Sam giggled at his

"Shimpai shinai, Paul-san. Mr. Moto says that dirty obake will soon be dead."

"What's an obake?"

Yoshi grinned through sleepy eyes. "Japanese for ghost."

Sam giggled. "He's already dead, Yoshi."

"Not enough." Yoshi stood. "It's been a long day. I'd better turn in."

"You're in the guest room just off the foyer," Sam said. "Paul's in my dad's room? Shall I show you where it is?"

"Nope." He rose and bowed to them. "I'll find it." He left them and went into the foyer to find the bedroom.

"He must be exhausted," Sam said, leaning into Paul's arms.

"Yeah, it's a five-hour flight from New York, and he got here early."

"What did you tell him about us?"

Paul playfully tugged her earlobe. "That I asked you to marry me, but you're not sure marrying a pauper is a good idea."

She sat up and punched his arm. "You did not. What did you tell him?"

"You really want to know?"

"Yes."

"I told him you're playing hard to get and that before you agree, you want a bigger share of my uncle's estate." He grinned.

"You liar."

"Well, what should I have told him?"

Her face became serious as she leaned in for a quick kiss.

"I don't think I can tell him that?"

She snickered. "You better not."

"So, what should I have said?"

Her eyes sparkled. "That the next time you ask me, I'll say yes."

She jumped up and ran, laughing, up the stairs.

Paul scrambled after her. When he caught up with her, she was standing in her bedroom door, smiling.

"What took you so long?"

He caught both her shoulders in his hands. "Did you mean that?"

"Yes."

"You sure?"

"Yes."

"When did you decide?"

"I think it was when I read Uncle Justin's letter. It took me a while to realize it."

"So, it's not just pheromones?"

"Does it matter,?" She tip-toed and whispered in his ear, "I do love you, Paul. I'm astonished by it, but it's true. I... we seem to belong together, but everything is so..."

"Crazy?"

"Yes."

"I'll ditto that."

He cradled her in his arms. "Maybe I should stay in your room with you," he said. "Never know what dirty tricks our nasty ghost has up his sleeve."

She pushed away. "Oh, no, you don't. Not with Yoshi downstairs. Besides, you come up with a creative way to propose."

"How creative?"

"Very. Memorable." Giggling, she entered the bedroom and closed the door.

Paul stood astonished, incredulous. *She said she will.*

His hope jumped up two notches as he realized the enormity of her decision. He would be her husband, she, his wife. He would no longer be alone. They would be a family to love and cherish 'til death did them part. He trembled, resisting the urge to pound on the door. He wished his mother was still alive so he could tell her about Sam. She was beautiful, intelligent, helpful, cheerful, brave and loving, everything he could ever hope for, the perfect partner for life.

He turned away from the door and to Gerard Duet's bedroom. "Find a good woman," his mother had said. Well, he had done that and more. He had found the best.

Now he needed a memorable way to ask for her hand. What the hell did that mean?

SIXTY

SAMANTHA BLINKED TWICE. For a moment, only blackness engulfed her. Then her vision cleared, and she recognized the shapes of familiar objects in her bedroom. She turned toward the bedside table. The light green glow of the digital clock winked the time at her. 10:30. Something woke her. She sat up. A light breeze brushed her face, causing her to shiver. She squinted to see across the room at the balcony doors. Open. She frowned. They had been closed when she went to bed an hour earlier.

Puzzled, she swung her bare feet off the bed and tiptoed to the balcony to see whether Paul was there.. She stopped at the threshold and peeked outside. The balcony was empty. Puzzled, she touched the nearest door. What had opened them?

She stepped out onto the balcony to investigate and what felt like a giant hand grabbed her and sent her soaring into the night sky. She screamed. Her rate of climb sucked her stomach toward the ground as when rising in a high-speed elevator. Ahead of her, the stars winked a brilliant hello, and the moon smiled a giant welcome. The chilly night air sliced through her pajamas like a knife made of ice. Panic gripped her, but she quelled it as she realized what was happening. Fortune Montmartre had somehow awakened her and enticed her onto the balcony. The realization helped only a little, but understanding brought rational thought. What could she do about it?

She twisted her body to peer down at the cottage, where a weak yellow light glowed in her bedroom. As she watched, her dad's bedroom lit up. Her scream had awakened Paul. Her heart leapt when he rushed onto the balcony outside her bedroom. Dressed in khaki boxer shorts, his head swiveled every which way, searching for her except up. The cottage continued to shrink at an incredible rat"Paul, help!" She screamed as loud as her lungs and throat would allow. "Help!" She wriggled her feet like an underwater swimmer, fighting to control her motion, but to no avail. Paul's shadow figure craned its neck upward toward her and waved. He saw her. Why wouldn't he? Her black silhouette would be as visible against the moon as a witch on a broomstick. The idea caused her to compose herself. He would find her.

"Sam, hang on. I'm coming," Paul screamed. She didn't know how he would come to her, but her heart told her he would find a way. She grew calm despite her fear.

Fortune's invisible force continued to lift her higher and higher into the night. And then her momentum stopped, leaving her to hang motionless. Why? Was he deciding what to do with her? Her heart pounded wildly, stealing her breath. Was he going to drop her? There was nothing but hard ground below. The impact would crush every bone in her body.

As if in answer, she began moving lower, this time toward the chateau. Now what? What new evil scheme had he devised for her? Did he plant to kill her? Torture her?

The ground was at least two hundred feet away. Dear God, please don't let him drop me. She thought of Paul standing over her broken remains and fought back tears. No! It can't happen.

She twisted her head to look down at the cottage. Paul had left the balcony. What would he do? What was even possible for him to do?

Her heart tried to pound a hole in her chest, making it difficult to breathe. She willed herself to become calm and oriented. Where was she? She looked and saw the chateau's outside basement door below. She yelped as she abruptly plunged toward the basement entrance. Oh, God, I'm dead. Fear engulfed her. She closed her eyes to wait for the inevitable final blow. She sucked air through pinched lips.

The wind rushing past her ears slowed. Her body rotated to a horizontal position. She opened her eyes and found she was floating headfirst into the basement. The automatic lights came on. Her motion stopped and her body rotated into an upright position, but her feet remained above the floor.

Fortune left her hanging until the outside doors slammed shut. Then she continued onward into the empty side of the cellar. She caught the wall as she passed through that door, but the power and momentum of her motion prevented her fingers from getting a grip. Her fingernail broke and burned like a hot poker had hit it.

The light came on. Her destination was that hellish room filled with torture equipment! Was he going to murder her as he did those young girls? Her heart pounded so fast she could not breathe.

She looked back as she flew through the hole. Paul knocked on the brick wall. This time she didn't grab for the wall. Fortune was too strong.

Inside the torture room, she realized where he was taking her. The iron coffin. Its door stood open, which meant he had decided in advance what he intended to do with her. Fortune maneuvered her body like a small rag doll. He spun her around until her back was to the iron box, then shoved her in and slammed the door with a loud, metallic clang. She heard the latch clack, locking her in. Pictures of terrified young girls in that same hellish prison flashed into her mind. Sam vowed not to panic.

Fortune's grip released her, but she didn't collapse. Not enough room. Samantha tried to lift her arms. Lack of space pinned them to her sides. She tried to turn. That, too, was impossible. No room. In the suffocating blackness, claustrophobic panic threatened to drive her mind into a dark and frightening place.

"No!" she hissed. "No! Think. Think."

She relaxed and the pressure against her body dwindled as her muscles became less rigid. She took a long breath. Okay, I'm trapped. What can I do?

She answered her own question. Test the strength of her prison. The box was old. She used her knees and elbows to press with all her might against the icy walls. She laughed at herself. Only a silly fool to expect them to break. The iron walls didn't flex even a little. All she accomplished was a sharp pain in one knee cap and her right-side elbow. "Damn."

She held her breath to listen. Was Fortune Montmartre still out there, waiting to enjoy her panic? If so, she would not reward him with success. Maybe I can reason with him. Could a person reason with an evil ghost? Helena seemed reasonable, but she wasn't evil. She had nothing to lose by trying. She remained silent for another moment. Not a sound outside the coffin. She took a breath and called out, "Mr. Montmartre, if you're still here, I beg you, let me out. This will do you no good. Please!"

No response.

"Mr. Montmartre, if you're there, please give me a sign."

She pinched her brow and listened. No sound. Only her breathing. Where was he?

Teardrops welled in her eyes and trickled down her face. They tickled, but she couldn't reach up to scratch.

She screamed for help as loud as possible. The sound reverberating inside the iron box was deafening.

"Stop," she ordered. "Paul will find me. I know it."

Warmth spread through her as she thought of Paul. She had said yes to his proposal. Now, facing she knew not what, she realized she wanted to spend the rest of her life with him.

He loves me, she told herself. She smiled. She was certain he would tear the estate apart until he found her. All she had to do was wait for him. The notion calmed her. What was he doing right this instant?

She slowed her breathing while experimenting to find a comfortable position. She closed her eyes to wait.

He loves me, and I love him. He will find me. He will.

SIXTY-ONE

PAUL RUSHED BACK to his bedroom and scrambled into his clothes. Samantha's screams reverberated in his thoughts like an echo in a chamber of horrors. Fortune had taken her and he had to get her back. He grabbed a flashlight from his suitcase. As he did so, his phone rang. It was the gate guard.

"Sir, did someone scream?"

"Not yet. Thanks. I'll call you if I do."

"Right."

Paul galloped down the steps to Yoshi's room and found him just finishing dressing.

"What happened?"

"Fortune took Sam. The last time I saw her, she was floating a hundred feet or more in the sky. Come on. We have to find her."

They hurried outside to search the sky. No sign of Sam anywhere. They looked toward the mansion. Dark and brooding as a haunted house should be.

Paul slapped his hip. "Damn," he yelled. "Damn, damn." His heart pounded in his head. "If he kills her, I'm not sure what I'll do, Yosh. I'll—"

"No, Paul-san. We must be positive. He won't harm her.

We'll find her, but we'll need a flashlight."

"I have one," Paul said. From his pocket, he retrieved his long black-bodied flashlight and swept the mansion with it. Nothing but walls and windows. He turned it off and searched for Fortune's reddish glow. If he found the ghost, he hoped he'd find Sam, too. He turned the light back on. No sign of the creep anywhere, but his gut told him Fortune was there, most likely laughing at them.

Yoshi put a hand on his shoulder. "Paul-san, we have to think. The estate is too big to search without a plan."

Paul expelled a deep breath and nodded. "Agreed. But why take her? It's me he wants."

"Yes, but perhaps he took her to lure you to him."

"Hell, yes. That's it." He forced his brain into gear. He squinted toward the chateau. "The question is, where did he hide her?"

"My first guess would be in his favorite room."

"The torture chamber!"

"Hai."

"Bless you, Mr. Moto. Wait. Those bricks are still in there, which—"

"Means he'll have lots of ammo."

"Right." Paul thought about it.. "I'll need my hard hat," he said.

"We'll both need our hard hats. She's my friend, too."

"Yosh…"

"I'm going with you."

"Thanks. I appreciate it."

Moments later, they were back outside, peering toward the mansion.

"Paul-san, if we're right, he'll be waiting for us."

"You can count on it."

Paul stood back as Yoshi opened the outside basement doors. He peered in. No sign of Fortune. He stepped down into the room. The automatic lights came on. Yoshi hurried in and stopped beside him. The door across from them was open.

He looked at his friend. "We'll have to go in fast to catch him off guard. You swing left, and I'll go right. He can't watch the two of us at once."

"Agreed. Divide and conquer."

"We hope."

"Yeah."

They walked to the door and stopped. "Okay," Paul said. "Whoever reaches the torture chamber first will rush in and rescue Sam. The other will keep Fortune busy. Not much of a plan, is it?"

"What if she's hurt? How do we get out?"

"I'm in the market for ideas. Got any?"

"Sorry, fresh out."

"In that case, we'll do it the old-fashioned way."

"Which is?"

"I'll carry her and shield her with my body."

"And?"

"We run like hell."

"Oh, great!" Yoshi grinned. "Come on. I'll race you."

Paul stuck his hand through the door. The lights came on. "On three. One, two, three."

They dashed into the basement and split up as planned. Paul aimed straight for the hole in the back wall, but halfway there, he stopped. Yoshi followed his lead and stopped, looking puzzled. The bricks were on the floor. Fortune hadn't touched them. His gut told him Fortune wasn't there. He lifted a finger to his lips to caution his friend to be silent. Yoshi nodded. Then he pointed to the hole in the wall and tiptoed toward it.

When they reached it, Yoshi seemed puzzled. Paul shrugged. He pointed his flashlight into the darkened room. He wanted to call out to Sam, but didn't dare.

They entered the torture chamber, walking as quietly as stalking cats. Paul shined the light around. He suppressed a groan when he realized Samantha wasn't there. Where could she be?

Yoshi surveyed the room, but he said nothing. Paul gestured for his friend to stay put and tiptoed to the skeleton room. He shined his light inside that one and looked around. It was empty, too.

"Damn," he said, breaking his silence. He turned back to Yoshi and joined him beside the torture bench. "She's not here." His voice was hoarse with disappointment. "Where the hell is she?"

The door of the iron coffin squeaked open, startling them. Sam stepped out and laughed. "She's right here. What took you so long?"

Paul aimed his light toward the corner. Sam stood before them, grinning. Shock froze him for an instant before he rushed to her and engulfed her in his arms. "Are you okay?"

"A little claustrophobic, but I'm fine." She gave him a hug. "I knew you'd find me."

"But what were you doing in that coffin?" Yoshi asked, joining them. He grabbed her hand and pumped it three times.

She pushed Paul away and said, "Fortune locked me in it."

"Locked? How did you get out?" Paul shined the light on the coffin.

Sam shushed him. "We'd better get out of here. He might come back. I'll tell you everything when we're safe."

"Smart. Let's go."

Back in the cottage living room. Sam grabbed drinks from the fridge and joined Paul on the sofa. Yoshi was in his usual seat.

"Damn it, Sam, talk to us. Start at the beginning."

She took a sip of her Pepsi and then told them everything. "When he threw me in that damned coffin," she said. "I almost panicked from claustrophobia, but then I told myself you would come for me. I relaxed and waited. Almost fell asleep."

"But... how did you unlock it?"

"I didn't. The latch clicked open just moments before you

arrived to rescue me. I didn't move at first, because someone Helena screamed in pain near me. Also, something hit the floor with a loud bang next to me. So, I stayed quiet until you I heard you."

"What do you think happened?" Yoshi asked.

"I'm not sure. It had to be Helena who unlocked the coffin, but I figure Fortune caught her and did something horrible to her. I stayed quiet, fearing Fortune would return, until I heard your voices."

"In that case, with your permission, I'm going back to bed," Yoshi said, yawning. "You're in the best of hands now. now, Paul-san." Yoshi stood, bowed, and went into the downstairs bedroom.

"I knew you would save me," Sam whispered.

"I'll always be here for you, Sam."

"Always?"

"Yes."

She wiggled against him. "So, what now? We can't sit here all night, can we?"

Paul smiled. "We're going upstairs to bed."

"We?"

"Yes. I'll lock your windows and guard you like a faithful watchdog. No more being alone for you."

She smiled and kissed him. His phone interrupted. It was Helena. "Did he hurt Samantha?"

"No. She's safe, thanks to you for opening the coffin door for her. I owe you."

"Wish I could collect, but I didn't do it."

"Who did it, then?"

"I don't know. I wanted to, but Fortune chased me away. Maybe he did it."

"Well, thanks for trying anyway."

"I have to go. I'm playing hide and seek with him again. He's angry and wants to punish me. Night." Paul cut the connection.

"I like that kid," Sam said, standing.

Paul stood and held her. "And I love this one."

"Prove it."

"How?"

"Take me upstairs and I'll show you."

And she did.

SIXTY-TWO

PAUL TURNED AWAY from the stove when Samantha entered the kitchen.

"Good morning, sleepyhead. Have a seat," he said, smiling. "Coffee's ready." He poured a cup and placed it beside a plate topped with a fork, knife, and spoon.

"What are you doing?"

"What's it look like? Making breakfast. Hope you like scrambled eggs, nuked bacon, and toast. Be ready in a minute."

"But, I should—"

"Nonsense. I'm a bachelor. I could be a short-order cook."

Yoshi came in, looking groggy, but rested. "Ohio gozaimasu." He flopped into a chair.

Paul served coffee for him. "How do you feel?"

"Like I'm half here and in New York. Can't tell which part is where, though."

Sam giggled as Paul served up two platters with bacon, eggs, and toast. "Compliments of the house. Help yourself."

When they were halfway through the food, Paul said, "I've been thinking. John gave us a solid lead to the bones, which means we're sure to find them. So, I'm changing the plan a little."

"How so, Paul-san."

"I don't trust those hard hats. They won't protect our bodies from falling stones or bricks. We need better protection, something that can withstand a heavy blow."

"Like what?" Sam asked,

"Football uniforms could work. They design the helmets to take a heavy battering, and the padding protects the shoulders, chests and thighs."

"That's a great idea," Sam said.

"There's a problem, though."

"What?" Yoshi was waking up.

"Where to get them? I found a store in L. A. that carries the shoulder pads, but you have to wait for them to be delivered. We need them sooner."

Yoshi took a large swig of black coffee. "I can run a search for them. L.A. must have a local source for uniforms."

"I found nothing."

"I have an idea," Sam said.

"What?"

"I went to high school with a boy named Noah Gonzales. A friend wrote to me and said he became the football coach at the co-educational Santa Monica Hill Military Academy. He'll know where to get them."

"Good idea, Sam-san. Do you think he's available today?"

"Let's find out." She checked her cell phone. "Today is Friday. It's eight-thirty. He'll be at school. Hang on." She punched a button, scrolled a list of names and dialed. She waited, then smiled and said, "Noah, hi. Yep, it's me. I'm home for good now. How are you doing?"

She listened, then said, "That's what I heard. Congratulations."

She listened, nodding. "Noah, that's great," she said. "Listen, I'm calling because I have a problem. I need to find a place to buy three football uniforms today. I—" She laughed at something said on the other end. "No, we're doing some excavation work here at the estate, and we're worried about being hit by falling rocks and debris. Football uniforms seemed the perfect solution. I—no. We don't need new uniforms. Why?"

She listened again, then said, "Noah, hang on a second." She turned to Paul. "He says he has a lot of old, worn-out uniforms at the academy. They're functional, but they have new ones with a new school logo. What do you think?"

"You're a genius, is what I think."

Samantha smiled. "That's perfect, Noah. When can we drop by?"

She listened. Then, "Would ten o'clock be okay?" Pause. "Yes, I remember how to get there. We had a game there once. By the way, did you ever marry that girl you were dating?"

Sam let loose a big laugh. "Wow! Four! Congratulations. See you soon." She listened for a moment and hung up.

"So, what did he say?"

"He said come on over. He has two full teams' worth of old uniforms for us to choose from."

"You're amazing, Sam," Yoshi said.

Sam giggled. "Ask and ye shall receive is my motto."

Noah Gonzales wasn't there when they arrived. He had been called to a faculty meeting, so he left an apologetic note to Sam with his senior quarterback. The young guy lost his voice when Sam smiled at him, but he gained control and croaked out that the coach had ordered him to provide whatever they needed. His eyes said he would have preferred to show Sam how to don the uniforms instead of Yosh, but he was helpful. He explained how to don and tighten the padding. After checking the uniforms, they elected not to take the pants and thigh pads, only helmets, shoulder pads, and jerseys. The kid stood watching as they loaded Yoshi's Mercedes and drove away.

Two hours later, they were back in the pool house staring down at a pile of football shoulder pads, including numbered jerseys for each of them. No one seemed eager to climb into the bulky padding.

Paul broke the impasse. "I suggest we scan the area in front of that old door. If Fortune built a tunnel from there to the house, it will be easy to find. Once we locate it, we can dig a hole anywhere to reach it.

"I agree," Yoshi said, "though I suspect the construction will be like the old western mine shafts with overhead supports. When we start the dig, that may give us a problem."

"Right. The scanner should show those, too. We'll follow the same procedure we did before. Sam ties herself to the tree, and we'll lash together like mountain climbers while we're scanning. Once we start digging, you can anchor yourself to the tractor."

"Makes sense to me." Yoshi stood and, as the young football player had instructed, put his jersey over the padding first, then lifted the entire rig and lowered it over his head and onto his shoulders. As they watched, he reached under his arms, pulled the retaining straps forward, and locked them in place. When he finished, he grinned at them. "Piece of cake. Where's the big game? I'm ready to go."

Paul donned his armor and lifted Sam's padding to help her, but she backed away. "I'll wear the helmet, but I won't need the padding. The tree will protect me."

Paul hesitated, then smiled. "You're right. Besides, I like you better without armor, but..." He frowned.

"What?"

"My bones are telling me their bones won't be there.."

"Well, you tell your bones to stop worrying. They're there. My intuition says so."

"I hope you're right." He lifted her helmet, pulled the bottom edges apart, and slid it over her golden hair. He patted the top of her head. "Smartest and most beautiful player on the team."

"Hai, so desu." Yoshi chuckled. "Let go dig up some bones."

SIXTY-THREE

THEY FOUND THE TUNNEL almost immediately by scanning near the work road across from the door. The shaft was four feet wide, six feet deep, and four feet below the surface, which put its floor ten feet below their feet. Unlike old western mine shafts with hard rock ceilings, this one had a thick earthen roof. As a result, Fortune had built a complex grid of beams and boards supporting the tunnel's ceiling. It was a very professional job.

Paul turned away from the GPR and said, "That was easy, Yosh. Now let's see where it leads."

As before, Yoshi had planted colored flags to mark the edges of the tunnel. He nodded. "Looks like it's following a diagonal path from here to the house. I suggest we map an area closer to the house and plant flags to mark off the path."

Paul grinned. "Great minds run in the same tunnel, Yosh. I had the same idea."

The tunnel ended at the outer wall of the skeleton room. Sam sat, legs crossed, on her folded chair, spying on them through her binoculars. Paul gave her a thumbs up. She lowered them, smiled and waved. When he turned back, Yoshi was frownin"What's wrong?"

"Nothing. I was just imagining how terrified those girls must have been. That sick creep dragged them through that tunnel into a dungeon. We have to make him pay for his evil."

"We'll try, Yosh, but first we have to find his bones.."

"So where do we dig?"

Paul eyed the house. "We should start at least eight feet from the house wall. If the tunnel caves in, we'll need room for another try."

"Sounds right, but those heavy beams may give us trouble."

"Yeah, we'll need a saw, a pick and shovels, a ladder and flashlights."

Yoshi's gaze wandered around. "Any sign of our friend?"

"No, but you can bet he's lurking somewhere watching. Let's get our gear."

They spent half an hour rummaging in the tool shed what they needed. Wen they finished they had a rusty pick ax, a gasoline-powered hand saw, and an extensible ladder. Back at the dig site, Paul retied Sam's lifeline to the tree and gave her a quick kiss. "You okay?"

She smiled and touched his cheek. "Yes, but it's frustrating when you two are talking and I can't tell what it's about."

"Sam. I'm sorry. If there was any other way, I…"

She giggled at his seriousness. "Don't worry about it. I know we need a lookout. Just don't forget I'm here."

"That'll be the day."

She giggled. "You better go dig."

Yoshi pulled the tractor in a line over the tunnel, placing the backhoe shovel between flags eight feet away from the house. They unloaded all the tools, and Paul climbed into the backhoe seat. "We'll dig in a small area. Sixteen cubic feet is a lot of soil to remove."

"Hai, wakatte. Just tell me what to do. I'm getting good with this thing."

They used the same digging pattern as before, and forty-five minutes later, Paul yelled, "Stop!"

The tractor stopped. "What is it?"

"I thought I heard something crack."

"What did it sound like?."

"Like a beam snapping."

"You think the tractor's too heavy?"

"Yes. These supports are old. I don't want it to fall through. Pull to the side and we'll dig across the tunnel."

Yoshi backed up and steered the John Deere onto safe ground and turned to place the backhoe above the ditch Paul had dug.

Paul hopped down to examine their progress. The trench was about four feet long, three feet wide, and almost as deep. He turned toward Samantha, who had the binoculars trained on him. He blew her a kiss. She grinned and returned it.

Yoshi chuckled and Paul said, "She agreed to marry me, Yosh, but there's a catch."

"What is it?"

"Her condition was my proposal has to be creative. I dont know what that means."

"Ah, so. That may take some hard thinking."

"No kidding."

He climbed onto the backhoe and told Yoshi to pull forward a foot. He stabilized the unit, dropped the shovel, and drove it deep. When he dumped the dirt away from the dig, he realized he had hit the tunnel ceiling. Two thick gray planks were now visible. One more good scoop would give them access.

Yoshi backed up a little, and Paul scooped another huge load of moist soil. This time, there was a distinct sound of breaking timber. He offloaded the scoop with a thick, gray piece of lumber sticking out.

Yoshi pulled the tractor back, set the brake, and cut the engine.

"Time for picks and shovels," Paul said, climbing to the ground.

Yoshi found a steady footing for the ladder, and Paul climbed into the hole to study the dirt-covered timber. "Give me the big shovel and the pickax," he said.

He shoveled the dirt away and hooked the point of the pickax under the broken plank. Then he put all his weight on the handle and tugged hard. The board ripped loose with a squeak of nails. He tore up several more twelve-inch wide planks until the hole was large enough to pass a man through. A musty, sweet odor rose from the tunnel.

Wrinkling his nose, he climbed up the ladder to join Yoshi. "I have to go in," he said. "Can't see much from up here."

"Paul-san. Are you okay?"

"Sure. Why?"

"You look worried."

"Well, I am a little. Every thing's riding on our finding those damned bones. We don't even know whether burying them will work."

"It will work, Paul-san." Yoshi patted Paul's shoulder. "I have faith."

Paul smiled. "I wish I did. Nothing has ever come easy for me. But I'm hoping this time will be an exception."

"Paul." Samantha's voice.

He waved and yelled, "We're coming!"

His watch read 12:30 P.M. "Let's go make some sandwiches. I don't want to face on an empty stomach whatever evil that hellhole may have waiting for us."

SIXTY-FOUR

Helena called when they were halfway through a lunch of ham and Swiss sandwiches on rye bread, with dill pickle slices and frosty cold soft drinks. Paul held up his phone for the others to read and punched the dictate button. "Helena, are you okay?"

"Yes, but I'm scared."

"Of what?"

"Something weird is going on. Fortune rushed past me like he didn't see me or even care. He didn't chase me or try to hurt me, but he was angry and worried."

"You can't tell why?"

"No, but if he's afraid, it must be horrible. What should I do?"

"Just hide and stay safe." A picture of her beautiful, unprotected, youthful body flashed into his mind. "Is there anything we can do?" Dumb question.

"I wish. I just needed to talk. It's lonely here, and I'm scared. I wish you and Samantha were here. With Justin gone, there's no one in the house, and I get confused. It's so weird."

"I'm sorry, Helena. Can you guess what's frightening Fortune?"

"No. I've never seen him like this. He's always dominating. Now he's afraid, and that frightens me."

"That is odd, but right now, we can't be with you. But there is some good news. We're close to finding where Talon buried you. If we do, your days of living in fear will be over. I promised you we'll do everything possible to save you, and we will. Do you want to discuss anything else?"

"No."

"Then I'll go back to work. Okay?"

"Yes. Bye."

"Helena, wait!" Too late. In his mind, he could imagine her young girl's sobs. Stricken, he turned to face his friends.

"Paul, I feel so sorry for her. She's sweet and lonely and frightened. There must be something we can do." Sam's expression matched his own.

"There is. Find and bury those bones and pray that it works."

"Paul is right," Yoshi said. "I can understand why Mr. Davenport wanted to help her. Her case is pitiful, but we're helpless. We exist on different planes."

Sam grabbed her shoulder pads and slipped her jersey over it. She lifted the rig and poked her head through the hole.

"What are you doing?"

"We're going to find those bones, and I'm going with you."

"Sam."

She glared at him. "You want to stay here and argue or help Helena?"

He wolfed down the last of his sandwich and said, "Let's go."

They walked to the dig site and peered into the hole that led into the tunnel. From their angle they could see nothing but gray floor lit by the afternoon sun.

"I'll go in first," he said. "If it looks safe, I'll signal when you can join me."

Sam caught his arm. "Be careful."

He grinned and patted her cheek. "Take care of Yoshi, will

you?"

He turned away and put one foot on the ladder, but a loud metallic clatter coming from the tractor stopped him. They all whirled to see what had happened. As they did so, the backhoe attached to the end of the John Deere lifted two feet above the ground and hung there for a few seconds before it fell back to the ground with the loud clatter of steel connections slamming together.

Paul grabbed their arms and pulled them to a safe distance. They watched as the backhoe struggled to escape gravity. It seemed almost alive in its efforts. Fascinated, they gaped as the machine made a final valiant effort and this time, the entire tractor rose three feet off the ground. They held their breaths while it hung motionless in midair and then fell to the ground, bounced once and lay still.

"I've heard of bucking broncos before, but this is the first bucking Deere I've seen," Sam said.

Yoshi guffawed at the pun. "Good one, Sam."

Paul, however, was serious. "Don't get close to the tractor while I'm in the tunnel. You can bet Fortune didn't do that little trick to entertain us. Remember what Helena said. Something weird is going on, so keep your eyes open.

He grabbed the ladder and skidded down it to the trench. At the bottom, he moved the ladder and lowered the end into the tunnel. With his high-powered flashlight tucked into his belt, he climbed down and then stepped off the ladder. The details of the underground construction were impressive. Montmartre had gone to a lot of trouble to build his tunnel to hell.

Vertical 4 x 4 beams spaced on four-foot centers supported the walls and the ceiling. To keep the dirt at bay, a solid lining of one-inch thick twelve-inch wide planks filled the gaps between the beams. The tunnel had remained unchanged for nearly one and a half centuries, so he decided it was safe. He looked up the ladder and called, "Come on down."

There was shuffling above him, and then Sam's legs came

down the ladder. He stepped aside to make room. When Yoshi joined them, he shined his light around the tunnel and said, "This was quite an operation."

"Yeah. From an engineering point of view, it's well built."

Sam looked toward the work road. "Talon must have filled the tunnel near the mountain door to conceal his skullduggery."

Paul turned his beam toward the house. The construction technique used was the same everywhere. He walked slowly toward the chateau, examining the floor, walls, and ceiling as he went. Talon had built brick walls on sides of the tunnel near the house and another wall across the end. When he saw that, his hopes crashed. Thick dirt and dust covered the brickwork. "Damn," he said.

"What is it?" Sam and Yoshi peeked around him at the wall.

"Nothing, and that's the problem. I had hoped to find something resembling a burial site."

"Maybe they're buried between that brick wall and the house," Yoshi offered. "He was a brick mason, remember?"

"Why else would he build a wall there?" Sam asked.

"The walls in the house were lath and plaster, not brick. So, this must hide something." He studied the bricks more closely. The mortar was still tight. "I'll need tools to break through this."

"The ones you left in the basement?

"Yes."

"Paul, you can't go back in there," Sam said. "It's too dangerous."

"We'll get new ones at Home Depot," Yoshi said. "Quicker and safer."

"Okay. Majority wins. The air here stinks anyway. Let's go."

SIXTY-FIVE

HALF AN HOUR TO the store. Half an hour of shopping and a half hour to return. They hadn't found a battery-powered work light in stock, so now Yoshi held the flashlight while Paul prepared to knock a hole in the brickwork. All three wore safety goggles.

Paul turned to Sam. "Stay back a few feet."

She nodded and backed away.

He lifted a heavy, double-faced sledge hammer and swung hard. The powerful blow sent a shock wave up his right arm and caused his ears to ring, but a red brick flew through the wall and fell with a thump. Another swing and two more bricks followed the first one. Three more blows did it. He put the sledge aside and took the light from Yoshi. He leaned in to examine the cavity and bumped his forehead against the house wall. "Ow!" He rubbed his head and shined the light through the hole. The wall was less than a foot from his nose. Not enough room to bury a shoe box, much less two bodies.

Disappointed, he turned to his friends. "Dead end," he said. "Two times at bat, two strikes. Damn." He leaned against the brick wall behind him.

Samantha came close to him and shined her light at the wall

behind his hip. Puzzled, she bent for a closer examination. She brushed the dirt away with her palm. Paul stepped aside to give her room. She kept brushing until she uncovered a cross made of light-red bricks inlaid in the of darker ones.

"Paul, look. It's a cross." She moved aside, excited.

"A cross?" Yoshi said.

"Yes. Remember what the clipping said? An upside down clue?"

"That's not upside down," Yoshi said.

Paul bent down and rubbed dirt away from the opposite wall. A bit more cleaning and another cross emerged.

"Paul, it's an upside down cross." Sam's voice was high with excitement. "He buried them on opposite sides of the tunnel. I'm sure of it."

Paul rose and gave her a grin. "By Jove, I think she's done it."

Sam giggled. "He separated his love from the man he hated. Makes sense to me."

"Right. Talon knew she hated Fortune, and he did, too, so he kept their bones apart."

"Yeah. Too bad it didn't work," Yoshi said., "They're still together in the mansion."

Paul waved them back and lifted the sledgehammer, preparing to bash another hole in the wall with the upright cross on it.

"Paul, wait." Sam caught his arm.

"What?"

"Falling bricks might damage the bones. Is there another way to open this?"

"Yep. I'll use the mason chisel and take out one brick at a time."

Excitement rose within him as he studied the old mortar and chose a likely candidate. Three good taps later, one brick came loose close to the floor of the tunnel. Then two more bricks. He stuck his hand through the hole to prevent falling bricks from hitting whatever was on the other side of the wall. Bu tapping lightly and catching the loosened blocks, he soon had a two-foot square hole in the wall and borrowed Yoshi's flashlight.

He knelt again and shined the light into the hole. What he saw sent his heart racing. He sucked in a deep breath of musty air and felt his face flush with warmth.

"Paul, what's wrong?" Samantha sounded frightened.

He rose and stumbled backward. "Have a look." His tone was breathless.

Yoshi and Sam both fell to their knees to peer into the hole. Sam screamed with excitement. "Paul, a coffin. This has to be Helena. We've done it."

Paul chuckled. "Sure looks like it."

Yoshi rose, faced Paul, and bowed. "Omedetou, Paul-san. You're a rich man now."

Before he could answer, Samantha wrapped her arms around him and kissed him.

"Whoa," he said, holding her at arm's length. "Let's not get carried away. We think we've found the bones, and I'm sure we have, but let's save our celebration until we're certain Fortune's gone."

"Killjoy," Sam said, mimicking Helena.

"So, how do we proceed?" Yoshi asked.

Paul spent a moment calming his racing brain, and then a wonderful inspiration struck him. He fell to his knees before Sam and said, "Samantha Duet, will you accept my love and vow before these three witnesses, Mr. Yoshiru Kawasaki and the corpses of Fortune and Helena Montmartre, to marry me and love me forever? If you will, I solemnly swear to do the same."

Sam fell to her knees, too, and took his face in her hands. "I do so swear, you silly man." She wiped his cheek with her fingers. "Your face is smudged.

Paul beamed. "So, was that creative enough?"

She rose and pulled him to his feet. "I'll say. How many girls have men dig trenches and holes in the tops of tunnels to ask for their hands before two one-hundred-thirty-year-old corpses?"

"Pretty creative, Paul-san."

Paul grinned. "The main thing is it worked, didn't it?" He turned to Sam. "Thank you, Mrs. Paul Davenport, to be."

She curtsied. "You're welcome."

"By the way, your face is smudged, too."

"Paul-san, what's next?"

"First, I'll open the other side and clear out the debris. Then there's the problem of removing the coffins without damaging the bones." His heart was pounding as he thought about the next steps. "We have to warn Helena about our find. She deserves that. Then, tomorrow, we'll bag the bones, dig graves, buy coffins, call a minister and have a funeral. Once that's done, we get the lawyer and Madam Song to come here to sign our report card."

"Don't forget the inheritance," Yoshi said, grinning. "Remember, I told my dad I should help you because you're going to become a rich contact."

Paul grinned. "Right, I forgot that little detail. Well, what say we clean up and celebrate the luckiest man alive?"

"And who might that be?" Sam demanded.

"Me, of course. Few men ever get to marry their dream girl."

Sam put her cheek against his. "Sounds good to me."

"Amazing," Yoshi said.

"What is?"

"Mr. Moto's best friend is going to be rich and have the most beautiful wife in America!"

They all laughed at his Peter Lorre accent. Paul was ready to pop with happiness. But then a loud thump and clang came to them from outside the tunnel. Fortune was still playing with the tractor. Weird.

What the devil was he up to? "I think we'd better save opening Fortune's side until morning. He must be mad as hell the way he's banging the tractor around. I suggest we exit this hole fast." Paul caught Sam's hand and led the way up the ladder. He climbed first, then waited for the others to emerge. When they joined him, he moved the ladder to a stable place, and they climbed out of the trench.

At the top, they found the tractor floating five feet in the air and rotating in slow circles. They watched, spellbound, for a few moments until it fell and hit the ground hard. The impact tore the backhoe loose from the tractor, which bounced on two wheels, causing it to teeter toward them. It righted itself and then remained still.

"What on earth is he doing?" Sam's eyes were wide.

"I don't know, but whatever it is, it's not good for us," Paul said. "If he can lift that tractor, he can smash us like flies. We'd better go fast. Now."

With Samantha in the lead, they went.

Running.

SIXTY-SIX

PAUL WOKE FIRST the next morning, dressed, and hurried down to make coffee. The kitchen clock said 5:45. All night long, two problems had run nonstop through his head. One was finding a good excuse to go next door and check on Samantha. The second one was tough. Figuring a way to remove the coffins without destroying them or the bones. They might crumble if not handled the right way. He feared their entire plan might fail if they lost even a single bone. He tossed it aside when Sam came into the kitchen.

"What an early bird. Oh, good. Coffee's on." She came to him, gave him a peck on his forehead and said, "I missed you."

"You did?"

"Oh, yes. I'm already having withdrawal pains."

He grinned. "Damn, I'm in love with an addict?"

"Maybe it's the pheromones, after all." She grabbed cups and saucers from the cupboard and put them on the table. Then she stood by the coffeepot until it finished growling.

She poured three cups just as Yoshi came in. He plopped down and looked at them through bleary eyes.

"What time will they deliver the coffins?" Sam asked.

"One o'clock." Yoshi stared at the coffee cup before him. "I hope this is mine. Oh, yeah. Good morning." He took a long sip of coffee, then said, "I solved it."

"Solved what?"

"How to get the coffins out of the tunnel?"

Paul studied his sleepy-eyed friend. "I worried about that all night myself with no luck. We can't afford to lose any of the bones."

Yoshi put down his cup. "Yeah, that's the essence of the problem. Here's how I figure it. First, we get tarps under the coffins. Then we pull out the tarps with the boxes on top. Once they're out, we wrap the tarps around the boxes for reinforcement so they won't crumble. Next, we put planks under them and tie the entire package with more rope. The last step will be to pull the wrapped coffins clear and remove them from the trench to the truck. Piece of cake." Grinning, he slurped more coffee. "What do you think?"

"I've said it before, Yosh. Mr. Moto's a genius, and we have everything we need in the tool shed."

"Yeah, I saw that yesterday. I hope we don't have to do this on an empty stomach?"

"Not on your life," Sam said, jumping up. "Give me ten minutes."

After a quick breakfast, they gathered the needed tools from the tool shed, donned their football gear, and Paul drove his truck across the lawn to the dig site to transport the coffins once they got them out of the ground. He parked with the truck's tailgate close to the trench to make it easy to load.

Yoshi's plan worked, except for one problem. It was slow to put into practice because the coffin bottoms crumbled when they tried sliding the tarps under them. They solved that by digging shallow trenches under one end to get the tarp started, then alternated lifting and sliding until the tarps were under the old boxes from end to end. After that, inch by inch, they pulled them out into the main tunnel. The rest of the plan was easNow, still in their football gear, while Samantha waited nearby, Paul stood admiring their handiwork. Altogether, the operation took three hours. And there had been no sign of Fortune. Was keeping his word on the truce, or was he frightened of something as Helena suggested? The minister was scheduled to arrive in three and a half hours, and they still had two graves to dig before he came. With Yoshi riding in back to keep the coffins safe, Paul followed his original path back to the work road to avoid messing up the landscape any more than necessary.

The cemetery was beside the work road, halfway between the pool house and the big live oak at the end of the estate.

Paul stopped and backed the tail of the truck close to the cemetery gate. His stomach gave a nervous lurch. An uncle he didn't know existed lay in rest here. He had intended to visit the site earlier, but now that he was here, he wasn't sure how to feel.

"I visited Uncle Justin's grave once when I first got home," Sam said, opening the gate for them. "I cried my eyes out because I missed his funeral."

And I missed his entire life, Paul thought.

A white wrought-iron fence about ten yards wide and ten yards long bounded the little cemetery. It was clean and well kept. Two headstones six feet apart were at the back of the square. One was wider than the other. Paul walked over to study the larger one. It was his uncle's. Made of polished stone, it had a sculpture of a naked angel lying across its top. Under that, a small inscription said: My angel, Helena Longmore. His uncle had refused to put her married name on the inscription. The main headstone inscription said:

Justin Davenport
Birthday and day of death.
Adventurer • Recluse
Faithful lover of Helena Longmore

"He must have been an interesting man," Yoshi said at his side.

"He was," Sam said. "I used to sit on his lap and listen in fascination to the stories of his adventures. He treated me like his own daughter, and I loved him for it."

"Too bad he wasn't my father," Paul said. "Things might have been different for us." He walked to the other headstone. Its inscription said:

Rest in Peace
Franz Heimlich
Loyal friend
Dates of birth and death

Paul checked his watch. The minister would arrive within three hours. "Where should we bury them?"

"Put Fortune against the fence near the street." Sam's jaw was tight. "Put Helena close to Uncle Justin. He would want that."

Paul grinned. "You're a romantic, too, aren't you?"

"Well, he loved her. Didn't he?"

"Yeah, he sure did. We're running out of time. I'd better get digging."

"Yeah." Yoshi said.

"I'll make sandwiches and bring drinks," Sam said.

She left.

Yoshi brought two shovels from the truck, and they stripped off their football gear. The mortuary had provided the dimensions of their coffins, and Paul now marked off the size of the holes they would need. It was a lot of dirt to remove in a hurry, but the ground here was soft. They could do it.

"You take Helena," Yoshi said. "I'll do Fortune."

They got to work.

SIXTY-SEVEN

SAM ENTERED the living room as graceful as a Cosmopolitan model. Her blond hair, again pulled back into a golden pony tail, glowed under the living-room light. She had changed into dark blue jeans and a fresh white blouse. Her eyes seemed to radiate their own glow from within. At her entrance, Paul and Yoshi both jumped to their feet to look at her in awe.

She walked to Paul and gave him a quick peck on the lips. He again detected the same delightful springtime scent she wore when he first met her. He reached to hold her, but she ducked under and sat on the sofa. Yoshi did his quickie bow and dropped back into his seat.

"We need to be super careful from here on in," she said seriously. "And we need a new plan."

"Agreed," Paul said, "but I want to go to dinner and celebrate our engagement first."

"I'll second that," Yoshi said.

Sam shook her head. "I've got a better idea. There's lots of food here and several bottles of wine, too. I can whip up a quick dinner, and we can eat at home, relax and make plans. Please." Her eyes were irresistible siren calls tearing at him.

"Who can resist a plea like that? How about you, Yosh? Home cooking?"

"I like any kind of cooking."

"It's settled, then." Sam gave Paul another peck on the lips. "It's only five o'clock. There's plenty of daylight left."

"Time for my report to Madam Song."

He dialed, and she answered immediately. "Mr. Davenport. You have news?"

"Yes. We found the bodies. Tomorrow we plan to remove them and bury them in the cemetery my uncle built."

"Congratulations. I wish you success."

"You approve of my efforts now?"

"No, but, but the burial of the bones won't harm him. It may not send him on either. Are you planning a ceremony?"

"Yes. We're ordering coffins and getting a minister. I'll keep you posted."

"You realize you're trying to evict a man from his own home. One he built himself?"

"He's not a man. He's an evil ghost that didn't move on when he died. If I could, I would destroy him."

"You and your uncle." She hung up.

Paul's phone rang. It was Helena. He answered and switched to dictation mode. "Helena, hi."

"Not Helena. This is Fortune."

"What?" Paul stood and slammed his brows together. "Did you say Fortune?"

"Don't be stupid. You can read. Read this. This is Fortune. I want to talk to you."

Paul stared at the phone. "I'm surprised to see you can type. Wasn't that unusual in your day?"

"Helena is typing. I dictate. She writes what I say. We need to talk."

"Talk then." Sam and Yoshi were reading over his shoulder.

"No. I want to meet face to face. You are like your uncle. You can see me."

"Where?"

"In the library."

Sam and Yoshi vigorously shook their heads. "It's a trap," Yoshi whispered.

Paul nodded. "Why should I trust you?"

"I give you my word."

"Right. The word of a Satanist, child rapist and murderer? You tried twice to kill me. After what you did to that tractor, I don't believe you."

Pause. Paul imagined a terrified Helena sitting at the keyboard. "This is Helena. He left. He went to see the tractor. Wait. He's back."

He's fast, Paul noted.

"What are you talking about?"

"You lifted it off the ground and dropped it."

"I did not."

"Who, then?"

"It doesn't matter. It wasn't me."

"What do you want to discuss?"

"An agreement."

"About what?"

"Our situation. We need to resolve it."

"How?"

"That's the point of the discussion."

"I see." Paul's frown deepened. "Let me mull that over."

"How long?"

"Why does that matter to you?"

"It doesn't, but you are a nuisance. I will make a deal with you. I want you to leave."

"Will you promise to make yourself undetectable to my uncle's psychic? If she declares the house to be clear of ghosts, I can inherit my uncle's fortune and will leave you alone."

A long pause, and then, "That's beyond my control."

"Other psychics didn't detect your presence."

"They were charlatans."

"In that case, I need time to discuss this with my friends, the ones you tried to kill. You can prove your sincerity by calling a truce until tomorrow noon. Call me then, and I'll tell you what I've decided. Take it or leave it."

"You're a bastard."

"If you harm Helena, you'll find out. There will never be a deal."

"I won't harm her."

"Will you call me tomorrow?"

"Yes. If I must."

Helena hung up.

Paul sat in stunned silence until Yoshi said, "Wow! What do you make of that?"

"Helena is right. He's worried about something. Otherwise, why would he offer a deal?"

"Don't trust him." Sam said. "He's a liar."

"Don't worry. It's obvious he wants to lure me close enough to kill me."

His phone rang. "Who is this?"

"Helena."

"You alone?"

"Yes. I'm scared. Fortune is acting too weird. You can't trust him. He's horrible."

"Have you learned what he's afraid of?"

"No. I've never seen him like this. What do you suppose it is?"

"I can't even begin to guess. Hey, I have good news for you?"

"What?"

"We found your burial site today, the place where Talon hid your bodies."

No response for a full minute, then she continued, "Is that good?"

"We hope so. We think it will free you of Fortune's domination. It's about time, don't you think?"

Pause. "Paul, what will happen to us?"

"What happens to other people who die?"

"I don't know. Fortune is the only dead person I know." Pause, then, "Do you think God will take me to heaven?"

Paul smiled at her youthful sincerity. "Helena, we're certain of it. You've suffered enough for a thousand people. Besides, I think you're already an angel. You belong in heaven."

"I am laughing. My mother said men who talk like that are full of blarney. I like it, though." Pause. "What are you going to do?"

"About what?"

"My bones."

Paul nodded. She wasn't fighting the inevitable. "First, we'll dig a grave in a beautiful spot next to Uncle Justin. We'll call a minister to give you a proper Christian funeral and burial."

"Will I have a headstone?"

"Yes, a nice one. Do you have an epitaph you'd like to put on it?"

Longer pause. "I've wondered about that. Can I put three lines?"

"Sure. What would you like?"

"First line. Please, God, take me to heaven. Second line. Thank you, Justin, for loving me and teaching me. Third line. Thank you, Paul and Sam and Yohshee for saving me." Pause. "That's it, I guess."

"We haven't saved you yet. But we're working on it."

"I mean, if you do, that's what I want."

"I guarantee it," Paul said. "You deserve much more."

"I hope so."

"We're sure of it." Sam asked for the phone. Her eyes glistened with tears. "Sam wants to say something, okay?"

"Yes, she's a wonderful girl. I hope you get married."

"Me, too." He handed over the phone.

Sam said, "Helena, this is Sam."

"Hi, Sam. I'm pretty scared."

"I would be, too, if I lived with Fortune. If you can, stay

patient a little longer. Then you'll be off to happier times. No more fear and no more pain. God won't punish you for what Fortune did to you."

"What about making love to Talon?"

Sam held back a snicker. "Just pray for forgiveness, and He'll do it. Loving someone is not a mortal sin."

"Are you sure?"

"I'd stake my life on it."

"Don't say that. I want you and Paul to get married and have lots of kids. You'll be so beautiful together."

"Helena, I think you're the sweetest, bravest girl I've ever known. I hope when my time comes, we can be best friends up there."

"Me, too. I'd love that. You're so beautiful. I wish I could be like you. Oh, no. He's coming back. Have to go. Bye."

She hung up. Sam stuck the phone in Paul's shirt pocket. "That poor girl. I can't imagine the hell she has been through." She backed away. "Paul, we have to succeed. I can't bear to think of her trapped in that hell forever."

"Yeah, I know." His face was grim. "I'll save her if it kills me."

"Don't say that! You promised her a minister. Did you mean it?"

"Yes. We owe her that much."

"I can help with that," Sam said.

"You mean you've got a minister tucked away in your little bag of tricks, too? Like with the football uniforms?"

She giggled. "Yes. I stayed in touch with my school friends while I was away. One of my girlfriends told me that Mark Abrams, who was also one of my school mates, became a minister last year. I suspect he'll help us."

Paul grinned. "You're the most useful person I've ever known. Go for it."

"I have to make a phone call." She sat on the sofa, skimmed her cell-phone contacts and dialed a number. After a moment, she said, "Mark, hi. This is Sam."

"Yes, I finally graduated."

"Yes, still at Montmartre. How about you?"

"That's great, Mark. Listen, I called to ask a favor. I need a minister." She paused and then explained the situation. When she finished, she turned to Paul and said, "He wants to know when."

"Today's Friday. How about tomorrow?"

She told him. "Four o'clock. That's wonderful. You remember how to get here?"

She giggled. "Of course." She hung up.

"What kind of minister is he?" Yoshi asked.

"Methodist."

"You're amazing," Paul said.

"What about coffins?" Sam asked.

"Oh, damn. You have any school mates with a funeral home?"

"Not that I know of."

"Paul-san, Sam's right. We should move to the cottage. Once there, I'll run a search for coffins."

"Right." Grinning, he extended his arm for Sam. "Let's do it"

Things were working out. He hoped.

SIXTY-EIGHT

HIS PHONE RANG at twelve o'clock sharp. Fortune. He switched to message dictation mode and said, "Hello."

"Paul, this is Helena. I'm typing for Fortune. Here goes. What have you decided? Do we meet or not?"

"No. I don't trust you."

"That's what I expected. Unlike your uncle, you're a coward, afraid to face me. In that case, never set foot in my house again. If you do, I'll crush you like a cockroach and tear your limbs off your body one at a time. If you want to live, get as far away from my home as possible. This is your last warning."

"Two wrongs out of two. One, this is no longer your house. It's mine now. Two, you don't have the power to crush me. You're dead, and I'm alive."

"Paul, this is Helena. He's gone, and he's furious. I'd better hide now. He'll want to punish me."

"I understand. I'm sorry. Just pray what we're doing works. We care about you."

"I have to go." She hung up.

"I can't believe I'm saying this, but I'm worried about a ghost!" Yoshi shook his head. "Poor thing."

"Yeah, we'd better dig."

The coffins they ordered arrived at one-thirty P. M. Two men got out and walked them into the cemetery and sat them to one side. Yoshi signed for them, and they left.

At two-forty-five they finished digging the holes and transferred the bones to their new homes. To accomplish the transfer, they placed the tarp-covered boxes on top of the new coffins, then removed the tarps from under them, like pulling a tablecloth from under the silverware on a fancy dining table. The rotten bottoms of the old boxes caved in, dropping the mummified bodies into their new coffins. The skin on both bodies resembled tanned brown leather. It was ugly and sickening to see. One body was smaller than the other, so it was easy to tell which one was Helena's.

"I expected them to be dust by now," Sam said, wide-eyed.

"Yeah, this is pretty weird," Yoshi said. "Mummies." He searched for causes for the mummification. Finally he found was he was looking for and said. "Three things can cause this. Really dry or wet or frozen environments. I'd say it's the first one. These mountains are both hot and dry. And Talon buried them deep underground, so not much oxygen got to them. But it's still pretty surprising."

At five past three o'clock, the gate guard phoned to say Mark Abrams had arrived. They watched as minister four-year-old Chevy parked next to Paul's truck. The man's face broke into a smile when he saw Samantha, who introduced them all around. His smile was pleasant and manly, but he also had that special caring expression Paul always noticed in ministers. He wondered what caused that. Paul liked the man the instant he shook hands with him.

Now they were standing with the reverend, staring down at Fortune's and Helena's remains in their new caskets. The young pastor seemed shaken by the mummies.

"You say they died a hundred and thirty years ago?"

"Close enough." Paul pointed. "That one is Fortune Montmartre, an evil man who built the original estate. The one on the right is Helena Longmore, a sixteen-year-old girl he kidnapped and forced to marry him. He murdered her when she was eighteen. We also uncovered the bones of thirty-six young girls under the age of fifteen he tortured and murdered. Our information is he was a practicing devil worshiper whose cult was driven out of San Francisco."

Mark Abrams nodded. "I saw that story about the girls on TV yesterday and this morning." His face showed concern and puzzlement. "Sam, if he was so evil, why do you want to give him a Christian burial? Why not let the police handle it?"

"I can answer that," Paul said. "My uncle, who owned this estate, recently died and left his fortune to me on one condition. That condition was that in two weeks I had to find Fortune's and Helena's bones and give them a proper burial." He hesitated. "My uncle believed the ghosts of these two people haunted the mansion. The fate of young Helena troubled him. He hoped that finding and burying the bones would send the ghosts on their way. He was... well, eccentric."

"I see." The minister's face became grave. "So, without a proper burial, you won't inherit?"

Paul grinned. Mark had got straight to the point. "That's about the size of it."

"Will you do it?" Sam asked in a worried tone. "I mean, say some words over them?"

The minister hesitated, as if thinking about his answer, then grinned at her. "I said I would, Sam, but it would help if I knew more about them? Something to make it more personal."

"I can do that, too," Paul said.

He gave the minister a detailed account of everything he knew about Fortune Montmartre, Talon and Helena. When he finished, he said, "Well, that's it. What do you think?"

Mark smiled at Paul. "Do you believe in ghosts, Paul?"

Paul squirmed a bit and answered. "Yeah, I guess I do. Stupid, huh?"

The minister rested his hand on Paul's shoulder and grinned.

"Don't tell anyone, Paul, but I do, too. Most modern translations of the Bible use the word 'ghost' in Luke 24:36, where Jesus is trying to convince his disciples he is not an apparition, but a real man risen from the dead. In older versions of the bible, such as the Geneva version and the King James Bible, they substituted the word spirit for the word ghost. According to the new translators, however, Jesus used the word ghost, not spirit, as the older versions reported, so I guess I'm in good company." He chuckled. "How should we proceed?"

"Can we do it here, now, and then move the bodies to their graves? Would that work?"

"Don't see why not. St. Paul said wherever three or more gather in the Lord's name, there is my church. Why don't we form a semicircle around the coffins?"

They did, and Mark retrieved a small book from his inside coat pocket. He opened and studied it for a minute. After a moment, he shook his head, closed and returned it. He looked at the bodies and said,

"Lord, we have gathered here to say goodbye to two people who died long before our time. We offer to You the body of Fortune Montmartre, who murdered his beautiful young wife, and was then killed by his own son, Talon, while trying to murder him. We especially commend this beautiful young woman, Helena Montmartre, whose sweet life was destroyed when the man Montmartre kidnapped her and forced her into marriage.

"We pray, Lord, that You have taken young Helena into Your arms and given her the peace she deserves.

"As for Fortune Montmartre, we commend his body unto You and bow to Your wisdom as the creator of the universe. We pray that You will find it in Your heart to wrest this man's soul from the hands of the evil one who held it until his death.

"We are all Your creatures, even though we may choose not to acknowledge You. And, for that reason, we ask You to care for our souls and those we now commend unto You.

"Amen. Let us pray."

They all bowed their heads as Mark launched into a familiar version of the Lord's Prayer.

When he finished, he looked at Paul. "Thank you for the opportunity to do this. This is an experience I'll carry with me to my grave. I pray your uncle will rest in peace."

"Mark, that was perfect." Sam said. "Won't you come to the cottage for a snack and a drink?"

"Sorry, Sam, can't. A minister's work never finishes. I have an appointment to visit and comfort an elderly woman who just lost her husband."

"May I have your card?" Paul asked. "I'd like to send you a donation, if you don't mind."

Mark guffawed. "I don't mind at all. We can use it. Our church is poor. Thanks for offering." He handed over a card. "I have to run now."

They shook hands all around and watched him drive away.

"Wow," Yoshi said. "That was educational. A first for me."

"We'd better get the bodies in the ground," Paul said with nervousness churning in his gut. These were the right bodies. He was certain of that. And they had given them a proper burial. But would it work? And how long before he would knowHe checked his watch. Too late to call Huckabee and Madam Song. He looked toward the chateau? Were they still there? If not, how did they go? Did they vanish in a puff of smoke, like in the movies? Would it have been pleasant for Helena or painful? Was Fortune still there, laughing at Paul's foolishness? Or was he now a rich man? He closed the lid on Helena's coffin.

They would know soon enough.

SIXTY-NINE

FRESH OUT OF the shower and dressed in slacks and a short-sleeved white shirt, Paul hurried down to stand on the front stoop of the cottage and peer across the grounds at the big house. They had done all they could. The bodies were now properly buried. But had it worked?

His gut churned with doubt. Was he now rich? Or was he still a pauper? He stared at the mansion, wishing he had X-ray vision. No sign of Fortune's red glow.

"Damn!" he muttered. Was Helena free now? A hopeful thought struck him. So far, Helena hadn't called him. If she was still at the mansion, she would call, wouldn't she?

Not if she's hiding from Fortune and can't call.

He let loose a quiet, frustrated growl. The suspense was almost unbearable. He took a deep breath. The early evening air was fresh and invigorating and normally would have energized him, but tonight the beauty of the estate mocked him, saying, "Dream on, you fool. You failed again."

Fortune's last words rose in his thoughts. "You're a coward. If you show up again, I'll tear your limbs off, one at a time."

Paul trembled with anger as he tried to analyze the situation. How would Madam Song know if he had succeeded? Would she tell the truth? What recourse would he have if she didn't? Hire a lawyer and contest the will? If it went to court, how could she prove the ghosts were still there? Or that they even existed? Impossible. They would laugh at her. He imagined a judge's stern face. Ghosts, Madam? Ghosts don't exist. Ruling for the plaintiff? A sane judge would throw the case out of court.

He studied the big house. A powerful urge to run to the chateau gripped him. He wanted to pound on the door and scream, "Hey, you evil bastard! Are you still here? If you are, come and get me."

And then he realized he was playing mind games with himself. If the house was clear, he would follow Huckabee's rules. If they hadn't vacated, he still had seven days to try something else. He stared at the mansion. He had to know now, not tomorrow.

Only barely conscious of his actions, he took off running at high speed toward the chateau. There, he bounded up the steps, through the massive front door, and into the library. He halted abruptly in the middle of the room. Heart thumping heavily from his sprint, he looked around, afraid of what he might find. He saw no sign of Helena or Fortune. He calmed himself. The burial ritual had worked, after all. The library was deserted.

He walked further into the room. The place felt empty. Exhilaration rose within him like a blazing rocket. He had succeeded. In seven days, he had gone from rags to riches. Even better, he had exchanged a selfish, mean-spirited woman for a beautiful golden angel.

Don't be stupid. You don't know that yet.

The negative thought crept into his mind unbidden. He felt his anger rising. He had to know.

He inhaled a huge breath and yelled with all his power. "Hey, Fortune, you son of a bitch. You wanted to see me. I'm here. Show yourself." At that moment, Helena's beautiful naked form appeared before him. Wide eyed and frightened, she shushed him with one finger to her lips. He blinked several times, trying to make the vision go away. It didn't. Instead, she came closer and stopped in front of him. Disappointment gripped his heart.

"You're still here," he blurted, instantly feeling stupid.

She nodded, pointed to the computer, and hurried to it. He followed and read what she typed.

"Paul, you must leave," she wrote. "He's furious. He wants to kill you."

"Yeah, and tear off my arms and legs." He took a deep, calming breath. "At least we gave you a nice funeral and buried you next to Justin."

"Thank you." She turned from the keyboard. Then she turned back and typed. "It's not working, is it?"

"I'm afraid not. Sorry. We'll order your headstone as soon as we can."

"Paul!"

He turned as Sam and Yoshi hurried toward him. Sam grabbed his hand and Yoshi shook his head in disapproval. "You shouldn't be here," he said. "It's too dangerous."

Helena typed furiously. "That's what I told him. Fortune wants to kill him. You'd better go."

"Hi, Helena. Glad to know you're okay." Sam was gazing at the computer.

"She's right, Paul-san. We'd better get out of here."

"Too late," Paul said.

Fortune was floating a foot above the floor near the wing-back sofa. Sam suddenly lifted off the floor, rising toward the ceiling. Paul grabbed her legs. "Help me." Yoshi jumped up and caught her arm. Together, they pulled her down. "Let's get out of here."

Fortune released her, and a barrage of heavy books flew at them from the first-floor shelves. They scrambled for the door. Paul looked back and blocked a large book inches from his face. Helena had vanished. Fortune vanished and reappeared before them in the foyer.

"Take her," Paul yelped to Yoshi. "Go."

He ran straight through Fortune and came out behind him.

Yoshi and Sam scrambled out of the house. Paul glared at Fortune. "This is not over," he growled. "I'll get you one way or another."

Fortune's face twisted into a smirking grin. A powerful force slammed Paul's chest, lifting his feet off the ground, and drove him backward toward the stairs. His heels hit the bottom step. He twisted his body, hoping to break his fall with his arms, but he was moving too fast. The ribs on his back hit something with a sharp edge. The blow drove the air from his lungs. A sharp, dagger-like pain stabbed his spine. But his anger was greater than the pain. In one swift motion, he pushed to his feet and dashed straight for the grinning apparition, swinging his fists as he moved. His blows met only air. Impetus took him through and past the evil apparition.

Paul tried to break his momentum and turn back, but the ghost gave him a powerful push that sent him sprawling through the still-open front door. This time, he used his forearms to break his fall. His face missed smashing against the porch deck by a fraction of an inch. The effort caused another spasm of pain in his back. He ignored it, and with all his strength, performed a power push up and used his legs like locomotive wheels to regain his feet. He spun around, intending to go in for another round. The door slammed shut in his face.

Paul stopped moving and stared at the ornate door. Suddenly, common sense over-rode his anger. He knew defeating the ghost physically was impossible. He had to find another way.

He looked toward the cottage. Yoshi and Sam were already at the front stoop and were watching him. They were safe.

He hurried down the steps, stopping in the driveway as the immensity of his failure hit him with the power of a battering ram. His stomach lurched, and he realized he had no desire to face their sympathetic faces. He needed time to get his head straight. Seven days of wasted hope and effort pressed on him like a heavy, smothering blanket, and Fortune was still king of the mansion.

With his thoughts dark with swirling eddies of emotion, he turned toward the back of the estate where Gerard had dug the graves.

It seemed a fitting place to think about his future.

SEVENTY

SAMANTHA STOPPED at the cottage's front stoop. She turned, expecting to find Paul right behind her. Instead, he was still on the mansion's porch, looking at its door. Puzzled, she watched as he left the porch and walked zombie-like toward the back of the house. Her father had walked that way, too. She lifted clenched fists to hold back a wave of fear. Had Fortune taken control of Paul, too?

Yoshi, who had entered the cottage, rejoined her on the stoop. "Where's Paul?"

"Look." She pointed at Paul's vanishing figure. "I'm worried Fortune did something to him."

"I doubt that, Sam. Paul is too strong-minded."

"Then why didn't he follow us?"

"He lost seventy-five million dollars and failed to fulfill his uncle's last request. I suspect he needs to lick his wounds."

"If that's true, I should go to him. He'll need me."

Yoshi caught her arm. "No, Sam. He wants to be alone. Otherwise, he would have followed us. Let him be. He'll come back when he's ready."

"How can you say that? He's alone. Fortune may have hurt him."

"You really want to know?"

"Yes."

"I'll tell you, but you must promise not to tell him. He's my best friend, and I want nothing to come between us. Can you do that?"

Yoshi's face was more serious than she had ever seen it. She nodded and gave him a brief grin. "Cross my heart and hope to die. Tell me."

Yoshi sat down on the stoop. "We drank too much sake one night after jogging ten miles. He told me some things about himself he would have regretted later if he even remembered telling me. He was really out of it."

"What things?"

"He believes it's his fault his mother died in poverty and his father ran away from home. He considers himself a coward for leaving her."

Sam sat beside him. "Yoshi, that makes no sense. He's one of the nicest men I've ever known. He's no coward. On TV, that detective said he received medals for his actions as a Marine, and he's smarter and more creative than any of the intellectuals I met at school."

Yoshi nodded. "I agree with you, but he doesn't. His father was an alcoholic who beat his mother. Paul was still in college the last time it happened, and he blew up. He threatened to kill him if he ever did it again. That's when James Davenport left home, just walked away, abandoning both of them." Yoshi shook his head. "Paul says his father leaving broke his mother's heart. He blames himself for that, too. He calls himself a coward because soon after that, unable to face his mother's unhappiness, he ran away to the marines and left her to die alone."

Tears bubbled in Sam's eyes. "So, he's never forgiven himself."

"Apparently not. It's a heavy burden he carries, even when he's smiling. He says he did a pitiful job of answering her letters, and when he returned for her funeral, he discovered she had almost no food. She had a job cleaning house for a wealthy family in Pasadena, but her bank account had only fifty cents in it. Ever since then, he's had a recurring nightmare about going home to visit her, only to watch her sink to her death in quicksand. He said he wakes up screaming sometimes."

Yoshi stopped speaking, took a deep breath. "When he told me that story, he was drunk, and he cried for an hour. All his pent-up grief poured out, and he couldn't stop it. I poured coffee into him and stayed until he sobered enough to go to bed. We've never spoken about that afternoon since then, which is why I think he's forgotten it." Yoshi hesitated. "You know how we met? Stupid me went jogging alone in Hahamonga Park near Pasadena. I tripped and broke my leg just below my knee. I lay in the blazing sun for two hours before Paul came along and carried me in his arms for three miles to his car. He saved my life."

Sam leaned in and gave Yoshi a brief hug. "So you love him, too."

"Yeah. There's one more thing. He left the marines to help his father, which is how his debt got so huge. But his father ripped bed sheets into strips, twisted them and hung himself from the shower rod in his bathroom. The nurse discovered him an hour later. Paul blames himself for allowing that to happen, too."

Sam's eyes lit up as understanding dawned. "So that's why saving Helena for Uncle Justin is so important. He's not after the money. He's trying to redeem himself for all the other times he believes he failed."

"Yes, that's my opinion. Please, don't—"

"Don't worry. I won't say anything. Thanks for telling me."

"You're welcome." Yoshi climbed to his feet and did a little bow. "I think I'll go rest for a while. I'm still hung over with jet lag." Sam touched his arm. "Help yourself. I'll stay here and wait for him."

Forever, if I have to.

Yoshi left her sitting on the stoop with her arms wrapped

around her knees.

She remained in that position for several minutes, pondering the events of the past seven days that had brought them to this point. With the death of Uncle Justin and the strangeness of her father, she had wondered what would become of her. And then Paul showed up and drew her into his world and his problems. In the beginning, she hadn't understood it, but now she realized he had filled the gap left in her life by Uncle Justin's death, a gap her father had never filled. She also knew their relationship was perfect for both of them. He was Prince Charming. She was Cinderella. All they needed was a happy ending.

She gazed up at the sky. The evening still held a deep purple glow. It was a time she loved.

She stood to get the kinks out of her leg muscles. She peered toward the back of the estate, trying to find him in the darkening evening. A chilly breeze wormed its way down her collar.

The far end was already deep in shadows. She could see nothing.

Shivering, she hurried inside the cottage. As she closed the door, she whispered, "Paul, where are you? What are you doing?"

Please, God, let him be okay.

SEVENTY-ONE

A POWERFUL SENSE of déjà vu rolled through Paul as he ran up the front steps of the old duplex where he lived with his mother in Pasadena. At the door, he stopped and adjusted his marine uniform. His visit would surprise and make her happy. He would give her a big hug and a kiss and tell her he would take care of her. A sudden dark cloud of fear raced through him. He frowned. This was his home. There was nothing here to fear.

He sucked in air, rang the bell, and waited. No answer. He pushed the button three times in quick succession.

The door opened. An older man peered out at him. Surprise caused him to stammer, "Uncle Justin, what...?" His uncle exactly resembled his portrait hanging in the chateau's foyer.

The old man smiled. "Come in, Paul. Your mother and I want to talk to you and we have little time." His voice was strong, friendly. He stepped back and held open the door.

"But—"

"Hurry, son. Our time is short."

He obeyed, fear rising like a storm tide within him. Am I dead, too? His mother, looking far prettier and healthier than the last time he saw her, smiled up at him from the living room's shabby sofa. Anxiety screamed within him that something was wrong, that Fortune had murdered him.

"Mom!" He started toward her.

"Sit down, Paul." She gestured to the only easy chair in the room.

He sat. "Mom!"

"Don't speak, lad. Listen," Uncle Justin said, joining his mother on the sofa. "What we have to say is important."

"But—"

"No buts," his mother said. "Listen to me. I know you think you shouldn't have left me, but—"

"Mom, I'm sorry." Heat rose to his face. "I should have stayed home and helped you. Can you ever forgive me?" Tears formed and blurred his vision.

"No, Paul, please. There's nothing to forgive. You did the right thing. Young men have to go places, expand their horizons, learn about the world. You didn't abandon me. Your father abandoned both of us."

Startled by her words, he sat speechless.

"Unlike you, your father was weak from childhood," Justin added. "His only ambition was to play around and gratify himself. Your mother was a beautiful girl when they married, and he destroyed the happiness she deserved. I admire you for your efforts to help him, but his death was his own fault."

"Paul, James was a drunk. And he sometimes hurt me, but I couldn't help myself. I loved him as I love you." His mother's voice sounded almost like that of a young girl. "It was James, not you, who broke my heart when he left. If he cared about either of us, he would not have run away. He was weak and a coward. I know that now."

"But…"

"Look, boy, you joined the marines like a million other young men to build your character." His uncle leaned forward. "I ran away to South Africa. The sins of the father are not visited upon the son. James was the coward, and his way of life robbed him of dignity. You were a dutiful son and left the service to help him. But it was a futile effort. What he did was inevitable. Alcohol destroyed his brain. Understand that, forget the past." He hesitated. "I've given you a way forward. Take it. Marry Samantha, build a home. Follow that path. Use the opportunity and be happy."

"But—." He was speechless, yet felt a growing sense of relief. They were removing the guilt that had plagued him for years.

"Hush, Paul," his mother said. "This is your chance. Take it. Marry that girl. You deserve to be happy."

Uncle Justin touched his mother's arm, then turned back to Paul. "One more thing, son. I've tried to return to the chateau, as did Fortune, but so far my returns have been short-lived and intermittent. Something, a bright light, keeps pulling me away."

"You've come back?" Paul blurted.

"Yes, for short periods only, but..."

"Did you release Sam from that iron coffin?"

"Yes."

"Did you lift the John Deere and drop it?"

"Yes."

"Then it must be your presence that has frightened Fortune."

"Frightened?"

"Yes. Helena says that Fortune seems frightened of something,"

"Good. Listen, Paul. I've been fighting the force pulling me away from here. I have been able to remain only for short periods. It's frustrating, but if that evil monster attacks you and you can't escape, call me for help. I believe that may pull me back. Remember that."

Paul sat stunned until his mother said, "Paul, did you understand?"

"Yes. I love you, Mom."

"I love you, too, Paul.

"Annie, we have to go."

She nodded as their images grew weaker.

"Wait, please!" He jumped up. "I tried to get rid of Fortune, but I failed," he cried. "I don't know what to do. Tell me, please." Their bodies and the room were fading.

"Revenge, Paul. Use revenge."

"Revenge? I don't understand. I…"

"Be happy, Paul," his mother's voice whispered. "I love you."

"Duck!" Justin gesticulated wildly as they vanished.

Galvanized by the fear in his uncle's voice, Paul snapped awake and rolled away from the tree.

Above him, a breaking limb cracked, followed by a powerful thud, the unmistakable sound of an ax blade being embedded into the trunk of the tree. He scrambled to his feet and stared at the spot he had just vacated. Moonlight glinted on the blade of an ax stuck in the trunk. If he hadn't rolled away when he did, he would have joined the rank of the headless horseman. The ax handle began rocking back and forth as if someone was trying to pull it free.

Paul glanced toward the mansion, saw the distinct, glowing shape of Fortune under the big oak. "Damn!" He rushed forward and grabbed the ax handle with all his strength. It jerked free of the tree as he did so, yanking him aside with incredible force.

He hung on like a man trying to subdue a bucking, wild stallion. The ax dragged him away from the tree, causing his feet and arms to flail in all directions. Realizing the danger of letting go, he hung on with all his strength. Once free of the tree's coverage, he moved into Fortune's field of view. When the ghost saw Paul held the ax handle, he let it go and the unexpected release of pressure on the tool caused Paul to fall forward. He tossed the heavy tool away from him as he hit the ground on his elbows. A severe pain stabbed his back. Fortune remained under the tree for half a minute longer and then vanished like a switched-off neon bulb. Paul imagined the ghost's face had been glowering at him. He inhaled and got to his feet. It was over for now. He hoped.

To play it safe, he tossed the ax into the bushes behind the junipers. As he made the throw, another painful spasm struck his back, almost taking him down. He remained motionless for a moment, taking shallow breaths until the pain went away.

He looked at the night sky, trying to replay and understand what had happened to him? When he first got there, he had stood under the big oak, staring down at the three empty graves. A scurrying noise from behind the Junipers caused him to twist around. Pain hit him again. He had limped to the big oak and dropped to the ground. Resting there, waiting for the pain to subside, he had fallen asleep leaning against the big oak's trunk. He had dreamed, and then Fortune had tried to behead hiA strong desire to recall the dream gripped him. He searched his memory, trying to dredge it up, but found nothing. Oddly, his effort to remember caused a sense of warmth and happiness to wash over him. Everything was going to be fine. He sensed his prospects offered future happiness, especially with Samantha. This was amazing. What had he dreamed? It wasn't his regular nightmare.

He strained to remember, but nothing emerged. Only the powerful sense of wellbeing and the notion it involved his mother and Uncle Justin came forth.

Use revenge.

A fuzzy idea nibbled at the edge of his thoughts. He tried to examine it, but it scooted away like a slippery ice cube. The idea seemed important, but he wasn't sure. At the cottage, light spilled from the downstairs living room window. He imagined Sam and Yoshi there worrying about him. He started walking, limping to favor the back muscles on his right side.

As he walked, the desire to remember his dream grew with each step. How could he have dreamed about both his mother and his uncle? And why was he so much happier?

Use revenge.

What did that mean? He knew the thought was important. But how? Why? He had to think about this.

SEVENTY-TWO

AGAIN SITTING on the cottage stoop with her elbows on her knees and her chin cupped in her hand, Samantha sat up. Something white moved near the far end of the estate. Paul! Coming toward her.

She watched his progress for a minute and then went into the kitchen to prepare three stiff vodka and tonics. She held back the ice until she heard the front door open. She dropped the ice and hurried to meet him.

When he turned toward her, she handed him the drink and said, "I don't know about you, but I needed this."

He took a big gulp and grinned, "Whoa, that's good, but it's not what I need."

He pulled her to him with his right arm. "This is all I will ever need." He kissed her and then broke away with a pained expression. "Sam, I have to sit down. I hurt my back. Where's Yosh?"

"Up here, Paul-san," Yoshi was standing at the top of the stairs. "You okay?"

"Yeah, I think so. Can we meet in the living room?"

"I'll be right down."

"Your drink is in the kitchen," Samantha called, looking

worried.

They left the foyer and sat on the living-room sofa. Paul cuddled her tight against him.

"I love you, Sam. Never forget that."

Puzzled by his words, she tilted her head back to look at his face. He wasn't acting defeated, but his eyes were grim, pain-filled, nervous.

"How bad are you hurt?" she asked.

"Bruised rib," he said. "It hurts, but I'll live."

He lifted his glass and took a long swig.

"Paul…"

He put his finger to her lips to shush her. "Wait for Yoshi."

She sipped her own drink and peered at him over its top. She hoped her puzzlement didn't show.

He wasn't smiling, but she detected a mischievous twinkle in his eyes. Why was he acting so mysterious?

Yoshi came in grinning, but when he saw their faces, he hurried to a stuffed chair across from them. "What's up?" He seemed as puzzled as she felt.

They exchanged glances and sat waiting for Paul to speak.

SEVENTY-THREE

PAUL CHUGGED DOWN HIS drink and searched for a place on the table to set his glass. Sam grabbed a coaster for him.

He nodded thanks and said, "Here's the deal. We had a setback today, but I still have a week left. So, I've been trying to figure out what else we could do. Unfortunately, all I have are vague notions. I'm frustrated as hell."

"Paul, I was worried to death," Sam said.

"How long was I gone?"

"Three hours."

He gave her an embarrassed smile. "I fell asleep, Sam. Before I left the chateau, I tried to fight Fortune, which proves I'm not too bright." He grinned. "I understand now how Don Quixote must have felt. Fortune has amazing strength and threw me around like a stuffed doll. I landed on the stairs and hurt my back. Then I made another mistake. I got up for round two. That time, he tossed me out onto the front porch and slammed the door in my face. Lucky he didn't kill me."

"But why didn't you come home with us?" Sam's face showed bewilderment. "We could have helped you."

"I don't know. I felt disappointed and pretty bummed out.

Anyhow, I walked back to the graves your dad dug, and while there, my back spasmed. I leaned against the old oak to ease the pain and fell asleep." He hesitated. "I had a weird dream."

"Ah!" Yoshi said. "What kind of dream?" He seemed eager to know the answer.

"I couldn't remember at first, Yosh, but I remember my uncle woke me. I opened my eyes and rolled to one side just in time to avoid being beheaded by a double-bladed ax. Fortune had swung an ax with amazing accuracy to chop off my head." He told them about his fight with the ax.

"That's incredible."

"Yeah, but real, Yosh."

"Thank God you're alright." Sam took his hand.

"We should thank Uncle Justin, too." He frowned.

"You haven't told us everything, have you?" Yoshi said.

Paul nodded. "The whole thing felt surreal, Yosh. On the way back here, the words 'Use revenge' kept nibbling at me. And then the details of the dream flooded back to me."

"Will you tell us?" Sam's eyes pleaded.

"Yes, I want to. You've both been more loyal and helpful than I deserve, so you should know everything." He lifted his drink. Empty. "Any more where that came from?"

"Hell, yes." Yoshi jumped up. "I'll fix them, but don't start without me." He hurried off to the kitchen.

They sat holding hands, listening to the sounds of an ice tray popping open and the clink and stir of drinks being made. Yoshi returned and handed them fresh drinks. He dropped into the easy chair, grinned at them, and said, "Okay, Paul-san. Shoot."

Paul took a long pull on his drink and said, "Ever since my mother died, I've had a recurring nightmare. It always starts the same way with me coming home on leave from boot camp, running up the steps, and ringing the doorbell. No one answers, so I open the door and almost fall into a room filled wall-to-wall with deep quicksand. My mother calls for help from the back of the room. Her head and one arm sticking above the quicksand,

and she's sinking fast. I cry out, 'Mom, hang on,' but she can't. I look around. There's no way to reach her without sinking myself. She faces me with pain-filled, sad eyes and says, 'It's okay, son. Don't worry. I love you.'

"As I watch, horrified, she disappears under the quicksand. I scream and wake up." He stopped and tried to bore a hole in the coffee table with his eyes. "After tonight's dream, I understand why I have that nightmare. It's because I joined the marines and left her alone to support herself. I never should have done that. Never." His voice broke. "But tonight the dream tonight took a different twist. It wiped away all my feelings of guilt. It's so weird. I..."

Sam touched his arm and whispered, "Paul tells us. Please."

Paul nodded. "It started the same as usual. I was running up the steps of our rental house in Pasadena. I rang the bell as usual, but this time someone opened it."

"Who?" Samantha gasped.

Paul grinned at her. "Uncle Justin."

"Uncle Justin?"

"Yes. It was amazing, Sam. He was exactly like his portrait. I mean exactly. Same face, same coat, everything. I've never met him, so I guess in my dream I reinvented him that way."

"Weird," Yoshi said, "but it makes sense, too."

"What did he say?" Sam asked.

Paul chuckled and told them everything that had happened. "He invited me in and said he and Mom wanted to talk to me. I went in, of course. Mom was sitting on our old sofa, smiling, and she didn't look sick or tired anymore. She looked younger. Pretty."

"God," Sam sucked in a breath. "What was your mother's name? You never told me."

"It was Anne, but uncle Justin called her Annie. He said she was beautiful when she was young... Anyway, I wanted to give her a hug, but she ordered me to sit in the chair across from the sofa. Uncle Justin sat beside her. The whole thing was surreal. I was like an obedient kid, but to be honest, I feared I was dead, too." He paused for a breath. "I tried to ask questions, but Uncle Justin ordered me to be quiet and listen to what they had to say. He said it was important."

"Instead, I told Mom I was sorry and asked her to forgive me. She shushed me and said there was nothing to forgive. After that, they both explained that everything that had happened was my father's fault. That none of it was mine. Uncle Justin said my dad always had been weak and irresponsible and that his death was his own fault because of his lifestyle."

"Wow!" Yoshi said. "That's some dream."

"Yeah."

"What happened then?" Samantha wanted more.

"Uncle Justin said he'd given me the path, and they both told me to marry you and be happy. About then, they began fading away. I begged them to wait and tell me how to get rid of Fortune. Uncle Justin said, 'Revenge, Paul. Use revenge.' And then he screamed for me to duck. I woke up and rolled clear."

"Wow, Paul-san. He saved your life."

Paul smiled at his friend's amazement and winced. "Yeah, I guess he did."

"Did you believe them?" Sam's voice was low.

"You mean about not being your fault?"

"Yes."

Paul thought for a moment. "I must have, Sam. If my back wasn't painful, I'd be happier than I can ever remember."

"You sure you don't have a broken rib?"

"Yes. If it was, I couldn't take a deep breath." To prove it, he took a deep breath. "It only hits me when I twist the wrong way, which means it's a bruised muscle. I've had worse, so let's not worry about it."

"Why do I get the idea you're holding back something?"

Paul grinned. "You are a mind reader."

"What is it?"

His face flushed, and he squeezed Sam's hand. "Sam, Uncle

Justin said he's been trying to come back from wherever he is. He said there's a force pulling him away, but that he's resisting. He can remain here only for short spans. I asked him if he's the one who let you out of that iron box. He said yes."

"Ah, so!" Yoshi hopped up, unable to contain his excitement, then fell back. "Helena said she didn't do it."

"Right. He also said he's the one who lifted the tractor and broke the backhoe. My guess is he was practicing to do battle with Fortune,"

"Paul, you said you were dreaming. It can't be real, can it?" Her voice was fearful and hopeful at the same time.

"It sounds crazy, but it seemed real to me."

"That was no dream, Paul-san. Dreams don't save you from a flying ax."

"I hope you're right, Yosh. There's one more thing. He said I should call to him if Fortune tries to murder me."

"Why?"

"He thinks my cry for help will be enough to bring him back permanently."

"I believe it was real, too," Sam said. "It had to be Uncle Justin who let me out of that box."

"So now we need a new plan." Yoshi said, becoming practical.

"Yes."

"Any ideas?"

"Well, his last words may be a clue."

"Use revenge?"

"Yes."

Sam's eyes widened and sparkled with excitement. "Paul, I think I know."

Paul's phone rang. Helena.

SEVENTY-FOUR

H E HELD UP the screen for Sam to see. "Helena, are you alright?"

"Yes, I saw what Fortune did. Are you hurt?"

"I'll live. Actually, we're worried about you."

"Me, too. I've been hiding. He's furious, and he still looks scared. He keeps looking around like someone is after him. It's frightening."

"Tell her," Sam whispered.

"We believe Justin is causing it," he said.

"Justin?"

"Yes. He's trying to come back to protect you from Fortune."

"Is that possible?"

"I'm not sure. Seven days ago I thought ghosts were fantasy."

Helena's typing paused, and then, "I'm sorry your plan failed. Are you going to give up?"

"No. We still have a week, and we're working on a new approach. Don't forget, you're the reason for everything we're trying to do, so don't lose hope. We won't quit on you."

"I won't. My father used to say a little poem. Tis a lesson you should heed: Try, try, try again. If at first you don't succeed, try, try, try again. I wish I could see all of you. "

"We wish we could see you, too."

"Helena, I asked Samantha to marry me. She said yes."

"That's wonderful. Congratulations."

Samantha giggled.

"How often do you check for new messages from me?"

"I hang around here a lot, but you don't write often. It's dangerous, though. Fortune looks for me here first. Why?"

"I may need your help."

"Oh, okay. I'll keep watch. I have to go now. Bye."

Paul stuffed the phone in his shirt pocket and grinned at Sam. "Well?"

"What?"

"You were about to tell us what 'use revenge' means."

Sam smiled. "Do you remember what the professor said about vengeful spirits?"

He tugged his earlobe. "Yes. He said they're the most fearsome type of ghosts because they died in a high emotional state. What…?"

"Fortune died in a fight to the death with Talon, didn't he?"

"What are you getting at?" Yoshi asked.

"Well, when Paul asked the professor whether ghosts ever voluntarily leave places they haunt, he said—"

"They might leave if they can gratify their desire for vengeance."

She smiled. "Right, and I believe that's what Uncle Justin meant. That we should use Fortune's desire to kill Talon against him?"

"Interesting idea," Paul said. "The question is how?"

"Maybe Fortune isn't aware Talon is dead." Yoshi leaned forward, the excitement of a new puzzle to solve on his face.

"He has to be, Yosh," Paul said. "They've been here a long time. Nobody lives this long."

"What would he do if we told him where to find Talon?"

Paul grinned at his friends. "I'm surrounded by geniuses. He may go after him."

"Paul, do you think he would?"

Paul shrugged. "We have to assume he will. Otherwise we're wasting our time." He turned to Yoshi. "What does Mr. Moto propose?"

"Elementary. We must convince Fortune that his reason for staying here no longer exists." Yoshi chuckled. "Give him a reason to go somewhere else."

"You mean like that cemetery in Colorado Talon is haunting?"

"Yes, if, as the professor believed, he's strong enough to leave here."

"What if he can't find it? Ghosts may need maps, same as we do." Sam asked.

"They must," Paul said, "unless they possess built-in knowledge of the entire universe, which I doubt. The worry is, he may no longer care. They say passion dims over time."

They fell silent for a moment. Finally, Paul said, "I think Yoshi has provided a good definition of the goal. Induce Fortune to leave here to go after Talon. And that poses several questions. Does Fortune still desire revenge? Can he leave here if he wants to? Does he know where to find Colorado? Damn!" The whole idea seemed insurmountable.

"Perhaps we can teach him," Yoshi said.

"How, Yoshi?" Sam was frowning.

"We could try the computer, of course, but..." Paul's thoughts were racing.

"We can't ask Helena to do it," Sam said. "Too dangerous for her."

"I have an idea," Yoshi said.

"Shoot."

"We could make up a couple of large pop displays containing the information we want to give him."

"Did you say pop?"

"Sorry. P.O.P. Point-of- purchase displays. We use folding poster stands in our lobbies to advertise things we're featuring at our hotels. We can produce new posters overnight, so I'm sure

L. A. has that kind of service, too."

"That's a great idea, Yoshi," Sam said.

Paul: "What would you put on them?"

"Well, we need to rekindle his desire for vengeance."

"Like an easy-to-read blowup of Carter Franklin's story about Talon," Sam was beaming. Her eyes were sparkling. "We could make the part about Talon's desire to kill Fortune bigger and bolder. Easy to see."

"That ought to do it."

"And don't forget his little poem." Sam was beaming.

Paul grinned. Their brains were cooking. He loved it. "What else?"

"Well, I suggest a simplified map to show him how to find Talon," Yoshi said. "We don't know Fortune's navigational capability. Don't want him to get lost, do we?"

"Only if he tries to come back. That's another great idea, Yosh."

"Arigato."

Sam wasn't convinced. "It sounds good, I agree, but how do we get him to read them?"

"I'll take them in and confront him."

"Paul, no!"

"How then?"

"I don't know. It's too dangerous. He wants to kill you."

"It can't be helped." He stopped as an idea came to him. "What did the diaries say about installing a sound system?"

"Uncle Justin played loud rock and roll, hoping to drive Fortune out of the house. It didn't work. Why?"

"If it's still working, we can use that to communicate with him."

Yoshi, gazing at his phone, said, "One more thing, Paul-san. We should order a riot suit for you."

"Riot suit?" Sam's voice held surprise.

"Hai. It's the protective gear worn by police during a riot." He held up his phone. "I found a perfect suit for him."

"Good thinking, Yosh, but it won't work."

"Why not?"

"Federal law prevents stores from selling that kind of gear to civilians. Otherwise, rioters would be the equal of the police."

"How about a suit of armor, then?"

"Armor? You mean like the knights of old used to wear?"

"Yes. They're flexible enough nowadays that you could move around easily enough."

Paul choked back a laugh. "I like the way you think, Yosh. In fact, your idea just gave me another idea, a slight variation on it."

"What are you thinking?"

"Motocross body armor. Those motocross cyclists wear some heavy-duty protection for their bodies, shoulders and arms."

"Ah!" Yoshi turned back to his phone. He left his chair and stuck the phone under their noses. "Something like this?"

Paul took the phone. It showed the torso of a body protected by heavy, black protective armor. It was what the motocross riders used to protect their bodies from handlebars, stones, or other objects they might hit during a spill.

"Perfect. It's lightweight and strong enough to help, if Fortune uses me as a ping-pong ball."

"It looks tough enough," Sam said, "but will it protect a man your size?"

"Some of those motocross riders are heavier than me. If it protects them, it will take care of me, too."

Paul handed the phone back. Yoshi took it but didn't return to his chair. His thumbs clicked away for a few seconds, and then he smiled. "It's called a body protector, and it says here it's designed to protect front, back, shoulders, flank, and elbows. There's a motocross cycle shop less than ten miles from here, and they have three extra-large units in stock. I like it." Satisfied, he returned to his chair.

"Me, too. Even if our friendly ghost throws me against a wall or into a stairway, that will keep me from breaking my back. Another problem you solved. Thanks."

"Dou itashimashite."

Paul checked his watch. Eight P.M. He turned to Sam. "Looks like we have a plan now." He stood with a little groan. "Only one thing left to do tonight."

"What's that?"

"Eat. I'm starving."

"Ha! Forget that. You guys need a break. We're eating in, and then I'm going to rub some stinky hot stuff on your back. Dad has some liniment and pain-relief plasters in his bathroom. Both of you need rest. Any questions?" She looked stern.

"No, sir." Paul saluted and sat.

Yoshi snorted his amusement. "What's on the menu, Sam? Guess I'm hungry, too."

"I don't know. I'll dig up something. You two stay here and rest."

She spun on her heel and scooted into the kitchen.

"She's quite a girl, Paul-san. You're a lucky man. And she's right to worry. If your back is still painful tomorrow, we should get it x-rayed."

"I agree. I'd hate to tangle with that creep the way it is, but..."

"What?"

"Well, when I say I fought him, that's not true. He kicks the hell out of me every time we meet. There's no way I can hurt him, but he can kill me anytime he wishes if I get close to him."

"Then why go?"

"I have to, Yosh, but..."

"What?"

"Don't tell Sam what I said."

"You have my word."

"Thanks, but this whole plan strikes me as pretty Mickey-Mouse? How can posters do what my uncle failed to do? He tried dozens of things and failed."

Yoshi chuckled. "My grandfather used to say, 'Nana korobi ya oki'"

Paul tilted his head, waiting for another of Yoshi's old Japanese proverbs. "Okay, Mr. Moto. I give up. What's it mean?"

"It means, if you fall down seven times, get up eight. Your uncle fell down many times and kept trying. So far, you've fallen only once."

"You're right, Yosh. But he didn't have a deadline. We do"So, how will you handle it?"

"Guess I'll stand there and take whatever he dishes out. If it gets too rough, I'll run like hell."

"I don't like it. It's too dangerous."

"I don't either, but I can't just walk away."

"I understand."

Sam came back then and gave them a choice of frozen dinners. "Sorry," she said. "That's it. We need to restock."

Yoshi chose chicken and gravy with corn and mashed potatoes. Paul decided on beef teriyaki and rice. Sam decoded on chicken pot pie. "And wine," she added.

Forty-five minutes later, she brought their food into the dining room. "Gentlemen, dinner is served. Come and get it."

Paul's back hit him hard when he sat at the dining table, but he ignored the pain. Only one problem dominated his thoughts as he ate and chatted.

Would their new plan work?

SEVENTY-FIVE

A WONDERFUL WARM odor of spicy cinnamon drifted into his half-sleep state. He blinked once and opened his eyes to find Samantha standing beside his bed, holding a tray. She was wearing a light-green print dress with pale-orange flowers and the same white apron. Her hair glistened like gold in the morning light, streaming through the bedroom window.

Paul gave her a sleepy smile. "I must be dreaming. Only in dreams do angels serve me breakfast in bed." The bedside clock said 8:15.

"How's your back?"

"I'm pretty sure it's painful. It needs another treatment." He faked a groan to prove it.

"Pretty sure? Isn't that what they call malingering in the Marine corps? Behave and sit up. Your breakfast is getting cold."

He sat up and bunched two pillows for props.

"Can I expect this kind of service every morning after we're married?"

"Hey, don't get greedy." She put the tray on his lap and stepped back. "I want the truth. How do you feel?"

He took a swig of coffee. "Pretty good, I'd say. No spasm when I sat up. Must be because I had a brilliant and beautiful doctor."

"Of course, or maybe the patient is a tough marine. Hurry and eat." She took off for the kitchen.

An hour later, Paul followed Sam into the living room, where Yoshi was already waiting. Paul was eager to get their new plan underway.

"How's our patient?" Yoshi asked Samantha when they joined him.

"Our patient is just fine," Paul said in mock irritation. "We have things to do, Yosh."

Yoshi guffawed. "What do you have in mind, Paul-san."

"Well, it's not that much. We have to edit the Carter Franklin news story for the posters and create some kind of travel map for Fortune."

"Don't forget the poster stands and the sound system," Sam said. "I checked the notes we made when we read the diaries. The sound system controls are in the apartment over the garage. Uncle Justin put them there to keep Fortune from destroying them."

"Yeah, I remember that. First, though, I'd better type up Carter Franklin's news story and edit it for whoever produces the displays."

"No, you don't. That's my bailiwick!" Sam exclaimed. "I majored in English lit, remember? You two go fix the sound system. Call me if you need anything."

Yoshi hopped up. "We've got our orders, Paul-san. Let's do it."

"Hang on. First things first." He leaned close to Sam, gave her a quick peck on the lips and whispered, "I love you, miss."

"I love you, too, sir. Now shoo. Can't get rich sitting around on our lower posteriors."

They left Sam and walked along the work road to the upstairs garage apartment.

To Paul's amazement, there was nothing to fix. The sound system was in the living room, housed in an expensive wooden console. It was in perfect condition. A silver microphone stood atop the console. Inside the console, an expensive preamplifier fed into a high-powered stereo amplifier. A small bundle of speaker wires led from the amplifier down through the floor. A wireless system would have worked just as well, but Paul figured his uncle didn't know about things like that. The wires led over to the house through underground plastic pipes. A shelf on the wall above the console held two stacks of CDs. Half were rock and roll and half were classical works by Mozart, Beethoven, and Vivaldi.

"Nice set up," Yoshi said. "Wonder how it sounds in the mansion."

"Let's find out. Fortune likes Mozart, so let's give him a treat." He pushed the power switch on the preamp and the CD player. All three units lit up. He grinned. "So far, so good." He pressed the eject button on the CD player and put in Mozart's Symphony No. 40, then pushed the play button and turned up the volume.

He listened and frowned. "It's not working."

"We're too far away. Let's go closer to the chateau."

Halfway to Montmartre, the sound of the Mozart symphony drifted to them.

"Wow," Yoshi said. "Old Mozart must be rattling the walls in there. I wonder if loud noises can hurt a ghost's ears."

"Good question. Didn't work when my uncle tried it, though. Wait here and listen. I'll go back and test the microphone."

Paul jogged back to the garage and climbed the stairs to the apartment. There, he found the mike already plugged in. He flipped its power switch, lifted it and said, "Mr. Moto, what do you think? Hello, hello, hello. Moto-san, I'm speaking to you. Hello, hello. Can you hear me now?"

His phone rang. Yoshi. "Yosh. Did it work?."

"Hai. I'm fifty feet away, and it's loud and clear."

"Okay. Hang on."

He turned down the volume about a quarter turn, lifted the

mike and said, "Testing. Testing. Testing. How about now?"

"Not this time."

"Okay, come on back. I'll meet you outside."

He turned off the system power and hurried out of the apartment.

When Yoshi joined him at the foot of the stairs, he said, "At least we can communicate with Helena and Fortune now. Let's go see how Sam's doing."

His phone rang. Helena, the beautiful ghost. "Hi, Helena. What's up?"

"Your voice was talking all over the house. Why did you do that?"

"We need a way to converse with Fortune without getting killed. Also, we can give you messages, too. Was the sound clear?"

"Very."

"Was it too loud?"

"Not for me."

"Good. I think we should invent a word that tells you to call me as soon as it's safe to do so."

"You mean like a secret word?"

"Yes. Whenever I say it, you'll know we need to talk."

"I love the idea. Can it be a phrase?

"Sure. Whatever you like."

"How about I miss you?"

"That works for me. If I say, 'I miss you', you'll call me. Okay?"

"Yes. This is fun."

"I think so, too. Helena, we're still working on your rescue plan, but now you can help. Take care, okay?"

"You, too. Bye."

"God, I hope this works." Paul said as they walked back to the cottage.

"What's your plan if it doesn't?"

"How'd that proverb go? Fall down seven times, but get up

eight?"

"Yes."

"Then, it's simple. If I fall down, I'll get up, marry Sam and live happily ever after."

If I'm still alive.

They found Samantha hard at work when they returned to the cottage. She was at the dining table, pecking away in concentration on a laptop computer. A small portable printer sat beside it.

"How goes it?" He stopped behind her to peer over her shoulder.

She greeted them with a smile. "My typing is rusty, but this was easy. Go sit down. This won't take long."

Paul followed Yoshi into the living room to wait.

Moments later, they heard the printer humming and Samantha's chair scraped as she pushed back from the table. She joined them, handed two pages of typewritten notes to Paul and sat beside him.

Paul scanned the story, which held the revised version of Carter Franklin's story, along with Samantha's modifications. She had used boldface type on certain parts, hoping to anger Fortune enough to rekindle his hatred of Talon. Those sections included the question and answers where Talon said he hated his father and planned to return as a ghost. She also made Talon's poem stand out. The final bold-face paragraph was the reporter's note about the cemetery being haunted.

When he finished, he said, "This is great, Sam. If our idea is valid, this should do it."

"I left out the part where Franklin says he visited the cemetery years later. I didn't want it to seem too dated, so I substituted the words 'I checked the cemetery later and found people reporting an angry ghost haunting the place.' Also, I think it would be a good idea to use red ink on the boldfaced sections."

Paul laughed. "Trying to make Fortune see red, are you?"

She giggled. "No, but that's not a bad idea."

"Now we need a graphic artist," Yoshi said. "Somebody hungry enough to work fast."

Paul raised his eyebrows at Samantha, not expecting her to deliver another solution. He should have known better.

"You won't believe this," she said, "but I know someone who can handle it. He used to draw comic book characters during class and sketch the girls in embarrassing situations. He started his own business right out of high school. Everyone called him Donny, but his real name is Don Juan Giovanni. He tried hard to live up to his namesake. Should I try him?"

"You're batting a thousand so far. Go for it."

Samantha checked her phone contact list, dialed, and pushed a button to put the sound on speaker.

A tinny voice answered, "Donny Graphics, the Mozart of Art."

"Mozart of art? Is this Donny?"

"Yes? How may I help you?"

She paused and said, "I don't know whether you remember me, but this is Samantha Duet. I was a year ahead of you in high school."

An almost gleeful laugh. "Are you kidding? The beautiful princess?" He chuckled. "How can I help you?"

"Donny, we have a graphics-art problem we need handled as soon as possible."

"We?"

"My fiancé and a friend."

"Fiancé, eh? Oh, well, c'est la vie. Tell me about the problem. I'm not busy right now."

"Great. Look, I'm handing you over to Paul Davenport, okay?"

"Your fiancé?"

"Yes."

Paul took the phone and said, "Hi, Donny. Paul. Where are you located?"

"Outskirts of Malibu on the northern side. What do you

need?"

Paul described the entire project to him, including the two large posters and the fold-up stands. He closed with, "We need it yesterday. Money is not a problem. But time is."

"If money is no problem, I can handle anything. First, two questions. How large is large and how soon?"

"What's the largest you can handle?"

"I have a guy who can do four-by-four blow-ups overnight, if that suits you."

"That's fine. What about the stands?"

"Yeah, I know a place in Ventura."

"That's great. Can you deliver a finished package, stands and all?"

"You bet."

"Good. When can we see you?"

"How fast can you get here?"

Paul chuckled. "What's the address?"

Donny gave it to them. Samantha took the phone. "Donny, Samantha. I know that area. Is twenty minutes too soon?"

"Hell, no. Can't wait."

She punched off. "If you're ready, so am I." She was smiling.

"We'll go in my car," Yoshi said.

SEVENTY-SIX

WHEN THEY PULLED INTO the driveway, they found him waiting for them, sitting on the front steps of a beige-colored California stucco home. He hopped up, ambled to Samantha's door, and peered into the car.

He was about an inch shorter than Sam, Paul estimated, but his gut said he liked his beer. His hair was brown, with a ponytail hanging to his shoulders. Tattoos covered his arms. A golden earring hung from his left ear.

Sam, seated beside Paul in the back, opened her door first and climbed out, causing Donny to back away with his mouth open in surprised shock.

"God, Samantha. You're as gorgeous as ever."

Sam stuck out her hand. "You, too, Donny. Nice to see you again."

"You can't bullshit me," he said, taking her hand. "I've added sixty pounds sitting on my ass doing artwork for the past four years."

He noticed that Paul and Yoshi had joined them. As they shook, he said, "Paul Davenport. You related to the guy who owns that castle where Samantha lives?"

"Yes. He was my uncle, now deceased. Do we work in your

house, or in a studio?"

"Gotcha. You don't have time for gabbing. Too bad. Haven't seen Sam in over four years. The studio is in the pool house. Come on back."

Donny Juan led the way around the side of the house into a spacious, well-lit artist's studio with a view of the swimming pool. He scooted behind a cluttered drawing table and hopped up on his chair. "Let's see what you got?"

During the next hour, Donny sketched four or five different layouts for the news story, but not for the map. The map layout was tougher, he said, because they didn't know the Colorado cemetery's location. Paul gave Donny all the information they had, then sat back and waited.

"I'm a computer geek, too," he said. He turned his back to them, bent over the keyboard of a large-screen computer system, and began typing. He grunted several times in the next forty-five minutes, but finally yelped, "Got you. Take a gander." He rolled his chair aside to make room and waved them to come look. He seemed happy and excited.

As Paul bent to view the screen, his doubts about Donny Juan Giovanni vanished. He liked the man, long hair, ponytail, tattoos, earrings and all.

He blinked at the monitor. "What am I looking for?"

Donny rolled closer and pointed to a spot just north of a place called Mount Pisgah Cemetery. "That spot doesn't have an official name, but I found a reference to it in a forum for Colorado cemetery readers. Can you figure that? People look for old grave yards. They record the names and take pictures of the headstones. Then they post the names and data on the internet. Anyhow, in the past, Benedictine Nuns operated that place, but over the years, various local organizations and the City of Cripple Creek have maintained it." He shrugged. "Best I can do, I'm afraid."

"Your best is good enough for me," Paul said. "I'd say you nailed it."

Donny beamed at Samantha. She rewarded him with a smile and said, "I say so, too, Donny. I'm positive that's the right place. What kind of map would you suggest? We don't want too much detail. Perhaps a few key cities highlighted in color. You know, kind of like a guide for a bird flying over. It has to be easy to read."

Paul almost laughed aloud. If Donny had been a puppy, his tail would have banged the floor wildly with happiness.

"So let me recap," Donny said. "You want a map easy to read with just major cities acting like stepping stones, and the map has to guide whoever reads it to that exact spot. Is that it?"

"Yes. Exactly."

"Where's the first stone?"

"Right here. Malibu."

"Got it, but we ought to give that cemetery a name, don't you think?"

"How about Talon's Burial Place in big, bold letters?" Yoshi suggested.

"Who's Talon?"

"He's an ancestor of the man we're doing this for?" Paul said.

"Ah! Got it. I'll work all night if necessary. That way you can approve it tomorrow and have a finished product by Wednesday afternoon. How's that suit?"

"Sounds great," Paul said. "How much do you need up front?"

Donny frowned. "Would two hundred be too much?"

"No, but don't you think five hundred would be better?"

"Hell, yes, it would. Sorry, Samantha, but I just fell in love with your fiancé."

"Get in line, buster." She giggled.

They left Donny bent in heavy concentration over his art board and walked around the house to the car. Once inside, Samantha took Paul's hand and asked, "Alright, sir. What's next?"

"Good question." He lifted her hand and kissed it with a gallant flair. "I suggest we go shopping for body armor and then find the best seaside restaurant on coast highway. After that, we'll treat ourselves to whatever delicacies they offer and drink ourselves silly. I'm not sure why, but I feel like celebrating."

"I know why, Paul-san."

"You do?"

"Yep." Yoshi grinned at them.

"Want to tell us?" Sam asked.

"Sure. You're an optimist. You believe we're going to win."

"Yes, but in the meantime, what do we do?" Sam asked.

"Hmmm, yes," Paul said with teasing thoughtfulness. "We play popular old marine game."

"What game is that, Paul-san?"

"Marines call it hurry up and wait. We've already done the hurrying part. Now we have to do the waiting."

Yoshi laughed and started the car.

SEVENTY-SEVEN

A ND WAIT THEY DID for the next two days. The only
breaks they had were phone calls. One was from lawyer
Huckabee saying he had Paul's second check, which Paul asked
him to hold for a few days. With collectors breathing down his
neck, he didn't want it visible in the bank. The guards called
twice about reporters wanting interviews. Helena phoned a dozen
times to ask what was happening. He put her off by telling her
he would implement their new plan soon. Sam said she called
because she was lonely.

"I didn't forget our secret phrase," she assured Paul with
every call. "Just call me. I'll be ready."

"Thanks, Helena. We're depending on you."

On Tuesday afternoon, in response to a call from Donny
Juan, they drove to his place to approve his layouts, which
everyone agreed were perfect. The finished displays would be
ready at three o'clock the next day. Paul appreciated the man's
fast service because if the current plan failed, that still left him
five days to try something else.

Now at four o'clock Wednesday afternoon, and they were
standing in the cottage dining room examining the completed
displays. They were better than Paul expected, especially the

map. The letters on the news story mimicked an old newspaper page with typography large enough to read from a distance. Everything was correct. The proper paragraphs were in bold type, but not printed in red. Donny said the red type would look phony. They all agreed. Donny had rendered the nap beautifully, and it was clear enough even for a child to trace the route from Malibu to Talon's burial place near Cripple Creek, Colorado.

"Well, Yosh, what do you think?"

"I'm happy. Mr. Giovanni did a good job."

"Me, too," Sam agreed, "but I'll be a lot happier if you'll put on your armor."

"Might as well. I want to get going."

He tore open the box, which held what the manufacturer called its Pro Protector. He raised the all-black shield over his head and slipped it on over his T-shirt. The unit used Velcro to strap it tight. Once it was in place, he put on a light blue sports shirt to cover it and turned to Yoshi. "How's your kick these days?"

"Huh?"

"Kick me. Hard. Let's see if this thing works."

Yoshi was doubtful. "You sure about this?"

"Do it."

Yoshi shrugged and landed a high-speed kick in the center of Paul's gut. Paul grunted and fell back onto the sofa. He took a deep breath and stood. "Wow. Good one."

"So?"

"It works. Didn't hurt a bit." The protector's padding covered all vulnerable areas. "I'm ready to go ghost hunting. He tested his body motion. Not bad.

"What about these?" Sam held up the elbow and forearm protective pads.

"I'll skip those," he said. "It's time to leave."

"Paul..."

He looked at her.

"Suppose Fortune won't go away? What if he wants to kill

you more than Talon? What...?"

"Sam, I'll be safe, you'll see."

"But..."

"No more buts."

"So, how do we proceed, Paul-san?"

"I've been thinking about that, Yosh. I have a plan. We have to go to the garage apartment to implement it."

"Why there?" Sam asked.

"The sound system is there. I'll explain when we get there."

The air in the apartment smelled like old mildew and motor oil from the cars below. Paul entered the living room and raised the front window to let in fresh air. Sam and Yoshi stood near the sound system, waiting for guidance.

"Grab a seat," he said. "I'll explain."

They sat on the sofa. Paul chose an old rocking chair. "First, I announce our secret phrase over the speaker, so she'll call me. Next, I have to swap phones with one of you. I'll leave my phone so Helena can call it if I get in trouble. When I have the displays set up, I'll call and ask Yoshi to use the sound system to tell Fortune I'm waiting for him in the library."

"What would you want me to say?" Yoshi asked.

"Maybe something like, 'Mr. Fortune Montmartre, Paul Davenport has information for you about your son Talon. He is waiting for you in the library. He is not there to fight, only to present you with important information about your son.' Repeat it a couple of times. If he's interested at all, he should show up."

"And then what?" Sam asked in a worried tone. "If he's not interested, he'll try to kill you. What then? Paul.."Don't worry about it." He pounded his chest. "I've got protection. Besides, if he gets out of line, I'm a fast runner. Okay?"

"No. What if you can't?"

"Sam, I've fought with him before and survived. I'm getting good at it." He grinned.

Seeing the doubt remaining in her eyes, he rose and crossed to her. Yoshi jumped up to give Paul the sofa. Paul sat and caught her hands. "You trust me, right?"

She met his gaze, worry still clouding her normal sparkle. "Yes, but it's too dangerous. This time, he won't let you go. We don't need Uncle Justin's fortune. We can make out without it, just like everyone else in the world. Please."

He sighed. "I can't do that. There's too much at stake. It's a debt I owe my uncle. Do you want to forget the promise we made to Helena? Should we leave her to the tender mercies of Fortune for God knows how long? I can't break my word, not when success is so close. I..." he stopped. "Sam, I give you my word. I will not let him kill me. You're the girl I've dreamed about my entire life. I won't let that evil creature take you away from me."

Her eyes bubbled with tears, but a weak smile found its way between them. "I know you have to do this, Paul, and I'll pray it works."

"Thanks. We need a lot of prayers to beat that evil bastard."

"Hai, so desu," Yoshi said.

His phone rang. Helena. He stood to answer it and walked to the window to peer at the mansion. "Hi, Helena. I was just going to call you. We're ready to go."

"Paul, I don't know where he is. It's almost like he's hiding. He's been out of sight all morning. I think you're right. He's afraid of Justin."

"I understand, but you need to be brave and help me."

"What do you want me to do?"

"Two things. First, would you mind typing for Fortune if he agrees to communicate with me?"

"I'll do anything you ask."

"Thank you. Second, if I'm hurt and can't escape, I want you to call my number. Samantha will answer, and they'll come to my rescue. Will you do that? "

"Yes."

"Good. Yoshi is going to announce to Fortune that I'm waiting for him. Then we'll see what happens. Okay?"

"If you say so, but something's not right."

"I understand. Give me ten minutes. I have some gear in my truck. Take care of yourself."

"You, too. Bye." They disconnected.

He offered his phone to Samantha. She rose and came to him for the exchange and then embraced him. He held her for several minutes before stepping back. "I have to go," he said. Then he grinned. "As Arnold would say, 'I'll be back!'"

She gave him a flicker of a smile that didn't hide the worry in her eyes and nodded in resignation.

"You both know the plan. I have to go."

He turned away and left the apartment, heading toward what? A future of wealth and happiness with Sam? Or worse. No future at all.

wavering. "No!"

His foot stomped the accelerator, sending the truck roaring toward the mansion before his courage waned. Wrong time to have doubts. The plan will work. It has to.

He stopped in front of the house and retrieved the displays from the truck bed, and went inside. He glanced up at his uncle's portrait hanging on the wall as he entered the library. Too bad meeting his uncle had been a dream. He could use the help.

He stopped inside the library door to be sure he would be alone. It was empty of ghosts. Good. He wondered where Helena was hiding. He hurried to the wall behind the desk and unfolded the displays, and stepped back to view them. The desk hid the lower halves of them. Not good. He moved them clear of the desk and further out onto the floor.

"Wait," he murmured. Which direction would Fortune come from? During their last encounter, he had entered near the fireplace. Paul shifted the displays to face the fireplace and then chose a spot for himself closer to the exit in case he needed to escape fast. Ready for action, he lifted his phone and dialed Yoshi.

"Paul-san?"

"Yes. I'm ready. Go for it."

"Watch your back, my friend.."

Yoshi's voice, mellow, educated and in what Paul thought of as a cultured Japanese accent, boomed forth the agreed upon message. "Mr. Fortune Montmartre. Mr. Fortune Montmartre, attention. Mr. Paul Davenport has important information about the death of Talon. Mr. Davenport is waiting for you in the library. He does not wish to fight or argue, only to deliver important information about the death and burial of your son. If you wish to learn about your son, please join Mr. Davenport in the library. Thank you."

Perfect, Paul thought. He swept the room. No Fortune. Where was he?

The announcement boomed through the house a second time.

Paul waited, watchful. Nothing. If the ghost didn't respond, the plan was dead on arrival. Disappointed, he called Yoshi and said, "No Fortune yet. One more time, Yosh." He kept the connection open to let his friends listen to his conversation, if Fortune showed up.

His friend complied, but this time added at the end, "Mr. Montmartre, if you don't meet Mr. Davenport, you will not learn the truth about your son and how he intends to destroy you."

Helena appeared suddenly before Paul and gave him a worried smile.

"Helena, where is he?" he asked.

She nodded and floated to he the computer keyboard. She sat and jerked her head back and forth between him and the keyboard while typing as fast as she could. "I don't know. I'm sure he heard your message. He seems afraid of something."

Paul frowned. "Do you think he's afraid of me?"

"No. Something else. I'm scared."

"Most bullies are cowards." Paul said the words in a near shout. "He called me a coward. He's the one hiding."

Helena jerked erect and began typing zombie like. "I don't fear you, Mr. Davenport. I suspected a trap and waited to see what you would do."

Paul's heart took a wild leap toward his throat. He turned and spotted Montmartre floating three feet above the floor, halfway between the fireplace and his own position. A crimson aura bright enough to be visible even in the lighted room surrounded his body. Paul wondered what caused that glow and why it was red. Helena's aura was faint-white with a hint of light blue and was much weaker. Fortune's long coat missing a sleeve together with his frilly shirt and dark trousers should have made him comical, but they didn't. They gave him a look of evil decadence.

Paul turned to Helena. "Are you alright?"

"She's fine," the girl typed. "I have control of her. What is your important information?"

Paul turned back. The ghost was a few feet closer. He stood

his ground, but decided not to give in to anger. You catch more flies with honey than with vinegar, an old sergeant always said.

Making his tone friendly, he said, "Mr. Montmartre, my uncle, advertised in newspapers all over the country and offered a reward for information about Talon. He wanted to learn where your son Helena's and your bodies. He received word about a news clipping from a Colorado weekly newspaper called the Cripple Creek Beaver. The original reporter's great grandson came here a few days ago, hoping to gain the reward. As a courtesy to you, I paid him for the clipping and enlarged it for you to read. Your son murdered you, so I figured you had a right to know what happened to him. You can read the story here on this display."

Paul walked to the display, touched it, and then stepped back. Fortune remained motionless for a moment, then drifted forward. As he did so, his aura increased in size. Apparently, the more energy he used, the brighter he glowed.

The ghost hovered five feet away from the display and read. As he read, anger distorted his face. After reading it, he faced Paul and gestured to the map display. Helena punched keys at high speed. "What is this?"

"We located the cemetery where his body lies, the one the reporter said that people have seen Talon there. That clipping says he is waiting the for a chance to destroy you. That map shows how to get there."

The ghost floated toward Paul. Helena typed. "Brilliant, Mr. Davenport. You expected this story to take me away from my home, didn't you? Why would I leave these wonderful surroundings?"

"Because you want vengeance. Your anger toward your son is the reason you became a ghost. I'm sure you appreciate the little poem he wrote about you."

"Talon was always a weak-minded idiot. I will find him and destroy him just as I did your uncle, and will you. Justin Davenport was a mush-brained moron mooning after my sweet young wife. All fools."

"Something else you should know," Paul said. "If you don't leave, I intend to burn your glorious home to the ground. If I don't survive this meeting, my friends have instructions about doing it. Maybe you would prefer to haunt a pile of ashes?"

"You're a fool, too, boy. You can't hurt me, while I can rip your frail body apart any time I choose. Still, I appreciate your finding Talon for me and for giving me this beautiful map. It's clear and helpful. For that, I thank you. But, since I'm leaving home to go after Talon, I see no reason not to kill you now. Except..." Helena stopped typing.

"What?"

"I plan to have a little fun with you first."

SEVENTY-EIGHT

PAUL STOMPED HIS BRAKES and screeched to a stop at the same spot he had when he first arrived. The mansion rose like a magnificent monument before him, but this time his knowledge that it housed an evil entity waiting to kill him tarnished its image. So enticing. So dangerous.

He clenched the truck's steering wheel, hesitating to move forward. In his heart, he knew he owed this to his uncle, to Helena, and to his own self-esteem. Yet Sam's appeal was almost irresistible. Common sense told him to walk away with her and live a happy life. You can't do that, his honor said.

Fortune Montmartre's leering, laughing face rose in his mind. "You're a coward, afraid to face me," the ghost had said. "If you enter my house, I'll crush you like a cockroach. Tear your limbs off one at a time."

Paul growled as he recalled the conversation. He also remembered his answer. "This is no longer your house. It's mine. And you don't have the power to crush me. You're dead, and I'm alive." The words seemed foolhardy now. The ghost was already dead. Fortune couldn't die again. But Paul could. And he does have the power to crush me, he told himself. Montmartre was king of the mansion, and that was a fact. Paul felt his resolution

Justin turned toward Paul, no longer smiling. He came toward Paul. From the corner of his eye, Paul saw Helena approach Justin. They both looked at him with worried expressions.

"Uncle Justin, I…" His world went black.

He fell back and lay as still as a corpse.

SEVENTY-NINE

T HE LIBRARY DOOR SLAMMED shut and a hammer blow far more powerful than Yoshi's kick sent him skidding backward toward the front of the room. As he slid along the floor, he rolled onto his stomach barely in time to prevent smashing his head into a wide window seat. The sudden jolt to his arms shot stabs of pain into both shoulders.

"Christ!" he murmured and twisted his body toward the library doors, scrambling to his feet at the same time. When he turned, he found the ghost grinning at him.

"Not bad. Try this," Montmartre mouthed.

A blow landed on his face and sent him toppling. Had Fortune broken his jaw? He jumped up and glowered at the apparition, now only inches from him. "Is that all you've got?" He dove straight into Montmartre's body and fell through it. When he hit the floor, he rolled and swept to his feet. Assuming the ghost was still behind him, he spun around, swinging his fist like a high-speed ball on the end of a rope. It passed through the leering grin, causing its expression to change to surprise.

Paul swung hard, driving his arm and hand like a scythe through the ghost's neck. Fortune vanished and reappeared near Helena. The girl started typing. He squinted to read it. It said, "Very resourceful, but I tire of this game. Goodbye, young Davenport."

Paul's feet flew from under him. He landed on his stomach, breaking his fall with his arms. He rolled onto his side to get up, but a powerful force pushed him onto his back and held him. Montmartre spun him around so he could read the computer screen. Helena typed, "I want you to know how you will die. It's the same way I killed your uncle and punish my wife when I grow angry. With her I stop, but with you, I will continue until there is no spark of life left in your puny body."

Paul twisted his head left and right, trying to unpin his shoulders, but it was as though a grand piano had landed on top of him. Helpless, he relaxed and tried to breathe, but the pressure on his upper body increased until he screamed, "Stop!"

It continued to increase. Paul stared up at the apparition floating above him, still smiling. He remembered what his uncle said about how the ghost punished Helena. "The pain is excruciating, and if he didn't stop, she would pop like a balloon, and her soul would forever vanish." Was that now happening to him? Would he explode and cease to exist?

He tried to suck in enough air to power a scream, but his chest muscles refused to respond. The weight on his body was irresistible. In desperation, he used the last bit of air in his lungs to cry out, "Uncle Justin, help me. Please." His voice was a weak and raspy imitation of Donald Duck.

The growing pressure on his chest caused his vision to grow fuzzy. Darkness descended like a black curtain being drawn to end his life. Was this how dying felt? And then, miraculously, the pressure vanished. He sucked in a huge gasp of air, imitating a drowning swimmer whose head just broke above water. His vision cleared, and he saw something amazing. His uncle, wearing his gray, pinstriped pajamas, was floating directly above his feet. "Uncle Justin! You're here," he cried. "Thank God. You made it." Justin looked down at him and smiled.

At that instant, something hit him hard and sent him spinning at high speed toward the wall of books. A flurry of books flew off the shelf and pelted him. Then Fortune Montmartre, glowing red and ugly, was floating above Paul, and the weight slammed his chest like a giant foot crushing the life from him. The devil was determined to kill him, no matter what else happened.

And then the pressure vanished again, and Fortune's face showed pain and fear. He twisted his head toward the bookcases as Justin floated toward him with his hands held out before him. Justin's expression was harsh with effort. He slowly brought his palms toward each other, and as he did so, Fortune appeared to let loose a blood-curdling scream. Paul wished he could hear it. Fortune glared down at Paul in pain and surprise. Paul now understood why his uncle had practiced lifting the John Deere tractor and what he now intended to do. He grinned up at the king of the mansion and waved bye-bye with the ends of his fingers. Fortune's feet flailed out of control. His expression grew more and more panicky. Justin's lips had pulled back from his teeth in a grimace of effort.

Fortune drifted to Paul's left and suddenly flew toward the ceiling to the floor and then back toward the floor, apparently with no control over his own movements. Paul struggled to prop up on his elbow to enjoy the show. Montmartre landed on his back, writhing in his effort to escape. but seemed to be pinned to the floor, which made no sense to Paul since the ghost was incorporeal. He should have passed through the floor, so Justin obviously was holding him there with the power of his mind.

Justin drifted toward Montmartre and stopped within two feet of the evil ghost. He smiled at Fortune, clearly doing something painful to the evil creature, because Montmartre'ss eyes bulged out of his head. Fortune shook his head in a pleading gesture, but it did no good. Justin continued to smile down at him with an expression that said he was judge, jury, and executioner. Fortune opened his mouth and released another scream. And then there was a flash as his body exploded like a brilliant firecracker. He was gone, with nothing left to show he had ever existed.

EIGHTY

THE CELL PHONE BUZZED in Sam's lap. Startled, she grabbed it and jumped up from the rocking chair. She answered instantly. "Helena, what is it?" No response. Then she remembered and switched to dictation mode. Her hand trembled as she spoke. "Helena, what's wrong?"

"Paul is unconscious. He may be dead. Hurry, please."

"Oh, God! On my way." She yelled, "Yoshi, Paul's hurt. Let's go." He tossed a magazine aside and followed her. Driven by fear, she rushed outside, galloped down the wooden steps, and then broke into a sprint across the lawn toward the chateau. A straight line was the shortest distance between two points. And the fastest. Behind her, she heard Yoshi's rapid breathing gaining on her.

She raced up the front steps, through the foyer, to the closed library doors. In a panic, she fumbled with the latch handle until Yoshi pushed it open for her. The first thing she saw as she entered the enormous room was his body, lying motionless on the floor near the desk. She ran to him and fell to her knees.

"Paul, wake up," she yelled. "Oh, God, don't be dead, please."

He didn't move. She touched the side of his neck with two

fingers, seeking a pulse. His skin was warm, but she felt no heartbeat.

She bent closer and shouted into his ear. "Paul, open your eyes. Please."

She probed again, and this time, a weak pulsation rewarded her effort. Thank God. He's alive!

He snubbed in a shallow breath, blinked once, then clamped his lids shut. Her own heart leapt in relief. He had responded.

Yoshi knelt beside her. "May I?"

She moved away and watched as he methodically touched and rubbed pressure points on both sides of Paul's hands and lower arms. Moments later, he groaned and opened his eyes, but he didn't notice either of them. Instead, his expression changed to shock. He inhaled in a huge breath and shouted, "Uncle Justin!" He struggled to sit up, but grunted and fell back. His eyes flicked back and forth between Yoshi and her, but settled on her.

"Hi, Sam. I guess this time it's no joke. I'm dead. Uncle Justin is standing at the computer beside Helena, wearing gray pin-striped pajamas. Why else would they be here together?"

"You're not dead, Paul-san, but Fortune gave you a pretty good beating. You must be still."

"No. I want to my uncle. Help me up, please, but take it easy. I'm in pain. That bastard tried to turn me into a pancake."

"Paul, no," Samantha said. "You may have internal injuries. Don't move."

"Sam, I don't care. Please. Help me." He struggled to smile, but succeeded only in showing his teeth. "I have to get up. Come on, Yosh, Help me." He extended his arms. Sam moved back.

Paul looked up as Yoshi straddled his body and caught both his hands. Paul tensed his body as his friend reared back and slowly pulled him to his feet. When he was able to stand, he said, "Thanks, Yosh. I'm good now." He gazed toward the computer where his uncle stood watching and waiting. "Sir, thanks for saving me. I was about to buy the farm."

Justin smiled and glanced at Helena. She typed, "You're

welcome, Paul, but your plan worked. You saved Helena. For that, I'll be forever grateful."

Paul grinned. "I followed your advice and asked Sam to marry me. She agreed."

"Uncle Justin is here?" Sam darted her eyes toward the computer.

Paul nodded. "As real as Helena, and he's wearing gray-striped PJs."

"I know those pajamas. They were his favorites."

Paul drew another long breath.

"I'll call 911," Yoshi said.

"Wait, Yosh. I'm better."

He smiled at Helena, who was back at the computer. "Helena, let's show Uncle Justin how we can communicate." He grinned at his uncle. "We have to talk."

The computer keys started clacking. "I agree. Samantha, my dear, this is Justin. I'm happy for you. I guess I don't have to worry about you anymore. You've chosen well."

Sam's mouth popped open. "Paul, where is he?"

Paul pointed to a spot beside the desk. She followed his pointing finger and, though she could see nothing, tears bubbled into her eyes. "Uncle Justin, I miss you. I'm sorry I was away when you... when he murdered youThe keyboard clicked. "It's okay, Sam. You lost me and your father, too, but you no longer need either of us. You have Paul now."

A cloud of emotion burst from Sam and she clung to Paul. He winced, but held her.

"Paul, do you need a doctor?" Helena typed.

Paul lifted his free arm to test its mobility. "Maybe later. Right now, I have a million questions for you."

The keyboard sounded like popcorn popping in a busy theater lobby. The screen said. "In that case, we'd better do it fast. You brought me here by calling for help, but I don't know how long I can stay. We need a chair for him to sit down. He's in pain."

Yoshi hurried across the room and hauled a small upholstered chair back. Sam stroked his face as he sat down and whispered in his ear. "I love you."

"Thanks. That's all the medicine I need."

EIGHTY-ONE

JUSTIN FLOATED closer to Paul and bent to study his face. Paul smiled at his uncle's worried scrutiny.

"What's wrong? I got warts or something? "

Justin grinned at him and returned to his place beside Helena. She typed, "Sorry, Paul. It's just that you have an uncanny resemblance to your grandfather. It's a bit spooky."

Paul grinned at him. "I'm spooking you? I thought I looked a lot like you."

"I agree," Sam said. "He has your eyes, nose, chin, and forehead. Good looks must run in your family."

Justin smiled. "You're right, my dear, but I, too, closely resemble my father." He turned to Paul. "You'd better get asking, lad. As I suspected, your cry for help gave me the boost I needed to cross over, but there's still a powerful force pulling me away even now, so time is precious."

Paul choked back a dozen questions he wanted to ask about his family. Instead, he said, "Just for the record, sir. You saved my life twice, didn't you? First, at the tree and again now."

His uncle shook his head. Helena typed, "No. I warned you about the danger. You did the rest. Today, I helped by knocking that ghoulish creature away from you. I suppose you could say I saved your life, but from what I've learned about you, I'm glad I did. You deserve a decent chance in life."

"Sir, what happened to Montmartre? Is he gone for good?" Paul needed to know. "I saw him explode."

The keyboard clicked rapidly. Paul read, "If you're asking, has he ceased to exist as a ghost? I don't know. I gave him a dose of the same medicine he forced on Helena all the years since he murdered her. When I saw him crushing you, my anger and frustration drove me to punish him until he exploded. If he no longer exists, I feel no regret. The universe is better off without evil creatures like him."

The keyboard kept clicking. "This is Helena. I'm glad he's dead, Paul. I hated him."

Justin smiled. Helena typed, "Justin wants to know if you have more questions."

"You told me in a dream it was you lifting the John Deere and dropping it? Did you?"

Helena got busy typing. "Yes, sorry about that. I was testing my strength to be able to fight Fortune. You had already found the burial site, so you didn't need the tractor any more. I thought if I could lift that, I could handle Fortune, and I was right."

"Why couldn't I see you, then? We thought Fortune was doing it."

"I'm sorry about that, son, but I had a problem. Something kept pulling me away so I could never cross over until you called on me for help."

"Helena said Fortune was frightened. I think you're the reason." Paul said.

"That may be. I hope so." Helena smiled at Justin as her fingers flew over the keyboard.

"One more question, please," Paul said. "When I dreamed, my mother was there, and she seemed younger and happier than I can ever remember. Was that real or wishful dreaming?"

"She was there, Paul, as I was. Annie was a beautiful young woman when she married James, but the years of hardship took its toll." Helena's typing paused and then continued for Justin. "Paul, we're almost out of time, so we'd better take care of business. You must phone Lawyer Huckabee and Madam Song as soon as possible. Demand that they come to the chateau tomorrow morning. Tell the lawyer to bring that letter I left for you. I want you to read it before he does. Clear?"

"Yes, sir."

"You are now in possession of my entire fortune. Some of it was ill-gotten, but most of it wasn't. Use it wisely. Make it grow."

"What about this house, the land?" Sam blurted. "What should we do with it?"

"Do with it as you will, my dear, but if it were me, I would sell it. I only remained here because of Helena." Helena stopped typing and smiled at Justin. Then she turned back to the keyboard and typed, "I'm sorry, but I can't stay. That light is pulling me away."

"Wait! I just want to tell you something," Paul said.

"What is it?"

"I… I guess I want to say that meeting you has been the high point of my entire life. I've always been alone, but when I read your letter, and I saw how it might be to have a real family. I thank you for that. It has changed my entire outlook about marriage and family."

Justin smiled at him. "I understand, Paul. I reacted the same way when my parents died. You marry our wonderful girl, Sam, and build a real family. Start a few traditions that will carry on even after you're gone. Traditions seem to hold families together. Do that, and you'll never be sorry."

"Uncle Justin, what will happen to Helena? You can't leave her here." Sam blurted.

"Don't worry about me, Samantha," Helena typed. "I'm going to a happy place with Justin." Helena typed.

"Do you mean heaven?" Paul asked.

"Maybe. We don't know where we're going, Paul. Only that

it will be peaceful and we'll be together. Of course, we can't do anything, you understand, but Justin is a strong man who is fun to be with. He loves me and will keep me safe. What more can a girl ask for?" She stopped typing and turned to Sam and Yoshi. "Thank you all for saving me. I love you." She floated to Paul and gave him a ghostly hug. The experience caused warmth to spread throughout his entire body. She flew back to the keyboard and started typing.

"I wrote in the diary you made for me," she typed. "You should read it." Justin reached for her hand. She left the computer, and they both waved goodbye. As Paul watched in fascination as the two ghosts floated hand in hand toward the fireplace at the end of the room. When they reached it, they faded from view, almost like a movie he had seen once. He stared after them a long moment after they disappeared.

"Paul?" Samantha touched his shoulder.

"They're gone," Paul said. "We did it."

Samantha bent down and laid her cheek on his forehead for a moment. He rested his hands on her hips. She smiled and straightened. "She sounded happy, didn't she?"

"Yes. They walked to the end of the room and faded away into the sunset."

"Sunset?" Yoshi asked. "I didn't see any light."

"A literary expression, Yosh. They just faded away."

"Ah! Paul-san, I wish to thank you for allowing me to be here. I'll never forget of this experience. I'm overwhelmed."

Paul smiled at his friend. "Welcome to the club, Yosh."

"Why do I feel as though I've learned something important?" Sam said, "But I'm not sure what."

"May I suggest something, Sam?" Yoshi asked.

"Please do. There's something happy in me that I don't understand."

"What is it, Yosh?" Paul asked.

Yoshi moved to the desk and sat in on one corner. "

"I can tell you what has affected me about all this." Yoshi

hesitated. "Billions of people on this planet believe in some form of life after death. Buddhists and Christians do, as well as many other religions. They're all forced to accept the idea on faith alone, but we're not. We have seen actual proof that it exists. We just experienced an amazing real-life drama, where an evil ghost was destroyed by a good ghost in order to save a young ghost he loves. That knowledge changes my view about a lot of things. There is life after death and apparently we won't be worm fodder when we die. Justin still cared about Helena and Paul after he died. I... sorry. Didn't mean to ramble."

Paul grinned at his friend. "Hey, you're not rambling. You're making sense to me. Keep going."

"I agree," Sam said. "Please continue."

Yoshi nodded. "Well, one thing I've always wondered about is what is it really like after we die. Will we be judged? Will we be punished? Do we just rot and turn to dust?" Yoshi grinned. "Sorry, Sam." He hesitated for a breath. "We still don't know the answers to those questions, but Justin said a light was pulling him away from here. Because of it, he almost didn't get back in time to save you from Mr. Montmartre. I guess my brain wants to learn where that light comes from and why does it have influence on us after death? Where did it take Justin and Helena? Certainly not to a bad place." He stopped and shook his head.

"My mother would say it was God taking them," Paul said. "My mother was a wise woman, so she may be right."

"You mean that light is taking them to heaven?" Sam asked.

"It's possible, I guess, Sam, but that's where faith comes in. If we believe that, we're in pretty good company. Wherever it is, Uncle Justin didn't seem afraid to go? It seems we'll have to wait until it's our turn to find out."

"I wish I could have seen them," Sam said.

"I'm sorry about that, Sam, but I appreciate that you both didn't doubt my sanity. I doubted enough for all of us."

Sam patted his cheek and said, "I'll always take your word, my love."

"I have to call Huckabee and Madam Song," Paul said when she let him go.

Yoshi coughed politely. "Uh, we can do that on the way to the emergency room. We have to make sure you're okay. One Davenport ghost at a time is about all I can handle."

"He's right, Paul."

"Mr. Moto is always right, but I'm fine."

"You think?"

"I'll go for the Mercedes," Yoshi said.

When he was gone, Sam said, "I love that guy."

"That makes two of us."

Paul made his calls, and both Huckabee and Madam Song agreed to be at the estate at ten o'clock the next morning.

"Only one hurdle left," Paul said.

"What's that, Paul-san?"

"Madam Song. Will she or won't she give us a go-ahead?"

They spent three hours at the urgent care clinic where Paul was X-rayed, poked and probed, and bandaged like an Egyptian mummy. After that, they stopped off at Jake's Place for takeout meals of fried drumsticks, chicken breasts, rice and gravy, buttered biscuits and homemade cole slaw salad.

Now they were back in the cottage living room, sipping coffee after their meal. Yoshi kicked back in the easy chair with a satisfied look of well-fed contentment and said, "Man, that guy can cook. He calls it hometown country cooking, but as far as I'm concerned, it's pure, hometown gourmet."

"I agree, Yosh," Paul said. "A perfect finish to a wild, adventure-filled day with good friends and good ghosts. What more could anyone ever want?"

"A good night's sleep for you," Sam said. "You look ready to drop." She looked at Yoshi. "The doctor said he's pretty badly bruised. Do you mind if I take him away? He needs rest."

Yoshi smiled. "Not at all, Sam. I'm ready to crash myself. Besides, tomorrow's an important day. He needs to have a clear head."

"Yeah," Paul said, rising carefully. "Decision day. Am I rich or am I still poor? I'll have nightmares all night."

With Sam at his elbow, he limped up to bed.

EIGHTY-TWO

LAWYER HUCKABEE and Madam Song arrived at ten
A. M. sharp the next morning. The gate guard, Roberto,
phoned and said, "Good morning, Mr. Davenport. You have two
visitors in a shiny new Caddy. The driver says he is a lawyer
representing your uncle's estate. A Mr. Huckabee. The other one
is a lady. Didn't catch her name. What's the word? In or out?"

"In, Roberto, thanks. Tell them to follow the work road to
the main house. We'll meet them there."

"Understood, sir. Will do."

They hung up, and Paul called through the wall to Sam.
"They're here. We'll meet them at the chateau."

"Coming," she called back.

Paul was much better now after a full ten hours' sleep and
a good breakfast. Pain hit him only when he moved the wrong
way or took too deep a breath.

To help him sleep, Samantha had rubbed him down again
with her dad's liniment. He had tried to hug her, but she jumped
back and said. "No way. That stuff stinks."

Now it was time to face the judge.

Yoshi joined them at the cottage door, and together they
quick-walked to the mansion. They arrived just as the lawyer's

Caddy turned off the work road.

Huckabee stopped the car and got out, carrying a shiny brown briefcase. Paul opened the passenger door for Madam Song. When she accepted his hand and stood, her height again surprised him. Her eyes were level with his own. She wore a bright-red two-piece suit.

Madam Song shook his hand. She wasn't smiling.

"Madam, how do you want to do this?"

She peered across the car roof at the front door of the house. "I told you, I'll never enter that house again."

"Then how will you know whether Montmartre is gone?"

"Good question, young man. I don't sense his presence from this distance. I did the last time I came."

They walked around the car to join the others.

"I assure you he's gone," Paul said. "He almost killed me yesterday, but my uncle crushed him the way Montmartre tortured Helena. At the end, Montmartre exploded in a bright flash and vanished. Helena believes he's gone forever."

"You saw this?" The woman's eyes never wavered from the chateau's front door.

"Yes. Just before I fell unconscious."

"You saw your uncle?"

"Yes. Wearing dark-gray pajamas, which I presume he was wearing when Montmartre murdered him."

As he spoke, the lawyer's eyes stared at Paul in disbelief, but he said nothing.

"Look. I have an idea," Paul said. "Let's do this in increments."

Madam Song faced him. "What do you mean?"

"Simple. We go onto the porch. If you feel nothing, I'll open the door. If you still sense nothing, we'll move into the foyer. Like that. One step at a time until you're satisfied."

"You're certain he's gone?"

"You have my word."

"It's true, Madam," Sam said. "Yoshi and I both were there."

"You saw Justin?"

"No, but Paul did. The house is clear."

Huckabee's face turned red, and he cleared his throat to show his impatience.

"So, what do you think?" Paul asked the woman. "You could just sign off on it and be done with it."

"No, I can't do that. Sorry." She eyed the door and nodded. "We'll try it your way."

Forty-five minutes later, after a quick tour of the entire house, they were in the library, gathered around the cold fireplace. Huckabee, sitting in one of the wing-back chairs, looked at Madam Song. "Well? What's the verdict?" His voice was impatient. His demeanor said he considered the entire process to be preposterous.

"He's gone," she said. "I didn't think it was possible, but Mr. Davenport has done something his uncle tried to accomplish for twenty-five years." She turned to Paul. "What happened to Helena?"

"She told me she was going with Justin. They vanished together. I assume she's safe now, whatever that means."

The psychic turned back to Huckabee. "Give me your paper. I'll sign it."

"We should be in my office," Huckabee said in a grumpy tone. He pulled a sheaf of papers from his briefcase. "We need a clipboard."

"I've got one." Sam hopped up from the sofa and went to the desk. She returned with a clipboard from the main desk drawer and handed it to the lawyer.

Huckabee clipped a single sheet document onto the board, rose, and gave it to Madam Song. "You've seen it before. It says you've inspected the house, and it's clear of the ghosts. You sign and date it at the bottom." His expression showed he liked none of this.

Madam Song signed and returned it. Huckabee sat and stuffed the paper in his briefcase. She smiled at Paul. "Congratulations, young man. I didn't think it was possible. I hope someday you will give me a full account of all the events that led up to this moment."

"Thanks. I'll be happy to as soon as we return from our honeymoon." He took Sam's hand. She smiled at the psychic.

"And now the letter from your uncle." The lawyer retrieved a sealed number ten envelope and passed it to Paul. Paul tore it open and discovered three sheets of paper in it. The top one was another note from his uncle. Undated and to the point, it said:

My dear nephew,

Please accept my apologies for playing a little game with you. In my original instructions to Lawyer Huckabee, I instructed him to state the terms of the will as you heard them. Save Helena or get nothing. I set it up that way because I believe in providing incentives when you desire a result. The second sheet in this envelope instructs lawyer Huckabee to invalidate the clause in the will requiring you to save Helena. In short, I always intended for you to receive my entire estate. You are the most deserving young man I know. I am proud of you.

Have a good life.

Your uncle,

Justin Davenport.

Paul grinned. The old rascal truly loved his Helena and strongly believed in the power of incentives. He read the second sheet, which was addressed to Huckabee, and said Sam was to inherit one hundred thousand dollars. The third sheet was also to the lawyer. He didn't bother reading it.

"These are for you," he said, handing it over. He passed his note to Samantha. She skimmed it and smiled as she gave it to Yoshi.

Lawyer Huckabee read the top sheets three times. When he looked up, he said, "My word. What a remarkable man your uncle was. You have inherited one-hundred thousand dollars, Miss Duet. Congratulations."

"Yes, I knew about that. Thanks."

The lawyer studied the third sheet. He cleared his throat and pinched his lips together like a bulldog. "This is a codicil, but it is no longer relevant. You met the terms of the original will. Therefore, let us proceed with the business at hand. I have another appointment this afternoon."

Paul spent the next half hour reading documents and receipts, transferring title to such things as Justin's bank account, which held a quarter million ready cash in a savings account and another hundred thousand in checking. Other assets included gold, stocks, the cars, and a lot of things that made no sense to him. The total came to roughly eighty-million dollars by Paul's count. The last item he signed was a receipt for the second fifty-thousand-dollar check Huckabee handed over in an envelope. The situation was overwhelming. Rags to riches in eight days. Such things didn't happen to him.

When it was all over, Huckabee stuck out his hand. "Congratulations, Mr. Davenport. To be truthful, you've far exceeded my expectations. Your financial worries are over."

Paul grinned at the lawyer. "Thanks. but I don't feel rich. And my chest still hurts."

The lawyer nodded and became serious. "Uh, this may not be the best time to bring it up, Mr. Davenport, but have you thought about managing your financial affairs? It's a rather complex set of finances and holdings."

"Who managed them for his uncle?" Yoshi asked.

"Mr. Davenport trusted me and several of my associates to do that. So far, we've added about twenty-five million to his original net worth."

"I'm a computer programmer, not a business man," Paul said. "It will take time to get up to speed on my uncle's finances. Until then, I hope you will continue for me as you did for my uncle. I also would appreciate it if you could pay off my debt to the hospital."

"I would be honored on both counts, sir. Thank you." Huckabee's cherubic features were beaming. "Call me when you're ready, and we'll settle everything."

"Great, but first we go to Vegas."

The lawyer smiled at Samantha. "I understand. First things first, eh?"

They walked out to the front and watched the lawyer and Madam Song drive away.

"Paul-san, I had my heart set on being your best man when you go to Las Vegas, but I spoke to my father last night. He will be in Los Angeles tomorrow morning. He wants me there. I'm sorry."

"Damn it, Yoshi, you have nothing to be sorry about. You're the best friend any man could ever have. None of this would have been possible without your help. We did it with four days to spare."

"He's right, Yoshi," Samantha said. She turned to Paul. "I should congratulate you, too,. You won your inheritance fair and square."That's a dumb thing to say. Don't you agree, Yosh?"

Yoshi grinned. "One hundred percent."

"I don't understand." Sam frowned, puzzled.

"We're joined at the hip, silly girl. What I have is yours. We're both rich now."

Samantha grinned. "I got it. May I try something?"

"Sure. Go ahead."

She gave Paul a quick peck on the lips.

"What was that for?"

"I wanted to see if it felt good."

He grinned. "Did it?"

"Yes. I think I'm addicted."

"You better be."

"Helena said she wrote in her diary," Yoshi said. "Maybe we ought to read it?"

"I almost forgot," Sam said.

"Let's go," Paul said.

EIGHTY-THREE

THEY RETURNED to the library. Yoshi got another chair for Sam. Paul sat at the computer and punched keys to read his cloud account. The first thing he saw was a heading outside any of the normal folders on the screen. Paul zoomed in on the text. They all bent close to read it.

Helena's entry read:

Dear Diary,

This is my first entry and probably my last. I can't believe I even have a diary, and I wouldn't have if it hadn't been for Paul. He's so smart and gentlemanly. I almost wish I could stay here with him. But I know that can't happen. He'll find a way to set me free, and then I'll be gone.

I've been trying hard to think of something important to say since this will be read by people still alive. So far, I haven't figured that out.

I am worried about what will to happen to me. Sam says I will go to a happy place with no more pain or torture by Fortune, so I guess she means heaven. I pray that is so.

My world since my death has been gray and hazy, with no interaction with anyone. My only excitement was to play a game of hide and seek, trying to avoid being tortured by my husband.

I have hated the long years of my life here because it was so boring. There was nothing to look forward to each day, except the same walls, the same furniture, the same everything. In fact, it's so monotonous I often tried to think of ways to end my life, but that was impossible. I'm already dead.

Justin and I talked about ghosts once. He said he had always believed that when you died, that was it, but when he saw Fortune and me, he changed his mind. He said we are proof that there is life after death. I laughed at him and said that my existence didn't much seem like life. No ice cream, no friends, no walks in the park, no buggy rides on Sunday. I don' call that life.

Paul has given me new hope for something better, and for that I thank him, Samantha, and his friend, Yohshee.

I just got an inspiration about what tell people who are still living, the wisdom of my experience, you might say.

It's this. We're all going to die, but if you're smart, you'll do everything you can to avoid becoming a ghost. A ghost's life is a horrible, boring, unending nothing.

That doesn't sound very wise does it, but it's the best I can do. I hope it helps someone in the future.

I'll try to do this again, but if I don't, I just want to tell Paul and Samantha how much I love them.

Thank you for caring about a little nobody girl ghost.
Helena Longmore

When they finished reading, Sam was teary-eyed again. "Paul..."

"Yeah, she was an amazing girl."

"I hope she and your uncle find happiness together," Yoshi said. He appeared stunned.

Paul's phone rang. He answered.

"Paul, Bill Johnson.

"Sergeant. You have news?"

"Yes. Good news. We hauled in all those drug hoods in and confronted them with the info we got from those suitcases. They spilled their guts, and the feds have already picked up two of the bosses. How are you?"

Paul grinned. "Sergeant, I'm perfect. I'm out of debt now, and I'm about to marry the love of my life."

"Congratulations, son. I wish you the best. Stay in touch."

"Will do. Take care." They hung up, and Paul gave them the good news about Dante and the gang.

Samantha squeezed Paul's hand. "That's great news, Paul. I was a little worried that they might try again, but..."

"What?"

"Well, I feel a little lost now that it's all over."

"Lost?"

"Yes. Like, what do we do now?"

Paul nodded. "I feel that, too, but I guess it's back to our daily routine."

"What do you mean?" Sam's eyes looked puzzled.

"Well, we have to decide whether we're going to move our stuff here and spend the night in our new home or stay at the cottage."

Relieved, Sam said, "I vote for the cottage."

"Why?"

"Because the cottage is my home. This place is like a museum."

"You mean mausoleum, don't you?"

She giggled. "That, too."

"The cottage it is, then. But, for now, I vote we start early and celebrate our transformation into monied gentry. How many young couples have such a fairy-tale change in their lives in just nine days?"

"You know what, Paul-san?" Yoshi said. "I think finding that drug money and being honest enough to turn it over to the police was a portent of things to come for you." Yoshi said. "You two are the prince and princess of orphans, and you both deserve a fairy-tale beginning to your lives."

"Well said, Mr. Moto.

"Arigato gozaimasu. I say we go celebrate."

"And then?" Samantha's expression was impish.

"I've been thinking about that. Now that we're rich, why don't we fly to Carmel and have a fairy tale wedding, as Yosh suggested, instead of an overnight fling in Vegas?"

Sam smiled and took his hand. "That's a wonderful idea. I always wanted to be a fairy princess. And after that?"

"Why shucks, ma'am. Don't you know how fairy tales end?"

"Yes, but tell me again."

"We all live happily ever after."

He pulled her against him and gave her a hungry kiss.

"Uh, I think I'd better go pack my things before we go," Yoshi said.

They didn't hear him.

— The End —

Made in the USA
Middletown, DE
29 May 2025